The Big Wheel

Scott Archer Jones

Published by:
Southern Yellow Pine (SYP) Publishing
4351 Natural Bridge Rd.
Tallahassee, FL 32305

www.syppublishing.com

This is a work of fiction. Names, characters, places, and events that occur either are the products of the author's imagination or are used fictitiously. Any resemblance to actual persons, places, or events is purely co-incidental.

The contents and opinions expressed in this book do not necessarily reflect the views and opinions of Southern Yellow Pine Publishing, nor does the mention of brands or trade names constitute endorsement.

ISBN-10: 1940869331
ISBN-13: 978-1-940869-33-9
ISBN-13: 978-1-940869-34-6 ePub
ISBN-13: 978-1-940869-35-3 Adobe PDF eBook

Author Photo: Wendy Woolley Photography
Front Cover Design: James C Hamer

Printed in the United States of America
First Edition
February 2015

Dedication

As always, this book is dedicated to my wife Sandra "Scandal" Hornback Jones, my co-dependent in wine, song, Scotland, and a particular chocolate lab mix named Siena Fiona Munro. Sandy owns this book as much as anyone, just as she owns her own charming and peculiar view of the world.

I'd also like to thank my writing coach and industrial-strength editor of many years, Phaedra Greenwood. There are several sections of the book that wouldn't have existed without her, and the way she pushed to develop "Sibyl Boxwood" makes me think she wants a book solely about that ambiguous character.

Praise for the Author

When cat burglar Robko Zlata robs powerful ex-Governor O'Brien of his political dirty secrets, he also steals what he thinks is an electrically charged recreational drug. It is, in fact, a digital soul, called the Artifact. This is the year 2020 and in this brave new world, friends, immortality can be purchased—but it ain't cheap. Soon enough O'Brien dispatches the wily Thomas Steward to recover the artifact, but Steward finds himself the target of the sociopathic hitman, LaFarge, and chaos ensues. As in the best of plots, nothing here is as it seems. Scott Jones is always is fun to read, and The Big Wheel is engrossing, unpredictable, and fast-paced, a twenty-first century morality play. So grab yourself a drink, settle into your easy chair, open the book, and begin. You're home for the evening. You won't stop until it's over.

John Dufresne, No Regrets, Coyote

"The unrelenting pace starts on page one of this near-future tale and doesn't let go. When Robert (Robko) Zlata decides to steal the financial and political dirty secrets of the wealthy ex-governor he inadvertently gets a whole lot more. What he thinks is a device for a recreational high turns out to be the source of the politician's ultimate power—immortality. Needless to say, the ex-governor is not going to stand for this and he sends a hired hand to get Robko. In a race across the nation, hunter and hunted begin to discover that they may have more in common than just the quest for the artifact. Get this book and then hang on for the ride—you'll find yourself totally immersed in *The Big Wheel.*"

Connie Shelton, author of the Charlie Parker and the Samantha Sweet mysteries

The great peril of our existence lies in the fact that our
diet consists entirely of souls.—Inuit Saying

Sors immanis et inanis, rota tu volubilis
[Fate is monstrous and empty, a turning wheel]
—Carmina Burana, O Fortuna

Fortunes Come and Go

Chapter One: The Wrong Rack

My heart thrums like a dynamo. I live for this. From the back seat of the van, I can see the silver hair of the Gray Man. The tires hum on the rainy street in tune with my heart, and the water splashes up into the wheel wells and across the rusty pan below my feet. The chemical cruze in my head runs like a slow, compelling orgasm, but soon I must steal, and little Robko must be straight for that.

I have no reason to be here except greed—that, and my pockets will soon be empty so greed grows to inevitability. Still, I like this rack so much I might have paid the Gray Man for the privilege of being here. I pop the upper in my mouth to flush out the trank, and swallow dry. The van stops at the curb by an old-fashioned newsstand. I jump out with the hot box, coffee and food in a big case zipped shut. I march up to a Nouveau-trash building, a good idea gone bad. I flash an admiring scan across the bottom five floors; they squat there like an old Chicago bank. Hollowed out and left as a façade, they carry a massive building that muscles up forty floors and more. The upper floors are a grid of rough concrete and large glazing in garish bronze. It makes the GE building in Rockefeller Center look graceful. I feel the game begin as the pill kicks in. Right in front of me, a man trips and dumps all his change from the newsstand onto the ground. An excellent omen.

I enter the tower of money, stride across the black marble littered with shining crystals. Inside there is a giant stock ticker in LEDs running across the lobby, "4 June 2020, FTSE up 0.5% gaining 24.75 pts and HSI up 0.6% gaining 246.1." Another good omen—more money to steal.

I put on the ugly Delancy Street accent and announce myself. "Coffee and cake for Insurance on 4. They shoulda caw'ed it down."

The guard inspects his screen and his activity log. "No, not here."

"Yea're shittin' me. Dey order sixty bucks of cake and latté and den dey can't 'member to email you?"

"Happens all the time. I'll have Tina walk you in."

Tina tricks out as a fat, black girl in a blue uniform, taser and radio on her belted waist. She takes me to the glass fence, scans her card, and releases the gate. We go through and she frog-marches me into one of the elevators on the lower bank. She leans in beside me, scans the card again, and presses the button for the fourth floor. Stepping out, she grins. "Have a nice day." I'm up and away.

The elevator door opens. First, I listen. I sidle out using the hotbox to hide my face from the camera. As we've planned, I step into the men's restroom and get rid of every liquid molecule I can. A joe in a suit comes out of a stall and ambles out behind me without noticing me.

I find the closet—an oversized wiring cabinet. I open the hotbox, and I drag out a blue uniform and a bottle of water. I message the Gray Man.

It will be a long wait. After I change clothes, I slide down to the concrete floor. My downers are still working a smidge. They create rainbow rings around light sources. I entertain myself by watching the phone circuits wink red and green as they feed calls into the building's wireless system. It's mildly entertaining, if I don't think at all. In a few hours, I'll ride the elevator up as far as I can, then I'll climb.

Swinging out into the space beyond, I stand on the sill and reach in to tug the closet panel back into place. My toes hold me up, but my left hand, wedged into a vertical crack, keeps me from falling back, down forty floors. All through this, I strain to hear a rumble—and I'm feeling a thrill a second, because it's a gamble. At this time of day, the elevator will hurtle past on average every four minutes and scrape off any careless intruder. I hear its thunder and shuffle myself over to the next shaft. The chance of two elevators passing here at the same time is forty-to-one. If the small chance happens, I get smashed like a dog on the freeway. The money makes the risk worthwhile. The risk makes the job a grin and a half.

To cover my tracks, I have to get that closet panel tacked back up. With a bit of one-handed fumbling, I'm able to start two screws and ratchet the metal up snug. I scale the rough interior of the shaft to the

4

next floor in seconds. With a thin punch, I knock screws back into a sister wiring closet. The elevator comes once more, and I crab and swing out of its way again.

Finally I'm safe. I'm in the closet, out of the shaft. The elevator hurtles by again, kicking up eddies of dust and rumbling like a train. With a sneeze, I'm through security level two, into the upper section of the building.

The floor holds the corporation's big computing and a new generation of data servers. A floor-to-ceiling glass wall with a slider door fronts this IT department. I enter a four-digit code into the keypad beside the door and get the expected blinking light. I take out a latex cylinder from my breast pocket—a fake finger—and I press the fingerprint into the glowing pad above the keys. The door opens as I expected. Beyond the door, an expansive computing room sits dark, surrounded by a ring of office space. I see only two people in their dwarfish glass cubicles—they stare into the green flicker of code and data, extensions of the machines they serve. It's an anachronism of a room, huge to fit old style computing, but now a few small boxes crouch in the center. The slider door trundles shut behind me, and I pace around the periphery of the room. As I pass each of the lighted cubicles, I raise my hand to wave. They don't even look up. "Evening. Just making rounds." I am a blue smudge of invisibility. I find the printer room. This is so easy; my heart rate is at a crawl.

I'm as close to my next destination as walking will get me—now I have to crawl. I pull up a tile from the old-fashioned flooring and wiggle down into the eighteen-inch cavity. Six feet away is a vertical pipe. Once it carried fat bundles of copper up and down the spine of the building—now it carries four optical cables. I climb into the conduit. I'm standing on a grate that's welded into place. I switch a light on my headband, casting an intense beam that tracks with my head. I keep my arms up over my head and scrape my chest as I go. Up eight feet. I love tight places like this.

I have my toes wedged into a horizontal seam. A motion detector blinks its red light ten feet above me. I wait, wedged against metal walls in a forty-story tube that slices down through the building below. A work light a few floors up casts a frail glow down to me. It blacks out; the power to the building has just gone off. The Gray Man.

I scramble up the pipe. I get a floor and a half up before I hear a

5

general bang. The work light comes back on and I freeze. The building is now running on generators. In a half minute, another loud noise echoes down the conduit, and we're back on city power. Within two minutes, the work light goes out again. I climb in a sprint before it comes back on again. I stop dead in the conduit a half-floor from my destination. I need one more power outage, but the Gray Man will give me two more. Just in case.

The light blinks off and I rush up. I double onto my belly into a fat, horizontal space and follow the optic cables into a side tunnel. I wiggle forward and dig in with my elbows. My feet just clear the shaft before I hear the bang of the power coming back on. I feel ecstatic, a true rush of well-being and happiness. I lie in the dark, wait to catch my breath, and revel in the thrill.

A day before the rack, Robko paced back and forth, trapped in the Gray Man's apartment.

"Let's go over it again." The Gray Man brought the floor plans up on his desk tablet and showed them at the same time on the screen on the wall.

"Let's not." Robko narrowed his eyes. Robko, Robert Zlata, strode back and forth in front of the screen. One of the apartment windows had been replaced with a white panel, a plastic sheath shot through with antennas. Robko could see the mesh of copper that covered the room's ceiling and the walls. The Gray Man had created a radio wave shield, a Faraday cage. "You know," Robko said, "this apartment is a microwave oven. I've been in here on slow cook for two hours." He fished in his pants for one of his floating pills but didn't find one.

"Boosting something this big from Governor O'Brien is both lucrative and dangerous."

"Big deal. You think just because he's mega-rich, he's dangerous?"

"He is...," the Gray Man sighed, "and if you work with my crew, you rehearse. You know the rules."

The furniture, dark oak and ornate, looked like some grandmother's possessions. The gear did not. Robko answered, "The crew is you and me."

"Not quite true, Robert. There were those who came and went

before you ever entered the scene. This has been a one-year job. Months of surveillance."

"I'm sure it was fascinating."

The Gray Man shook his head and ground on. "You have to bypass four levels of security. Now, let's start again. Lay it out for me."

Robko took a sip of hot sweet tea. "Level one, standard first floor reception, guards, and elevator banks. Employees get in with keycards through chest-high glass while deliveries and guests are signed in and escorted. I come through as the coffee boy, and they bang me up to the fourth floor to Insurance." Robko eyed the apartment instead of the floor plans on the wall. A seven-foot-tall metal box protruded into the room, its end framing a cheerless steel door. This brutal airlock was another layer of security, and the Gray Man insisted all electronics be left in it. Even now Robko's iMob phone—his little electronic world— lay on a shelf behind that door.

"The guard will program the elevator to carry you there. You can't change that without cracking open the control panel. You also can't get out of the elevator. The hatch is wired."

Robko waved a hand. "But once I deliver the coffee, I can take an unsecured return trip. I punch three and get off on the maintenance floor." Dim afternoon light filtered through the windows. The tiny copper mesh across them flickered bronze in backlight.

The Gray Man's voice plodded on, through Robko's hiding place, the disguise and the journey through the building. "At eight p.m. you take the elevator to the fortieth. Go up when you can get on and hide in a crowd. Lock yourself into the next closet. The back wall has an access hatch into the elevator shafts. It's not monitored—no sensors this low in the building. You enter the elevator shaft and ascend one floor."

Robko said, as he stifled a yawn, "You mean I make a one-floor free climb with no rope in a shaft that has a busy elevator."

"Yes. That's basically what you do and why you're here." The apartment doorbell rang and the Gray Man fluttered his fingers over the tablet, opening camera views to the hallway and into the security airlock.

The first camera showed a dingy hallway, painted red and poorly lit. A girl stood there with a white plastic bag in her hands, holding it up in view, the bag open and the lip rolled down. The Gray Man opened

7

the hall door. The girl stepped forward and let the door lock behind her. Quite beautiful, she stood in the harsh light, a goth in dark lipstick and serious eye makeup, looking a lot bored. "Let me in, already." The steel door into the apartment clacked four times—top, bottom, sides.

She minced in, scowled at Robko. She dumped the bag onto the dining table in the middle of the room, shoved aside papers and memory devices, placed out small cartons of Thai food. With a haughty glance over her shoulder, she slipped through a glass door into the back of the apartment.

Robko said, "She looks pissed."

"She didn't want to come back to the city, not during the summer."

"Come back from where?"

"Someplace more—copacetic. Hand me chopsticks." The two men distributed the food. Robko chose soup with rat-shit chilies and stirred its noodles up with a white plastic spoon.

The Gray Man started again. "Now, you crawl out of the closet into the elevator shaft and make the climb."

The apartment was stiflingly hot. Compelled to take up the narration, the Gray Man supplied his own soundtrack. "That gets you to the IT floor. From the IT floor you can climb up to the executive floor in the old cable chase. Once you are onto—or at least under—the executive suite floor, you'll move along until you get to the printer room behind Reception. There you have to get up and out through an access hatch after moving a copy machine forward out of your way. The machine weighs one hundred sixty-three pounds without the paper. More than you."

"Stop with the drama. I use an air-powered skid your people hid there some time ago. Did I mention I could have set up the machine myself? Or for that matter, just gone in direct as a copy repairman and done the job without all this climbing?"

"You would never have gotten from the printer room to the vault— we have to get you in before everyone comes to work. At this point, you've already run three major risks we can't control. The guard could have called the fourth floor and found out the coffee and cake order was fake. You could have been stopped in the hallways by real security. You could have... um... encountered an elevator."

"You're reminding me why my rates should go up."

"Yes, but we've already fixed the deal."

8

"For this job."

The Gray Man's gaze swiveled to Robko. He showed thin lips in a death-head grin. "Yes. So, by this point you're on the right floor. Now you have to get into the executive suite. Up here it's eye scans, not fingerprint readers. This is simple. We have a device here," and the Gray Man held up a small box that resembled a digital camera. "You use it to project the retinal scan of O'Brien's personal assistant and unlock the door."

"How did you get the scan, by the way?"

"Let's just say we have a tame optometrist. Go down this hallway to the double doors."

The Gray Man peered at the plan, his back to Robko. Robko flipped him the bird, then shrugged.

The Gray Man droned, "Use the scanner to the left of the door to enter the executive suite."

Robko pursed his lips. He reached for the Gray Man's wallet lying on the table. He took the hundreds out, stuck one back in, replaced the wallet. The Gray Man strobed his chopsticks in a shimmy at the images on the wall. "I've marked the cameras inside this section—and the dead spots. Keep your head ducked, and don't look up at the cams. So tell me, what comes next?"

"O'Brien's office lies behind the secretaries. I use the same projector for the eye scanner on his door, enter, and let the system lock me in. The nice thing about the Governor's office is its low security. No motion detectors, no cameras."

"Except the vault's security."

"Yes, the vault."

The Gray Man has brought me all this way for what is in that vault.

In front of me are spread the usual trappings big bosses require: the couches, the bar, the immense desk, and the panoramic sweep of glass. But what's important lies through the double doors to the right. I open them and lights flicker on. I can see the vault waiting there in all its transparent simplicity. The glass box crouches six feet away from the walls on its own pedestal. Huddling inside are a data server, a translucent desk with a holographic monitor, and several lustrous boxes.

First I have to get into the vault. The dog that guards this glass cube is a dual tumbler bank lock mounted in the door. A case-hardened steel box holds the lock suspended on the glass. It's a simple, elegant, mechanical lock with no electronics and no timer. We don't know the combination.

I drill two holes, each to the right of a tumbler knob. If I drill in the wrong place, I rupture a manifold that holds an acid. It will ruin everything in the lock, just like ATM machines. Once I've drilled through the safe spots and into the mechanics of the lock, I use a standard needle listening device and unlock each tumbler set. I hear the last click; now I can throw the handle.

Disarming the lasers and the pressure switches inside the vault is the final trick. Before I jerk the door open, I start my timer. I've only got a minute to rush the keypad and enter the right password. The code this year is the names of O'Brien's ex-wives, entered backwards. A bitch, or two in fact.

It is indeed close, since I mistype once. My iMob counts down, tolling out seconds, and it reaches "three" before I get the code in. Silently I scream for joy, and my adrenalin pumps around in a waterfall of delight. I have an aching erection. I've cracked through level four, and all I have to do is steal the data off the server and unlock the boxes.

I jack my memory device into the server and start a huge download. Next, the translucent glowing boxes. The boxes each have a keypad; I have the codes because the keypads face the window. Days of surveillance from an adjacent building have revealed all. O'Brien's boxes hold portable memory devices, and as instructed, I drop each into the bag. But in the last cube, I find something I've never seen before. The Gray Man hadn't prepared me for this.

It's an acrylic box, one by two by three inches. The box holds a gray mass of powder or crystals. Notches on the outside allow it to connect or couple into something. I see sets of contacts on each end, maybe two hundred in an array.

What? Are the crystals some exotic compound to provide O'Brien with a unique experience? Could it be an electrically activated drug, like a Singapore Slam? Could it be gene replacement to prolong his life? Maybe the crystals could cure his cirrhosis, or relieve his diabetes, or give him the circulation system of a twenty year old.

10

Whatever this little gem is, it's something only the very rich could afford—important enough for him to keep close at hand. Maybe the contacts are either an alarm or lock, or the crystals are inert until activated by way of the contacts. A mystery—how charming!

The Gray Man doesn't have to know about this drug. It's not part of the negotiated deal, but it could get me killed. Killed dead. Either by the Gray Man, or O'Brien. Of course I'll keep the box—I'm doomed by my blood to keep it.

The day before, they looped over and over the plan. It wasn't enough to get in. Robko had to get out.

The Gray Man's voice wheezed on. "You exit by riding on the elevator roof down to the ground. It's a cinch from O'Brien's floor. The doors protect against someone breaking in, not breaking out."

"The reverse of a lobster trap."

"A simple switch disables the alarm on the stairwell door. You unlock the elevator maintenance door with this key." The Gray Man held it up. "Their security is laughable on this end."

"It will improve after I'm gone."

"There is that. You'll have to wait, but you can stroll onto the roof of either of the executive elevators when they come to the top. Don't move after you're on the elevator—interferometer scans in the shaft. Once the elevator is on the ground floor, drop down the side into the basement and proceed to the loading docks. You can exit onto those docks with no challenge. Use this key card." The Gray Man gave Robko the card.

"And then I walk away."

"You know the place where we'll meet. Message ahead, and I'll be there for the exchange. We'll transfer your fee from my bank to yours right away."

"Anyone else coming to the drop?"

"No. And it's a public place. I probably won't shoot you."

"And I'll probably bring the stuff."

"See that you do."

11

Chapter Two: Slave to Fortune's Service

Robert Zlata, known to his family and friends as Robko, often met the Gray Man at this particular coffee house in the Bowery. Big, mirrored, plate glass windows faced the street, and he could see out without being seen. He liked the hours—always open—and the escape routes. The shop occupied a corner; two exits reassured him and he knew about the window onto the alley. Robko sat in his favorite chair. Through the window, he watched the Gray Man stride up the street under the streetlights. He also watched himself reflected in the glass, saw a small man dressed in black, with a massive mono-brow above two deep set eyes—a somber expression. He pushed his fingers through his pelt of raven wing hair and watched the image in the glass preening. He grinned at himself. Mink-like, his small, sharp incisors flashed out and then hid themselves.

The Gray Man relaxed—for once he wasn't all about business. He laid his pad on the table. "Best coffee in the Bowery."

"You like this place, don't you?"

"I've got to get out sometime. This place is better than okay." He nodded towards the baristas. "I'll be a minute."

The Gray Man took his time. Placing his cappuccino on the table, he sat with one hand across the chair beside him and crossed his leg. He dangled the foot. The Gray Man asked, "You're from Chicago, aren't you? Nice town."

Robko narrowed his eyes. A little late for a personal relationship. "Some parts. My neighborhood left a lot to be desired."

"Mean streets. The usual story."

"Pulaski Park and points northwest. Very ethnic, working poor—but not dirty. We had everything from Bohunks to Puerto Ricans."

"And your ethnicity?"

"Zlata doesn't give it away? A good Slavic name, Polish in this case."

"What does Zlata mean?"

"Gold."

The Gray Man pushed the tiny spoon around the lip of his saucer, leaned forward. "Well, you've had a pretty golden day, haven't you?"

"In by ten in the morning, and out by midnight. Long day, but successful."

"I was eager to meet up with you, after."

"It's only been an hour."

"True," said the Gray Man. He lifted an eyebrow.

"Yes, I have them with me." Robko shoved the satchel under the table to the Gray Man's feet.

"Forgive me for a moment." The Gray Man brought the satchel up from the floor to the seat beside him and unzipped it. Dipping his hands in, he rummaged for a bit. He turned the contents over in his hidden hands, everything still in the bag. "Yes, here's the disk for the full server. The download went okay?"

Robko nodded.

"And O'Brien's memory devices. I see there are eleven here, and not the ten we expected."

"I've been thinking about that. One lockbox had two flash drives, one smaller than the other. Maybe older. Who knows what it could hold."

"I appreciate the honesty, Robert. Not all people in our trade would have delivered the extra."

Robko's shoulders twinged. The twelfth item hung as a weight in his pocket. He diverted the conversation. "What do you think is stored on these devices?"

"One is what I expected—it's even marked with a tape label. It holds financial information, instantly useful. I hope to recover your fee thousands of times over within the hour."

"And the others?"

"Ah. My future buyers expect they will hold trade secrets of various kinds."

"O'Brien has labs, factories, and offices all over the States to hold his trade secrets."

The Gray Man just hummed.

"So we had to crack his office rather than just jacking the info from his flunkies?"

"Two reasons—O'Brien gathers it all together for us, in one place. Very tempting. Second, Dennis Malley O'Brien is first and foremost a politician. He wouldn't keep the data I want in a lab or a factory or an employee's office." The Gray Man zipped the bag shut.

Robko tapped his spoon on the tabletop. "Now on to why I'm here. You've got yours. I'd like mine."

The Gray Man stirred his milk foam under and pushed his pad towards Robko. "I'm ready when you are. Just fill in the account."

Robko got out a piece of paper.

"Paper and pencil. How quaint."

Robko grinned. "Some things shouldn't be digital." He typed in the number.

The Gray Man, assessing him through drooping, secret eyes, slurped on his coffee. "Tap 'Send.' You should see a confirmation in a moment."

They both stared down at the pad. "Yes, there it is." Robko said, "If you don't mind, I'll check directly." He got out his vidi and slid out the expanded screen. He typed in the enquiry. "Okay, just arrived."

"All as agreed," said the Gray Man.

Robko got up to go. "It's been great fun. Don't call me for a while. I'll call you."

"You'll soon be looking for work. You enjoy it too much. If anything comes up, I'll keep you in mind."

Robko slid out the side door. He needed to move the money now. The Gray Man was too good.

Robko lived quite close to the coffee house, not that anyone knew. The Bowery held most of the restaurant supply businesses of the city, and he lived in one of the cookery warehouses. He tramped down Delancey past the storefronts and into his narrow stair. As he turned in, a man pushed out past him. Curious, Robko pivoted to watch him stroll away—a tall, emaciated black in a dilapidated topcoat. The black glanced over his shoulder, and Robko noted expensive Honecker sunglasses. Maybe knock-offs, or stolen.

The stairs led Robko two flights up to a single enameled door. No doorbell; the door was scratched and dirty. A jink pipe lying by his doorsill—he shook his head. He couldn't understand people who sucked drain cleaner into their lungs.

14

He fished out his keys, noticed the nonsense " been cut into the door's enamel, neat. Could be the thi Robko unlocked the two deadbolts.

Behind the door lurked two offices, glasse wainscoting up, and facing each other. They had been long abandoned, and he left them locked and full of dust. The loft lay beyond them down the hallway they framed. At the street end, he kept his working space, the tables with goose-neck lamps and small devices for disarming alarms, the recorders and the transmitters, the desk tablets and computers. Scattered further back in this rough, unfinished place, a series of expensive purchases squatted, made after racks and scores— from flush times. A recreational space circled in the middle, with couches and media, and beyond gleamed a minimalist kitchen. Robko strode across the creaking floor to the first workbench and picked up a pad. He rubbed his index finger across the tablet and spoke to it, "Password RobkoZlataFour. Home page financial. Tap third down. Insert password Iberia bank. Tap transfers and payments. Tap transfer to. Tap all. Choose name on account. Type Dragomir. Tap continue." He stared intently— the screen pasted up several pop-ups, flashed blue text, and then scrolled down to a status line. He blew out a breath—the money had gone where the Gray Man couldn't find it, jumped three times through three aliases, four accounts, and ten time zones.

Robko ambled back to his bed behind the kitchen. The buzz from the job had floated out of his system, leaving him just tired. Dead tired. He needed four or five hours sleep before he started the party. He dropped the acrylic box—the manifestation of his betrayal—into the bedside drawer.

Thomas Cabot Steward got the call from O'Brien's assistant at about ten in the morning. He sat across town in a commandeered conference room. It was his because it was the best in the building. The usual wall of reports he needed marched across the big table. Two assistants chased data for him through the piles and through desk tablets. An intimidating guard was parked in a chair outside the doorway.

The call interrupted his interview with the company's CFO. He was about to decide if the woman would stay or go. He already knew e wouldn't continue as CFO. He remained calm, polite, urbane. She sweated; her forehead shone through her makeup.

One of the assistants took the call on Thomas's iMob, turning her back on the people in the room. She hung up, wrote something down, and brought it to him. She held it over his shoulder in front of his eyes so the CFO wouldn't see.

He looked at the note and blanked his desktab. He glanced at the CFO. "I'm sorry, we'll have to continue this another time. Something has come up." Thomas stood, took a suit coat from the back of his chair, and leaned his head close to the assistant's ear. "Have the car come around immediately."

Ugly traffic snarled up Manhattan, but it wasn't his problem—the privacy of the town car insulated him from the city, and it drove itself, optimizing the route using satellite. He focused on two things. First, he mentally sketched out a preliminary report on the new company and his progress. Second, he counted through O'Brien's companies like rosary beads. Somewhere in that list lived CEOs in disfavor, moving up, or about to retire. Those few companies were his best opportunity. By the time he reached O'Brien's headquarters, he had a list of three. He also knew what to say about the new acquisition.

One of the O'Brien secretaries waited for him in the lobby. He wrinkled his forehead—an escort meant something big was up. She wasn't his type—very tall and very thin, like a crane in heels. They both badged through and took an executive elevator. The door shut, and the secretary turned to him. "Mr. O'Brien said to tell you right away that we had a significant robbery here last night. We lost some intelligence of great value. He didn't want you to be surprised, so he told me to give you a preliminary heads-up."

He kept a bland face, but disappointment hung like a stone in his stomach. This wasn't The Call. O'Brien had summoned him to Olympus to receive new instructions. There wasn't a CEO job with his name on it, just another round of problem solving for the Governor.

People hurried back and forth in a frenetic mess at the secretaries' desks. The phones rang, and new arrivals waited to be escorted back. The secretary led Thomas smoothly down the wide hall to the CEO's domain. There at the inner sanctum, the Personal Assistant greeted him and ushered him in. The PA was a guy who wore a bespoke suit as nice as Thomas's.

16

Men surrounded the small conference table and filled the couch and chairs. The ones actually around O'Brien conferred in excited tones. Thomas shook his head. He saw a packed space, heard the adrenalin in the conversations, and smelled irrationality.

O'Brien stood up and lumbered forward to take Thomas's hand. "Tommy, I'm glad you could come right away."

"Always glad to get involved, Dennis." Thomas smiled. Still first names. No banishment to the couch then with the also-rans. Maybe his luck was in; maybe this was an opportunity he could play.

O'Brien stood just under Thomas's height but outweighed him two to one. The CEO kept Thomas's hand and swung around to place his arm over Thomas's shoulder. He drew Thomas in close and pushed him forward toward the table. "Sit down here with us. You know Don Garland, head of Corporate Security?"

"Yes, we've worked together some in Acquisitions." Together they had evicted the unwanted from the building.

"And this is Egan LeFarge. He's handled several tricky things for us in the past, and he's on retainer with us."

LeFarge looked like a British officer from a Mideast station. Clipped close, sun-burned brick red, black-pencil mustache. He had canine teeth like a dog of war.

O'Brien directed his players. "Don, could you show Tommy the list of stolen items and what we know about the crime? Tommy, lad, you catch up."

Garland, with a look like he faced the guillotine, handed his desk tablet over to Thomas. "It's the top two files, Steward."

Thomas slashed through the two documents. An absolute disaster! He handed the pad back.

O'Brien cut off his conversation with LeFarge. "Well, Tommy. What do you think? What's your first impression?" O'Brien's head swung bear-like, first to Garland and then to LeFarge. He expected Thomas to be brilliant.

Thomas half-bowed. "Follow the money. Whoever got your personal accounts will move money out of them rapidly. If Corporate Security doesn't have resources, there's a firm we use during hostile takeovers. They can follow disappearing money through the banks and can determine who owns those accounts. They move fast, and they have some not-so-legal contacts."

Garland looked sour. "We've already got some resources on this."

O'Brien waved Garland down. "No, this is good. I'd rather have two bloodhounds on the trail than one. Tommy, give Don the name and the number."

Thomas said, "I'll just flash it to your phone, Don."

"Sure."

Thomas added a barb. "Let them know it's Thomas Steward on behalf of Dennis O'Brien, and you'll get a lot of traction." Garland nodded, but scowled.

O'Brien leaned forward. "What else are you thinking?"

Thomas tugged at his lip, cleared his throat. "We have to know whom we're chasing and not just thrash about blindly. If we don't have a name, we certainly have characteristics, and those will make the thieves more predictable. It's like reverse engineering." He paused. "I don't know about crime and how to read crime scenes, so I can't help there."

LeFarge said, "I know crime." He looked down his nose at Garland and Thomas and smiled. A tight hard mouth. "Let me think out loud. First, we definitely have enough surveillance, so we have a picture of the thief or thieves recorded somewhere. This is less valuable than you think, except as a link—the guy who did the physical work won't be your planner and leader. Second, we have a rough idea of how they got into the building, into the vault, and out of the building again—but no idea yet how they got onto the floor or into the suite. That tells me they're smart, and they don't work by smash-and-grab. The way one of them finessed his way into the building shows they can grift—they ran a plausible con on Garland's rent-a-cops downstairs. The vault shows they know traditional safecracking. They had good intelligence to get them the other passwords needed. They knew about the weaknesses in your elevator security. All this requires long lead times, big investment up front, and patience." He paused and looked around at his audience. "Finally, they knew what they were after. Again great intel, very expensive intel."

O'Brien wagged his big head and growled. "What are they going to do with my data?"

LeFarge lifted his hands and shrugged. "They maybe planned a sale of the materials for later, maybe an auction, but I don't think so."

Thomas brushed the tabletop, and without looking at LeFarge, asked, "Why is that?"

"They're a crew, not an entire marketplace. They most likely have a buyer up front—and that buyer commissioned this piece of work."

O'Brien said, "All fine and good, but I don't feel any closer to my data."

Thomas watched the corner of LeFarge's mouth turn up. A wolf's canine glinted out.

The Governor banged on the table. "Keep going... say something encouraging."

"There are a limited number of people who could do this thing. That tells us that the thieves—or at least the mastermind—is known in the business. That means we can find him through snitches. Last, their leader has the biggest balls in the world, and he's willing to take on anything. We look for an arrogant son of a bitch."

O'Brien smiled, his lips fat, moist. "Good speculation. But I want a name, I want a location, and I want my data back. All of it. Tell me exactly what you think we should do, Egan."

LeFarge said, "Work the money trail, as Steward said. Work the security footage to find the safecracker as he got in—focus on the footage in your outer office. With faces, we should get one or two names. Hire a security firm that specializes in snitches, both foreign and domestic. Make a list of your enemies who would be this bold. And finally...."

"Finally what?"

"You have to decide whether you want to hand the answers over to the police or bring in your own extraction team."

The Governor and LeFarge stared at each other. O'Brien said, "Build the team for me, Egan. Don't involve Don with the set-up; I want his hands clean. Don, you have to handle the basic search for these guys. Get me a name."

O'Brien took Thomas aside, into the room where the vault sat open and plundered. The Governor positioned his back to his office and faced away from the crowd. Over O'Brien's shoulder, Thomas kept an eye on the head of Corporate Security and LeFarge, their heads together. LeFarge spoke in a low voice to Garland.

Thomas asked, "Why am I here, sir?"

O'Brien said, "Because of what else they stole. I can't get it all back without hauling out every trick I have. You're one of those tricks."

"Can you give me an idea of what else they took?"

O'Brien breathed twice. He hemmed. "Just the data is bad enough. You already know about the memory device that holds my total finances. Every bank, every offshore account, every password, years of books and shadow books, fraudulent tax returns, deals I've made that I don't mind being in the daylight, and the midnight deals I've made that should stay in the dark."

"Enough for most people to go all out to get it back."

"It's worse. The rest of the memory devices are purely political. They document who I own and how much I paid, files on everyone I ever pressured, dirty tricks and illegal activities, what payoffs I got as Governor, and what we did for it. A real bitch's brew."

"All in one place... all pure poison."

"I can't have anyone—FBI, enemies, blackmailers, journalists—I can't let it stay in anyone else's hands. Christ, I spent a bloody fortune to protect it, and now here I am spending anything—anything—to recover it."

"You've got a good team with great backing."

O'Brien waved his hand dismissively. "There's another thing they stole. I want you to take personal responsibility for recovering this one. I don't want anyone else, inside or outside of this building, to know what it is."

Thomas waited.

"They stole a device, the greatest artifact our civilization has ever produced. There are only three, and until last night I controlled all three. It's a new form of data storage that can map the brain. It can be used to store all those things that make up a man."

"Huh."

"As technology advances, it could be downloaded into new computers to form an artificial intelligence based upon a man. It could be used to archive and search the greatest minds of the world. It could be used to download a man's mind into another human host—and very soon at that."

Thomas thought about that. "And who is stored in the stolen device?"

"You don't think I would waste this on anyone else, do you? They've got my soul, Tommy, and I want it back."

Thomas opened his mouth, thought better of it, and closed it.

20

O'Brien gripped Thomas's arm and looked into his face. "You're my boy, Tom. You've always been lucky as well as smart. You go along for the ride, and if these other guys can't get this Artifact back by accident, you get it back on purpose."

Thomas said, "Dennis, this isn't finance. You don't need a Wharton graduate for this; you need trained investigators."

"I've got those already, and we'll see how they do. You're my dark horse, Tommy."

This was all so wrong. "Oohkay. I'll give it my best shot."

O'Brien beamed. Got what he wanted without committing anything. "Of course, you tell anyone—I would be very unhappy."

So, he was basically doomed—to secrecy, and probably to failure.

"Good boy. I knew you would understand."

"I have to operate independently of Security and of LeFarge. I would have no purpose in their teams, and they won't accept oversight from me."

"Agreed."

Maybe he could make it easier. "I'll need access to you and to reports from the two teams, night and day. And I need any resource I ask for. I want Ryan Haevers to come in behind me to take over the acquisition I'm doing now while I go onto this full time."

"Agreed."

"I'm new at this—I'm bound to screw it up."

"No you won't. I trust you. You and your luck. Just remember, don't betray my trust. Get my soul back." The bear gripped Thomas's bicep. Hard.

21

Chapter Three: Cracks

Poking around, that's what Robko called it. A hot shower didn't help. Gazing in the refrigerator, the door hanging open until the stainless box talked to him—that wasn't any better. Anyway, the grapefruit juice had turned a suspicious brown and smelled like rotting peaches. He checked the news and saw nothing of interest. He internetted talk radio, and within a minute clicked it off. Eight hours before, life had been sweet; now it ran... flat. No high this morning.

About eleven, he wandered out for coffee and a roll. He browsed the Daily on his pad for a while as he sat on a tall stool on the street outside Bennie's. He added two packs of sugar to the coffee and dropped in one of the bitter pills, a sodie, to get a little cruze on. In a couple of minutes, Robko began humming the theme from "Dragnet." He first checked the paper's front page, then turned to the crime section and scanned through it. No mention of his boost.

He powered off the pad and slipped into unthinking vacancy, gazing off down the avenue. The waiter popped up at his table and jarred him back to attention. His name was Kevin, and Robko had a soft spot for him. Robko knew it was narcissistic. Kevin came off as a second edition of Robko. Like him, the waiter was short but muscled. He was languid because he took the same drugs. He had a face full of flat planes, a duskiness in his skin, eyebrows like a thicket, and cheap-dyed blond hair. And a nice ass.

Kevin also sulked in front of the customers, practiced rudeness, and slouched a lot. You couldn't have everything. "Kev, how's the play going?"

"What play? The dead play?"

"C'mon, can't be that bad."

"I got a hall for performance, but it's a real dump and needs a lot of TLC. The audience will have to stand up, not sit down—how frickin' off-Broadway is that? I got a friend who agreed to direct it, as long as it doesn't interfere with his day job. We'll try casting, if we can raise a little money. Phuttin' actors all insist on scale, even if they never been on the boards."

"How much you need?" Robko glanced offhandedly down the street and pretended disinterest.

"Four grand buys me a week. Then we either fold, or the gate takes care of the next week."

"Huh. Success sounds as rough as failure."

Kevin stared at him from under that black fence of eyebrow and batted his lashes. "Don't tell the cast, but I just want it on my résumé." He appeared downcast, but the corners of his mouth turned up in a secret grin.

"I can give you the four flip. Anonymous. But I get an invitation to the cast party."

"Kram, man! That would be great!" Kevin reached over and rubbed the back of Robko's wrist. Robko took Kevin's hand in both his hands.

Kevin slipped his hand away. "Oops, got a customer." He slunk off, smirking as he wove between the tables. Robko was pretty sure he'd been played. He looked down in his hand, as if surprised to see Kevin's watch there.

Back to crime and fame. A search on the newsosphere didn't turn up any mention of the rack. O'Brien might not report the crime, but it should come out anyway. There weren't many secrets in a big office. One of the rags should have picked it up from a gossiping employee and made a splashy to-do. Maybe tomorrow. As he swallowed the last of the coffee and stood up, the store across the way, or at least the graffiti on its lockdown, shouted for his attention, "Luck Gonna Run You Over." The signature was complexly unreadable, its own glyph. Robko decided it was a wanna-be-artist's statement, a step above the other vandalism. But he thought it wasn't a very hip saying, was it, and it wasn't applicable to him. He was on top of the world. Or should be.

The black man squatted on his heels in the alley mouth, the paper bag of spray cans at his feet, watching the world roam by. His face was hidden by huge sunglasses.

In the acquisition's palatial conference room, where splendor couldn't disguise abject corporate failure, Thomas Cabot Steward spoke at length while Ryan Haevers took notes with pen and paper and recorded him with an iMob. This marathon session with Ryan included narratives for all the executives from the acquired company—the boys and girls for the chop. Thomas summarized his thoughts for Haevers, "Watch the COO. He's the dick who ran this company into the ground to get his hyped-up stock price. The VP in charge of new-store startups is okay. VP Sales is a joke. The CFO should go back to her job in advertising—or go away. It's all up to you now. I won't second-guess you. O'Brien does that enough for all of us."

"Thanks for the chance, Thomas."

"What chance?" Thomas reached for his coat, snapped his briefcase shut.

"I know you gave me the step."

"Not me. Good luck, Ryan. Move fast; don't get stuck." He left his fifth takeover in someone else's hands and descended to the street. The car tooled him down to Manhattan.

He worked in the car again, glad to leave the confines of the take-over's depressed, angry office. All the way, he turned over ideas—where to start?

As he strode back into O'Brien's empire, it felt like home. The acquisition's office had smelled of a combination of flop sweat and basement air—not this place. Success had a smell made up of good aftershave and cinnamon. Again a secretary met him in the lobby, nodded, and charged off for the elevator. He followed her. No nymphet like the anorexic crane who had brought him up yesterday. This one marched fast, eating up the marble floor.

She led him to a conference room off the executive row and swept open the door. "We don't have any office I can give you, but you can use this space for the interim. Here's your in-house phone." She handed him a wireless and an earbud with mike. "I'm your support, and my TinyURL is Pound Six." She took his phone back, showed him "#6 enter," and dropped it back into his hand.

"What's your name, Pound Six?" He smiled a disarming preppie smile he had practiced over and over.

"Angie. Angelina Tommo."

Thomas appreciated Italian; it was so different from the white Protestant landscape he had grown up in. "Angie, call me Thomas. Come back in ten minutes. I'll have a list of the documents and feeds I want."

"Ten minutes... got it. Would you like coffee?"

"That would be great. Latté if it's available. And, Angie?" She turned back to him in the doorway. "Doing anything after work? Want to catch a drink?"

She grinned and shook her head. "Maybe." He watched her draw the door shut, and she watched him watch.

Thomas sat at the table figuring angles. Angie represented a chance to find out who were the winners and losers around O'Brien. She might be difficult to crack open—she wouldn't have gotten where she was by telling tales. The losers would be more interesting than the winners. One of them might be an insider who had sold the layouts and the passwords. He would take an approach of drinks and flirtation with Angie. There might be something else in there between them, something personal.

He also needed his own information feed, not just the ones used by Garland. A feed tuned to the way he thought. He talked to his pad, his finger adding a period, a colon where needed. "New note. O'Brien's active enemies: Carstairs, Thurgall. O'Brien's successor: Gallagher, Tuerno. O'Brien's children: Allison, Dennis Junior, maybe others from previous marriages that I wouldn't know. O'Brien's VPs in central office: too numerous to count. Copy the Executive VPs file in here. O'Brien's accomplices in the state house, Search Local Knowledge to list top three."

Thomas leaned back in his chair and cocked an elbow up behind his head. He caught a whiff of perspiration and looked down at his shirt to find it was losing some of its crisp edges. Small damp spots in his armpits betrayed his humanity. He'd have the town car run him home for a shower and a change before lunch.

He touched his iMob, said, "Call Brent." The vidi complied. "Brent, Thomas Steward here. How's the political blog going?—I can't see you. The video is blanked.—Oh, subway?—Listen, I need you to check out political activities and financial aspirations of ten or so people for me, people associated with my boss.—Uh-huh. Indeed, usual fee.—Also, you can use the stuff for the blog, but not right now—wait till I tell you. The other bloggers will be watching you search around, so leak it that you think O'Brien might want to make a run for the Senate.—No, I don't think it's true, but your heat-up might make him think about it, and you'd be first in if he decided to come back into politics.—I'll flash my names here over to you now. I need you to start feeding to me as you get it. Don't wait to package it all up; I'll take it raw.—All right, bye." He emailed the padtop to his source. Where was Angie with his latté?

Irritated, he jumped up and started pacing around. What about O'Brien's in-house resources? There should be some useful feed there that no one else would think of. A knock on the door interrupted him. Angie stuck her head in. "You should hear this, Mr. Steward. There's a report that just arrived, and it's causing some excitement. They're in O'Brien's office."

Grabbing his coat, he strode past her, tossing flattery over his shoulder. "Great, thanks for looking out for me, Angie. I owe you." Screw the wait for coffee; this was more important. He had a spy on board.

O'Brien sat ponderous behind his desk and three men stood before him, facing the executioner. Thomas strode in as if it was his meeting and took a place at the end of the desk, away from the guys on the carpet. Two of the men up in front were Garland and LeFarge.

Thomas cast his eyes over the Governor. A beast, a bear. Even his bespoke suit looked inadequate for the task of holding in all the fat, those huge shoulders, those bulged-up arms. His big bullet head with its ring of gray hair hung forward, his whole face a glower of disappointment. Probably an act. O'Brien shot Thomas a grin, swept his gaze over the other three, and said, "You remember Tommy Steward." His voice, a growl, rumbled right over the three in front of him.

Two of the men glared at him, and the third faltered in his narration. O'Brien smiled at Thomas and wagged his fat finger at the other three men. "It's okay. I invited him. If I didn't, I should have. Can you back up, please, for Tommy's benefit?"

The mouse that had been talking began again. "Well, as I said,

26

we've gotten two pieces of information. Our local security contractor provided one. He's been able to tell us there is only one crew planning a large job in the City. Our guy tells us the crew chief has hired surveillance people and worked for at least six months. They're angling something that sounds like corporate espionage. Two independent informants confirm it. The snitches were, and I quote, 'Impressed by the guy but can't figure out what kind of corporate theft would be big enough.' This criminal normally does banks or diamond exchanges, so it's a change-up for him."

Thomas asked, "Does this organizer have a name?"

Garland, his voice heavy, said, "Not from this intel—just a nickname. He's known as the Gray Man. Highly respected, never caught, and his people are seldom arrested."

Thomas looked at Garland—standing there in front of the desk he appeared dog-eared, half-whipped. Thomas asked, "Does his style match our break-in?" LeFarge shot him a look—what did that mean, that LeFarge thought he was meddling?

The mouse piped up. "Well, yes and no. The Gray Man is known for technical types of theft—he likes to tunnel in, or come through the ceiling, disarm alarms, and make invisible exits. He doesn't often use violence or run a confidence game, and his jobs display simplicity. Another interesting thing is his style. He's not afraid to handle big materials. He's supposed to be the guy who took the four pallets of money off the dock at the Chicago Federal Reserve two years ago."

O'Brien pushed on. "You said you got two pieces of information."

"Yes." The mouse nodded three times at O'Brien, tock, tock, tock. Everyone could see his Adam's apple swallowing. "People following the money traced it out of your accounts in four jumps. It is now in an account listed under a Carl Dupont, a Canadian in Montreal. We got lucky—the money shipped offshore but circled back." His voice cracked. "Dupont's bank is ready to cooperate with your bank—after your CFO called and cranked up some pressure. The Canadians placed a watch on Dupont's account, but they're not ready to freeze assets. That requires the right US government requests. Mr. Garland here," and the mouse nodded sideways at his boss, "asked us to hold off."

Thomas wanted the question asked and LeFarge obliged. "Did our security team find this out?"

"Oh no, Acquisitions' contract firm in London found the money."

27

Garland winced and O'Brien threw Thomas another toothy grin.

O'Brien asked, "What do we know about Carl Dupont?"

The mouse added detail. "A low-level VP at the bank in Montreal gave us Dupont's phone number and address." Thomas thought there might be some Canadian regret over that disclosure. "When we back-trace the number, it's an import-export company named Ultra-World Trading."

O'Brien pressed. "Is that all you have? After twenty-four hours?"

The mouse ducked his head. "That's all we've got now."

O'Brien swung his chair around to stare out the big window. He hummed, quiet, detached.

"Well, we could—," began Garland.

O'Brien said, "Wait."

"—It's plausible Dupont —," Garland said.

"Wait, goddamn it!" O'Brien tented his fingers and hummed across them. Four men hovered in an uncomfortable pause. O'Brien swung his chair back to face them. He looked at Garland. "Well, you wanted to talk."

"If we can get a photo of Dupont, we can try to match him to the surveillance footage in the building. We can hire people in Montreal to watch his house and business."

"A start." O'Brien's jowls were mottled with extra blood. "Egan?"

"My team will be ready by tonight. If Dupont is our guy, he's more likely to be in New York than Montreal. If we can find him, we can send the team in."

"Thomas?"

"Since he's a business, we can crack him open. I can use the same techniques we do in Acquisitions. If he's legit, we'll know it. If he's dirty, we'll know that too. If he has holdings in the US, I can find them."

O'Brien leaned back beaming. "Something to work with! Don, I want you to try to match Dupont with the Gray Man. Egan, if we do get an address, I'll send you in, but if it's in Canada, you have to have transport across the border. Arrange the proper trucks to get your gear into Montreal without calling attention to the—you know. Thomas, you've got half an hour to get me Dupont's financials on my desk." The bear turned his chair to the window. They had been dismissed.

Thomas made it back in the thirty minutes. He dropped into a chair

28

in front of the desk and tossed a memory stick across the polished surface to O'Brien. "Dennis, we've got credit checks, annual statements to shareholders, and a photo from the company prospectus. Ultra-World Trading has received several fines from Customs, both US and Canadian, and has had one of its employees arrested for 'suborning' a Canadian official—it's a good guess that he bribed a customs agent."

O'Brien set a cut-glass tumbler down on a coaster and picked up the memory stick. He jacked it into a pad. "Where did you get the bribery thing?"

Thomas could pick up the faint, smoky scent of Scotch. "Easy. All that comes from an Internet search of the news agencies." Thomas went on, "The annual reports show the company recording high cash flow, exceptional return on capital investment, and its margins are much higher than its industrial sector."

O'Brien gave him a hooded look, his prominent brow hanging over his eyes. "All that means what I think it does?"

"Dupont is dirty and is flushing money through his company. Taking the company public was his first mistake—looks good on paper, but opens you up to scrutiny."

"Don needs the photo."

"Angie Tommo is flashing it down to him now. Dupont looks to be about sixty, and he has gray hair. Ties into the Gray Man nickname. He graduated from McGill in '80 with a technical degree."

"He's our guy." O'Brien sounded certain.

"Looks likely."

O'Brien picked up his glass, swirled the Scotch, scanned Thomas over the rim. "Do you have anything else?"

Thomas grinned. The Governor would always push for one more step. "I saved the best for last—the company does business in the US, and they have assets here, in New York. He has a long-term shared lease with another importer down on the harbor and an apartment listed as his US business address. There's a shed out at the airport in Queens." Leaning forward across the desk, Thomas handed O'Brien a slip of paper with addresses on it.

"It's the apartment." O'Brien swiveled his chair and spoke to his desk phone. "Allen, get LeFarge in here now."

Thomas rounded off. "We'll have more later, Dennis, but it's liable to be down in the noise, not critical stuff"

O'Brien grunted. "Okay. Better get back to it, Thomas. I want the safecracker too, and his colleagues, so start looking at employees. Besides, you shouldn't hear the next part. Deniability."

Robko had landed at the Montenegro Club. He drank anise and vodka, rather than doing the stone. He stood shoulder to shoulder with old acquaintances, guys that didn't mind his buying one little bit. His mobile rang in his pocket, over the boom of the music. He turned from the bar and pushed his way back into the hallway to the restrooms. He wobbled a bit and grabbed the doorjamb with one hand. "Yes?"

"Robert, it's...."

Robko couldn't make out the words, but he recognized the Gray Man's voice. "Wait." He pushed into the bathroom, glanced around, and went into one of the stalls. The stench of urine rose around him, but now he could hear over the club noise. "Yes?"

The Gray Man's voice sounded tense, cracking. "I don't have much time. There's a team of men breaking in. I think it's the Feds. I don't know what they have on me, but they're not trying to serve a warrant. They're just crashing in."

"Christ, get out of there!"

"Can't. They've got me blocked front and back. They even have men on the roof across the way."

"You're caught. Lay down on the floor spread-eagled. Don't get shot by accident."

"No accidents here. They know what they want. Robert, take care of her for me, if you can. Get her out safe, drive her where she says. If you can find her, it will only take you a couple of days to do as I ask."

Robko stared at the stall's partition. It was painted chocolate, with obscene figures gouged into the paint.

"Are you there? I don't have much time." The Gray Man's voice was high and tight.

Robko coughed. "Why should I get involved?"

"You owe me."

"You don't believe that. But I'll slide by to take a look-see. After you're arrested."

The Gray Man's words tumbled out. "Okay, this sounds like it. I'll leave the phone on... chunk it under the couch!"

"No, don't! Kill it! They can trace—" Robko heard a long sliding sound, a thump, shuffling. A loud bang. Feet pounding, a voice shouting. Crashing.

He hung up. The Gray Man had made a disappointing mistake.

Robko ran to the bar and emptied his front pockets of money. "Got to go," he said to the bartender. Once outside, he ran several blocks back to his place. Fumbling in his haste, he synced his vidi to his desk tablet. Once he had his data on the tab, he scrubbed and ruined the vidi's memory. Still wound up, on a nervous edge, he took a cab to Central Station, crossed through, and took a bus. He left the phone on, jammed down between a seat and the wall. He got off where he saw a taxi rank. The Gray Man had been caught. Robko had covered his tracks, but what if his boss gave him up?

Chapter Four: Poverty and Power Melt Like Ice

Wearing a Yankees ball cap tugged down low and a pizza joint delivery jacket, Robko slid around the corner to take a gander at the Gray Man's building. In the morning light, the block showed off the same dull thirties style that lined the entire neighborhood. The front showed nothing out of the ordinary. If he went straight in, they could box him up in the stairwell or elevator—if they were there.

He ducked around the block and found the building behind the Gray Man's. He entered the foyer. He pushed all the doorbells at once, leaned away from the camera, and someone buzzed him in. He hiked up seven flights to the roof. Ducking, he crabbed to the back wall and peeked over. His eyes found the Gray Man's living room. A large bulging web disfigured the glass; something substantial had been thrown into it from the inside. Robko grunted. "Of course he'd have armored glass." Yellow tape fluttered across the window that led onto the fire escape.

Robko clattered down all the stairs and cut through to the back, into the alley by the communal dumpsters. He couldn't reach the ladder to the fire escape, so he dug his fingers and toes into the cracks of the bricks and scrambled up to the first landing. He took the metal stairs to the Gray Man's apartment. The kitchen. He held his hands around his face and peered through the glass to see into the gloom. He saw an ordinary room, not trashed or tossed. Robko glanced at the yellow tape that read "FBI Crime Scene No Admittance." He tried the window and found it locked.

He moved across the back of the apartment, sidestepping down the window ledges. At each window, he checked for signs of life. He saw something disquieting in the living room—a chair sat in the middle of the open space.

He found no window open. He saw no girl present. He could

jimmy a window, but the alarms were visible—a hassle. But across the room he spotted something wrong with the front door. He took the fire escape up to the roof and strode to the roof's door. A screwdriver got him in. He crept down the stairs. When he reached the Gray Man's place, he found more police tape. The door lay inside the entry on its back. He stared at the huge split in the wood where the ram had struck and at the broken jamb where the locks had torn through. He whistled softly—this had taken some effort. He flipped the switch, but no light flicked on. The steel door at the other end had been blown off its hinges and sat propped up against the side, blackened on its edges. He could smell something like cordite—stinking, sharp. Gray light illuminated the living room beyond. He slipped under the tape and picked his way through the room. It took him fifteen minutes to work the place. Paperwork in a briefcase showed him the Gray Man had a name—Carl Dupont. Robko didn't find a name for the girl. She wore interesting underwear. He found a disturbing amount of blood in the living room, spattered up the wall and under the chair out in the center. Interrogation. That didn't feel like FBI or NYPD. Someone had sifted through everything in the apartment but repositioned it all instead of wrecking the place. They had been discrete when they searched the place—why, when they left the blood? Two teams? No PCs or phones, only dangling wires that went with them. Any digital records of the Gray Man's life had been taken from the apartment. A bust. All this sneaking around, just for a name. And they might or might not have the girl.

At home, Robko made quiet enquiries. A woman he had once known returned his call. She worked dispatch for a police precinct nearby. Things had been good between them; she told him NYPD had not responded to any call at the address he gave. He made the second call to a friend, the one person he trusted who had also worked with the Gray Man. Robko asked for the name of the Gray Man's woman. The friend turned out clueless. Robko rang the morgue and checked if there had been any corpse named Carl Dupont delivered. He called all the hospitals.

Without a contact in the FBI, he had nothing left to try. Hungry, he could have eaten. Instead, he fueled himself on coffee and downers. Lying on his back on the couch in his warehouse, he stared up into the dusty rafters and the dimness above him and conjured his way through the problem.

The girl wouldn't know how to reach him, and he didn't know how to contact her. He didn't know who had taken the Gray Man. He didn't know if this was about the O'Brien rack. He didn't know anything.

All the scenes of the past four days rolled like a wheel through his head, around his tranked memory. He dropped a yellow jacket onto his tongue. Sooner or later, Robko thought, the drugs would unlock his mind. He felt himself slipping into an insensible stone as midnight crept into the warehouse.

Thomas escorted Angie into the usual New York bar, if there was a usual. Set up for couples and for twenty-dollar drinks, it illuminated everything from below with blue light, made double chins disappear, and gave everyone a glam-fabulous Mediterranean tan. Thomas smelled an air thick with a mix of very expensive colognes and perfumes. She sat across from him and did the interview on him. "Phillips Exeter and Yale? Or was it Groton and Stanford?"

"Neither, I'm afraid. University of Illinois at Urbana-Champaign and Wharton. Before that, the high school was pretty snotty, but still public."

The blue light showed her off as quite beautiful, with dark, dark eyes, black hair pushed back on one side behind her ear, a gold earring glittering in the light. "Not my fault you come off like an ad for an East Coast finishing school. The horn rim glasses. The expensive suit and the regimental tie. The golden hair so casually hanging down across your manly forehead."

"I don't suppose you'd believe I buy all my clothes on the Internet?" He stared down the front of her white silk shirt, down to where a lacy bra pushed her breasts up towards him.

"No." She stirred the olive in her drink with the swizzle stick. "How did you get in with O'Brien?"

"O'Brien Investments hired me out of a mutual fund to do valuation analysis. When O'Brien bought a couple of companies rather than just their stock, we worked the deal for him. Then he made me into a general fixer for a while. I traveled around helping with company re-orgs. I moved into Acquisitions three years ago."

"Sweet. You know Acquisitions is known in the hallways as Rape and Plunder."

"A calumny. We're all saints in Acquisitions."

Her eyes narrowed; she scrutinized his face… all part of sizing him up. "If you don't mind my asking, why is a young guy from out in the divisions in so tight with the Governor?"

"Beats me. I've been lucky. What's better, O'Brien thinks I'm lucky."

"Well, soon you won't have to do real work. O'Brien will bring you in from Siberia and make you VP of Knitting or something. You can begin infighting to see how close your office can move towards the Governor's, and how fast."

"What I want to do is stay out in the field, run a small company, work up to a big one. That's pretty much what my father did."

She rolled the stem of her glass between her fingers. "How dull. I thought you would be more interesting."

"You'd prefer I was a dancer, like my mother?"

"Really? Anyone I've heard of?"

"Alice Lisolotte Rinser Steward? If you say yes, you're either from Germany or Illinois."

"I'm from Staten Island. The Italian Staten Island." Her teeth flashed white in the blue light. "We have toe-tappers there, too."

"You're not dancing for a living up on O'Brien's floor."

"No, I'm a babysitter."

His babysitters had never looked like Angie. "And who's the biggest baby?"

"Not you… although you did hit on me on Day One."

"Sorry if I misread the signs."

"Maybe yes, maybe no. Unlike the Governor I don't make up my mind in a hurry." She flicked her cool glance up and down.

He could sense the scale's swing from hopeless to hopeful. He channeled the conversation back where he wanted it to go. "O'Brien does judge the quick and the dead." He raised an eyebrow. "I've noticed he changes his mind at least once a month. Who's getting the hammer now?"

35

"Office gossip? I wouldn't have thought it in you, Mr. Thomas Cabot Steward."

He grinned. "All corporate men are little old women. You know that."

"You would know as much as I about the hammer. You're invited into the inner sanctum."

"The only guy on the skids I know is Garland. I'd help him out if I could—he got a bum rap."

She said, "Bum rap. How George Raft."

"Okay, it's a canard and a slander, if you like that better. Garland's organization did the right things, but they banged up against someone who was better and had more invested. Playing defense is tough."

"Nice of you. Mr. Garland wastes no affection on you."

"Anyone else I need to watch out for?"

"Weeell." She toyed with her glass. "I hate to say. But I'll give you a freebie, being you're new and a preppie on top of it. Stay away from the VP of Research. For some reason he's the fair-haired boy right now. He doesn't play nice."

"Thanks for the warning." He slipped his hand out across the glass table towards hers.

She glanced down at his hand, then glided her hand back. She crossed her arms, framed the gorgeous V of her cleavage. "Don't expect this type of revelation again. You wouldn't want me talking about you at work, would you?"

He leaned back and made the leather and chrome chair squeak. "Depends on the context… and the amount of admiration you express."

"My, and he's vain, too."

"Realistic." He waited to see the result of this claim.

She smiled, her teeth phosphorescent in the blue light. "Men are seldom realistic. For instance, they think they're loners, but they're really pack animals."

"And O'Brien has a pack?" Amused, he showed his own teeth.

"Oh yes. For one, he has Garland as his beagle. LeFarge is his pit bull."

"And me?"

"You're the Labrador retriever. No, the wolfhound."

There were worse dogs than a wolfhound. "You've finished your drink. Another? Or maybe dinner?"

36

"We both know what dinner means, Thomas Cabot Steward. I won't go up that road. I'll take the drink, though. I'll put it on your expense account when I fill it out. You've certainly been working."

I'm on the sofa. I'm lying on the couch where I started hours ago. I am profoundly stoned down, just where I want to be. I say it aloud. "Profound." My muscles twitch in a startled little jerk. Why? I hear something back behind the kitchen. I ease up off the couch on cat's feet, tranked cat's paws. I creep through my house to scan the back.

At the fire escape, I stare down to see black SUVs in the alley. Men move around like snakes in a pit in their black jackets with large yellow letters on the back—"DEA." Christ and Kram, this is a raid by the dope police. There's no way I'll go into a Fed Scuzz Bucket just for my benzos and jackets.

Running to my bed, I fish the paper bags out from under and also the windbreaker I wore today. I shake the yellows out into my hand and throw them in one of the bags. Whoa, what's this? The acrylic box from the score, all lustrous and white in the dark of the room. It, too, has to go so little Robko can live the next few years free. There's also a hundred grams of Phenobarbital under the sink—Jesus wouldn't that get me sent up for dealing! I jam the box and the pheno into the garbage disposal—turn on the water. Flip the switch to hear it grinding. Run for the bath, throw all the pills in the toilet, shake the bags out over the porcelain, flush-flush-hit-the-handle. Back to the kitchen to turn off the water, turn off the grinder—tiptoe back to the window where they creep up the fire escape. I know there's got to be someplace in here I can hide till they're gone. A big thunderous sound at the front door, kram it all, they're blasting away at the front door with a shotgun! Now a ram. On second thought there's no hiding. I've got to run from these guys because they don't act like cops; they act like a death squad—I've gotta get out, but the freight elevator in the back opens onto where their trucks are parked, and the front door is down—they're coming in. I snatch up the run-bag from under the bed. The hatch in the living room—I run as quiet as I can across the room—I've got a trap door under one of the tables—I pry the floor up. They're insanely loud, or maybe it's in my head. I've got seconds to get out of sight. My salvation exists as a black hole under a table. I twist around to drop my legs through. I can feel my feet catch on the rafters below on the metal truss. I squat down below the floor. I curl up into the space below and drag the hatch closed over me. I'm in the restaurant supply under my loft where I hang by my hands and drop down onto the shelving. Thank You Mary and Joseph—boxes not piles of plates. I slither across the top to the end of the row. I climb down the side. Oh Christ on a Crutch… I wish I wasn't so stoned. I would know how to get out of here in one piece. The yellows roar in my head fighting with the adrenaline. But now I remember my bike—this warehouse connects to the next one over. The boys let me store the bike there. I scurry rodent-like down the aisle to the back. Through the bars and glass, I can see them in the alley with their guns and their toys. At the door in the side wall—a key over the jamb—I can feel my hands shake. I drop the key. Of course I have to scuttle around on the floor. Feel for it. Ah there it is. Unlock the door. Slip through oh I do know how to slip don't I. Here's the bike up against the wall under the tarp. Draw the tarp off softly… softly. Crap, I dropped the helmet didn't I? I drag on the jacket, zip it up… and the helmet—can a helmet stop a nine mil? Now push the bike to the back crafty… crafty. Turn the alarm off. Slide back the door. Oh God don't squeak—it leads to a loading dock that sits on the back. The door is a black hole in the shadow, but can they hear it creaking open? No one hears me. Hoist my leg over the bike. Oh careful I can do this. Breathe and turn the key. Fire the bike—she catches. She growls. She's in gear. She howls and shoots forward. I fly off the dock at an angle, down the alley into freedom. The bastards are shooting. What is this? These aren't cops. They're the Nazis in Poland. I lean into the corner out onto the street. She cuts the New York night like a laser running ahead of me. I take a left onto Delancey to run up through the lights so fast I can't glance down at the speedo—here's the Williamsburg Bridge— bomb across into the next borough. Then I'll decide what to do and where to go.

Across the bridge, I slow down from eighty to thirty. Can't afford to get caught by some patrol car after outrunning a death squad. I'm panting like a winded runner, but I've burned the downers out of my system. Where am I going? Sibyl, of course, I can go to Sibyl. She can kill me instead of these boys. Small difficulty. Sibyl lies back across the water behind me. I'll go all the way around, cross Manhattan, and cut through Chinatown.

I better pull into an alley and slow my heart down some. Here, turn in here, behind a club I know. Park by the dumpster and this slab of a back door. An alley light hangs over me. I wish someone had busted that one out—no matter. Breathe. Damn. A person—tall—moves away from me down the alley, into the blackness.

On the wall I see the same graff as I saw at Bennie's, the same basic shapes, the quote marks, a signature that is a block of visual gibberish. This one says, "Plunge Me Into The Shit And Raise Another Up." I'm beginning to feel I'm following this guy around. Screw him. Screw this omen.

Chapter Five: Hide in Plain Sight

Robko couldn't approach Sibyl straight on—God knew how she would react. He chose the Cumberland Hotel on the edge of SoHo because they knew him. First, he parked the bike deep in their garage on a day ticket. He retrieved his Black-Irish alias from the run-bag, pocketed it, and hung the bag over his shoulder. Rather than pop straight in, he ambled around a bit to clear his head—he had just been through a lot.

Since he had first noticed the graff on the shop outside his coffee house, he paid more attention to street art—it calmed him and excited him at the same time, like a barbiturate gork. He studied the clues and searched for the prophecy. He ranged down a street, away from SoHo where it turned grittier, where bits of trash traveled along the walls, gossiped, whispered. He saw various admonishments painted up on the walls: to do impossible sex acts, an opinion about the current mayor's mother, and a strange graff that said, "Sweet Mouth Make Me Well." That one reminded him of Sibyl. The graff mirrored the new style—the type he had picked up on only yesterday. He scowled at the tag beside the graffiti—an image of a black silhouette in a long coat. The black man again.

He caught a cab back to the hotel as a cover and made a formal entrance at the front door. He recognized the clerk, but the clerk had forgotten him.

Robko handed over a driver's license. "Hi, Johnny. I'm checking in. I don't have a reservation, but since I stay here so often...."

"I believe we have a room available, Mr.—Abernethy? One moment." The clerk clattered away on his keyboard. "Yes, I've got you here. You're a member of our loyalty program I see, and here is all your data. Still Boston?"

"Yes, I'm just in from there today. You keep a bag here for me. If you'll have the concierge find it please."

"Very good sir. I'll need a credit card."

"I hate all those receipts, don't you?"

The desk clerk shot him a look.

Robko coughed, arched his eye. "I'd prefer the wife not know about this one, and she's my bookkeeper. I'll just pay for three days, like always, and a couple hundred for incidentals." Robko, now Sean Abernethy, counted out fourteen hundred.

"Very good sir."

"Is the kitchen still open?"

"We can do light snacks sir. Breakfast starts at six."

"Great. I may have a visitor this evening or tomorrow. Send her up when she asks for me."

"Yes sir, I'll leave instructions here on the computer. I'll have a bellboy bring up your bag as soon as we retrieve it."

Robko rode up in the old gilded elevator, sauntered down the Beaux Arts hallway, and entered his funky, tawdry room. Four hundred a night didn't buy much in Manhattan. Still, he had lived in a lot worse. He picked up the hotel vidi-phone and got an outside line. He dialed, and the other end picked up on the second ring. The man answering was in a starched, striped shirt with a deep maroon tie. He gazed serenely into the screen and said, "Box Office Entertainment." With his eyes at half-mast like that, he looked like a dressed-up snake.

"I'd like to make a booking for the evening."

Box Office produced a clipboard and a pen. "Yes sir. Which show?"

"Sibyl."Snake-man riffled back a page. "I'm sorry, sir. Sibyl is sold out this evening. Not even SRO. Perhaps you'd be interested in another of the shows?"

"No, I'll wait until I can attend a Sibyl performance. When the ticket booth calls in, let her know it's Sean Abernethy at the Cumberland. Tell her no hurry; an afternoon matinee is fine."

In a polite echo to the desk clerk minutes before, Box Office said, "Very good sir. I'll let the show know you called."

Sean Abernethy didn't feel hungry; he felt famished. He dialed room service.

Thomas had been cut out of the loop by LeFarge and Garland, and the workarounds didn't make him happy. He had the name Carl Dupont, and he had access to raw data from Corporate Security, delayed by at least a day. He didn't receive their analysis or any clues on where LeFarge and Garland were headed. In spite of the printouts and memory sticks on his conference room table, he saw only a barren field. Not acceptable. On the other hand, Garland and LeFarge hated each other enough, maybe, that the two wouldn't partner up to screw him. Small consolation.

In the meantime he was pinned to this room with its brown, rich carpet, its white walls, and its sheet of glass overlooking Manhattan.

Angie strode in to the conference room with coffee and a memflash. "Breakthrough! Mr. Garland's assistant slipped us these files and said Security doesn't want these on the network. 'Please treat with utmost confidentiality,' she says."

"Good morning to you too, Angie." He cheered up immediately at the sight of the memflash.

"Here's your latté, and good morning, Mr. Steward."

"Thomas. I prefer Thomas. Any calls?" He was watching her tight, lustrous blouse, with its slashing neckline. He had to remind himself to look up into her eyes.

She grinned, her teeth flashing white. "I suspect you've been here for some time, so you would know."

He could smell a faint scent from her, the scrubbed smell of a good shampoo. In spite of himself, he leaned forward to breathe in more of it. "Well, yes, I did come in early. It was worth it. I have a source that claims everyone wants Dennis Malley O'Brien dead and that O'Brien doesn't give a rat-shit what they think. I know quite a bit more about Carl Dupont, but nothing about his associates or employees. I also know there's been an earthquake in northwest China."

"I'm impressed." She pointed at the memdevice. "Um, if I were you, I'd look at the action log for Captain LeFarge's team. Corporate Security's folks are all rushing back and forth whispering about it."

She was bringing him good luck as well as the data and advice. "Excellent. Maybe I can catch up with what's happening." He waved his hand at his tablet. "And when in doubt, follow the money. A friend of mine has done some extraordinary data search that cost O'Brien forty thousand because of its alleged illegality. I now possess two years

42

of Mr. Dupont's bank transactions."

"Can I help?"

"Yes, you can. Bring your desktab and start looking at Mr. Dupont's cash flow."

She sat down on the opposite side of the table, sliding into a chair like slipping into a swimming pool. She loaded the transactions that he blue-toothed to her and said, "What am I looking for?"

"Where he gets his money… unusual large payments, travel, rent or mortgage payments for buildings we don't know about. Also regular ATM withdrawals to cash—and where the ATM is. Large equipment purchases like getaway vans. Oh, and any check labeled Safecracker, payment for—"

"Ha ha."

The memflash she had brought startled him. "Can I read you some of this while you work?"

"Sure. I can multi-task with the best of them." She sneaked him a sly look and grinned.

"LeFarge's team raided an apartment—the apartment that I found for them! They took down Carl Dupont and wrung a fair amount of intelligence out of him. Listen to this; it's cop-speak for a beating. 'After some difficulties with the criminal, he was induced to surrender the name of his B&E man and of the two other persons in the crew. Only three employees…' blah blah. Now it picks up. 'The safecracker's name is Robert Zlata. According to the perpetrator, the other two suspects are out-of-state already….' Blah blah, 'one in jail for car theft….' There is a fourth person to check according to the file. 'Dupont's last phone call traces to a local name, Tim Boxwood, linked to an address nearby in the Bowery.' They don't say what they did with Dupont, but they're bound to have him locked up somewhere. Working him for information."

She let out a breath. "That's a lot of laws to break."

"They're up for breaking and entering, multiple counts of impersonating a police officer, assault and battery, kidnapping, and conspiracy to commit criminal acts. Murder might be next." He shook his head, half in admiration for LeFarge, half in chagrin for how over the top it all was.

"The poor bastard." She had long since stopped work on her desktab. Her mouth angled down, her face dead serious. "Sounds dangerous, for you as well as Dupont."

"For me?"

"It's the big time, Mr. Steward. Rules are for other people, not O'Brien. He's not on the firing line for this."

The air in the room hung humid, drenched in threat—she was right. O'Brien could need a scapegoat sometime in the future. "Then we'd better catch our thieves before LeFarge goes any further. The fellow who broke in here and got away may be the same person as this Timothy Boxwood they found on Dupont's iMob. There's more. They raided the Boxwood place down in the Bowery, and one of the team shot another in the confusion. Boxwood got out the back door on a motorcycle."

She paged back on her desktab, her fingers flicking. "Wait, I've got a tie-in! I have regular payments to a Tim Boxwood on a bi-weekly basis starting four months ago. I've got the account number too—SoHo bank." She beamed it over.

"The money, that means that Boxwood is Zlata."

"Okay, that's a jump, but what do you do with it?"

"Maybe SoHo is where he lands. Maybe the Bowery. Let's try to find out who this Zlata-slash-Boxwood is, using trails the police wouldn't. I want you to start credit checks on Zlatas, all the Zlatas in America if you have to."

"Not the Boxwoods too?" she said with a touch of irony in her voice.

"I have a reason. The coffee and cake deliveryman on the footage looked more Bosnian than English. Ergo, Zlata is the real name. Start with NYC first, and do the big cities next."

She muttered something he didn't catch.

He said, "I'll call my friend again. We'll pay through the nose, but we'll get Boxwood's bank transactions."

"What about Boxwood's phone? The built-in GPS?"

"Garland will be looking for Boxwood's vidi. It's either a quick win or a dead end, and Garland will already be on it."

"What are we chasing besides Zlata-slash-Boxwood, Mr. Steward?"

"It's Thomas, please. We'll check real estate transactions in SoHo and the Bowery to see if Mr. Boxwood has purchased anything else in the last ten years."

"I have a friend in realty, Thomas. For a small fee, she'd do the search for us."

"Would she do it in a tearing hurry for a big fee?"

She flared her eyes and broke out into a smile. "Oh yeah."

"Call her." He tapped his way to the white pages for Zlata, Robert. He found five in New York City. He discarded three who had registered to vote, and threw away the other two because, according to the City website, they worked for NYC. Dead end. Not as easy as compiling corporate data. Genealogy next—he'd hire a firm to give him the US family trees for the Zlatas. At this rate, he could expect very long days or a short career. He tapped on the edge of the desktab. He had missed something. It ate at him, but what was it?

A knocking. At first it reverberated in Robko's head, but then it repeated and bounced around the room. He dragged himself out of bed. Throwing on the bathrobe, he shuffled over to the door. He peered through the peephole, and opened the door. An explosion in the shape of a woman swept in, raised a hand, and whacked his ear hard. The explosion swept on past into the room.

He fell back. "Damn, Sibyl! That really hurts."

"You're lucky I wasn't holding anything, like a club or a hatchet."

"Good to see you too. Just like old times."

"I'm still mad at you. Mr. Abernethy again? Why I put up with this, Robert, I ask myself." She was still whipcord thin. She had gone to blonde, cut in an expensive shag. She had an X&G bag over her shoulder, but knowing her habits, he figured it was a knock-off. She perched on the end of the bed. "A thousand. Up front this time."

"This isn't about sex. Or it's not all about sex."

"Meeting me in a hotel? Why didn't you just come home?"

"Not my home anymore. If I remember the last time we talked, you were waving a knife around and threatening to cut off my little robko. Besides, I may be in trouble. I don't want any blowback coming your way."

"Trouble?" Her face took on a familiar pinched look, like a worried fourteen-year-old. He gazed into her small face with its absurd blue eyes. Contacts, no doubt—big eyes in an elfin face anyway.

45

"Hmm." He sat on the bed beside her. She didn't move away. Slow, hesitant, he ran his forefinger over the back of her hand.

"Trouble," she repeated. "Money?"

"No, I'm set right now."

"Bluemen? The Fedzilla?"

"Not so's you could tell."

"Then what are you talking about?"

"My loft in the Bowery got raided last night. It's another crew, but not the usual. These guys are violent. Smash and grab. Shoot-you-dead types."

Her eyebrows pinched together, a vertical line up into her tall forehead. "A crew? Why are they after you?"

"Jealousy? Revenge for my last employment? Maybe they think I have something they want. I don't know yet."

"Why am I here?"

"I'm not really sure. I wanted to see you. I wanted to tell you to watch your back."

"That's just so nice. Two years you waited."

"And look at the reception I just got. Thank God I didn't come over the week after."

She reached up and touched his ear. "It's a bright cherry red."

He thought she sounded a little pleased. "I wonder why."

She picked at her lower lip with a thumb and forefinger. "Tell me, why should I watch my back?"

"They can follow me to you. The name on the loft is Tim Boxwood. The names on your condo are Tim and Sibyl Boxwood."

"Oh." She sat quiet for a long minute. "What are you going to do?"

"Get a phone. Watch your place for a couple of days; see if anyone sniffs around. Move out of here into a furnished apartment. I'll try south of you in Chinatown. Lay around and see what happens."

She slapped him on the arm, hard. "You're the most do-nothing I've ever met. That's not a plan."

"Best I've got."

She muttered under her breath, "Piece of shit."

"That too." He fell silent. She sat cross-legged, with a red shoe wagging, wagging on the end of her boney foot. Fake Celetti, he thought.

She stabbed him in the thigh with a painted nail. "Give me five

46

hundred."

"I thought you wanted a full flip."

"Family discount. I wanted the afternoon off anyway. Saturday is a big night for me, and I can get some sleep beforehand."

"Here?"

"You're naked under that robe, aren't you?"

Chapter Six: Love Turned on The Wheel of Torture

Thomas sat in the Adirondack chair out on a windswept lawn that perched on the edge of the Sound. Loutish, unformed, O'Brien sat beside him, grunting into the phone. He was wearing a terrycloth robe and Mexican sandals.

Thomas waited. He planned what he would say and what he would ask. O'Brien hung up, angry. "Damn fools. Don's people got caught watching Dupont's Montreal relatives. Sooner or later one of them will go looking for Dupont." He flung the vidi on the table at his elbow.

"Did Dupont give up the memory devices?"

"That would be a no. He had already passed them on to his buyer."

"And he didn't have a name for the buyer?"

"No, dammit, not a real one." It was hard to tell if O'Brien was feeling petulant or savage.

"Then we should have a plan for containment."

"Don't be goddamn mysterious. What's that mean?"

"Wait for the buyer to make the first move to use the data against you."

"And then? Hire an army? Done that."

"Hire a bunch of lawyers and set up financial attacks on your enemy. Serious predatory attacks."

"Meaning?"

Thomas dipped his head. "For example, have a bunch of patent-infringement and unfair-trade-practices people ready to file something within twenty-four hours, once you have a target. Deny your enemy access to any ongoing favorable deals. Build a cash pool to buy stock. Threaten a hostile takeover, and then trade for the data."

"An army of bureaucrats."

Thomas blinked. "You know LeFarge's team calls itself 'The Foreign Legion?' Also, the 'Kill Team?' They're risk takers. You need a capability for risk taking, but—"

O'Brien waved a hand and shut him off. "I get your point. Now, why are we here?"

"I wanted to talk to you privately at your house. How much you want out in the open later will be your decision."

The Governor grunted. "The office is safe."

"We have proof it's not."

Annoyed, O'Brien snorted. "Tell me what you gotta tell me."

"We know the safecracker. If the Artifact didn't turn up with Dupont and he didn't confess to selling it, I believe it possible the safecracker didn't give it to the head thief. We should pursue the burglar, not the buyer who has the memory devices."

"Tell me about him."

"His name, his real name, is Robert Thomas Dragomir Zlata."

"What kind of a name is that?"

"Slavic. Polish."

"Frickin' Polacks."

"His family is from Chicago, and they call him Robko, so he's grown up deep in the local culture in spite of his Christian names."

"What do we know about him?"

"He didn't finish high school, and the US Military refused to take him. Sealed record of course, but we guess personality issues or he failed a drug screen. Got picked up on drug charges as a kid—weed— but has no adult criminal record. That in itself is a surprise."

O'Brien asked, "What about his folks?"

"His father is dead, died of a heart attack in prison. Had an older brother, but he's dead too, from leukemia. Robko is estranged from his mother; she's only seen him occasionally over the last ten years. It's for the usual reasons. According to her, Robko's not a good Catholic boy, not much good at all. She's religious, in spite of the fact she ran a bar for forty years. She works, and he doesn't. She thinks he's a drug user. She knows he's stolen from her. She wants grandkids, and he wants— what? We don't know him that well yet."

"How did you find this out?"

"I flew out to Chicago on the red-eye and asked her."

"You got balls, Tommy. And luck."

"I also talked to an uncle and some friends in the neighborhood. The interviews cost you a bunch. Robko used to be in a gang or crew, boosting cars for a chop shop. They suspect he moved on to burglary, what they call second story work. They don't know what he does now. He's not around much."

"What else do we know?"

"He was born July 10, 1988. Five foot eight, a hundred and thirty, black hair, light brown eyes—school friends admitted his eyes look pale and spooky. In good physical shape, likes basketball in spite of his height. He spends a lot of money judging by his loft here in New York, but he's off the financial grid. Zlata is a cash-only type of person. For instance, he had a serious motorcycle accident in 2002. He used no medical insurance, paid everybody in cash."

"But where is he?"

"We worked forward through his alias. You know, Tim Boxwood, the name on the Bowery loft? We followed Boxwood to another alias, Abernethy."

"You have a name. Do you have a location?"

"Approximately. He's gone into hiding here in NYC, and I think I know within a few blocks where he is. I want a favor though, Dennis."

"I'm listening."

"I want to look for him myself first. Give me some time to hunt up his acquaintances, drink in his bars, find his old girlfriends. Don't send in the storm troopers, not just yet."

"Huh. Fewer feet on the ground."

"They wouldn't know what to look for."

O'Brien dropped his gaze to the grass, tilted his head, scuffed at the green with his toe. "No promises, Tommy. You found this guy, or at least found out who he is faster than anyone else—so that earns you something. But like I said, I will have the Artifact at any cost. And quick."

"So for now, it's a yes?"

"Stay in touch. I mean it. Two or three times a day, or I unleash the hounds."

"I understand." Thomas stood up and nodded—a little medieval bow. He always shut up and left the meeting when he got what he wanted. He had bought some time, and now he needed some luck.

Robko looked for an apartment the morning after Sibyl's visit. He found a walkup above a Chinese grocery store. The apartment would be ready in two days, and he knew enough not to push the landlord. Scoring this sublet as a white-eye in this neighborhood—that was a special deal. Both Robko and the landlord liked the week-by-week cash aspect. The tenant on the lease had to be pulling a short jail term somewhere, unaware of and cut off from this side deal.

He spent afternoons on Canal Street, the seedy side of SoHo. Sibyl had a condo in one of the graceful old five-story, cast-iron buildings there, but this far south, the blocks hadn't turned posh and gentrified, and the real estate prices weren't catastrophic. He wandered back and forth a bit, in and out of the cheap clothing stores. He looked at electronics only the poor would buy, browsed the news at the stand on the corner, and got a haircut. A Middle Eastern restaurant squatted across from her door, perfuming the street with cumin and coriander. He ate too many falafels and drank enough tea to float himself inside out. He saw NYPD patrol cars and some private security, fat-looking and ineffective at best, but he didn't see anybody in a good suit. He didn't see a van by the curb or patrolling the area. Still, he had an itch. Someone in the neighborhood was watching somebody. A bugman hid somewhere around here, he could feel it. He decided the condo should remain off-limits.

On Canal, he bought a phone and loaded money into the card. As vidis go, it wasn't very smart, but as long as he could get onto the Net, listen to the news and make calls, it kept him happy. He also bought four baseball caps in various colors that he rotated in and out of a plastic bag.

Seeing Sibyl had put him in a sentimental mood—he called his Ma. He hadn't seen the old bitch in a year. She wasn't home, and the answering machine picked up. He didn't leave a message.

He videoed the Matchmaker, out on the coast. He was at a table under an umbrella, sucking on a margarita. Judging by the beach and boats behind the Matchmaker, Robko got him close to a marina, maybe one of San Diego's. Robko could hear discomfort in his voice. The conversation was marginally helpful but so round-about as to be a pisser.

The Matchmaker's voice came through fruity, plush. "Yes, who is it you want?"

"Hi, I'm trying to reach the Castelon Dating Service."

51

"Who's this? There's a glare on the screen, and I can't quite see."

Robko coughed. "An old client. You set me up last year, you know, on the Milwaukee thing. And the year before there was a girl on the—the Florida thing."

"Oh yeah. I remember you. You're that really tall guy."

So this was how the conversation would go. "No, I'm the short one."

The Matchmaker picked his glass back up and inserted the straw into his face. "Sure, I remember you. What can I do for you this fine day?"

"I ran up against a strange girl on a date, and I wondered if you had anything to do with her." *With my door being kicked in and me being shot at.*

The Matchmaker pushed his sunglasses up onto his forehead. "Tell me about her."

"Well, she had a lot of hangers-on. A lot. And she liked it big and loud. She was capable of slapping someone around pretty good."

"And where did this date take place?"

"Within sight of Greenpoint across the bridge. You know, back East."

The Matchmaker sucked on a tooth. "Greenpoint? Out by the airport? I don't think we've got anyone like that on file. That's a woman who would seek a specialized relationship. We haven't had anything like that come up in a while. There are a few old clients, you know, who do the—"

"The rough stuff?"

"Yeah, you know, who are looking for it rough or give it out rough, but—"

"You're telling me they don't live near Greenpoint?"

"Yes, that's right. They date around more in California and out on the Lakes. They wouldn't be interested in someone like you, I'm afraid. They tend to hook up with bankers and…. um, truckers."

"Well, thanks anyway. I'll call maybe, the next time I'm free for a date."

Thomas wandered SoHo off and on for a week, when he wasn't

working with Angie and the data. O'Brien allowed this only because nothing else was coming together. Thomas wore his lucky shoes, carried his lucky jacket, avoided cracks in the pavement—but it wasn't working out very well.

He took a turn past the apartment on Canal Street at different times of day for a look. By now he had a dossier on Sibyl Boxwood and knew she was a prostitute. His information showed she made the mortgage payments on the apartment—Tim Boxwood didn't shell out for it. He saw Sibyl on a frequent basis. She left for work at three in the afternoon and often didn't return until the morning. She didn't use the condo for business.

Boxwood had morphed into Abernethy, or at least they saw money going out of Boxwood's account and showing up later in Abernethy's. Angie had commissioned a very expensive hacker to tunnel the SoHo and Bowery hotels. Digital desk registers showed an Abernethy had checked into the Cumberland the night of the loft raid. He checked out three days later and left no trail. The address he had given in Boston didn't exist.

At night Thomas moved from bar to bar, not expecting to spot his opponent. He just wanted to find where Zlata had been in the past, who he was, what he liked… what women he was attracted to. Thomas carried a photo, a clever fake that showed a young Zlata and an equally young Thomas in basketball uniforms, arm in arm. After a drink and maybe a bar appetizer, he'd ask the bartender, "Say, I'm trying to find an old buddy of mine who used to live around here. See…." He'd show the photo. "I've lost track of him. I'm trying to find out where he moved."

The bartender would lean over and look at the photo. Most of the time the bartender would say something along the lines of, "Whoa, a long time ago. You're a lot older now!"

"Do you know him?"

"Nah, never seen the guy, or he's changed so much I don't recognize him from this."

Late in the week, Thomas twigged that he had the style wrong. He had been in and out of restaurants and bars he liked. On impulse, he ducked into a bar near Zlata's loft. The old storefront sported black painted glass overlaid with green and red paint scrawls. A homemade poster on the door advertised the night's musical entertainment, the

Zombie Howlers and the Pukers.

Inside Thomas found an interior so dark he tripped over chairs twice getting up to the bar. He ordered a beer and watched two young people beside him slurp jello shots. He doubted this was the place to order a scotch. The background music was some sort of trance threaded through with industrial noise in a loop. It made the hair on the back of his neck stand up.

"Yo, buddy!" A voice beside him cut through the sound. "You look lost."

Thomas turned to see a serviceman, a mere baby in uniform. "No, I just wandered in out of curiosity. Interesting place."

"What?"

Thomas raised his voice. "Interesting place."

"You ought to see it when the bands start up about eleven."

"What kind of music?"

"Oh, thrash, hard buzz, some old-timer punk."

"I have a friend likes that kind of stuff. He used to live around here, and I'm trying to find his ex-wife, so I can track him down for old time's sake."

"What's the babe look like?"

"Short, lightweight, blonde."

The serviceman shrugged. "Come on, man, that don't help. They're all freakin' pixies down here. How about the guy?"

"Here, let me show you his picture." Thomas handed over the photo.

His new friend held it under the edge of the bar where neon girdled it. "Nah, don't know him, but I've only been coming here for a year. Hey, Lew." He motioned the bartender over. "Do you know this guy?"

"Sure. Name was Sean. Major 'klono-dude,' used to come in here a lot but hasn't been around for a while."

"Klono?" asked Thomas.

"Klonopins, man," said the serviceman. "Your friend's a stoner."

The bartender said, "Nothin' wrong with that, except I prefer drinkers. That's where we make the money."

Thomas said, "So do you know where he lived?"

"No. Why should I? He was just around... you know what I mean?"

"Any friends of Sean's still coming in?"

"No. He likes women and men, both. Prefers small, butch women to the soft, squishy type. He ran with one who was pretty hot—and domineering. She ain't been in since I don't know when." He picked up Thomas's empty beer bottle. "Anything else I can do for you?"

"No thanks. But if you see him, let him know Tom Steward was looking for him."

The bartender raised an eyebrow. "Right. That'll be four seventy-five, and a twenty for the info."

Thomas handed over two twenties. "Thanks for talking with me." The serviceman caught him by the elbow. "Say man, try the Dumpster. It's two blocks over on Greene."

"Thanks. I will." But not in a blazer, khaki pants and a pressed shirt.

Robko lay on the couch; he watched the changing lights from the street on his ceiling. Flickering reds and greens filtered in from the Chinese medicine shop across the way. The shop was filled with fake rhino horn and most likely pig teats.

He hadn't been out at night since he had moved into his apartment. Chinese takeout littered the coffee table beside him, and he had a cruze going from some klonopin. A major sense of chemical-induced peace had pushed his troubles to the far edge of his mind. At three in the morning, a rapid knock shook his door. He rolled off the couch, staggered a bit, and ambled over to open the door.

"Thanks for letting me in so fast, you gozo." Sibyl slipped in, whipped around, and slammed the door. She slapped the deadbolt over. "Great neighborhood. Hot-and-cold-running Tongs, Chinese kids panhandling at all hours, and all the crank you'd ever need. I even saw a black Chinaman. The graffiti is cool, though. I saw one on the edge of Chinatown that said, 'In the Balance is Love and Chastity.' Fits my career."

"Don't slam the neighborhood, Sibyl. I feel comfortable here. No white person can come within a block of us without looking like a bonfire on a hill."

"Next time let me choose the apartment." She looked around the place—it had a single window that faced the street. Old metal blinds hung askew. Inside, the walls were toffee colored, flaked in places, and showing blue underneath. On the floor, a distressed lime green rug stretched out. "Interesting. Run down enough to make good photo." She pulled out a slim little camera and fired off six shots.

"Still taking snaps?"

She walked over to the breakfast bar, scratched at some grime with her fingernail, and glanced at him.

He nodded. "Yes, I know it's all a bit tawdry, but the servants' quarters in back are quite generous, and the pool is an added bonus."

"Robert, you always thought you were a smooth talker. Well you're wrong. Stoned again, aren't you?"

"Just floating along with a mild feeling of euphoria, and most of that is your presence. Thanks for coming by."

She reached up to rub his cheek. "You look good... compared to my last customer."

"I always look good. It's my Gypsy charm."

"You're a Polack, not Romany."

"Well, I am a thief. That makes me kind of Gypsy."

She held up an exotic shopping bag from one of the stores up on Prince Street. "Look, I brought vodka for myself...," she hauled out a premium Scandinavian brand. "and a bottle of hair dye for you."

"Hair dye?"

"It's for your persona. The Black Irish aren't really black you know. They're mostly brown-eyed with dark brown hair."

"How do you know these things?"

"I'm in the people business. Folks brag more about where they came from than where they're going. They give you the whole spiel— everybody from the German Lutherans through to the Greek fishermen—they all have illustrious ancestors. Come on in the bathroom, and I'll get started."

She took off his shirt and pushed his head down into the sink. Tugging on cheap vinyl gloves, she wet his hair and applied the dye, working it in. She held him by the back of the neck when he tried to straighten up. "Not yet. The dye sets for thirty-five minutes." She stripped the gloves, threw them into the brown-spattered sink beneath his nose and disappeared. He could hear her in the kitchen. When she got back, she set a glass that tinkled with ice down on the edge of the bathtub.

56

"How long's it been?"

"Couple of minutes. Uncomfortable?" Sibyl planted her hands up on his shoulders and ran them from his shoulders down to the small of his back. "You've stayed in shape."

"Virtuous life."

"Yeah, right."

"No, really. Most days I eat right, and I go to a climbing gym."

"A what?"

"A place where you climb... on walls, with harnesses... so you don't fall on your head."

He felt her dig her fingers into his shoulders, kneading the muscles. Then she slapped him on the ass. "The dye's dripped out enough so's you can straighten up." She fished out a shower cap from the dye box and snapped it around his head. She wrapped his shoulders and neck with a towel. "You can write this towel off, white to chocolate brown. I wish I had contacts to change your eyes from cat-yellow to dark brown."

He said, "I like my eyes."

"That's your trouble. You're not into self-criticism. Sit on the john here, and don't move around. This stuff can stain everything if you let it. You've already got a spot of it on your chin." She scrubbed at him with a wad of toilet paper.

"I just sit here for thirty minutes?" He could feel the plastic of the shower cap over his ears. It made her voice muffled.

"No, I'll do your mono-brow also." Sibyl applied petroleum jelly around the eyebrow hair and used a toothbrush, his toothbrush, to push brown die into the single long bar of black hair. She sat back on the edge of the tub and took a hard swallow out of her glass.

He liked this, the lazy feel, the way she touched him. "My, this is so domestic." He sensed the air in the little room steaming up, even with his wet hair and a naked torso. His shoulder blades rippled out a tiny quiver—she was sitting so close, touching his knee with hers.

"As domestic as we'll ever get, bucko."

"I appreciate you thinking of me, helping me out."

"It's just hair color, Robert, not a commitment."

"But you're not waving the knife around this time."

"Can't carry it when I'm working. I don't need a weapons charge if I'm busted. I could go get a paring knife from the kitchen if you want, if you feel more comfortable around armed women."

She took a sip of the vodka. His turn. "I've been watching your place a bit."

"Oh?"

"Nothing yet. I've got a bad feeling about it. Maybe you should move in here for a while."

"Give up a perfectly wonderful condo for this dump, a dump with a resident stoner? I don't think so."

"Well, then, let's go out together. I can keep an eye on you part of the time if you'll let me hang around."

"I work nights."

"Every night?"

"Wednesdays are slow. I don't normally work Wednesdays."

"Tomorrow is Wednesday."

"So it is. What did you have in mind?"

"How about the Comet Kitty?" He glanced at her to see the reaction.

"Christ, Robert! Even when you're on the run, you want to party." She tucked the cap back behind his ears and swabbed at them with a corner of the towel.

"Officially, I'm between jobs, not on the run."

She wrinkled her nose. "You're officially frightened about a crew chasing you."

"I prefer not to think about that part. Yellows help a lot. I could use one about now."

"Stay still—the color isn't done setting. Where are they?"

"In one of the Chinese takeout boxes on the coffee table."

"Okay, I'll get them for you, but only this time." She got up carrying her glass and in a moment sauntered back with a new drink and a cardboard takeout box. "Your food looks about two days old. Congealed." She stopped in the door and cocked her head at him. "That mono-brow is a trademark. We should change more than just the color."

He took the box from her hand, opened the top, and poured out white, blue, and yellow pills into his hand. He chose one, swallowed it dry, and dumped the rest back into the box. The pill was chalky and bitter—he shuddered. "Okay. What did you have in mind?"

She looked him over. "We'll make it, *them*. Less of a forest. I'll pluck out about a pound."

"I'm all right with that. After all, it'll grow back when this is over."

She got out tweezers and leaned over to him from her seat on the tub. He turned his face to her. In a moment, she said, "This isn't working. I'll twist my back at this angle." She got up and straddled him on both sides of the john. Her tush was very firm, hard, nearly boney. She took his chin and tipped his head back, jerked the first of the hairs out.

He could feel tears collect in the corners of his eyes. He could smell her, and he could feel her small breasts pushed against his chest. He wanted her to lean down just that little bit and kiss him.

She shifted her bottom and continued to pluck out a center section of hair, a trench that would allow the skin of his nose to link up to his forehead. Tears ran back towards his ears. He sucked a gulp of air in hard. He could feel her breath drifting down onto him.

"Ah," she said. "Stop that!" She slapped him lightly on the side of his jaw and continued, "I'll slap something else down if you can't control it." Perverse in all things, she rotated her bottom again, screwing it into him.

Chapter Seven: Too Clever by Half

Thomas began anew. Bars for young professionals were all wrong. The thing he needed was fast and loud. The SoHo provided a population of bars that catered to the thousands of tragically ace and rebelliously hip, the young and unemployed, the self-marginalized trust babies. He couldn't do much about his short hair, but he could dress to fit. He sought advice. Angie referred him to what she called old-school gangsta boutiques on the Lower East Side. Thomas transformed, even if still white and professional, into the type of guy who spiked his hair and dressed like a slam wannabe... or a film director.

He bar-crawled down one of the party streets of SoHo on his way to a definite club. On the journey, he wrapped his mind around the types of patrons and the nuances of alcohol and loud music. With regret, he passed by a jazz joint. He knew his own feet wanted to turn in, not Zlata's. Thomas strode around the corner onto Greene Street; there in a walk-down, under the steps hunkered the Comet Kitty. One of Sibyl's neighbors, a loser named Arnie, had told Garland's people this was her local bar.

The club wailed hot and rolling, even at ten p.m. He caught blasts of sound each time the door at the bottom of the stairs opened. Taking a big breath, he started down and slid into the chatter and party of three couples on the way in.

Comet Kitty shown forth as a glam-punk slammer, dressed out in hot pink with much emphasis on strobes and flickering floods. A red bar ripped across one wall with leopard print stools. The male bartender wore heavy eye makeup. Above the bar, they had hung a banner he took as a warning, "Join In With the Rogues at Kitty's." Black silhouettes bracketed the sign, shapes of something he took to be cats or squirrels.

In spite of the joint's little-girl colors, many of the patrons draped themselves in black, drab browns, and olives, the perennial uniform of NYC cool. He found a place at the bar where he could watch the dance floor and the surrounding tall tables. He determined to settle in. He would let Zlata come to him, if possible.

The band alternated between pure thrash and lovely ballads about drugs and death, often within the same song. By twelve, he had separated out the crowd into archetypes. Those who came for the music surrounded the stage where the band played. Other patrons dropped in to hook up. A third crowd patronized the club to buy, sell, and use various mood enhancers. From what he could tell, a fourth group, which included female impersonators, came to strut their stuff. Kitty opened her welcoming, eclectic arms to anyone who liked their music loud.

Not him—loud was boorish. The place didn't smell lucky, at least not for him. He tried laying out a broken pentagram of bar straws, just in case, to lure the black cat in.

At the moment he was about to give up, full of sour disappointment, he saw her. Sibyl Boxwood appeared from the back and made her way through the crowd. He lost sight of her a couple of times because of her diminutive size, but each time, her sharp face, bruised-looking eyes, and shag blonde hair reappeared in the blue and pink flashing lights. She had someone in tow, a man. She joined four of the music lovers near the stage. They all bumped heads, and she nodded at the man. Heads bobbed and lips semaphored greetings back and forth. Thomas craned his neck to peer at Sibyl's date. His coloring was all wrong. On the other hand, he appeared to be the right size, the right age—older than the average Kitty-danian. High cheekbones, cut chin and a scowl. Forget coloring. It had to be Zlata. In a city of ten million people! Thomas knew it; he was certain.

By one a.m., he had proven to himself—by use of subtle tests of dexterity with his swizzle stick—that inebriation had captured him. The band took a break, and the house music roared up. He teetered on his bar stool and caught a glimpse of Zlata and Sibyl as they wiggled down a crowded hallway towards the restrooms. Maybe intent on sex? Or making an exit? He wound his way through the seething mosh with those high steps of pretended sobriety. Once in the hallway, he found a door propped open that led up stairs to a narrow dingy yard. He tripped in his haste and fell across a trashcan, followed by a spill across an uncomfortable, dismembered bicycle. Both shins burned. The yard led him to another in back and to a gap between two buildings. He sucked in a breath as he spotted his couple up ahead. Chin down, he followed them for six blocks. He didn't recognize the last blocks. He felt lost—not a good thing in New York. A red dragon in neon—the edge of Chinatown. Two blocks later, a real Chinese street—not the streets tarted up for the tourists. He lost the pair.

Storefronts lined the street—groceries, cleaners, furniture stores, herbal pharmacies—and apartments stacked up overhead. They had gone to ground in this block; he knew it. He stumbled back to the corner and read the street signs. Even drunk, he would remember. Feeling conspicuous in an Oriental world, he tramped back a block or two to restaurant row.

He tripped on sidewalk cracks and fought hard not to weave or lurch. He told himself he was sharp and on top of it, in spite of the evidence. His brain told him that a little food would temper the booze, so he stopped by a harshly lit food stand and bolted down three palm-sized mu xu pork, slathered in hoisin sauce. Limp and drooping at the counter that ringed the stand, he slurped a cup of green tea.

A thought crawled through the vodka and into his forebrain—he could get a look at Sibyl's condo. She and Zlata would be blocks away in Chinatown.

No taxis, no luck. Hustling fast, he wove off north for Canal Street—it must be north, he thought—stopping to pee between two dumpsters on the way.

At her building, a small box van squatted all akimbo up over the curb, and a couple moved furniture into the foyer. Only in New York would people be moving at three in the morning. The door to the foyer had been wedged open by a wad of packing paper; he slid in. Two flights up, he found her door. The foolishness of his plan struck him. He was an MBA, not a professional burglar. He squinted at the two serious deadbolts and a keyed doorknob between him and his goal. He sighed, placed his hand on the door, and willed it to unlock. The door inched away and swung into the apartment.

Jesus! Someone had broken in here before him, maybe before he even had the idea. Someone pro. He glanced at the jamb and saw the deep marks of a crowbar. He eased the door further, made himself a narrow gap, and wriggled inside. A bright light in the hallway behind him cast a spear of light into her front hall. Once in, he half-closed the door and froze, listening. He tried to breathe as shallow as a whisper. He could hear nothing beyond his own wheezing, the panicked bass beat of his heart.

A small, lancing light in the room beyond flickered across objects—so fast he couldn't recognize anything. Someone prowled the apartment with a flash. He took a careful step forward, his hands out, timid.

A force like a truck crashed into his left side and threw him up against a wall. Something smashed him in the gut with two quick blows. He doubled over, with no way to breathe. Someone picked him up like a floppy toy and threw him down onto the hard floor. In a second, two-hundred-and-fifty pounds slammed down onto him. He tried to roll out from under but only ended up on his back. He sobbed for air. A big man on top of him spat out curses in a stream. Thomas writhed, an eel trying to wriggle away. The man hit him again, pinned his throat with one hand and squeezed hard.

Thomas panicked. He was choking! With both hands, Thomas shoved. His left hand slid across metal—gun? He slapped his hand on the steel, grabbed the grip, and shoved as hard as he could. A flash lit the space between them, and a concussion rocked his senses. His head spun; his eyes blinked. Rolling away, his attacker screamed, "I'm hit!" Now free, Thomas still sprawled on the floor, a turtle on his back.

The lights in the apartment blazed on before Thomas could move. He lay blinking, blinded in front of two men who glared at him. His attacker, wrapping a forearm across his gut, crawled away looking over his shoulder. To his left crouched another giant.

They all froze. Then, Thomas saw the man on the left lean slow into a lunge. Thomas jerked upright, and a heavy object slithered down his chest onto his belly—the gun! He seized it with both hands—jerked the trigger twice. Two casings soared out of sight, and the smell of cordite filled his nose. The brute's face fell open in shock. He plummeted past Thomas and collapsed as a heap against the baseboard. The back of his head was a chewed up mess.

"Oh Christ!" Thomas's first attacker collapsed onto his side in slow motion and rolled up into a sitting position, legs out in front of him. He had both arms cinched up tight across his stomach. Blood pooled up across his arms and dripped down onto the floor. Clutching

63

the gun, Thomas crawled over to the guy and stuck the pistol up in his face.

"Who the hell are you?"

The guy's eyes were unfocused, glazed. "I know you. You're that financial prick who's been bugging LeFarge."

Very bad. These must be two LeFarge men. Thomas leaned into the bastard and grabbed him by the shoulder. "Why are you here? Listen to me, I said! Why are you here?" He spaced out the last four words and screwed the muzzle of the gun up into the man's chin.

"What are you going to do, kill me? Christ, you already done that."

"Then tell me why you're here, before you die."

Saliva dribbled out of the corner of the man's mouth. "God! I wish I could rip your throat out. You held out on us, didn't you? You knew all the time Zlata's whore lived here."

"Why are you here?" Thomas's voice sounded tinny in his own ears.

"We busted in to search the place, to take him alive or kill him— and to take her if we couldn't grab him. And now look; you screwed us over good, Jack." The guy groaned. "I just shit myself. It won't be long now."

Thomas rocked back onto his heels. He had interrupted a planned murder or two. Now there would be two different corpses. The wrong corpses from O'Brien's view.

He crawled towards the door—nausea washed up over him. On his knees in the hallway he revisited his mu xu pork. He struggled up to his feet, lurched into the wall and wiped his mouth on his sleeve. Moving to the head of the stairs, he stared down at his own hand. He still held the semi-auto. He jerked out his shirttail and stuffed the gun into his pants. He stared down at his new clothes and picked out dark flecks and damp spots everywhere. His legs felt weak; he trembled like a nervous Chihuahua. He stumbled down the stairs and out into the street. A block down Canal, he collapsed onto a bench. What the hell was he doing? What had happened?

He muttered, "Why are you running? It was self-defense. Call the police—and tell them what? Tell them it was an accident, but the conspiracy was on purpose?" He paused. Afraid. Of whom? What?

Canal Street hid, cloaked behind its roll-down shutters, not answering, somnolent under its streetlights, waiting for dawn. He made

64

out a wad of newspaper with a fish smell at his feet—his stomach lurched, tried to escape. He hunched over, wrapped both arms around himself. Tell the police that he left a man to bleed to death. Tell the police he's an accessory to Carl Dupont's kidnapping. But it's all justified because Dupont's a thief. Tell them Dupont is dead or soon will be. Tell them LeFarge is a murderer, and therefore, O'Brien is too. Turn state's evidence. Right. He didn't have much to incriminate anyone but himself.

Thomas gazed goggle-eyed at an early riser walking a pug dog. The pet lover stared askance at the disheveled man on the bench and scurried his fat little beast past. Nobody except O'Brien would ever make him a CEO, not with blood on his hands. Was it too late to get out? Or did he even want to?

He still wanted that step up, still wanted the Bishop's ring. He wanted to pretend he had never crossed the line… that things were like yesterday—competitive, clean, on-the-edge-of-legal, narcissistic. Was he running from the police? No. He was making sure O'Brien wouldn't find out. O'Brien had been Thomas's shot at the future, but now he could be the end of it. Run from the police, sure, but lie to LeFarge and hide his treason from O'Brien. He lurched up off the bench, spattered in blood and wondered what he would do next. Like a boat loose in the flood, he bumped his way down the sidewalk, caught in the eddy, spinning around as he made his way downstream.

Chapter Eight: Weep Over Luck's Change

Thomas Cabot Steward might as well have had the words "Murderer" cut across his forehead for all to see. The shooting had transformed him into a forensic stockpile of self-incrimination. He couldn't go home and contaminate his own house. He wandered around until he remembered the gym. He caught a cab to his racquetball club. There in his locker, he had a sports bag and a spare set of office clothes.

Outside the club he dropped the gun in a storm drain. He couldn't avoid the check-in at the desk, but once in, he had access to his big locker and the showers. First, he stripped off everything and dumped it into a trashcan. He scrubbed his hands hard in the sink, paced back naked through the room and opened his locker. He got his kitbag and padded into the showers. Back in the marble booth under the shining spray, he showered with the hottest water he could tolerate and shaved standing up. To remove the stink of cordite, he snorted soapy water up his nose from his palm. He sneezed it out… couldn't think of anything else.

After tugging on clothes, he opened the trashcan that held last night's debacle and tied the trash bag shut. He dragged it along with him. He stopped in the coffee bar to bury the clothes beneath yesterday's barista grounds and garbage. He knew that was no guarantee. He had littered New York with the crime's traces.

Down in Chinatown, Robko rambled out for breakfast and strolled back in with steamed eggs and rice noodle rolls. They ate in the narrow bed off of plastic plates, Sibyl propped up against the footboard and he against the headboard, with the diminutive cartons nestled into the heap of bedding.

Sibyl wasn't a fan. "See, if I had chosen the apartment, we would have had kolaches and coffee, or empanadas with fruit filling."

"Hey, when I cook, we eat what I want. When you cook, we eat what you want."

"Take-out isn't cooking." She poked at an unravelling noodle roll like it would leap up and bite. "What are these little square things?"

"That's tofu. The green things are scallions."

"No wonder I left you."

"Um, I left you." He poured an entire steamed egg out of the carton into his waiting mouth.

"Well, this time it's my turn to leave. I want to go home for a few hours, accomplish some things before I go to work." She rose up from the bed, stretched, and began to wander around the room, searching out her clothes. "You don't mind washing up, even though you did the cooking?"

He watched her disappear from view. She folded herself into her underwear, slipped on a cotton shirt and black jeans, and an oversized black sleeveless tee. She thrust both hands up into her hair and shook it out. He told her, "You should wear that outfit to work. I like it a lot. I'd love to see you take it off."

"And spend the day here, I bet." She hesitated at the door. "It is tempting, but I have a life… unlike you."

"I need to teach you the meaning of the words stop-and-smell-the-roses."

"I need to teach you the meaning of the words lazy-ass. Lock up behind me."

❀

Sibyl never made it to her condo.

In the street below, a friend caught her arm. "Sib, are you all right? Come in here, in the diner. Come on, come on." Anxious and frowning, he hid them away in a café. Down an aisle past tables and patrons, he hustled her into a booth.

With tea and coffee ordered, she said, "Okay, Arnie. What's this about?

"You don't know? There was a shooting in your condo last night. By the time the cops got there, the killers were gone."

"Killers? In my place?" Her vision sharpened down to only his face, puffy and yellow colored.

"Well, maybe one killer. Maybe more. Yeah, you had two dead dudes in your place."

"Dead?"

"A black and a white. All the commotion woke me up, so I popped down the stairs—just before five. They interviewed me, so I got to see them tagging and bagging the guys. There's blood all over your entry and I guess spattered across your living room."

They shut up as the tea and coffee arrived. As the waitress bustled away, Sibyl leaned towards him and hissed, "A shooting in my place? Why? Who?"

"The police want to know that too. They're looking for you. They want to talk to you."

"Did, um, did you say anything about what I do for a living?"

"I only said you worked nights and probably hadn't been home."

"That's okay then." She shot a glance down the café towards the front and then back at Arnie. "I'm all shook up—it hasn't sunk in yet. No lie, two dead men in my apartment?"

A tiny smile teased the edge of his mouth. "Oh yeah."

It wasn't his place, the bastard. "It has to have something to do with—with Tim. You remember him, my ex."

"He was before my time, before me." Arnie touched her hand, tried to cup it in his.

"Christ Arnie, I told you it was just mercy sex. Besides that was two years ago. I can't be bothered with that crap right now."

"I know." He drew his hand back and hung his head all sheepish.

"So my ex has landed me in it."

"Maybe. Better find out before the police talk to you."

"Okay, you're right. I need to bug out of here. You should stay as far away from me as possible."

"I'll go with you, Sibyl. They're on the lookout for a single woman, not a couple."

"No, no." She dropped five bucks on the table. "I'll call him on the way. Get as far away as I can. I'll go out the back. I can't stroll up Canal, not today."

"Hire a lawyer, Sib."

She nodded.

68

❀

Thomas left straight from the gym for work, thinking hard and dragging with exhaustion. He knew he couldn't bounce back to full form. He was drained by a major shock, a serious drunk, and no sleep. Coffee helped though, even as it amped up his jitters and soured his stomach. Angie arrived; he donned his blandest face.

"Mr. Steward, good morning. Another early day?"

"Angie, you could at least call me Thomas."

"Hmm. Office etiquette and all. We'll see."

"We've known each other less than ten days. An intense ten days, though. We've gotten involved in a criminal conspiracy together, even if we're tangential to it all."

Leaning on the door jamb, she cocked her head. "Where's this going?"

"I want to ask you to take sides… my side, in this case."

"All right."

"Just like that? You say all right?"

"Sure."

"Think it through. I'm in big trouble."

She considered. With a nod, she said, "Let me lock my purse in my desk and snag us some coffee besides that perked dreck you've got. I'll decide if I want to hear this by the time I get back."

When she returned with her coffee and his latté, he watched her. She leaned forward and placed his latté in front of him. Her mouth was straight, her eyes still, reticent.

His hands jittered on the tabletop. "What did you decide?"

"To trust you for a while, to hear you out." She slid into a chair, not opposite him, but closer, at the corner.

Thomas cleared his throat. "Last night I was in the right place at the wrong time. Egan LeFarge had two men in Sibyl Boxwood's apartment, and I ran into them. During a struggle, I accidentally killed one of them. He was choking me while we fought over a gun. I killed the other one on purpose when he attacked me. Both times it was self-defense."

She met his gaze head-on. "I'll say one thing. You know how to start the workday with a bang. Better tell me about it—all of it, every

69

single detail."

"Indeed. The one thing I figured out is that O'Brien or Garland leaked the word on our thief's identity to LeFarge." He narrated all the twists and turns of the night and included the clean-up.

"Are you going to the police?"

He shook his head hard. "Definitely not. How could I explain why I was there without implicating O'Brien and the rest of you?"

She raised an eyebrow. "Great of you to think about us. You let a man bleed to death and didn't call 911. And besides, you were breaking into the place and you used a firearm, even if they acquit you of murder. New York gun laws—big jail time—but you could turn state's evidence."

"True. Only I have nothing for evidence. Zero documentation."

She drummed her fingers on the table. "Not quite. You've got LeFarge's reports on the apartment invasions. Will you go to the cops and ask for a deal?"

"I like my life too much to turn state's evidence. Why should I let the death of a couple of flunkies ruin it? I ride this one out, O'Brien gives me one of his small companies to run, and I become one of the good citizens, a friend to law and order."

"Cynical." Her voice crackled with dryness.

He spread his hands out on the table. "Yes, and self-centered. I just don't care enough about LeFarge's two strongmen to feel responsible or remorseful. Also, what are LeFarge and O'Brien like when they're crossed?"

"Scary."

He nodded. "My thought exactly."

"Okay, at least you're not doing this out of panic but out of calculation."

"So, now what?"

"You've gotten rid of the gun, the gunshot residue, and your bloody clothes. No problem there unless you're unlucky. What about fingerprints?"

He slumped back in his chair and stared down at the table. "No good. I left prints on the door, the floor, the wall, the taxi—you name it, I may have touched it."

"Have you ever been fingerprinted for anything?"

"No." He breathed out in a whoosh. She had found the key point.

"So there's nothing to match against."

"How about DNA evidence? Did you leave any blood?"

"I hadn't thought so, but about an hour ago, I noticed I had been cut. See?" He showed her the web of his left hand. Two gouges, now scabbed over. "I held the gun wrong. The top slider thing cut me."

"So they might have your blood as evidence."

He felt his eyebrows crawl clear up to his scalp. "There was an awful lot of blood in the room. Maybe they won't find mine among all the rest."

She said, "I assume you're not in a DNA data bank anywhere?" He shook his head. "So you're off the hook for now. That doesn't mean you don't have a future problem. You need to avoid ever giving up your fingerprints or DNA."

"A ticking bomb." He thought about it, a permanent threat, a dark secret.

She waited, quiet, like a promise that it was all fixed.

He tried to shake it off. "So, are we good?"

Angie glanced at him. "Yeah, for a while. You're more the victim here, even if you are taking the selfish-bastard route. If you play it smart, you might even get away with it."

"God, wouldn't that be nice." He needed luck as well as smarts. "Thanks for standing by me."

"Yeah, well, we'll see how it works out. I'm going to run down to Security to get those stale, day-old reports they're giving us." She sprung up, charged to the door, and jerked it shut behind her with a clunk.

Maybe she wasn't a hundred percent on board. Yet.

Angie was gone about an hour, but he didn't worry. Much. She was probably pumping friends down there for info. She swept back into the room, her pad in her hand. "Nothing downstairs. Nothing happened yesterday or the day before for them. They haven't glommed onto the shootings yet."

She lit the screen of her desk tablet. "Speaking of victims, I did what you asked about Dupont's family. Here's the data and a photo." She handed over her desktab.

"Hmph. Wife long gone and now in Hawaii. A daughter gone missing. Isobel Dupont. Traveled down to the US with him, I see. Early twenties, pretty in a black-lipstick-and-fingernails way."

"Yeah," she said, "some men like that death-and-anorexia look."

He peeked over at her. "I prefer Mediterranean."

One corner of her mouth twitched up. "Would this daughter have the memflashes? Where do you think she is?"

"Ah." He stared up at the ceiling. "Three possibilities. She's running silent and deep, or she's with Zlata, or LeFarge has her. In the first case, her dad sold the memflashes or she has them." He paused there.

"What does the second case mean… if she's with Zlata?"

"Dunno. We still look for him, not her. In the last case, she's given them up to LeFarge if she had them. If she gave them to LeFarge, then he's selling out O'Brien because he hasn't delivered."

She frowned. "LeFarge is the outsider here."

"Meaning we should be most suspicious of him?"

She nodded.

He tipped his head. "He's a ruthless man, hand-picked by O'Brien to do those things none of the rest of us will. He could be arrested for two home invasions, one or two kidnappings, and maybe one or two deaths. I'll bet he sleeps fine at night."

"What will LeFarge think about his men's deaths?"

"I've tried to puzzle that one out. I hope he assumes Robko Zlata killed them."

"Our workup on Zlata didn't show a propensity for violence."

"LeFarge's men intended to take or kill Zlata. LeFarge will believe Zlata would react violently if cornered, because LeFarge would."

She got up and paced back and forth. As she marched and counter-marched, she crossed her arms and settled her chin in her hand. "But from here on, you have to consider LeFarge your biggest threat."

He watched her, first her breasts framed by her crossed arms, then her backside as she turned. "Yes. No more information sharing. In truth, I've been withholding information from LeFarge already."

She stopped and faced him, one hip cocked. "Have you withheld any information from me?"

"Only the name of the street in Chinatown. It's Kenmare."

She waved a hand. "Too late."

"Too late to tell you?"

"No, too late to use, to catch Robko Zlata. Won't they be on the run? Sibyl Boxwood will know by now the police are at her place."

She had knocked him for a loop... obvious when he thought about it, but he hadn't seen it before. "Yes. Robko's pattern is to run. We don't know if Sibyl is attached enough to run with him. Or frightened enough. She doesn't know LeFarge's men will kill her."

She dropped both hands on the table and leaned towards him. "How will he escape?"

"I bet he assumes the cops would use the usual law enforcement techniques—watch the terminals and stations, use the surveillance cameras on him. Just like TV. He won't use an airport, at least not close by. Same for bus and train." He watched her face—his involuntary glance flicked down at her breasts.

She caught the glimpse, straightened back up, and turned from him. "Chancy. There are a lot of bus stations. He could pick a far-away one like Yonkers."

"Does it matter? We need to know where he's running, not how he's running."

She had doubt in her voice. "Nooo. That's logical. But if he stole a car? We can track him through the police."

"Right, you're right. How is important. The last time he ran on a motorcycle. He was prepared and went to ground quickly."

"Yes. The bike would work for the two of them, if they travel light."

"We've got no evidence he's been back to his loft. Corporate Security has been watching it. They haven't reported anything, right?"

She paced back and forth again. "Uh-uh. Will Sibyl talk to the police?"

He held both hands up. "She's a high-priced call girl. She'd be reluctant to trust the police."

She said, "So they travel light, but where to? His home base is Polish Downtown in Chicago."

He nodded. "Maybe he'd go there. Any place closer?"

"Like friends here in the City or in upstate New York? Maybe the Hamptons?" She flicked her eyes at him to check the reaction.

He pursed his mouth. "Let's check for his friends in his graduating class and the one before and after."

Her eyes opened wide; her mouth became a sharp straight line. "Sure, must be only a thousand people... and who knows, he could have made friends after high school."

"Charming optimism. What else did I miss?"

Angie pivoted towards him and grinned. "Give the Chinatown connection to Garland."

"Hah! No, wait. That's a good idea. No one here knows about the killings yet, so Kenmare Street will appear to be virgin intel. He'll think I'm doing him a favor—letting him in on the win."

"So you go make Garland feel good, and I'll start searching for Zlata's friends. We'll need help processing all those names."

He jumped up and came out from behind the conference table. "Is there someone here in Corporate you trust? O'Brien promised me any resource I asked for."

"A woman in Audit and a man in Insurance."

"Call them; clear it with their bosses." She picked up the vidi. "Angie?"

She glanced up with the first number already ringing and the iMob cradled against her ear.

He tried for a disarming grin. "Thanks. You're a natural at this."

Her lips clamped hard, thinned to a narrow line. "Don't screw this up, Thomas."

In The Summer of My Life

Chapter Nine: Leaves in the Strong Wind

Robko and Sibyl paid a small fortune for the bike's ten-day stay in the Cumberland parking garage, roaring up the ramp hundreds of dollars lighter. They caught the Holland Tunnel west into New Jersey and began their two-hundred-and-fifty mile trip. He stopped along the road at a big-box store to buy her clothes and a motorcycle helmet. They ate and got back onto the Interstate. By the time they crossed into Pennsylvania, Robko had lost himself in the day. He cruised along with the traffic as he enjoyed a bluebird he'd swallowed and its imprint on the summer day. Sibyl would be uncomfortable—sport bikes are not designed for passengers. The backpack they had purchased wouldn't help as it lay heavy across her kidneys. She clung to him and leaned over his shoulder to see ahead.

They crossed a chunk of Pennsylvania and rolled back into New York. They dumped onto two lane roads. Four hours gave them Ithaca. The town opened up to them, first the reservoir to the left, next the view of two hills. He spun into downtown where he parked at the curb. She got off, stretched like an athlete, and sauntered into a café.

He slumped on the bike, indolent from the drug that hugged him. Down the way, Ithaca fought to keep its downtown viable. The main street busied itself tarting up and glamorizing its shopping. On the side of one old building, two black men clambered around scaffolding, their goal to paint over some graffiti. He recognized the flowing shapes and the illegible cubist signature. The graffiti said, "I Rule." Maybe this style was a break-away movement. Maybe it was the same guy on tour. He admired the idea—to "Rule," but still….

She sashayed from the café to the bike. Ten feet away, she pulled out her camera, planted her feet like a gunfighter, and took his photo.

"Where do those photos go?"

"In the Cloud, under a pseudonym." She tapped the screen for the upload.

He pointed. "Look, graff that quotes some classic. College towns are even more la-de-da than the City. It should be in Latin." Something about the graff made him feel uneasy, or maybe the barbiturate winding down weighed on him.

She said, "Like you know Latin."

"And you do? Don't forget I'm a lapsed Catholic."

She made a poofing sound with her lips. "The people in the diner knew of a bed and breakfast up on South Hill. I called, and they've got a vacancy. I know the way, and they're expecting us." She cinched on her helmet and mounted up behind him. She slapped him on his helmet, rocking his head over. He pulled away from the curb, and slipped up the hill.

Robko found the B&B. as far from his style as he could imagine. It nestled pink on the hillside, with colonial brick-a-brac worked in here and there. She held her arms out to embrace the view. "Look at this place!"

"Yeah, look at it."

"Well, think of it this way. No one would ever search for the great Zlata in a pink house."

"I wonder what the bedroom is like?" He patted her butt.

A stern woman with hair bunned up on a scrawny neck led them upstairs. She insisted on showing them each detail. "And here is your room, one of my favorites." Two beautiful oak beds—two—as narrow as coffins and five-and-a-half feet long awaited. "The beds are two hundred years old. Some people complain about the length, but you two won't have a problem. You have a sitting area."

At the end of the long room two doily-covered chairs crouched wing-to-wing with a butler's table in front. "And there is a lovely balcony." She opened two French doors to display a balcony stuck out by two feet, surrounded by a massive white railing. "Here is the bath," she said, and announced, "The last visitor dyed in here… awful to clean up."

Sibyl's mouth hung open. "Died?" She took a step back.

"No, not 'died' dead but 'dyed' as in hair. It made a horrible mess."

"Oh. Well, that does make a difference."

"I'm sure." The stern woman didn't like being misunderstood.

"It's all so beautiful. I'm sure we'll enjoy the room."

78

"Breakfast at seven sharp. The rules are on the butler's table."

Sibyl conciliated the dragon. "We'll read through them; I promise."

Robko grimaced at the beds, separated by two feet of dark flooring. Still, it would only be for a day or two. And it would keep Sibyl happy. In the morning, they would go down to the church, and he'd talk to Father Mirko.

Angie got her assistants, and the conference room suddenly resembled a telemarketing call center. All four of the team had desk tablets, iMobs, and internal building phones in front of them. Each marched down their part of the high school list. Incessant voices filled the room—Thomas hid in the noise and activity. It helped him block out the images of blood and dead men. Even as he videoed and talked and called again, part of him thought about his prey, what Zlata was like, what he could be doing.

Incoming calls were the exception. They all jumped when Angie's internal phone rang, and gawked as she answered. "It's O'Brien's PA. O'Brien wonders if you have a minute and can step in."

As Thomas strode down the hall, he rehearsed what he would say, what he would reveal, how he would spin it. He reached the suite, and the Personal Assistant showed him into the sanctum. Crisis had been replaced by a quiet center of executive power. Thomas peeked to the right and saw the vault now closed, sealed. He turned back to the seating area and found Garland slumped into the couch.

Garland waved a hand at the rest of the leather expanse. "Make yourself comfortable, Thomas. O'Brien's on the executive crapper. We're lucky he didn't invite us in."

Thomas nodded to the head of security. "Don."

"Vault's back up and running. Some good news there, but I'll leave it for the Boss to tell you."

"I imagine you've been making some changes?"

"Closing the stable door after the horse? Yes. We found some traces of our thief in two wiring chases. Somehow he beat the motion detectors there. I had steel gratings installed on all of them with magnetic locks that can only be triggered from the security office. We found he'd been up on the roof, so we added some pressure switches there and on top of the elevators. We have interferometry scans in the elevator shafts, but turned them off years ago because of pigeons. Those flying rats gave us regular false alarms. Got a guy looking at alternatives."

"Maybe you could kill the pigeons."

Garland glared at Thomas. "That did occur to me, you know."

"Sorry, thinking out loud." Things got quiet.

"You know…." Garland stopped.

"Yes?"

Garland coughed into his hand. "When you showed up, I thought, great—here's another one of the Governor's prep-school types, seven foot tall and blond, come to tell the peasants how to do their jobs."

Thomas dropped his eyes. "Yes, well…."

"But I got off on the wrong wavelength. I think you're all right. You haven't screwed with me, and you've been respectful to my people. You gave me the stuff on Chinatown. I don't appreciate the competition part of all this, the way we're matched up against each other, but that's more O'Brien's doing than yours."

"It occurred to me we're both in the same business for the same guy. LeFarge, though…."

Garland nodded, his eyebrows jumping upward towards his hairline. "Yeah, dangerous man. The two of us are trying to get the data back. He's more interested in disappearing anyone who ever touched it."

"That's the fundamental problem. LeFarge could bring all this down on our heads."

"Yeah. I don't want my kids to visit their daddy in prison. You get any ideas on how to handle LeFarge, talk to me. Maybe I can help, or at least not get sandbagged."

Thomas said, "I will. I also want to ask a favor. Can your people provide me with a taser?"

"I'll think about it."

Thomas half-closed his eyes.

"No, you're right. I just offered my help. I'll send one up. If you use it on LeFarge, I'll buy you a drink."

O'Brien lumbered out of the wall on the left side of the suite, the concealed door sweeping shut behind him. "Tommy, glad you could step in."

80

"Of course, Dennis."

"What progress?" O'Brien looked ready to smile, or to crush Thomas.

"Bad, since the killings."

"That's not what I want to hear."

Thomas started again. "You know after I trailed Sibyl to Zlata and Zlata to Chinatown, we were in good shape. We could have staked out the neighborhood—Garland's expertise. We informed Garland first thing in the morning. To help his people, we were working the digital trail, the rentals in the neighborhood."

O'Brien flipped his hand to the side, brushing away the explanation. "I know all that."

"The shooting in the Boxwood apartment means we start all over again. Both Garland and I agree that Zlata and the girl ran, once there were murders and an official police manhunt, or ex-wife hunt."

"Christ, finish the story! Do you have him?"

"No. All we have is my hunch. He wouldn't run far, and he'll also stick to family and friends. We're running down his old school classmates. Some should be out here on the East Coast, and we'll check them first."

"And? What's the problem?"

"It's a list of nearly two thousand names for three classes, big school. So far we've got a hundred we can't find and seven hundred that are still in Chicago. We'll ignore Chicago for now. The missing hundred are more interesting because one or more of them could be in the same business as Zlata."

O'Brien inspected Thomas levelly during his explanation. "Eight hundred. That means twelve hundred to go. Plus the ones that are missing."

"We sorted those first eight hundred in twenty-four hours. The staffers have been killing themselves to deliver." Thomas smiled his most confident smile. He knew his case sounded weak.

"Get four more people on it. Get six. Use the room next door—it's the conference room for the head of patent law, and I can make him book space downstairs." He turned the spotlight on Corporate Security. "Don, what do you have?"

Garland wrinkled his forehead. Things couldn't be going all that well for him either. "Three things. We had a couple of potential locations for Zlata—Chinatown and a hotel where a snitch had seen him. We purchased the security footage at the Cumberland Hotel for the three days around the shootout. We identified Sibyl Boxwood as a passenger on a motorcycle in their garage about eleven a.m. on the third day. No positive i.d. on the driver since he wore a helmet, but you know it was him. For the murders in the Boxwood place, we're monitoring the police and the condo. We have a man on site even though NYPD Forensics completed its work and sealed the apartment. We're listening to police radio and watching the electronic desk blotter for arrests. As for the third thing, we've hired people in Chicago to keep Zlata's family under surveillance. Nothing illegal, like I said."

O'Brien buried his right fist in his left palm with a thump. "I don't give a hairy shit about legal, get me?"

Garland shifted on the couch, silenced.

"Well? What does all your legal activity mean?"

"What surveillance shows is that Zlata's apparently not in Chicago, at least not in his home neighborhood. The NYPD doesn't know where Sibyl is. We don't know where they zoomed off to after he left the Cumberland."

"And LeFarge? What does he know? They were his goddamn men!"

"Haven't seen him."

Thomas confirmed the same news on his side with a shake of his head.

O'Brien voiced a growl.

Thomas asked, "Any change in how we should deal with LeFarge?"

"No. Just keep me informed."

Thomas asked, "Garland said there was some good news?"

"Yes," said O'Brien. He waved his hand at the vault. "We have two of the memory devices back. One memflash cost me ten mill up front at an auction. In London, of all places. The other we worked more as a business exchange."

"Hmm?"

"I took your advice and set up a finance and legal response team. My General Counsel runs it. We got word on a politician in the state house who was twisting some arms up in Albany—the arms I twist. One of the twistees videoed me and asked for protection from this

Senator."

"What happened?"

"The Senator's money comes from his wife, and that's where the pressure points are. I made the creditors of one of his wife's companies call in their loans. I bought out a couple of partners in another company. The Senator suddenly came across. But get this, the bastard wanted to recover his initial investment." O'Brien bared his teeth.

Obedient, the two employees chuckled. "Two down, nine to go," said Garland. "Well, if that's all, Governor, I've got to get back on it." Garland and Thomas marched out together. Thomas knew next time they'd better have something to deliver.

Chapter Ten: A Mark of Devotion in the Heart

The sport bike swept them down the hill to Immaculate Conception. Their black-clad figures hugged the garish machine, a mélange of bright colors and sculpted fairings, through a community of porches, green grass, and cracked sidewalks under old, old trees. The bike leaned into time, cast an echo up against the middle-class houses, cut through another way of living. They parked up against the white stone of a Norman Gothic church, clambered down, and hauled off their helmets.

"Are you sure?" asked Sibyl. "You said it's been a long time."

"Mirko will remember. What he does with the memories—now that'll be the interesting part." The big black doors led them into the church. "Let's find the office."

"Wait a sec. Look at that dust floating in the air." She fished out her camera and photoed the nave illuminated by the stain glass behind and above the chancel.

They wandered off to the right through a covered walkway into the converted residence next door. They found the parish priest's office on the first floor. Robko knocked on the doorframe.

A large chair spun around and revealed Father Mirko. Zlata saw a dark, dangerous Slavic face. "Yes, can I help you?" With the words, the priest's face moved from sullen repose to a real smile.

"Maybe, maybe not. Ithaca is a long way from Chicago."

The priest's eyes squinted and he said, "I know you! Robko Dragomir Zlata! You've changed your hair color, and you've cleaned up your eyebrows, but it's still the same shifty kid I grew up with." He jumped out of the chair.

"Shifty, huh?" The two men met beside the desk. They exchanged a hug and pounded each other on the back.

Robko said, "Let me introduce you to Sibyl, the most important person in my life. Sibyl, this is Mirko and vice versa."

Mirko stuck his hand out to Sibyl. She stared down at the hand. "What, no hug?"

"I thought the uniform gave me away. I have foolishly taken a vow of celibacy. Hugging you, well... sit down, drag up that chair, come sit down."

They both sat down with him, separated by the bulk of a scarred metal desk. Robko said, "Mirko and I grew up within three apartments of each other. We went to school together. We played ball together. We both dated Nadia Miroslawa Radoslaw, maybe at the same time. We whipped the Murphy brothers together. Why, we even... maybe we shouldn't go there."

The priest guffawed. "No, let's not. How did you find me in Ithaca?"

"My Ma of course. She holds you up as the almighty powerful example we should all follow."

"And when was the last time you saw your mother?"

"Now, Mirko, don't play the guilt game. I live in NYC, and besides, Ma and I spend every visit fighting." That was all true, but it was also true that there was some comfort in the arguing.

The Father said, "And you were such an obedient child."

Sibyl snickered. "Robert? You're kidding."

The conversation circled, wove back and forth, looped back on itself and plunged off again before it flattened out. The priest cleared his throat. "Why now, Robko, after all these years? Is there some way I can help you? Did you come to ask for something?"

"I want you to hear my confession, Father."

Mirko broke out in laughter, long and hard. He wheezed.

"No, I'm serious. I want you to hear my confession. Then I can ask my favor."

The priest cocked up one eyebrow. "Uh, you're gaming the system, aren't you? What I hear in the box is bound by the sanctity of the confessional. You tie my hands, then you ask the favor."

"Works for me."

Mirko leaned over to Sibyl and whispered, "And you hang around with this man?"

"Actually, he's kind of my ex. I'm available if you're in the market."

Mirko sat with his elbows on the table, his hands folded together. Then he slapped the desk with both hands and hollered, "Okay, let's go hear the grís grís. Mirko sat with his elbows on the table, his hands folded together. Then he slapped the desk with both hands and hollered, "Okay, let's go hear the grís grís. Confiteor Deo omnipotenti! Or Robko will confess to me, and to God." He led the way through the church. They followed behind, hearing his slippers whisper on the stone flagging. With a flourish, Father Mirko indicated the confessional— shiny wood, pierced panels, and a trinity of doors. Robko slipped off to the left, and Father Mirko took the middle.

Robko had a lot to say. Sibyl circled around the church three times inspecting everything, her camera out and busy. She took a place in a pew in the transept and waited, sitting still and silent in the dimness. She inhaled the dust of old masses and older stone. Silent, she could hear the melody of Robko's voice, punctuated by the drum of the priest's words. When the doors opened and the men stepped out, Robko looked shaken and the Father's face glowered dark and brooding. Robko paced forward to the altar and knelt at the rail. Father Mirko strode over to Sibyl. "Come back to the office. I'll buy you a cup of coffee. Come, child, he's going to be a while." As they ambled out of the church, he shouted over his shoulder. "No faking it. He'll be watching, and so will I. And leave the collection box alone. I'll be checking." His slippers scuffed along, smoothing out her hard clattering footsteps. "Now, tell me who this Sibyl is and why she gave up her marriage to Robko Zlata."

Robko showed up in the office in fifteen minutes, popped in to find his ex and his friend conspiring. "Glad we got that over."

Sibyl said, "You've got a smirk-and-a-half, Robert."

Mirko flashed out a crooked grin. "My son, you may think you've put one over on the Church, but for a moment, a small moment, you've received some absolution. Of course, in your case, it was a drop of absolution boiling away under a hot sun."

Robko grinned. "I admit it; I feel better. Just don't tell my Ma."

The priest folded his hands. "Now, what's your favor, my old friend?"

"I need two things, Father. First… a place to hide."

"That's one."

"And I need to know who's chasing us. People around us are starting to die."

"That's two. Why me?"

"I can't trust anyone I've worked for or with. They took my last boss down—whoever they are—and he gave me up."

"I repeat, why me?"

"You still have the contacts. My uncle says you were the confessor for half the Polish criminals in Chicago."

"True. God chooses a priest's flock. I had thought I left most of that behind me when the Church sent me here."

Robko said, "Sorry."

"No you're not." Mirko tented his fingers. "Who would have thought you'd come back to the Church?"

"I'm the prodigal son, aren't I?"

"More like a Trojan horse."

Sibyl reached across the desk and patted Mirko's hand. "I know just what you mean. You open the gate and let him in, and pretty soon, you're overrun. Do it because of who you are, not who he is."

"Let me think about it. Come back tomorrow after early Mass. I'll know by then what God wants."

Sibyl said, "Thank you, Father."

"Be prepared for me to say no. I'm not in the business—or that business—anymore."

Outside, Sibyl asked her personal skanker, "So what is the story with the Father?"

"You mean besides my Ma liking him better than me? Mirko got sent up to do hard time. In prison there was a Polish gang united under a rock-hard leader. The way I hear it, Mirko got promoted to enforcer and made quite a name in there. Nobody in that jail screwed with the other Polish, any of them. But the big Pole…," Robko twitched his head back towards the church. "The one fried up on phencyclidine, everybody scraped and bowed to him."

"Phen—?"

"Angel dust. Bad, bad drug. The Bluemen never pinned a murder on Mirko, and he rode out his term. No extra time, but no parole either. Prison changed him. He did something he's ashamed of, and it wasn't just a killing."

"And where were you?"

"I met him at the gate as he walked out. He took my hand and told me, 'I've got to change, Robko.'"

"So that's where all this came from."

He nodded. "Mirko also said, 'Hell waits beyond my death.' Pretty dramatic talk, but he meant it. After that, he went off into the Church, and I moved off to jobs out of town."

A woman from Accounting, dressed in black and as severe as a nun, said to Thomas and Angie, "I've got it! There's a Polish boy who shows up in several of the yearbooks with Zlata, from junior high into high school. He's a Mirko Kazimierz." She carried a stack of index cards and slapped one down in front of him.

Thomas said, "Polish is good. Kazimierz was a saint right?"

Accounting ignored him and snapped down another card. "One of Kazimierz' four sisters married a Zlata, a cousin."

Angie said, "Close family ties. Good."

"Mirko's got a criminal record." She produced an index card with a rap sheet summary.

Thomas shook his head. "Good, but so does another twenty percent of Zlata's class."

"He has a page on a social site. It's more interesting than many pages. He tells us prison reformed him, and he's now a priest."

Angie asked, "Relevance? Old friends, but now one is a priest. Maybe Zlata would go to him, maybe not."

The woman shook her head. "I like the Church tie. That makes it more likely Zlata will seek him out, not less. I'm Catholic—I know. There's one thing more." She leaned back, and pleasure flooded her face.

Thomas grinned. "What's your punch line?"

"He has a church in Ithaca, two-hundred-some-odd miles away."

He snatched up the card and jumped to his feet. "That's it! Thank

88

you so much—this is going to work. Angie, call the town car. I'll go by my place and pack a bag. You'll run things on this end, and I'll call in each step of the way."

"Wait, Thomas. This is all a gamble. What if you're wrong?"

"Only one way to find out."

Angie asked, "Can't you call Ithaca?"

"The priest won't tell me anything over the phone." Thomas packed his briefcase. "This is all a wish on a guess on a hunch; but if you examine it, it's rational. It's one of the possible solutions. Smile, everybody—the sun's just popped out from behind a cloud. What could go wrong?"

Chapter Eleven: Daniel in the Lion's Den

Ithaca—the type of place Thomas pictured for retirement, not that CEOs really retire. The town car took him past Queen Annes, Richardsonians, Cape Cods, bungalows—neighborhood after neighborhood of 1920s suburbia mixed in with 1890s wealth. He nodded again and again—he could live in this one, or that one. Even the student slum seduced him—the old houses made up for their descent into tiny chopped-up apartments by housing beautiful young people, as Ivy League and white-bread as any nostalgist could want. Realism intruded; he would also have to keep an apartment in ugly, messy New York.

He checked into a chain hotel on Seneca—not the usual standard he booked on O'Brien's travel account. To balance it out, he took a suite. He rented a robocar at the desk and gave voice commands to the town car to return to New York. As the clock on the mantel of his room struck four, he headed out to the church.

He found the priest as Mirko shuffled in slippers down the stairs from the classrooms. They met in the doorway of Mirko's office, on the faded linoleum and the cracked threshold. The man in black habit said, "Can I help you? Are you looking for someone?"

Thomas took stock of the priest. He appeared six foot tall, six foot wide, with a dark complexion, high cheekbones, and dark impenetrable eyes. "I'm looking for Father Mirko, and based on the Chicago accent, I think I've found him."

The wall of a man inclined his head, reserved. "You have the advantage over me."

"Sorry. My name is Thomas Steward." He held out his hand.

"And how can we help you today?" The priest's handshake mangled Thomas's hand.

"We have a mutual acquaintance."

"God's world is a small place."

"Robert Zlata. I have to find him. I need to talk to him, pretty desperately."

"I once knew a Robko Zlata. I grew up with him in Chicago."

"Same man. Can we go in your office, Father? Sit down? Talk?"

Father Mirko waved his hand into the room. "Go right in."

The room smelled of institutional cleaner and stale cabbage. Seated, the priest cast a neutral gaze upon him. Thomas said, "Perhaps I should begin. Zlata took a certain object from my employer. It's placed him in a great deal of danger."

"There are a number of ways I can interpret that, Mr. Steward. Are you a threat to Robko Zlata?"

"I'm his best option."

"Well, I don't know what I can tell you. Priests can't always be forthcoming when discussing their parishioners. Besides, I have no reason to think you mean well for my old friend."

"Is Zlata one of your parishioners then?"

"More like family, I suppose—once upon a time." A silence deadened the room.

Thomas looked for another approach—apparent candor. "Um, I see your dilemma. Anything I say might be tainted by my own agenda, and any assurances I give could be less than trustworthy."

"As you say."

"And you're not ready to say if you've been in contact with him recently."

A single syllable answer. "No."

No could mean no Zlata or no betraying of Zlata. "But you'd tell the police if they asked you?"

"The Church and its priests are full members of the community. That gives us obligations to the authorities."

"But I'm better than the police, in this circumstance."

"Bring me a policeman, and I'll cooperate."

"Even if it would be better for this to remain a private affair for Zlata?"

"You can't pressure me that way. Robko will always have to pay the consequences for his actions, but with God."

Real candor then. "Let me start over. I don't know if you can represent Robko Zlata or contact him, but I have a message for him. I can offer him a private amnesty, a full walk-away from any repercussions from my employer. I can also help him avoid certain dangerous criminal elements and, of course, any legal prosecution. What he would give me in return is the full story and the restoration of the object."

"That's so generous, Mr. Steward… and sensitive too, not to offer thirty pieces of silver on top of it. Don't expect any commitments on my part, however."

"I'll leave you my card. I'm in the hotel down on Seneca. I'll write that number down also. I don't know how you can confirm who I am and what I say. Go online and search my name and the name Dennis O'Brien. I do urge you to pass the message on to Zlata." Thomas waited to see if the priest would ask anything else, but he only sat motionless. That black-cassocked force had damped all the sound in the room, like a wool shroud. Thomas rose to his feet.

"Mr. Steward."

"Yes." Maybe the priest was reconsidering.

"Just one thing. To my knowledge, my friend has never physically hurt anyone. He has always been indifferent to the concept of ownership, but he's never been violent."

"Thanks for the picture. Why are you telling me this?"

"Robko is like all of us. He doesn't deserve to have pain or death brought to him."

"Then give him my message."

Father Mirko rocked back in his chair as Sibyl and Robko strolled into his office. "Are you still riding motorcycles, even after that ghastly accident?"

Robko grinned at his friend. "You know me and bikes."

"Where did you park your motorcycle?"

"In front."

"Move it now. Park in back, and then come here." He nodded to Sibyl, "You, lovely child, can stay with me while he does my bidding."

In two minutes Zlata slunk back in and asked, "Now, what was that about?"

"Do you know a Thomas Steward? He's a tall man, dirty blond

hair, horn-rimmed glasses. He dresses well and carries a leather attaché case. He works for Governor O'Brien."

"Hardly my type, Father."

"There's more. You may not know him, but he knows all about your last job. He'll give you a free drop and a certain amount of protection. Protection includes no criminal charges... all in return for an unnamed object and your autobiography."

Robko jerked bolt upright. "And he said, an object, as in a single object?"

"One object, quite clear on that."

Robko turned to Sibyl and shook his head. "Then it's not the memflashes he wants. It's the acrylic box."

Father Mirko said, "There's a potential trade, if you believe him."

"No, I'm afraid not." Mirko raised one eyebrow, and Robko ducked his head. "The box was kind of destroyed in a raid on my place. I don't have it to trade."

"Complicates things. He found the connection between you and me, and he's followed you to Ithaca. He has resources."

Sibyl said, "But so do we. We have you."

Father Mirko sucked in a big breath and trickled it back out. "I told you I would know today what God wanted from me. This Thomas Steward is God's sign. He shows me the consequences if I say no to you. I can't guess what the consequences are if I say yes. But that is what I do say. Yes."

Robko revealed his pleasure as he touched Sibyl's hand.

She said, "You're smirking again, Robert. Thank you, Father. I'd hate to ride that motorcycle clear to Chicago."

"Here's what I can do. We run a summer camp. We require our employees to live in the camp—pay is room and board and peanut money. I'll send you to the camp director—you do have I.D.s in other names, don't you?"

"I do, but Sibyl...."

"Robert, I've got a driver's license in my maiden name. It's not all under Boxwood."

The priest said, "Then you're set. I can hide you. As a penance, you'll mop floors and clean bathrooms."

Robko asked, "Done deal. What about the other? Our need for information?"

93

"I made some vidi calls last night. I think I've found your wet mob. There's no Pole on the crew, but you might remember a guy who is a member. Jerome Powers?"

"AKA Jerry the Squeeze?"

"That's the man."

Robko nudged Sibyl. "This guy is so huge, he once turned a four-hundred-pound coke machine over and bounced it up and down until it delivered all its soft drinks and money."

The priest said, "Turns out Jerry used to be military before a dishonorable discharge. Now he runs with a crowd that purports to be a private army. He told his brother who married a Czech whose brother married my niece who is deeply religious. Let me give you a second to unthread that one."

Sibyl said, "So you got it fifth hand."

"Best kind. Jerry blabbed to family and, therefore, to the whole neighborhood that he's a sergeant in a muscle squad. This squad pretty much does what it wants to anyone it's pointed at—and someone else has to clean up afterwards."

Robko said, "That sounds like a possible."

"It's more than possible, it's probable. His captain is a merc named LeFarge. Jerry says LeFarge is the tame hitter for a rich man named O'Brien. And this Steward works for O'Brien too."

Sibyl said, "Oh. So Steward is a direct danger to us."

"Not the way he talked. He's much slicker and softer than someone who runs a private army, different background altogether."

Robko wrinkled his face up. "That's worrisome. I have to know more."

"That's all I have."

"Not from you. From this Steward."

College towns need their beer halls and their taverns, cheap eateries with cheap booze. In the evenings, Thomas combed the college bars for the man and the woman, without much luck. In two nights he ran through the entire string Ithaca had to offer. He admitted to himself the University town felt quite homey—not Zlata's feel at all.

But he found one bar that matched. It didn't have that Ithaca Ivy-

League squeakiness but ran more to urban angst and anger. Thomas did his "looking for a friend" there, but got laughed down. He resolved to stay until closing, to see if Sibyl and Robko showed—it had worked at the Cosmic Kitty… knock on wood.

※

Robko showed, all right, but on a different side of town. He suspended himself from the roof of the hotel in an improvised climbing harness, a rope taken from a Catholic garden shed. Slipping down the face of the building, he counted three floors—he remembered a time in Philly when he had ended up on the wrong floor in the wrong office. Dropping onto the stunted balcony, he knelt and inserted first a screwdriver and then a crowbar under the sliding glass door. Defeating both the lock and a charley bar, he lifted the door off the rail, pivoted it inward, and scrambled in through the thin triangle that opened to the side. With a bit of grunting and one pinched finger, he got the door back on its bottom track.

He opened the door, and Sibyl slipped in from the hallway. "Did you bring the pizza?"

She handed him a pair of yellow cleaning gloves. "You gozo. Always the smart remark. What can I do to help?"

"Admire me while you stay out of the way. Sit on the couch or on the bed. I'll search the place."

First he sorted through Steward's clothes, felt through the seams and pockets. Then he moved on to the toiletry items.

She bumped him, crowding up against him in the palatial bathroom. "What are you looking for?"

"For memflashes, drugs, of course, and weapons. Always disarm your enemy." So close together it could have been a sack race, they moved back into the suite's living room. He shuffled through a few scraps of paper on the desk—meaningless—and took out every drawer in the place to check for anything taped on the bottom. He stood on a chair to inspect the top of the armoire and peeked behind every painting. "Saved the best for last." He moved to the probable target, a safe bolted to the floor of the walk-in closet.

He said, "This will be too simple. Why bother locking it at all?" He inserted a length of air-conditioning hose into his ear, held it against

95

the safe face, and dropped the tumblers in under a minute. Opening the door, he leaned back over his shoulder to wink at her. "This is it. I've got his desktab and some files." He handed them out to her.

She carried the files out to the living room and laid them on the coffee table. "There are three. One's labeled Isobel Dupont. Another is a double header that stars you and me. The big one is a file from a research office stamped 'secret'."

"I've got the Dupont file. You take us on first. What do they know?" He flipped through the Dupont file.

"Three good photos… one of you and two of me, as a blonde and as my natural brunette. Also photocopies of drivers licenses, two for me and three for you."

"Three?"

"Zlata, Boxwood and—wait for it—Abernethy. They must know about the Cumberland. What are these numbers?" She showed him a page.

"That's bad. They're bank accounts. They've burned my money. They'll either take it or freeze the accounts."

"All your money?"

"Of course not. Just most."

Sibyl asked, "What do you have in your file?"

"I've got two photos and a Canadian driver's license. The license is for this Isobel Dupont. I know the people in the photos."

"Who are they?"

"One of the photos is my boss on the O'Brien job, the Gray Man. I flip it over and ta da, it says, 'Carl Dupont' on the back."

"So the name of your boss turns out to be Dupont. Doesn't help, outside of the fact it tells me you'll work for strangers."

"I already knew the name. He had a girl at his place who never introduced herself. I always thought she was his steady squeeze. This is her photo and the back says 'Daughter—Isobel Dupont.' The two misled me."

"Fancy that. Why's this important?"

"He called me the night they hit his place, just as LeFarge kicked the door in. He asked me to find this girl and take her to wherever she told me."

"But you never found her."

"Doesn't look like Steward has found her either."

Sibyl leaned over the table and peeked at the third folder as he opened it. "What's the final file?"

"This one is important. Let me read it through; then I'll summarize. You photograph each page on my burner phone as I hand it to you." They spent fifteen minutes scanning through the fat file.

Robko said, "Comes from O'Brien's VP of Research. He's reporting on a new device they got when they bought up a lab. It's never been patented or gone to the FDA."

"Well?"

"My little box of electro-drugs turns out instead to be a hugely compressed memory device. It works by placing tiny charges across a network of powder. They use this device to store both the contents and the neural map."

"Of what?"

"The human brain."

She snorted. "So you stole—and then lost—the world's only cyborg?"

"No, no, it isn't a cyborg unless you hook it up to something. It's an archived mind."

"Whose?"

Frowning, he waved his hand. "I don't know. The interesting thing is there are two more in existence, but only two." They both stared at the photo of the device. Not a vial of a super drug... something much, much bigger.

She bumped him back into action. "There is the desk tablet left to go. Let's download his files."

"We're hosed if he uses an old-fashioned password lockout. We don't have his code or the time to crack it. I'll have to steal the tablet."

She caressed the surface, and it flickered into life. "Just as bad. He's got a fingerprint lock."

"Hmm, that's actually good." Robko sloped off to the bathroom and opened up the kitbag. "He's got athlete's foot—probably a gym rat. There's a bottle of foot powder here. I also have a water glass and...." He cupped powder in the palm of one hand and with a sighing breath, scattered it onto the glass as he rotated it. "I have all four fingerprints and a major smudge where the palm touched. The thumb is smudged. This one is an index finger. Check the desk for some tape."

Sibyl reported, "Tape, stapler, stationary, labels. You never stocked your place this well."

He brought the glass to the coffee table, and she brought the tape. "I get one shot at this." He lifted the print onto the tape. "Wake up the screen."

She flicked a finger. He placed the tape over the icon of a fingerprint and rubbed it on. The screen unlocked; the pad said, "Welcome back Thomas." The pad's voice was a rich and fruity one, vaguely English and definitely female.

Robko wasted no time. Sliding a plastic box the size of a cigarette pack out of his pocket, he directed the pad, "Find new wireless device. Connect. Copy all personal files."

In five minutes they had done the job—a simple matter to restore the room and slip out into the hallway. Robko's head sang; he hummed the monotone tune. "I tell you Sibyl, we're finally on the right side of this fight. With what we know, and what we can learn from Steward's files, we can go on the hunt—not just get chased until we're caught."

"Hunting beats running for the rest of your life. Let's do it." She took his hand, just a couple wandering down the corridor of a hotel. She said, "God, this makes me hot."

"Holding hands?"

"Gozo. Stealing stuff. I could whip your pants off right now."

They took the elevator down and ambled through the lobby. "I tell you what. Let's stop in the bar before we pick up the bike in the alley. I'll buy you a drink, and, just to be fair, I'll bury a yellow to start a buzz."

She grinned like a ten-year old shoplifting candy. "There's no booze at the camp. You're on." They sauntered into the hotel bar of the man they had just robbed.

Chapter Twelve: Ashes of the Earth

Thomas, it's Angie here." He could see her perched on the corner of her desk leaning over the phone. She looked office-sleek in a double-breasted blazer and her trademark silk shirt.

Thomas lolled on the couch in his suite, in the same corner Robko had occupied twelve hours before. "Ah, you called to console me in my shame. I just got off the iMob with the Governor. He wants more progress, and I have none."

"Of course. You expected patience? Tell me about the priest."

"I wasn't very smooth. He vigilantly protected his friend and sounded rather sanctimonious about it. I still don't know if Zlata is here."

She shrugged. "How about the bars? Has your SoHo trick worked again?"

"No, but that was always a long shot." Even so, he had counted on it. His luck may have soured.

She frowned. "Really? Leaves you only the priest."

"I hurried up to Ithaca because of Father Mirko, and he's why I stay. How about on your end? Any other names panning out?"

She gave a sigh. "No, just depressingly good news about his classmates. It's a testament to life. Most of these kids, even the bad ones, grew up to have babies and pay taxes. We have a small running list of hard-to-find people, of course, and we've just begun the last five hundred. But no prize yet."

Thomas winced and shook his head. "Not what a man with a hangover and hearing impairment wanted to be told."

Her smile flashed out like sun from behind a cloud. "If you think I feel sorry for you because you spent last night in a bar, forget it. I've got some good news. Garland caught me in the elevator, all very casual. I think he timed it to bump into me."

"And?"

She leaned forward and dropped her voice. "He wanted me to know Sibyl still has her vidi. She turns the phone on and off, but she does use it. Beauty and the beast effect, if you ask me."

"The beauty...?"

"You were right. She's in Ithaca."

"And the beast part?"

She frowned, lines chasing across her forehead. "Garland provided this same data to LeFarge."

"Ithaca! I feel vindicated."

A shake of her head. "You should feel nervous. LeFarge and the bully boys must be on the way."

"Is Garland going to keep helping us?"

"I'm on his speed dial."

"That's good. I've got to see the priest again. I'm running out of time, and so is Zlata."

Father Mirko stood towards the back of the church. Parishioners filtered past; some of them stopped to thank him or say hello. Thomas hunched up in the last pew, hitched around to face Mirko. Thomas's voice muttered out low and intense in-between the interruptions. Unlike Thomas, the priest made himself at ease. He smiled, talked with his flock, and shook hands as parishioners oozed past.

Thomas felt the hair stand up on the back of his neck. This was too casual. "Father, we're down to the wire."

"I like to think about the eternal life, Mr. Steward, not about the day-to-day panics. It slows things down and renders things harmless in perspective."

"Zlata's enemies are on their way."

"Or perhaps they are already here, in the back of this church."

"Father, I only want the device."

"You work for a man who wants more, don't you?" The priest stopped to hold the hands of two women and talk about their children.

Thomas ran the possible angles through his head. He spoke the second the women turned away. "O'Brien may have unleashed something he can't control."

"Robko will be safe enough, wherever he is. My old friend may have some personal issues, but he's resourceful."

"He's here, in Ithaca. I had guessed he'd run here, but now I have proof positive. I'm not the only one who knows. What they call an extraction team is on the way."

"And what do you want, my son?"

"I need to take protective custody of Robko and Sibyl. I need the device in my pocket. I need to escort them into O'Brien's building and fulfill my promise of immunity. All that would make the extraction team obsolete."

"What makes you think—once in captivity—my friends would not be hostage to O'Brien's whims? Hit teams can have other uses. It was Pilate who sought Christ's release and then condemned him."

The priest had said 'friends.' Then Mirko had met Sibyl. Thomas tried personal charm. "I give you my assurances. I can make this work."

"But aren't you Captain LeFarge's partner in this?"

How did the priest know about LeFarge? "No, I'm his competitor. It's complicated. LeFarge is as dangerous to me as he is to you." There, he played the personal threat card, his voice sharp.

"To me? Perhaps you speak in generalities?"

"No. LeFarge's team is toxic to anyone around Zlata."

"Mr. Steward, you think you can intimidate me, but look at who I am. Prison taught me I could give and take the most awful things invented by man. Now I have the Church and God."

"There may be life eternal, but getting to it can be painful. Pity to throw your friends' chance away."

The priest glowered, his face dark and his brow drawn down. "I won't give them up to you. Or LeFarge."

Here in the Church's summer camp, Sibyl and Robko spent the nights apart in the staff dorms, but they could spend mealtimes together. At first, in the crowd of children and counselors, he couldn't find her. He popped up on tiptoe, gawping about for her. She would blend in to the background, because she looked much like a ragamuffin boy. A finger dug into his back and he heard, "Hello, skanker."

They found a table over to the side of the dining hall and plunked down across from each other. He said, "We need some time to think through a plan. And we need to steal a desktab to open up the files."

"You could buy one."

"What's the fun in that?"

The dining hall reverberated with the high pitched fervor of children and the dank smell of boiled vegetable. Vegetable that no one ate. Sibyl leaned close. "You always say 'we' but you mean 'you.' Don't forget, I'm just the person who brings the pizza." She pushed her plate away and hauled her phone out of her bag.

His mouth fell open. "What's that?"

"It's my iMob, gozo. I'm checking my messages." She turned the vidi on. "I've been saving the battery."

A bolt of pain ran through his head. "You've had it all this time?"

"Of course. It's one of the few things I had on me when we left NYC. I called Arnie and conned him into hiring someone to fix my front door and clean up the blood. I had to let Box Office know I wasn't available for work. Small things like that."

"Aaah. Did you know they can trace your location through your mobile?"

She dropped the phone on the table and jerked back like it was a roach. She drew her hands into her sleeves and hugged her chest. She swept her eyes around the hall as if 'they' would already be here. "What'll we do?"

"Turn the phone off, for one thing. Then lose it."

A deep voice rumbled out from behind Robko, "No, give the iMob to me."

She ripped out a squeak of surprise. Gathering herself, she stared over Robko's head. "You scared me, Father."

Father Mirko dropped down beside them. "I just had a chat with Steward. He made one last plea for your surrender." He held out his hand.

She handed Mirko the vidi. The priest continued, "Steward says the muscle squad is on the way. I have no reason to doubt that part of the story, so I drove out right away to talk to you. It's time you two children packed up and made your departure."

She leaned forward. "We've placed you in danger, haven't we?"

The priest wagged his hand. "Nonsense."

102

Robko said, "Come with us. Life on the road can be sweet."

"No, I'll stick to what I know. My church is here, and I wouldn't be up to your lifestyle anymore."

She shook her mop of hair and reached for his hand. "Please reconsider. It's not all booze and drugs."

The priest snorted. "It's also cheap motels and the clubs he loves so much, right?"

"Robert's got a plan, or will have one in a day or two. We're going to get our lives back."

Mirko grinned, toothy, and rose from the table. He patted Robko on the shoulder. "I've already got my life."

Waiting across from the church, Thomas slumped down in his anonymous robocar. He didn't know where to find Zlata and Boxwood, but he did know where to find the priest. Stomach acid burned the back of his throat, a foul taste. He had Garland's taser, and he had read the instructions. The extraction team would have something better than a taser. This could be bad... or horrible.

Thomas only had to wait an hour, a jumpy, nervous hour. A plain white van pulled up to the church's office, and four large men clambered out. The first one on the pavement scanned up and down the street. They tramped inside.

Thomas eased out of his car and stepped across the street. He carried the three-shot taser down by his right side. He armed the taser and dropped his finger onto the trigger guard. The muscles in that finger ached, tight as whipcord. He slipped through the front door of the church and skittered through the walkway. He hugged the wall as he moved up to the priest's office. Hesitant, he stopped at the closed door. He hung there and listened, his ear near the crack between door and frame. Inside something big slammed into the wall—a colossal boom. All the school memorabilia on the wall jumped and rocked. Thomas jerked back from the shock. With a ragged breath, he grabbed the doorknob.

He could only wedge the door partway open; legs stuck out from behind it. He wiggled through over a fallen man, into the room.

The odds sucked: the priest balanced himself on spread feet, defiant beside his desk, confronted with three men. Thomas jerked the taser and fired at the man nearest him. The nitrogen cylinder discharged, the barbs sailed forward dragging their wires and struck the merc in the neck. The man fell to the floor, spasmed, and thrashed like a fish out of water. Thomas turned his aim to the next man and shot him also, hooked his next fish straight into the shoulder. Not waiting to watch this one flop, Thomas fired at the only merc still standing. The barbs didn't penetrate the man's back but fell to the floor. Something had stopped them punching in—body armor. Out of gas cartridges and disarmed, Thomas stared down at two men who twitched with huge spasms on the floor.

The last bullyboy paid no attention to Thomas behind him—or his downed associates. Instead he charged forward, caught the priest around the chest, and lifted him as he ran Mirko backwards. Both men flew out the window. They crashed onto the porch beyond. Thomas leapt to the window and gaped out through the broken frame.

The situation flip-flopped. Mirko ripped himself out of his opponent's grip and twisted around behind his attacker. He had an arm over the man's head and a hand around his throat. Thomas shouted, "For Christ's sake, don't snap his neck!"

Ignoring him, Father Mirko pursed his lips and shook his head. "Forgive me, son," said the priest. Mirko pinched the carotid arteries with his hand and the man, struggling, passed out in ten seconds.

The priest dropped the merc onto his face and heaved himself up on his feet. Fishing in his pocket, he delivered a handful of large, black zip ties. "Here, take these and secure the men inside for the police. I'll take care of this one."

"You're prepared."

"Previous life experience. And I knew they were coming."

Thomas couldn't touch the men he had hot-wired without catching the charge that coursed through them. He switched off the taser. They lay limp and stunned while he zipped their wrists together. By the time he tied their ankles, they had recovered. They struggled against their bonds, cursed him with mouths that still quivered and spit. Father Mirko crawled in through the window and hog-tied the unconscious man he had thrown into the wall.

Mirko and Thomas panted, their breath rattling in and out. Thomas asked, "How long before the cops show up?"

104

Mirko said, "A good ten minutes? Neighbors might not even report it."

"You might have to call it in yourself."

The priest scuffled around the four mercs, extracted guns, and tossed them into the corner. "I owe you an apology. You've shown which side you're on."

"I'm not on Zlata's side, if that's what you're thinking. But I'm not one of them." His voice cracked.

Mirko said, "I will have to call the police, sooner or later."

Thomas shook his head. "I would prefer not to be here when they arrive."

"You've earned that."

"Let me call O'Brien while we're both here. He needs to know what these guys did in his name."

"Yes. I wouldn't mind listening in."

The CEO picked up on the second ring. "Tommy," said O'Brien. His voice boomed hollow into the office. His face was composed.

"Dennis, I'm calling to let you know what your extraction team did."

O'Brien's voice was full of honey. "I expect they did what was needed so I get what I want. Otherwise, I am disappointed."

"They followed the phone to a priest. He had parked it on his desk, in plain sight. They assaulted him, tore the place up, and ended up lying on the front porch in public view."

"This would be the priest you failed to convince?"

Thomas shook his head at the rebuke. "The same. He's tough enough to take two of them. He wouldn't have talked."

"I had hoped Sibyl Boxwood still had the mobile on her. The priest—that's an unforeseen complication." O'Brien didn't look at all worried. Why?

"They tried to beat up a priest in broad daylight!"

"You had two days to sort this out, Thomas. Where's the Artifact?"

"How should I know? I'm wasting my time cleaning up after your army."

"Careful, Thomas. I don't like your tone."

"The police will soon have your team. Then you can worry about something besides my tone."

O'Brien shook his head. "Unfortunate. Their bonuses rise

immeasurably if I have to buy their silence."

"This isn't about money. This's about effectiveness and consequences. These clowns screw up everything."

O'Brien was frowning, his face as dark as a storm. "Careful, Tommy. I'm not feeling very—patient right now."

"We start all over. Zlata's on the run again."

"Don't lecture me or point out the obvious, Steward. Just do your job."

Thomas stared into the phone.

"Do you understand me?"

"Yeah. I'll call in later, Mr. O'Brien."

"Get the Artifact. Now." The call ended. Thomas shook his head and dropped his vidi into his pocket.

Mirko said, "It appears your employer has more in common with these men than you."

"Maybe. I'm glad you were out of sight."

A new voice drawled into play. "How charming. Collaborating with the enemy, Steward?" LeFarge lounged in the doorway. He carried a pistol with a silencer screwed into the barrel. His man from the porch sagged against the doorframe beside him, rubbing his freed wrists.

Thomas dipped his head, inhaled with a rattle in his throat. "LeFarge. I should have known you'd come out to watch your operation."

LeFarge, stepping inside, spoke to his man. "Close the door. Cut the other three loose." LeFarge waved the gun. "And this would be the priest? I don't think we've been introduced."

"Father Mirko. I already know you." The priest backed up to the desk and faced LeFarge.

The room grew crowded again as LeFarge's men struggled to their feet and staggered about. LeFarge said to them, "Take Mr. Steward to his car. Make sure he drives away." Cocking his head, LeFarge said to Thomas, "You get a pass this once. If O'Brien rescinds his protection, I'll kill you myself."

"The Father comes with me."

"Now, that wouldn't be helpful to me, would it?" LeFarge aimed his gun at the priest. "I'll ask once, where is Robko Zlata? Where is Sibyl Boxwood?"

"I sent them away. I don't know where they are. Now there's no

106

way for you to know."

"Pity," said LeFarge. "I believe you. Makes all this so much harder. Thomas will have to find them again."

Mirko stared into LeFarge's face. He saw something there. "I forgive you." The priest made the sign of the cross.

Thomas had always thought silencers made guns noiseless, but they just suppress the noise to a powerful slap. The gun reverberated, and Thomas jumped.

At first they all stood there, waiting. A sigh, nearly a groan. Mirko slid down the desk to the floor. Blood oozed out of the hole in his face.

"As I said before, drag Mr. Steward out of here, stick him in his car, and relieve him of that stun gun, even if it's empty." LeFarge aimed his pistol at Thomas, squinted down the barrel. His cheeks hollowed and his lips blew out a popping sound—nearly a kiss.

Chapter Thirteen: End and Beginning

Sibyl leaned over Robko's shoulder; her finger pointed ahead. He saw a water tower to the northwest, a water tower emblazoned with graff. He nodded his head and strained to read the message. Hanging above the rolling upstate New York road, it offered a shout of joy to the place and the season, "Winter's Army is Defeated—Hot Summer Got It on the Run." Thinking he had just passed a sky-laid signpost meant only for him, he swept into a new set of curves.

Sibyl shouted to him over the keening of the wind.

He should have bought comm-helmets. "What?"

She banged her chin guard right up against the side of his head. "Do something for Mirko?"

He shrugged, telegraphing his answer back to her. Her chin sank onto his shoulder, and she clenched all the tighter.

He had already closed the door to Mirko and boarded it over with downers. He put all on hold in this sunlit world. He had a metallic taste in his mouth, a cruze building up behind his eyes, an image of his friend standing to his left smiling, dressed all in black. He didn't know what road uncoiled under him or where it headed. The right way to ride a bike.

In the early evening, they stumbled across Rochester. She shouted, "Middle America. Company town."

"Crap food. Crap clubs. Mid-America values," he shouted back.

"I want to stay in one of the luxury hotels down on the river."

"Can't happen. We lie low." He swept across the town and down to the West. He spotted a chain of cheap motels lined up on the interstate, and he took the exit. "Pick one."

"You gozo. The one in the middle, then."

The bike swept up under the portico. They pried off their helmets, ruffed their hair out, and took off their sunglasses. Synchronicity. He said, "We need to think, and I can do that in this type of place. I have trouble doing anything but the stone in those fancy high rises. All the juju centers on the room, not on people. Here you can scheme up good stuff.

"That's because the cheap mattress keeps you awake." She climbed down from the bike and stretched catlike.

He said, "Staring at the ceiling is the best way to work things out."

She sniffed. "Sounds like jail."

He booted the kickstand down. "Great things are planned and written in jail."

"So jails make the greatest intellectuals? I think not."

"Gandhi and Mandela both did their homework in jail."

She grinned. "So did Hitler." She followed him in and watched him check in and pay cash. The room hid around the back of the motel, just the way he liked.

The room. He nodded, feeling a good vibe. He watched her scan the interior of the concrete box, with two gloomy prints on the wall, a bathtub in need of re-grouting, and a huge, ominous TV that loitered on the dresser. Robko threw himself onto the bed. "Isn't this great? The soul of America."

"It's awful, Robert. Take me to dinner, right after I pee." She dropped her bag on the bed.

He needed to offer her something. "I saw Thai a mile back." He waited until she whisked off to the bathroom, then rolled over to the bag. He emptied it onto the cover, picked through the contents and kept four hundred dollars and a pair of earrings. He left the camera.

They found dinner, as Sibyl summed it up, to be "Okay." After New York, provincial Thai turned out less of a thrill and more of a misplaced expectation. Sibyl said, as she pushed phat Thai around her plate with a flatware spoon, "The owners must be Vietnamese... or Greek."

"A distinct possibility. I tried to talk you into the steak house."

"Ugh. Fat and gristle. A GMO animal full of steroids."

"There's package liquor in the strip next door. Let me buy you a bottle of wine."

"Will you help with it?"

"Not this time. I've got sodie in my blood and thought I might add a diazepam on top." He shoveled money, her money, onto the bill, and found his feet.

"Sure then, wine it is. At least I won't mind when you lie there saying dreamy things at random."

Rochester closed up shop at ten in the evening. They had little choice but to crawl onto the cheap mattress early. Robko lay on his back, his head on the world's thinnest pillow; Sibyl stared at the muted TV, a frown cut across her face.

He said to the ceiling, "I want to swing through Chicago and see my Ma. But Chicago is too dangerous for us long term. They'll know I come from Chi. I can't see us hiding in Humboldt Park looking over our shoulders all the time."

"Okay. Where will we settle then? Seattle?"

"The one place in America with weather worse than New York?" His eyelids hung at half mast, sleepy from the Valium. At last his brain was starting to turn off.

"It's not that bad. Rains more in Detroit." The over-priced bottle of Bordeaux towered up on the tiny bedside table with a plastic cup from the bathroom. The cup showed three inches of red.

"Let's try L.A. It's a good place for thieves like me to outfit and to operate." He threw his arms out like he was a cross on top of the slab-like bed. He toyed with the idea… a carved ornament on a tomb.

"Hmph," she grumped.

"I know you don't want to motorcycle across the country, but once we arrive, the bike would be great. That wonderful California weather."

She hunched her shoulders, "You're right about one thing. I don't want two thousand miles of wind in my face and bugs in my teeth."

"I got a plan."

"At last." She reached out her hands clear to her ankles and stretched.

"Let's buy a car here, drive it to L.A., and sell it."

"What about your sport bike? You can give up your Italian?" She gazed down; he stared into her violet-colored eyes, changed up from blue, courtesy of contacts. So fake—he loved it.

He said, "We can rent a trailer and take the bike with us. We'll look like Okies migrating to California. That's also the soul of America, just like motels."

"Sure. The great transcontinental road trip. I can even buy a real suitcase and clothes to fill it. Just so you have a plan." She turned and leaned over him, laid her hand on his chest.

He grunted. "The real plan comes later. We have to figure out O'Brien's weak spot. We need to buy him off or neutralize him. Or we have to run and hide where he's guaranteed not to find us."

"Hard to neutralize one of the richest, most powerful men in the world."

"Aah, he's not so tough."

She snorted. "So we can eventually go back, to the City?"

"Only when we're ready and only when they've called off the search."

"Robert, they won't call off the search. O'Brien didn't store just anybody in the brain archiver." She slid down the bed, lay on his outstretched arm and faced him.

"Artifact."

"What?" She had her hand on his chest, distracting him.

"The file we have calls the gadget 'The Artifact' over and over again."

"Don't change the subject. I think Dennis O'Brien loaded himself up in the box, all the nastiness of his black heart, and you ran him down the garbage disposal."

"You think he would back off if he knew it was gone?"

She considered it. "No, he takes all this personally. Take this army of goons he has. Look at this Steward and his mission to find you. If you told O'Brien you mangled his toy, he'd be worse, not better."

"I've been thinking about the Artifact. First, there's more than one—I just stole the one that he was using. Second, I'm certain that he wants to corner the market. Evidently O'Brien wants it for himself."

She sank down beside him, onto the thin mattress. "So? Why should we care?"

Robko scratched his nose and rolled over a bit towards her. "It doesn't figure. He loves money and power. This Artifact, it would be bigger than television, bigger than the Internet. It would be a huge change in the way people saw life. He'd sell one to every single American. And, that's without hooking Artifacts up to anything except desktabs."

"So why's he's hiding the Artifact? As personal immortality?"

"Possible."

"That doesn't make me feel any better." She dug her fingernails into his chest, to make the point.

He rolled on his side to face her. Lying knee-to-knee, nose-to-nose, he found it hard to see anything but her eyes. By squinting down, he saw her nose as an out-of-focus blob. "We'll get to him. He's a man of passions, so he's vulnerable. I'm a man who smooths passions out."

"Yeah, with yellow jackets."

"And diazepam. It makes me a good thief."

"I have my doubts about that. Hemingway wasn't a great writer because of his drinking. How come you don't talk much about what you do?"

"Maintains an aura of mystery. But you can be assured, you're my team now, and we can trust only each other."

She fiddled open two of his shirt buttons.

"Team, huh. What's the split, fifty-fifty?"

"Seventy-thirty. I'm the senior partner."

"Forty-sixty, my way. I'm better looking."

"Huh. You don't even know what the job is."

"That's true. How come you don't talk about what you do?"

"You asked that before. It's hard to explain. And we don't talk about what you do...." He drew back where he could watch her and determine what was safe and not safe to say.

"It's called whoring, Robert. You don't have to dance around it. In the business, I'm called an 'ivory,' a white whore." She nuzzled into his neck, to show it was okay.

"Being a call girl... isn't that like surrendering yourself?"

"Not at all. It's a simple transaction. They bring the money; I bring the fantasy."

"Fantasy means role playing?"

"No, it's deeper, closer, in the blood." She bit his earlobe.

"Is it dangerous?

"I wish. To be an 'escort' like me means great hotels, room service, and excellent client hygiene. It means I draw the high-stakes boys with the expensive cologne. I'm more dangerous to them, or to their reputations at least, than they are to me. They hate it when I take their pictures."

"You said 'fantasy.' "

"Yes. By the second time I screw them, I've figured them out. Some like a bit of pain." She jerked out one of his chest hairs, and he jumped. "Some like the booze or the drugs. Some like lingerie. Some like the idea of an underage girl. I can make them get off just by whispering 'Daddy.' Some are like you; they're ambivalent. They focus on the little-boy ass."

"Hmm." He reached over her hip to touch that ass.

"And they all want it to be good for me. Isn't that sweet?"

He wasn't much sure he liked that part. He'd have to think about it.

Back as fast as he could be from Ithaca, Thomas hustled into O'Brien's HQ at eight thirty the evening of the murder, knowing that NYC and this team, his team, would still be at work. Angie met him at Security. They rushed into the executive elevator together, and she punched in O'Brien's floor and badged the reader. He said, "Go back to our conference room; give me ten minutes. I need to talk to Garland."

"Will you tell me about it after you talk to him?"

"Yes. God forgive me. You're in deeper and deeper."

"He's on thirty-eight." As Thomas sprang off, she said, "In a few minutes then."

Thomas marched into Garland's office. He slapped his hand down onto the desk. "They killed the Father, right in front of me. And we lost Zlata again."

"Yes, I know. LeFarge alluded as much when he called in to ask for data. He wants us to tunnel the cameras in a zillion police cars, searching for the motorcycle on the road."

"How did LeFarge get to Ithaca so quick? Couldn't you have bought me some time?"

Garland chose anger, a good defense. "C'mon, we're under the spotlight here. Even the phone-tower data comes in with time stamps. I can't delay this stuff."

Thomas let it hang there, allowed silence to act as his disbelief.

"And what if I had bought you an hour or two? Could you have wrapped it up in that time?"

"No. Maybe a couple of days, maybe not."

"Right. Don't expect a miracle if you can't deliver on your side."

Thomas cocked his head. "You're probably right."

"Straight, I'm right. But in the future, I'll do what I can. I regret the murder as much as you."

Thomas smiled his ingratiating, practiced grin at Don. "I appreciate it."

Don traced a couple of circles with his forefinger on the glass desktop. "Here's a new development I can tell you, though I'm not sure how it fits with your search."

"What's that?" Thomas asked.

"Isobel Dupont has been seen."

"Really! Where?"

"You won't like it. One of my people saw her crawling into the black SUV LeFarge uses, out in front of this building—of her own free will. Or at least my guy didn't see any force."

Across from Garland, Thomas raised his eyebrows. A glass-domed clock on the desk spun its weights back and forth, several times. "What does that mean?"

"It means she's not dead like her father. It means she made a choice."

"Hooo. I don't know how to use that. I'll have to think about it."

"Well, at least she's not lying in a New Jersey grave."

"What happens now?" asked Thomas.

"You find Zlata—again. I support where I can—in particular, I'll arrive on the scene first before LeFarge. I'll swarm him with witnesses. But what do you think should happen now?"

Thomas shrugged. "I think we should retain good criminal lawyers. Just don't tell them what's up, not yet."

Thomas strode into the conference room where his eight staffers had assembled. They looked so expectant, so trusting. "I want to thank you all. The lead you gave me worked out and guided us to Zlata. The bad thing is that I couldn't capitalize on it, and he's disappeared again. But you positioned me there at the right place and time, and for that I'm grateful."

A moan, more felt than heard, swept across the room. One of the eight asked, "What happens now?"

"Now you go home. See your families. Go to dinner." He held his hands out in a fan-shape. "Drink wine. Come back in tomorrow, and we can start again. Maybe by then, you and I will know where to look."

They all filed out, except for Angie who leaned on the window sill. "What is it, Thomas? It's more than losing your safecracker."

"LeFarge killed Father Mirko. Shot him in the face, right there in the church office. Shot him just to tidy up."

She thumped down into one of the chairs. She opened her mouth, closed it again, stared at the carpet. Then her chin came up. "Thank God you didn't tell the staff."

He shook his head. "No comfort there. It's bound to be on the news by now."

"And O'Brien?"

"He's completely indifferent. He believes he can spread some money around and keep the problem away."

"He's right. It won't keep the problem away from us, though." She dropped her head into her hands.

"Two big problems. Zlata and LeFarge. I'm beginning to admire Robko Zlata, the shifty little bastard. I don't know what to do about LeFarge though."

"Is LeFarge your job?"

"By default. O'Brien approves of him. Corporate Security gives our mercenary full access, carte blanche. Garland practically wets himself when he's around LeFarge."

"What will you do?"

"I'll try not to think about it till tomorrow. My rational brain is worn out. Rational is leading me nowhere. I need that irrational voice inside to tell me what's what."

"I'll make you an offer. Come over to my place. I'll cook Italian. We'll drink dago red."

"Indeed." He lifted his eyebrows, like the first time they had had drinks.

She shot him a worried glance. "Oh dear. Thomas, there's something you should know, something I've kept from everyone in the office."

"You're married and have three kids?"

"I'm a lesbian."

He snickered all the way to the elevator. Punching the button, he

115

said, "There's another surprising story I can tell you, one that's not so funny. You know Dupont's missing daughter, the goth?"

Chapter Fourteen: Bitterness Speaks to My Soul

Let's buy the car in Buffalo." Sibyl forked a huge bite of scrambled egg into her mouth.

"What?" Robko's attention snapped back into the room.

"Lef buy va ka im Buffawo." She flared her now-blue eyes, waved the fork at him.

"Didn't your mother ever teach you not to talk with your mouth full?"

She swallowed. "I never do around my clients. With you, I figure, why bother with manners."

"Something about Buffalo." He leaned closer. The scent was confusing, her shampoo, the bacon, the stale coffee.

"Buy the car in Buffalo. The car... Buffalo."

"Why there?"

"It gives you another couple of hours on the bike. You deserve it for coming up with the plan. Let's motor over on two-lane roads, avoid the Interstate."

"Cool. That's a good idea anyway. Big-time criminals on the run should stay away from big roads and the troopers. Thanks for the offer. I'll take you up on it."

"Let's spend a slow day, ride over, wait to do the buying binge tomorrow."

"Sure." He leaned on one elbow, his fist to his temple. She wasn't done yet.

"And let's stay in a nice hotel tonight."

"Maybe. Okay. Buffalo is the last place I'd be... they'll never look there."

"A suite. I love spending your money."

"Keep in mind they know about three of my four bank accounts. We may have to find some money sooner or later. I'll have to go back to work."

She said, "Or I will. We're a team now."

Black top scrolls out before us like the yellow brick road. The ride is good, but the thoughts are bad. Mirko bothers me. The way he looked in that dining hall, so calm and confident. He knew about Dupont and Dupont's daughter, he knew about the two dead people in Sibyl's apartment. He knew all that, and he still insisted on taking a stand. Kram it! Never fight when you can hide; never hide when you can run. Mirko, you fat old bastard, no running for you. You missed prison and the hard life; didn't you? You missed it. You loved the blood and the broken teeth and a shiv in the ribs, but you would never admit it, would you? Even when we were kids it ran too strong in you, and you'd go too far—I had to jerk you off the Murphy kid to keep you from killing him… and nearly too late—the poor mick had a concussion. So I figure you made a stand against O'Brien's hired muscle because you wanted it and not because God wanted it—I figure you're either dead or taken now, and there's not a single holy thing I can do about it. I just rode away. Left you holding my bag of shit, and look what I do with a gift that huge! I get so Christ-like stoned, I see a halo around every bright reflection, and I try to hide from myself in this infinite day with this smooth-as-sex road. The bike thunders between my legs, zero to sixty in three seconds. Shift down for speed's sake and lean into the curve to come out like a rocket, changing up through the gears and traffic. Speed—the love of my life. A truck right on top of us. Twitch left. We're past it right up on a grandma in a fat American car. Loop around her and run down the yellow strip in the no-pass. Take a pickup on the right and a recreational barge on the left wallowing towards us. Did you see his eyes all lit up like runway lights as he watched me come at him on a curve at seventy? Shift down, down and touch the brake, into the next corner. Lean far over to the pavement but understeer on the throttle, and we're out the other end of the pipe. The cruze from the bluebirds has me hung motionless. I see all and touch every detail. I own the road in slow motion as the bike screams her heart out for me. A jimber like a steel bar connects my crotch to the bike. Like a guided missile, we're around a tractor. Why the hell is a tractor on the road?

118

And now the first buildings fill in space between the farms. We hurtle forward to seek the core of Buffalo. Road clogs up and becomes someone else's boulevard and someone else's ride. We have to back down, down, down. And doesn't thirty feel like we're standing still? Stop for the light with a squeal of the brakes. The barbiturate falls out of my blood, leaves me stranded. Now we come off the buzz to find Mirko is still there, still protecting my back just like when we were boys. Except now, Mirko, you're dead, aren't you? And I don't have a blessed idea how to deal with it. My old friend. Only….

After dinner at Angie's, Thomas caught a cab back to his apartment, a condo on the top floor he bought to show off his early success in business. He took a shower and grabbed a glass and a bottle.

With wet hair, he ascended a spiral staircase and unlocked a door that opened onto the roof, one of the perks of money. Only nine hours till work, and he still didn't know where they'd go from here. He could drink for another hour and sleep. Then he'd go to the gym. He'd show up for the meeting in time, but what would he say to those expectant faces?

They had signed up, for sure. For some reason he had their loyalty, and the team had brought itself together. They enjoyed the hunt. Anybody would find it novel, intriguing, gratifying—compared to Insurance or Accounting. Thomas Cabot Steward hadn't been what drew them in, sold them on the game.

He flopped prone in a deck chair, feet on the cornice of the building. The irrational side of his mind didn't say, "You brilliant devil, you know the answer." If Thomas had no answer, maybe Robert Thomas Dragomir Zlata did.

A full glass, a reflective sip. Zlata, who are you?

What did we know about Zlata? Smart enough to hide his money in three separate names and places. He hadn't moved money offshore that they knew—he probably intended to spend it all. An athlete—he had crawled up that wiring chase where most people couldn't have wiggled in.

A cat slunk along the balustrade. He knew that cat—it saw him and, with a hiss of alarm, dropped off the wall away from him into the

119

darkness. He knew the trick; there was a ledge below. Maybe it was an omen: a cat, an apparent suicide, a miracle survival.

Zlata. He was a small man with a good opinion of himself—all his actions spoke confidence. Did he have the short-man Napoleon complex? They knew he was a drug user who preferred klonopins and other downers. The guy was in his mid-thirties, but he chose angry music, young, screaming—what did that have to do with downers? Incautious, a risk taker, otherwise why would he have been out in a nightclub when he should have been hiding? He bought an apartment for—and lived with—a prostitute, at least until they had a falling out.

Thomas could hear the cat hidden from him by the balustrade. A sudden scratching, a scuffle, a tiny shriek cut off. The cat was a better hunter than he.

Zlata. Not the simple Catholic boy his mother raised him to be. He had lived for the last two years in a grimy warehouse loft filled with nice trendy furniture—secretive and an impulse spender. He had a thing for motorcycles, even though he had experienced a bad crash. Adrenalin or death wish? Maybe both. Thomas filled his glass again. When he put the bottle down beside his chair, it scraped on the gravel, louder than the hum of the city.

Plonk wine drop-kicked him into a million dollar idea. LeFarge had been right to focus on the motorbike. They didn't know where Zlata was, what name he hid under, what appearance he had adopted. They didn't even know if the woman was still with him. They did know he had left NYC on an aggressive, unusual motorcycle. He had probably escaped Ithaca on it. They had followed the money and the ex-wife as far as they could. Now they would follow the bike. He felt like his luck had changed.

When Thomas charged into work an hour early, Angie was waiting. She had arrived at work before him, before them all. She leaned against the conference table heaped with files, ringed with company phones, in wait for eight other staffers to arrive. She held one arm between her breasts up to her throat, one—inviting—curved down across her upper thigh. Venus on the half shell, unaware. "Mr. Steward, good morning."

He pushed his briefcase onto the table, shuffling back files, drinking her in the whole time. "Ms. Tommo. I see office etiquette is back."

"I'd be more informal if I had a good idea to offer. I figure when you're running on empty, you'd better be polite."

"I had planned on being more familiar until you made your announcement last night. Unless you'd like to use me for heterosexual cover?"

"I'm a big girl. I can take care of myself." She grinned. "No offense."

"Back to Zlata...." He leaned over the back of his chair, forearms on the upholstery, and tilted his head towards her.

"Yes?" He heard that uptick in her voice. She wanted him to save the day.

"We're not boxed in. I don't know how yet, but we're back in business. Let's give the team time to trickle in. I'll toddle back to Reception and arrange coffee and pastries, visit with Garland, check in with O'Brien's Assistant. Then I'll tell all of you my idea."

Eight jammed into the room when he returned. The original team had claimed their chairs while a couple of newcomers leaned against the windows. He said, "I've got donuts on the way. If we act like cops, we should eat like them too." He picked up a chuckle here and there. They waited. Would he deliver?

Thomas continued. "Enjoy the evening off?" Nods. "Any miracle ideas occur to you overnight?"

Accounting said, her red nails held up to her cheek, "His past spending might show us where he's comfortable—if he ran to an old, familiar place. We should go through the three bank accounts for some spending done in Chicago. Food, transportation, motel rentals, that type of thing." It was obvious she disapproved of anyone who would rent a motel room.

Thomas responded, "Good. I'll bet he won't go home to Chicago, but I've been wrong often enough over the past few days."

Accounting said, "If he's run to someplace new, his past spending is no guide."

"Not necessarily," said Legal. "If he consistently buys something unusual each time he changes cities, we could track that."

"Unusual, like what?" someone asked.

Angie said, "C4 explosive." They tittered.

Thomas knocked on the table. "Yes. That's one thing we'll do. Analyze the money pattern. Anything else?" Tapped, they all looked to him for something big. "I think I know the what. But not the how. Help me work it out. We'll follow the motorcycle—that's the what. We haven't done any work on the bike at all. What do you think?" A big sigh rippled across the room—good or bad?

"Not many bikers in the world. Means he's in a smaller gene pool," said a youngster who leaned against the glass.

A staffer at the table, so short you couldn't see a quarter of his tie, said, "It's a sport bike. Most enthusiasts his age would own a cruiser. Sport bikes are for serious speed freaks."

A heavyset man with a sports-television paunch said, "Rare—like Torentino shoes. The bike is an Italian import. There can't be many motorcycle agencies that handle the brand. We can track them to see if it comes in for maintenance."

The young guy polishing the glass with his back said, "License. We have the license number from the garage surveillance footage. We need to figure out how to search for the plate." The room buzzed with ideas.

"If he leaves the state, he'll want to re-license the bike rather than drive around with New York plates. He'll either go down to Motor Vehicles or steal one." People at the table nodded enthusiastically, heads like dipping birds.

Insurance waved both hands, his face beaming. "He's required to carry insurance in all states. If he re-licenses, he has to have proof of insurance which means we can watch the databases."

During all this interchange, Angie typed rapid-fire on the screen of her desk tablet. Patents wrinkled his eyebrows in worry. "Is that legal, hacking into databases?"

"Illegal for us. We're not the police. We need coppers." This came from a woman who would lie to anybody on the phone to get intel.

Number Four from Legal, said, "Are you sure? We need Information Technology. Here with us. And we need to be willing to bend the rules." Legal had voted for technology, not lawyers.

Angie laughed, a burbling fountain that sprang up. Her head tilted towards Thomas, her eyes merry. "We can get IT—and more space at the same time. I've found expanded room for the team. We're moving down to the computer floor at noon today. We'll get better security, more isolation."

Thomas guessed she wanted to wall off LeFarge. "Who knows someone in IT they can trust to play on our team?"

Angie's friend from Accounting raised her hand, "My husband works in IT. I don't trust his taste in clothes, but I do trust his discretion." Angie nodded and made a note.

Thomas said, "Let's look at the bike." He brought up a picture on his desktab, a stop frame from the Cumberland garage. He projected it onto the wall. "It's a sleek beast. Look at the body, the fairings, the large alloy spoke wheels. Even the paint is designed to scream. It's a speed freak's bike, like someone said. Where did he buy it? Is it custom? Where did he have the bike modified? Does he still have ties to the shop? Do we know a biker who could go see for us?"

Angie stopped the room cold. "We need surveillance to find the bike. Illegal surveillance. Nationwide."

"Tall order, Miss Tommo," said Thomas.

"But possible. O'Brien bought the controlling interest in Tran Cam three months ago."

"Tell us about Tran Cam," Thomas asked. He watched her, her calm and her confidence. She was his girl, all right. Only not.

She held up her hand like hushing a class. "They're the single largest US Surveillance company. Tran Cam runs the traffic cameras for most of the big-city police forces in America. They do corporate security for a lot of the Fortune 500. Tran Cam has a major contract with the Feds for surveillance at their installations."

One of the team said, "That's impossible! We can't hire ten thousand people to stare at TV monitors. And all those people would have to know what we're up to."

Angie said, "Facial recognition software. They can tweak that kind of software to search for the bike." Her voice was reasonable, firm.

"How do we get access to Tran Cam?" asked Insurance. His bald, doming forehead wrinkled in a pucker.

Thomas thought out loud. "We need clearance from the top. We need to feed Zlata, Boxwood, and the bike into the Tran Cam system. We need someone to insert the code to bypass their controls. We need the system to feed out to us here in this office."

Patents said, "So you need to suborn the CEO, his operations manager, a coder, and a communications engineer. Is that all?"

123

Thomas slapped the table with both hands and flashed his most charming grin around the room. "The CEO. If he tumbles, then all else is possible. Let me approach O'Brien, see what we can do."

The room murmured a soughing sound, a contented buzz.

Thomas felt delight wash through him. The consensus in the room was "this would work." He summed up, "In the meantime, I also want the three bank accounts searched going back as far as you can; see if Zlata paid for another residence somewhere or always buys weird traceable items. I want intel on everything about the make, model, and custom touches on the motorcycle. Let's bring our IT guy on board. We'll tunnel into all the Motor Vehicle Departments and insurance data bases that support major cities."

"Why major cities?"

"Ithaca was a one-off. Zlata is an urban animal."

"Can you do it?" Thomas asked O'Brien.

"I could make Georgie Patton cry. This is easy," replied the Governor.

"Good. If you can bend Tran Cam's boss, then I'll meet with him. Together we can figure out how to use their system but involve the minimum number of people."

"You're sure the cameras and the software can identify Zlata and Boxwood?"

Thomas hadn't said anything about the motorcycle—that was his ace in the hole. "Law enforcement uses the software every day, and the prisons are full. Zlata will turn up on camera sooner or later, and Tran Cam will inform us. Then it's up to Corporate Security to lay out a web of people in the right city and find him."

"Sooner or later? I don't have your patience. What will your people be doing?"

"We'll figure out Zlata's spending patterns. We'll also tunnel some databases. It's all across the line as far as legality."

"I don't care—and I don't want to know. Just do it."

"Okay boss." The boss wanted deniability, so Thomas could be the fall   guy.

Chapter Fifteen: End of the Idyll

Sibyl drove while Robko dropped in and out of sleep beside her. They puttered along in a twenty-four-year old minivan, a bit of a sad thing he thought. They towed a rented trailer, visible as an orange and white box in their tail lights. The enclosed trailer jerked as it ran over bumps and transmitted an irritating shudder up the trailer tongue into their van.

She pushed the search button on the radio for the millionth time, a most annoying habit. She joggled his elbow. "Are you awake?"

He jerked upright in the faded, stained seat. "Yes. Are we close by? I don't recognize anything in the dark."

"Still on I90, at the exit for Milwaukee. Central Ave is close by. That's why I woke you."

"Where?"

"Look at the map on your iMob, gozo. You're practically home."

He did. "Okay, let's go over it again. You drop me off—"

"Yeah, yeah, I dump you, drive around a big circle using Central and Parkside until you get right with your mother and magically reappear on the curb."

Robko hopped up on the dumpster and chinned himself onto the roof of the three-car parking unit on the back of his Ma's apartment block. The old, blond brick was crumbly under his fingers. His feet followed a route he had taken many times as a teenager. She never locked the kitchen window of the second floor apartment. The room was dark as hell itself. He crept in over the sill, pushing a chair away from him and back under the kitchen table. He swiveled his head around as he eased the window shut. An orange dot glowed on the other side of the table.

He saw the ghost of her face as she drew hard on the cigarette, then the swoop of the ember as it headed for the ashtray.

"That you, son?"

"Yeah, it's me, Ma."

"You shouldn't have come. I don't know what weasel thing you done, but there are guys hanging around, asking questions... watching the house."

"Sorry about that, Ma. It's not so much what I did; it's who I did it to."

The orange glow flew up from the ashtray, burned bright, and then disappeared in the smoke that swept out around it. "You and your old man. I thought he'd be the death of me. I think you'll be the long, sad song they use to take me to the graveyard."

"Aaah, Ma."

"Turn on the goddamn light. They aren't out in the alley, or you would have seen them."

He took the four steps and flicked the switch. Everything was in its remembered place. He pulled the chair out across from her and dropped into it. He waited.

"Brown-haired now? Well, it's good to see you. Been too long."

He nodded. "Three years."

"More like four. I pray at Mass every day you'll clean up and come home."

"Maybe someday." He looked into her eyes, red from the cigarette smoke and with little veins where the vodka had broken through.

"Robko, you don't mean it. You're thirty-two, too old to change."

There were lines around her eyes. Lines put there by ten-hour days running the bar... lines dug in by him. "I'm happy, Ma. Can you be happy for me?"

"You got muscle after you, son. How cheerful can I be, knowing there's always going to be someone after you? What I wouldn't give if you were a grocer here in the neighborhood or had a nice job at the Post Office. Or you were a priest." She shook her head and took a drag.

"Me... a priest?" He choked down the laugh. "I just came by to let you know I'm okay. I got Sibyl with me, and we're heading west."

His mother's second-hand smoke flurried out across the table and drifted across his hands and forearms. "Sibyl." She started a new cigarette with the old one. "I always liked that girl. Very finishing-

126

school—what a hoot, her with you. I always thought she'd dump you for Stannie."

Stannie. Stanislaw. His brother. Her firstborn. "She might have."

"Yes, she might have. Too late now."

Too late for the good son, dead for years. He crossed his arms and scratched both elbows, an old habit from the principal's office. He waited.

"West, huh? Don't tell me where, so they can't beat it out of me."

He flinched. "Can you get someone to stay with you, just for a little while?"

She wheezed a little chuckle, the smoke burbling out of her mouth. "I thought about that. There's a couple of heavies at the bar, but they'd think I was coming on to them. My old bouncer Teddy would do it, but he's got COPD. There's a new bouncer, a kid really. A tattooed wonder with huge muscles, but he's got nothin' upstairs."

"So you're alone?"

"No. I brought the bar shotgun home."

There didn't seem to be much to say to that. He waited again, like he always did.

"Mirko's dead, you know? Murdered." She stared deep into his face.

He nodded, gazed down at the red checks in the plastic table cloth.

"His sister called, the spinster one. I thought about you the moment she told me."

"Why? Because we are—were old friends?"

"Because I wondered if you were there when it happened."

Sibyl asked, "How was it? You look whipped." She snapped a picture of him slumped up against the arm rest and then pulled away from the curb.

"Mothers will do that for you."

"Gimme a break. Your mother's still around. Mine, she's in a nursing home and is scared to death of me. I can't walk into her room without her going off in screams." She reached across the console and rubbed his thigh. "I like your mom. She's seen it all."

"Maybe we should lay up close by for a couple of days."

"Unh-unh. You had your chance to go hide out in Polish Land. Now we're headed into my country where the corn is tall and the women are blondes."

"You're not blonde."

"Not anymore." She sighed. Rochester had changed her hair color again… back to brunette.

"Still mourning your blonde look?"

"No. I mourn the loss of good accommodations out here in the middle of America. Denver's the last chance at a suite before Los Angeles."

"I don't know. Omaha is a possibility… and they have steaks."

"I'd prefer albacore tuna. And sushi. Sashimi… and wasabi."

"Someone's hungry." He reached across the console and traced a pattern on her knee with his index finger.

"Aren't you hungry?"

"On the contrary. I'm quite horny—a well-known side effect of shaking off my downers."

"But if you're aroused when you're tweaked, how can you have the same problem un-tweaked?"

He splayed his knees and adjusted his pants. "Who said it was a problem? Why don't you pull off in the next alley, and we'll explore whether it's a problem."

She rubbed her fingers and thumb together. "Give me five hundred dollars."

"Now, there's the problem. I need to hit an ATM. I've got forty-five on me."

She scanned him and arched an eyebrow. "Pity. You could have negotiated me down to fifty, but forty-five… that's just cheap. And in the back of a minivan? I ask you."

"Well, if you want a room with a bed, we can find one. Chicago has plenty of flops."

"I'm wide awake. Why don't we drive out to Omaha, get in in the morning, and spend all day in bed." She paused. "Robert, I've been thinking. If anyone is watching, our ATM usage draws a line across America."

"Naah. I kept it all separate, and this is the fourth account. They don't have a clue."

"So you think we're safe."

"Safe and without any option. We need the money."

She shook her head. Her hair cascaded around her face, settled back on her shoulders. "And if you're wrong?"

"Then we'll have to escape their constricting net of evil villains, burst out of the trailer on the bike like Batman and Robin from the Bat Cave, and scream into the night. We'll live the hobo life, sleep under bridges and inside giant culverts, and travel only at night until we hit L.A. and pick up my other resources."

"Other resources?"

"I have a fifth account. It's a savings account. I thought I might one day be old and need old-people money. There's also diamonds. How about that motel? I want to get laid... soon." Robko pointed to an old-fashioned motor-court rolling into view.

"Puuleeze. Another four blocks and I catch the Kennedy Expressway. I'm driving on, so you can put your testosterone back in your testicles."

Robko stared through the windshield at the 30s building, focused on a scrawl in black paint down the side of the motel's cinderblock wall, saying, "Wanton Love: Who Will Love Me?" A block-shaped tag at the end finished off the graff—that signature. He shuddered. "You're right; drive right past this one." All these tags, maybe by the same man or same group, maybe speaking to him. The dickheads were creeping him out.

Thomas called this part of the chase "spidering." He had cast his web out and now waited to see what information would blunder in and be snagged.

The team had grown up so fast. O'Brien's CIO delivered the IT neuker who built them digital tunnels into eight DMVs. Angie relocated the team to open space on the computer floor and set up connections into the major insurance databases, courtesy of the Corporate Insurance division right in their own building. One other thing pending: O'Brien hadn't suborned the Tran Cam president yet. Thomas kept his hand on his spider web to see if it vibrated, but mostly he waited, dark and grumpy. His team glimmered shiny-bright and enjoyed themselves quite a bit. He grew bored... and nervous. He didn't know how to read his luck.

The team worked long and grueling hours, but not Thomas. He hid away in his carrel on the computer floor, projected Zlata's data onto the cheesy wall, and listened on his phone to the alt-bands he thought Zlata enjoyed. Thomas acclimated himself to an unexpected preference for the type of singer that would spit on the audience and insult the fan base. His cadre thought he searched for Zlata using some mystic method, but really he just messed around and tried to wriggle into Robko Zlata's head. Half-assed and surely moronic.

He returned to the Comet Kitty even though his prey had disappeared into America. He morphed, a fraud in his spiky hair, sunglasses, and black clothes, but he did enjoy himself. He visited with the singer and the drummer of a band named Red Knuckle. He bought them drinks and bar food. They enjoyed talking about themselves; the conversation circled round his admiration for their raw three-chord sound and their psychopathic lyrics about the current American war. They asked; he lied. "I'm a lawyer who specializes in entertainment contracts."

"You're in the business, man? Who do you know?"

"Not music. Actors. Theatre. Movies, TV adverts." He enjoyed becoming someone else, building his own fiction.

Red Knuckle invited him back for the next night. "Hang out before the gig, dude. It'll be phunk."

They lounged around a table about nine, eating carryout Italian and waiting for the club to open, yawning, quiet, waiting. "Is this the way it is with you guys most of the time?"

"Hell yes, my, my," replied the singer. She had done her best to make herself ugly—black-polished nails, a face painted chalk-white, flea market clothes, hair that escaped in shards from a Jamaican dreadlocks hat. But there was still an exotic beauty that shone out.

The drummer explained, "It's not so much a life as a train ride. We don't have time for anything personal. You wake up and you stagger off to work. You play, and you really pump up for that. About two in the morning, you finish up, and you go out to eat at some local dive and talk about how good the gig was or where you play next. If you're lucky, you get stoned on someone else's dollar, and you might go home with somebody or take that mysterious somebody to your place. If there're no surprises, you sleep for a while. Then the train pulls out of the station, and you do the ride all over again."

"And how often does this happen?"

The singer said, "We gig as much as we can. We're working six days a week right now. We'd tour if we could afford it, but the expenses on the road kill you."

Thomas asked, "What happens the seventh day?"

"We rehearse, work up new material, jam out. We're not any stinkin' cover band, man."

Thomas ate their food, and listened to the earnestness behind their brutish sound during three sets. He hovered at the edge of the stage when they closed. "Great sets tonight, guys. I just wanted to thank you. I'll see you around."

"Wait, man, want to eat Chinese? We know an all-night place up two blocks that stays open for the restaurant people. You can buy since you're a fat-cat lawyer."

"Sure. Why not? Even if my clients are out-of-work actors."

He followed people who had nowhere else to be into a red painted restaurant and ate MSG-infused food for two hours. After, he wrapped himself around the singer and followed her home. She rented an apartment across town, above Tribeca and way north of Canal. He coughed up for the cab.

"This is it," she said, as she led the way into an efficiency. She dropped her music bag and her keys on the floor by the couch. "Lock the deadbolt behind you. My neighbors are no better than they ought'a be, but at least they only try to break in a couple of times a year."

"Nice place."

"Frickin' liar. It's a dump. I haven't had time to clean since Christmas, and anyway, I'm not here much." She stepped in close and fingered his lapel. "Want to crank up? I got some LA Turnarounds left that we could powder."

He thought of all the elegant evenings he had manufactured on the way to seduction, all the good wines and esoteric food. He thought about his previous women with their finishing-school accents and preppie clothes, in the end revealed in their white underwear... giving just enough to honor the conventions.

Zlata would have understood this woman, poised on the edge of something in an apartment like this. Stage dust in the hair, the strong smell of performance sweat, tattered and ripped black clothes that revealed flashes of white, blue-veined skin—Robko Zlata would have been at home. "Sure. I can't reciprocate with anything, but if you have enough for two?"

"Straight. You popped for the cab. Fair warning, this isn't meth, just some jumpers." She found a mortar and pestle and ground up six powder-coated pills. "I don't do meth anymore. I like it too much, and it gets in the way of the music." Placing a pinch of the dust on a piece of foil at the end of a glass tube, she held a match over the assemblage and drew deep. His suck on the pipe imitated her hit with some competence. The smoke seared his sinuses and dissolved his throat into a burning mass of flesh. Clenching down hard, he kept himself from exploding into a cough.

The hit had an all-enveloping, soul-shivering effect. He had never had such a feeling of well-being in all his life. She worked with his belt and opened his pants. He fumbled within the rips and tears of her clothes, desperate to discover the woman inside.

At eleven the next day, Thomas made it back to his apartment. For all the high, there had to be the low. He felt as bad as anything he could ever remember. Twice he stopped on the subway to retch into a trash can, but the dry heaving did nothing. He knew his Chinese feast from the night before lay congealed in his belly, but his throat closed like a vise. By the time he reached his door, he shook like a train platform with an express roaring by. He dropped his keys. When he bent down to pick them up, a black-out swarmed up through his head. He dropped to his knees. His nose, his whole sinus passage sucked in a whiff of something that made him gag. It cleared his head, this smell. Some chemical, some cleaning compound. Shining in the hall light a small puddle, there in front of his kneecaps. Nasty stuff… it bled out from under his door. Dipping a finger into the liquid, he raised it to his nose. It was awful.

He lurched to his feet and wiggled his key into the lock. Opening the door a crack, he surveyed the gap. Near the floor, a thumbtack had been stuck in the doorframe with a thread that led away to the left. He pulled the tack with a gentle dig of his fingernails, dropped the thread, and eased the door open. A crude paper fabrication crouched against the

132

baseboard with some innocuous firework taped to it. Thomas stared down at something he recognized as a firebomb. An igniter waiting for him, and a foyer full of accelerant. *If this goes off, what will be left for them to find?*

Down in the Bars

Chapter Sixteen: Send a Message, Send a Message

In the tallest hotel in the Mile-High City, Robko got high and sought the low. The old night died, and a new day, welcome or not, crowded into his life. They had taken the suite Sibyl wanted. He thought it the opulence of a faked life, the irony of trash delivered upon a silver platter. He lay upon a leather couch as white as Sibyl's rounded belly, wearing the hotel's maximally-plush black robe. On the wall to his left, a fake Mark Rothko hung in splendor, the size of his ciotka's dining-room table. In his haze, he daydreamed of that aunt; she knew all the tales of the old land and all the stories of God's paradise. Always dressed in widow black, always with a pile of childhood's books and strange little wooden toys from Europe.

He found this bone-whitened place the flip of home—none of the children, the cats, and the dark massive furniture that towered up to the ceiling. Here it was stripped to the bone, all line-on-line, white-on-white. He could hide here, hide from them. Hide from Mirko.

The drug ratcheted up another notch, and he had the illusion the room rotated. The window wall across from him transformed into a floor beneath him; luxuriant air and glass suspended him over the horizon of the city. His body leaned out from the couch, ready to launch into the depths of a sunrise. The glass waited below, a thin skin between him and the sun.

"Robert, I'm back." Sibyl entered from the foyer where the piano hung, sauntered across the white-carpeted wall. She strolled round to the end of the couch between him and the sun and paused to watch him from below. His inner ear wobbled, disoriented as she cantilevered out from the wall. He pushed that rush of vertigo around in his mind like the party favor it was. "Sibyl, glad you got here before I fell off. Try one of these robes; they're so comfortable it's nearly like sex."

"You gozo, you've picked up another fetish... the black terrycloth fetish." She stepped around the arm of the couch and brushed him on the forehead with her lips. She peeled her clothes away, and he watched as they fell up against the wall beside the suspended couch. She revealed herself, metamorphosed into a sleek shape that crawled up into the leather cocoon and held him tight. "You're right; this robe feels great, feels like sable. Let me in." She tugged at the tie.

"We may drop off the face of the earth any second. I'm glad you're going with me."

"I see you scored. Well, I did, too. I shucked a desk tablet out of the hotel office. After all, the door was unlocked. The silly bitch even has pictures of her naked. Stored on a pad without a password! You remember how we first met—shoplifting makes me so hot."

"I should tell you I have a new drug. It's called Painted Desert. It lights up the world. Would you like one? It's a dream wrapped in a down."

"Halluso, is it? I always liked you on hallusos; they make you so mystic and full of holy universal shit."

"It's the curse of lapsed Catholics. We're all searching for God's grace and finding it in the Swiss cheese of our brains."

"See, that's what I mean."

"Don't fall off into the dawn, not yet. I'm ready for wild love, I think. Of course it could be a delusion, so I need you to check for me."

She felt down between them with a soft, wriggling hand. "No hallucination here. Do you feel like it, right now?"

"Give me five hundred dollars."

Still home at noon, Thomas lay in the chaise in the shade of the rooftop air conditioning equipment. He had nothing important to do, and he contemplated his death at LeFarge's hands with great idleness and melancholy. His iMob chimed. "Steward here."

"It's Angie." And so it was, in a white linen suit and a navy silk shirt. "We've got a lead on an Italian bike, an exotic one painted red, brought in for 'tires and tune.' The shop says a couple brought it in, and they had been running it hard—wear patterns on the tires show they'd used up the sidewall as well as the tread."

He tried the smallest of smiles. Still, it was a chance. They had to

138

take it. "Where is the bike?"

"San Francisco."

"Want to go?"

Her laugh burbled through the cell towers. "Sure. I'll get us tickets and two rooms near Union Square."

※

San Francisco turned out cold and drizzling, grayed to summer's end sooner than the East Coast. Thomas's mood matched the autumnal rain; he slumped on the couch. He gazed at the gilded cornice and the slate-colored window below it. She swayed in from her adjoining room. "The private detective texted me."

He flicked the fingers of one hand. "Dick."

"Of course. The slang is 'dick.' You guys enjoy that word. Our Dick is on location, but the couple hasn't come in to pick up their motorcycle."

"What arrangement did you make?"

"When they do show up, he'll use his vidi to send a picture. We can decide right then if he tails them."

"They'll be on a hot bike."

"And so will he. He can play the part. It's not like he's wearing a black suit and a brown, big-brimmed hat."

The corner of his mouth twitched up. "Carrying a snub nose and driving a 1941 coupe. So we wait…."

"Thomas, is something wrong? You seem down in the dumps." She leaned up against the back of an easy chair.

"I've got a new problem. LeFarge may be removing witnesses of Father Mirko's killing."

"You mean his four muscle men? Has he killed them?"

"I don't know about them. I was referring to yours truly."

She shook her head. "If he was going to shoot you, you'd be dead."

"Accident—he wants a plausible accident. Either O'Brien agrees with LeFarge, or LeFarge wants to hand the Governor a way to rationalize away my death… after the fact."

"What makes you think LeFarge is after you?"

"I found a booby trap in my apartment when I got home Wednesday." He made a fountaining gesture with both hands.

Her mouth dropped and she stepped towards him. "You're sure it was a booby trap?"

"What do you think?" He heard his own voice, too abrupt.

"We'll have to take precautions."

"We means you too. LeFarge wouldn't mind collateral damage, taking you out at the same time."

Her mouth drew down and her eyes narrowed. "None of this makes sense. He needs you to find Robko Zlata."

"Well, he needs the team. He may not hold me in high regard."

"Teams need leaders," she said with a faint smile.

He returned a grin. "Our team may have a leak. He may have someone on the team, and we don't know it."

She shook her head—her dark hair bobbed. "We chose our people carefully."

"And it worked, seeing we got good people, but it only takes one."

"Do you have someone you suspect?"

"No, but this trip makes a pretty good test. If LeFarge's people show up, there's a hole in our security."

She ambled over to the bar and made a drink: scotch neat, he thought. She leaned up against the bar's sideboard. "So what did you mean… precautions?"

"I haven't been home for a couple of days—I've hoteled it. I'm digging around for an old friend I can visit for a while. My problem is that most of the guys I know are competitors, not friends."

"How about women?"

"Hmm. They've moved on, or I have. There is one, but she's more dangerous than LeFarge. Lives on Chinese food laced with MSG. How about you, do you have a place to go?"

"Well," she paused, "I think I'll call my cousin down on Staten Island."

"They'll know to search for family."

"Yes, but it's hard for a stranger to pass unnoticed in our little version of Italy. It's a tight community."

He levered himself out of the luxurious sofa and joined her at the bar. He found a bottle of Pouilly Fuissé in the fridge and opened it. Taking a stemmed-glass-full over to the window, he gazed out at the lights of Union Square. "Want to do major room service tonight?"

"Sure. It's all paid for by the Governor."

"You can tell me about your girlfriends; I'll tell you about mine."

Her laugh ran like a waterfall through the room. "I have something in common with the boss."

⚘

In Denver, the desktab lay on the couch between Robko and Sibyl. The couch had restored itself to its normal position within gravity, with no physical manifestation of its recent metamorphosis. She said, "Find Sibyl Boxwood."

The desk tablet gave her three files to choose from. She opened one after the other, and said each time, "Read file." The tablet duly read each file in an Asian singsong voice. None of these files taught them anything except how well Sibyl had been profiled. When the Asian voice read her medical records, she peeked sideways at Robko and grinned, but didn't blush. Then she searched for Robko's aliases. Steward's master summary showed him unaware of the fourth and fifth identities. Or rather, he hadn't known at the time they stole the information in Ithaca.

Most of Steward's tablet was dedicated to financial crap. It took time to find the right part of the tree. As Sibyl searched down the promising branches for information on O'Brien's organization, the memdevice unfolded like a flower, a deadly nightshade. She and Robko listened to several cross-linked files gathered under "OBrienFriends&Enemies." They found notes on the head of Corporate Security, Don Garland, and on Egan LeFarge. Steward's voice, mid-American and without color, read his memos back into the room.

She snorted, "I know the type. Two-hundred-dollar Oxford shirts, weekends in the Hamptons, some kinky sex he would never reveal to his preppie wife."

But Robko listened for the hunter's voice, the man who had found him in the City and then in Ithaca. A shudder ran through his shoulders as Steward read out the Zlata data crisp, judgmental, hard. He asked her, "Don't you notice something weird about his voice?"

She said to the tablet, "Pause." Turning to him, she said, "What do you mean?"

"It's..., I don't know, as if I'm hearing myself talk. Doesn't he sound a lot like me?"

"Yeah, right, beyond the fact you're both tenors? Like he has your street punk accent, and you talk in his nasal business-school twang? Naah, his vocabulary is way better than yours. He's a Regular Joe; you're a Booster."

"No... there's something."

"I think you're still junked from those Painted Deserts. After-flash."

He frowned, but it was true. He could feel a little bit of trip kick in.

She turned back to the tablet. "Play."

The tablecloth was so starched Thomas could push drops of water around on it with a spoon. They had pulled out all stops, and the table held the most pretentious food he had seen in months. Wonderful presentation, but his mind roamed elsewhere. "It's no good trying to dodge LeFarge indefinitely. It could be a while before this is all done."

Angie said, "We're at a whole new level of corporate infighting, aren't we?"

"Yes, with firebombs and knives and guns."

He teased a bit of polenta with his fork. "O'Brien's the key. I haven't been able to convince O'Brien he doesn't need the Foreign Legion and Captain LeFarge. He doesn't see them as a liability. And if he thinks my luck has deserted me, I'll be the liability."

"Don't kid yourself about the military crap. O'Brien enjoys it. Think about it... O'Brien knows business and politics. Now he's got his own army. He's having a great time commanding killers—it's a new form of power for him."

He spread a big glob of paté on a crostini and handed it to her. "So O'Brien won't fire or eliminate LeFarge?"

"Not until Zlata is captured and probably killed. Could O'Brien give you some protective coverage even though LeFarge is the favorite?"

He scowled. "I'd first have to convince O'Brien that LeFarge had tried to kill me. If he doesn't believe me, I'll have destroyed the trust."

She shook her head. "How much trust do you think he has now?"

"Just enough to get what he wants."

She pursed her lips, a charming pout. "Can we get LeFarge

arrested for killing the priest?"

"Dangerous. First, I was there, so I'm implicated. Second, LeFarge could bring us all down to save his own skin." He sipped delicately at the wine.

"Can we blackmail LeFarge into backing off?"

"I could threaten him—tell him I'll turn myself in to the police and testify against him. But I think he'd just come straight for me. No more fake accidents—he'd go for the sure thing."

"Gunshot to the back of the head. Mob style." She cleared her throat. "Could we eliminate LeFarge before he kills you? And me?"

"Eliminate? You mean murder? Maybe, if it comes to that. Risky. Killing is LeFarge's specialty, not ours. And how squeamish are we?"

"Can you hire your own bodyguards?"

"Maybe, or I could maybe work the Zlata pursuit on the road, from outside NYC. I chase Zlata, and LeFarge chases me."

She flared those beautiful dark eyes, a moment of fright. "Leaves me hanging out there."

"Say no more."

188 Lincoln Avenue, Denver's hottest new restaurant could do takeout—that is, if the hotel manager calls ahead, and the doorman goes over in a taxi to get it, and if Sibyl speaks directly with the chef. Robko loved the plum soup, and his next Painted Desert—just one to help with the coasting—gave him the tiniest little flashes of connection. He leaned over the glass slab of the coffee table covered with plates and the serving dishes, but he also lay in an orchard outside of Warsaw, fat, purple fruit splayed around him, plums on the ground spoiling in great-grandmother's sunshine as it drooped hot out of the sky. The hotel room smelled like fruit sugar, like dust from the orchard road, like grass.

Sibyl, on the other hand, expressed great admiration for the field greens with mustard dressing. She waved her fork—he ignored her. She stabbed him in the back of his hand.

"Oww."

"Check this out. This file is a hyper-tree. O'Brien's Security must have turned over a bunch of raw data. This one is about headquarters, and here's O'Brien's residence. Look!" She opened up the branch for the mansion and touched a leaf. "It's a floor plan with the electric wiring."

"That's the alarm system. There, up in the corner, the symbol for a motion detector, and that's a camera."

"I want one of your Chinese parsley gnocchi. That buttery stuff smells so good. Look, here's a map of the grounds."

"Ground shakers. They installed geophones." He nodded sagely, and little lightning flashes went off. He listened to afternoon rain softly coming his way, and he huddled up against a Polish tree.

"Here's another part of the hyper-tree, flagged in red. Maybe an industrial complex."

He pointed at the lower right corner. "Research. In Georgia. Maybe where they built the Artifact?"

"This could take days. There's so much stuff in this memdevice."

"Of course it's huge—we stole raw data. The important thing is that it provides us with one of five pieces we need." He cracked his knuckles and stretched his shoulders. The dream of his Prababcia's orchard faded, even as he tried to tease it back.

"Which are?"

"The first is good intelligence—and this is a huge step forward. The second is a crew. That's you and me now."

"And the last three?"

"We need to know what would break O'Brien. That leads us to number four, a plan." He had lost count. How many pieces of the puzzle?

"Don't keep me in suspense. What's the fifth?" She raised one eyebrow, and his pulse leapt.

She wore his bathrobe, and he imagined how it could fall open. The grin started building up from within his chest. "Another heart-stopping bout of sex."

"Give me my five hundred back."

❊

After the Mousse Grenadine, Thomas and Angie had settled into coffee and cognac. The room hung around them, soft and ivory colored, like a linen tent. Trouble evaporated, disappeared from his horizon.

She was heartless. "So you don't have a clue on how to beat LeFarge…."

He grunted. "True. But I've got a good team to help, once we root out our spy."

"If there is one."

"An awkward point."

She forgave him. "And this trip is half about finding out."

"We need to keep our focus. It would be nice to capture Zlata—that's the key thing. With him in hand, I can come to terms with the Governor, and LeFarge's purpose will go away."

Her phone chimed; she picked it up from the white tablecloth. "Message. It's from our detective." She peered at it. "Goddamn! He lost them. He went next door for a burger, and they left before he got back!" She held the iMob screen out to him.

He stared. Staring did not change the message. "Aaah. Coast to coast for nothing."

She leapt to her feet and stomped about the room. He could hear her muttering under her breath. He thought it was Italian. With an angry gesture, she cocked her arm back to throw the vidi across the room. She stopped. Whirling towards him, she flashed out a smile like the dazzling sky. "Oh well. Sometimes you hire a ritardato." Those shoulders came up in a shrug and her breasts saluted him.

Too many disappointments had piled one on the other. His lip came up in a snarl. "We don't even know if it was them."

Angie grinned. "Cheer up. You got a great meal out of it."

It was true. A snicker toyed around at the back of his mind. He nodded. "Tell your private dickhead he can kiss his fee goodbye unless he comes up with something. Maybe he can get a description. Maybe they said where they were going. Maybe they paid with a check. Something."

She tapped away at the screen. "Done."

"That's half the trip's goals wasted."

"And the other half? We can't draw out LeFarge's people sitting in a hotel suite."

He was nonplussed. "So you want to go out?"

"It could work."

"Too late for shopping or sightseeing. It's clubbing, then."

She dipped her head. "Gay or straight?"

145

"Loud." Maybe he could score a little something.

"I'll ask the concierge."

"Now what?" asked Sibyl. "It's hours and hours before breakfast." She rolled up off the plush rug and grabbed the bathrobe up in her arms.

"Well, I could pay you the five hundred. Then you could spend it on me. I do feel like celebrating."

"And how do you want to celebrate?"

He fished at the dangling hem of the robe trying to get it back. The room was a little chilly. "Let's find a band."

"And champagne."

"And where do we find a punk club with champ?"

"I'll ask the concierge."

Chapter Seventeen: Yo, Bartender

The fourth day after they hit Los Angeles, Robko had a job interview in a location he found remarkable. The address was unmarked. A brutalized gate bent and bowed away from the parking lot towards the street, and it had a lock he didn't want to mess with. He ghosted up the chain link and dropped to the other side. He hiked across a desolate, pockmarked spread of concrete to an industrial building. Just beside a giant rollup door, an open man-door yawned. He slipped inside. The vast space opened out through the warehouse with some sky-walks, some portable toilets, and small job-site trailers crowding the sides. Halfway down, two semi-trucks were parked, their doors open. Men swarmed about unloading them. A man in a beret, leather jacket, and sunglasses paced forward and said, "Can I help you?"

"I'm here for the job interview."

"Who did you talk to?"

"I'd rather not say."

"And your name is?"

"I'd rather not say."

The man in sunglasses jerked around towards the crowd milling about the back of the trucks. "Manny," he shouted. "Your new dude is here."

Robko strolled over to an obese man waving at him. "You looking for me?" It came out a growl, but perhaps one not unkindly.

"If you really are Manny."

"Cautious little shit, aren't you. I'm Manny, all day every day. What's your name?"

"Steve Gordon."

"That's who they told me to expect. You don't look like no Gordon... or a Steve."

Robko shook his head. "The Gordons are on my mother's side."

Manny scowled. "Funny, too. Have you bartended before?"

"Yeah. A couple of roadhouses, a club back east, a restaurant in a ski resort."

Manny jutted a finger up in the air. Stiff, black hair covered the back of his hand. "What's in a Pink Lady?"

"Gin, cream, egg white. Normally served in gay bars."

Manny held up a second finger. "What's a Strangler?"

"Schnapps, vodka, rum, and cranberry juice. Normally served to people who plan to puke later."

Now Manny had three fingers in the air as he counted up. "What drugs and drink are you into?"

"If I said 'nothing,' would you believe me?"

Manny closed his fist and scrubbed it across the black bristle on his chin. "Yeah right."

"Downers. I don't drink, and I don't do opiates or barbs while I work." *On my jobs, not yours.*

"You're hired. Just for a week, to see if you make the cut. When can you start?"

Robko raised his shoulders and opened his eyes wide. He cocked his head sideways. "Now's fine."

"I hoped you'd say that. We're short-handed. Let me show you the set-up." They trod through the huge space.

Robko asked, "What do you call the operation?"

"We used to call it PowerUp. Now it's Phatal. With a 'Ph.' Get it?"

"How often do you move?"

Manny said, "We pick out a new joint every weekend or so. Sometimes we slip the owner something; sometimes it's abandoned, and we just move in. These trailers bring in the lights and the stage, including the sound equipment. My stuff, the bars, they come in catering trucks. We sell booze and only booze—we got customers in the crowd who handle everything else, and we stay drug-free. If I catch you stealing, dealing, high, or screwing the customers—either male or female—you're finished. I'll be watching. A little buzz is all right with me, but if you go space-cowboy, I will personally kick in your teeth while your replacement holds you down."

This suited Robko. He now knew where Manny stood on labor relations. "What days do I work?"

"We're only open Friday and Saturday nights, but we spend Thursday and Friday setting up and Sunday tearing down. We always tear down and park the trucks somewhere else, even if we're using the joint twice. The job runs four days a week, but they're long days. I pay at the end of each night, just in case the Bluemen interrupt us sometime during the weekend."

"What's the risk factor?"

"Big enough to make the pay worthwhile. We've been caught once in five years."

"What's the pay?"

"Four C a day. We take January and February off, so if you're permanent, the gig is fifty three large a year, tax free."

"Are there concessions besides the bars?"

Manny stuck his little finger into his nostril and dug around. He withdrew the fat digit and inspected the end of it as if an unusual gemstone perched there. "Curious little dick, ain't you? Well, you'll find out anyway, so there's no harm in saying. I got a couple of upscale restaurants that send us roach coaches. The celebs love the designer food. They like the performance art too."

"Performance art?"

"Yeah. Last weekend Dickie Bettson brought in his motorized pterodactyl. This weekend, they got two guys in gold lamé tuxedos with jack hammers. They'll bust up rocks by the front door." Manny held his hands out in front of him, clenched his fists, and jerked them up and down. His belly jiggled.

"How many customers?"

"Usually three to four hundred, sometimes more. It's all viral. We message a few of our outlaw hosts where the location is and who the bands are, and they spread the word around the community."

"So you draw in three hundred party animals a night. What's the cover?"

"Only a hundred and fifty a pop. And there's what you might call substantial markup on the alcohol and food." Manny rubbed his thumb and forefinger together—his hand resembled a fat, wriggling badger biting the end of his arm.

Robko cracked up, delighted by the whole setup. "Have you ever considered buying a liquor license and a legit location?"

Manny slapped him on the shoulder—it caused Robko to stagger a

149

bit. "Where's the fun in that?"

Thomas needn't have worried. The Tran Cam deal proved to be simple. O'Brien held a secret or two over the head of the CEO. Once the man rolled over to the pressure, a first Tran Cam stooge added the search for the bike into the stack of national security requests. Stooge two labeled the feed to the team as a real-time report to a secretive Federal department. It happened so casually, Thomas knew all other types of abuse must occur all the time.

Thomas gave three of his staff the job of tracking Tran Cam. Between them, they checked the data feed all day every day, a recipe for burnout that Angie remedied with rotation. The rest of the team moved on to the missing memory devices, the other nine. The team invented something called the Wolf Trap.

"Here's the deal," Thomas said to the assembled team. "We have nine loose memory devices out there that contain sensitive material, both financial and political. Zlata boosted them, and Dupont sold them on to a single buyer who's now auctioning them."

He talked about the recovery of the first two and segued on to current efforts. "O'Brien is paying some serious talent to search upstream for Dupont's buyer, but the buyer has masked himself well. The memdevices show up on the market through different salesmen—we know that by the first two."

"So, do we search for the buyer, or do we stay out of the way of O'Brien's other talent?" asked Accounting. She wore her glasses pushed up on her forehead, her mouth a block of teeth surrounded by red lipstick.

"Let's move downstream, see if we can find another path to the devices," Thomas said.

Legal drummed on the table with his favorite yellow number 2 pencil. "O'Brien had good instincts on the second device."

Angie said, "Look for the victim."

Insurance sniffed and blew his nose. "We can track the devices as they come into play. We need to single out the most vulnerable people in the O'Brien net, the ones who would be blackmailed, and watch them."

150

"Behavioral change," said another team member. "We keep track of what they do, and if it changes big-time, someone has their hooks into 'em."

The idea gelled right in front of Thomas. "So you stake them out like lambs and wait for the wolf to come hunting?"

Auditing bared her teeth... on the hunt. "Right. Focus on the high-risk targets. Either the ones who could do the most for a blackmailer, or the ones with the worst secrets."

Patents dug at his cheek with his fingernails. He needed specifics. "What do you look for?"

Legal twirled his pencil through his fingers like a drummer showing off before the cymbal crash. "Changes in voting patterns. Any financial change that smells like it gives up some control. Major liquidation of personal assets."

Thomas said, "It means slow going, trying to find each device one at a time."

Insurance rubbed his tall, shining forehead. "Chasing Miss Sibyl turned out a total bust. We don't have anything to do until Zlata and his bike surface anyway."

Angie said, "We go down through a list—"

Patents jumped on it like a dog, his head swiveling as he shot a demanding scan up and down the table. "What list?"

Auditing spoke the unspeakable. "O'Brien has to give it to us. He's the original blackmailer."

Patents slapped the table. "Yes! We take each possible lamb and make an individual profile for what to look for, and then we watch the lamb."

Auditing asked, "How do you watch?"

"That part is easy," said the IT guy. "I can make sofbots that crawl the news feeds and report back on pattern changes of your lambs. The first ones will be crude, but I can refine them over time. Add artificial intelligence, learning systems, that kind of thing." He beamed a round face full of joy. At least he was going to have fun.

Insurance wagged his head. "O'Brien won't want to give up the names and the crimes."

Thomas said, "I'll offer him compartmentalization. For each lamb, only three staffers—Angie, the profiler and our botmaster—will know who the lamb is." Thomas's phone messaged him. It read "I Once

151

Ruled," and the sender's i.d. was blocked. "Anyone else getting weird-ass texts?"

Blank looks washed across the room. "Never mind. I'll set up some time with the Governor, today if I can, and explain what you want and why. Good work, everyone. Jean, could you stay behind? I've got a side project I want you to work on."

Jean came from Auditing. Thomas knew her better than some of his staff; she had been one of the original four, all Angie's friends. A brusque, thick-skinned woman, she defined the role of career hard-nose. She had to be; she inhabited the world of corporate auditing. Thomas gave Angie the lead with a nod.

Angie hunched forward toward her friend. "Since everything we do is confidential, I won't say the obvious. I will tell you it's political. I need you to keep this from the rest of the team."

"Sure. Understood."

"We need to know what Egan LeFarge is up to. He's been there each time we've found and lost Zlata."

"You want to spy on O'Brien's private army?"

"Uh-huh. We think LeFarge will catch on to any ordinary surveillance, so we believe we should follow the money at first, till we know the ground."

"The money. I understand following the money. Can I have carte blanche on this?"

"What did you have in mind?"

"An open mandate for audit. It's what I know, what I do. Once we know where the money originates, in what department or which O'Brien company, we'll also know the account numbers that receive the money. Then we can buy additional information from your sources on those outside accounts."

Angie grinned the smile of a shark. "Okay. Go audit the right people. Be bold and wave around the Head Auditor's name, but let's keep this off O'Brien's level."

"Got it." She jumped up to go.

"And Jean," Angie said. Jean stopped. "This is something that has to go fast. LeFarge is a danger to the team's mission." Jean nodded.

"And to me and you," Thomas said under his breath to Angie.

❄

For his first night Phatal billed a New Zealand surf punk band as the headliner and lined out a Jewish hip-hop power crew as an opening act. Robko had trouble wrapping his mind around the bands, thinking it could be pretty awful. But by mid-afternoon, he could see as they focused on setup and sound checks that they were competent.

Part of his job was hooking up electricity, whether he was trained or not. The wires were run down the rafters and dropped to the trucks. While on top of a catering truck, he spied the flowing graffiti that swept down the factory floor. It ended with a flourish in the familiar cubist signature. When he got a chance, he ambled down the words. He wondered what message had been sent to him. Four black silhouettes of a man in a top hat and long coat formed bracketing quote marks. The message read, "The mimbo and the bimbo drop, the brainiacs pop, everyone happy does the stone." He repeated it to himself twice and laughed out loud. That was his bio. It was also as strange as he'd ever seen.

Phatal mixed every cult in L.A. together into a mélange of fans: the xTreme jocks, the boy racers, the hip-hop and slasher crowds, the surfers, the actors, the beautiful, beautiful girls with coke up their noses, the flannel-shirted lesbians, and the muscle boys so pretty. They worked Robko off his feet, and soon he dripped in sweat. During infrequent breaks, he grabbed the opportunity to check out the drug vendors and restock most of his pharmo, including some excellent designer barbs. At three-thirty, the surf punk band fired up its last set, and Robko messaged Sibyl "Catch cab cum spnd paychck. Im purple booze trck."

She showed up as the crowd hit a frenzied peak at the encore. He spotted her approaching the bar—since she had dyed her hair black recently, she dressed mechano-goth for the night. She wore black make-up and wrapped herself in the world's tightest dark-gray coveralls. "Any trouble getting in?"

"No. The guy on the door doesn't grade on celebrity status, just how cool you are. I avoided the cover charge by mentioning you worked here."

"Champers?"

"Oh yeah. Throw those bubbles at me."

He chose a particularly good French. "I charge seven bills for this

153

bottle. You, on the other hand, get it wholesale, for a hundred."

"I'm honored. And a real flute, not a plastic cup. My, you're moving up in the world." She had perched on his stool behind the counter.

"Don't get used to this life. It's just a bridge job. It keeps me connected, and I get clubbing for free. But it's not what I do."

"And how will you fill the other three days of the week?"

"Local racks. You'd be surprised how much preparation you have to do for a job. And then there's O'Brien, bringing him down."

She held the glass stem in her fingers at an angle and rolled the base across the drink puddles on the counter. Propping her cheek onto a delicate fist, she stared over at him. "You feel pretty bullet-proof here in L.A., don't you?"

"Yeah. I don't think they can trace us. New money, new I.D. We even changed our appearances. But we can't leave it forever. Steward's intel will only last so long before it goes stale."

"You forgot one other thing we have to do." She arched her eyebrow, lifting it up towards her black shag of a bang. His libido jumped in his briefs, awake, on the lookout.

Surreptitiously, he readjusted himself and wished he hadn't worn such tight jeans. "What?"

"Start training me. The switch from the golden-hearted Ivory to the steely-eyed cat burglar."

"Steely-eyed? More training, less late-night TV."

"I get my clichés from you, not from TV."

He gave in. "We'll begin with lock picks and work on your forearm strength."

"Will there be champ breaks?" She held the flute to her lips and sipped like a hummingbird robbing a flower.

"Every Friday and Saturday."

This week Thomas spent a lot of time either in the office or in a couple of SoHo clubs. He hadn't gone so far as to move into the office, but he lived in hotels half the time. The other half, he showered at the gym and picked up his dry cleaning there and went into work without any sleep. In the late evenings, he would escort Angie down to the town car and pack her off to Staten Island. Luck just hung there on the razor edge, not dropping either way.

A week and a day after the botched firebomb, LeFarge tried again. Thomas padded down out of the racket club, dressed in his anonymous NYC black. Street buzz said the Dumpster, a new bar south of Prince Street, could really cruze—he would check it out. As he drew abreast of some stairs that led down to a basement door, a man jumped in his face. A giant neon burst flashed through Thomas's mind—O Christ, a mugger! When he tried to back up, he ran smack into a second assailant. They threw him down the stairs. After a very long time in the air, he ricocheted off the wall before he fell into a pile of trashcans. The landing jolted him hard, knocked out his breath. He floundered. He stared up the steps to see a wall of muscle dressed in hoodies that plunged down towards him. He crabbed on his back further into the stairwell's shelter.

"Hey, what are you doing there?" Shouting echoed from the street. Thomas's attackers glanced up to see the racket club's doorman and one of the fitness instructors. The hoodies decided to run for it. They charged past Thomas's Samaritans, shouldering them aside. While the doorman watched the muggers pelting down the street, the trainer dropped down the stairs and helped Thomas to his feet. "Guy, you were nearly street kill." The instructor pointed his finger at a serrated knife glimmering naked on the concrete.

"Christ! They would have murdered me. Thank you for coming to my rescue." Thomas crept up the stairs, and more than a bit shaky, wobbled back inside the gym to collapse. Once the tremors stopped and the anger stoked up, he grabbed a cab up to the Bronx and moved into a residence hotel just off the expressway.

The place cost only one-eighty a night; dirt levels were not over the top, but his window faced the expressway and the air conditioning did little to mask traffic noise. Like so many solitary people in NYC, he stood at the window and watched other lives rush by. On the sidewalk below the expressway, people—mostly White and Hispanic—marched along, all on their way to somewhere. One black squatted on a blanket, back to the wall. He sold something spread out in front of him. He wore a pork pie hat and a long black raincoat.

Thomas turned the attack over and over in his mind, replayed it until he trembled like a Pomeranian once again. He had no skills, so he needed protection of some sort. Where could he hire his own mercs, and how could he explain the grotesque expense to O'Brien? How could he blackmail LeFarge into backing off? How could he do the job and yet drop out of sight?

He could make out a well-lit piece of graffiti, huge, stretching thirty feet on the elevated highway wall above the black man. In a loopy flowing style, it said, "Roasted On The Spit—Then Chewed Up And Spit Out." He couldn't make out the signature. He did get the sentiment, feeling chewed up himself.

He'd visit his apartment tomorrow. He'd take the Super upstairs with him and pack some clothes. Maybe he could buy a gun someplace.

Chapter Eighteen: Naked after Vespers

Robko and Sibyl took up L.A. life in what she called a 'repurposed motel.' He thought it had great advantages—he sprawled in a lawn chair outside his front door, living the California life. He held a lemonade, and the sun hung low in his eyes. He had a mild cruze down and running. As a plus, the glittering image of jewelry he had seen on a customer two nights before circulated around in his head. He also mused on his new friend, Dickie Bettson, artist and skanker. Nobody turned out clean in L.A., not even Pterodactyl Man.

The splintering of glass broke his contemplation. He leapt to his feet, fell back three steps, and twisted towards the echo of shattering. A hammer lay out in the parking lot in a spray of glittering shards from the window, his window. Sibyl banged the screen door open, marched out onto the communal walkway, her sandals snapping like gunshots. "I just can't tweezle that goddamn lock. It's driving me crazy. Show me one more time, and show me right, or I'll cram the picks up your ass."

"Sure. Why don't we have a little cool down though, and do something fun."

"Are you patronizing me?"

He could feel the grin bubble up—he screwed it down, didn't let it out. "I'd never do that. Let's break into a car."

"Which car?"

"The neighbor's here." Next door a Latino grilled meat on a cheap barbecue. "Hey, Alejandro, can I show Rhonda here how to break into your car?"

"Chure, man. Help yourself to anything you find in that piece of chite, too. You need any help fixing the window Rhonda broke, you shout."

Sibyl's eyes narrowed, and her mouth clamped down into a thin line. She followed him out to the car's side. "What made you choose

Rhonda? I hate that name."

"It's a song from a Pansy playlist."

"Tchaa. Next time I choose."

"Pay attention now. Recent cars have alarms, so you don't want to mess with them without the right equipment. Cars like Alejandro's pre-date alarms, practically predate internal combustion. We call this a slim jim." He held up a flat, supple piece of metal with an L shape at the bottom. "A lever controls the lock on the door. You fish around until you find the lever, and pull up on it." The door clicked; he tugged it open to demonstrate that he had unlocked it. He pushed the lock down and slammed the door. "Now you try."

Taking the slim jim, she said, "What about power locks?"

"An old power lock works the same as the manual lock—just a solenoid instead of mechanical."

After some hesitant attempts, she fell into the hang of it and popped the lock several times. She flashed him a triumphant glance. "Great! That gets me into the car. What if I want to drive away in it?"

"You've seen it on TV—we hot wire it. You shunt past the ignition lock, then you short the starter wire. Let's do that later, on our own van. Now, on to this mortise lock that's kicking your butt." They flip-flopped through one of their doors—three motel rooms had been knocked into a two-bedroom apartment. Sibyl led the way around the crimson motorcycle crouched in the living room, into the far bedroom. They had made it their workshop.

A deadbolt lock waited on the table, set into two pieces of wood, upright and defiant. He said, "Rest your hands on mine, and feel me work." He inserted the two picks into the lock. "This one is the torsion wrench. It helps hold the pins up as you push them out of the way. You try to turn the cylinder with a steady, small pressure. This one is the hook pick. It pushes each pin up and keeps it there as you work deeper into the lock. Feel how I reach back, pin by pin. It's all by touch."

"Are you being obvious or sarcastic?"

"Patient. I'm being patient." The lock snicked pin by pin until the torsion wrench drew the bolt back.

"You need to find different words. I'm tired of hearing the same thing over and over again."

"I'll say it in Polish next time. Now you hold the picks, and I'll try to guide your hands." He placed his hands around hers, and they

158

skritched the picks in. Over her shoulder, he watched her bite on her lower lip.

She said, "This stinks, and so do you."

"Hostile. Frustrated."

"No, you really do stink. Time for a shower."

"Huh." After a full, agonizing minute, the lock drew open. "Okay, now try it by yourself; now that you've felt the pins and the cylinder. I'll loiter here and watch."

By the fourth time, she picked the lock smooth but slow. "I prefer the bump key."

"Sure, but then you have to bring the right bump key for the right brand of lock. Better not to depend on luck. Pick the lock again."

She perspired with the effort. "It's hot in here. I want to move someplace with better air conditioning." The lock drew back; she flashed out a triumphant grin.

"Maybe in a month or so. Let's hang out here and keep a low profile."

"Yeah, hang out surrounded by criminals like Alejandro."

He waved a dismissive hand. "He's just a guy getting by. His wife is a nice lady."

"She tried to stab him last week."

"All relationships have ups and downs. Look at ours."

Thomas's head banged, and his pulse sounded like tin in his ears. He reigned over his afternoon staff meeting, brooding. He doodled, and each beat of the blood in his head made a sharp, savage mark on the paper. Red Knuckle had booked back into SoHo to play—and he had ended the night on a leaper called "white triangle," one he and his singer had chosen from a pharmacopoeia behind the Chinese restaurant. He had a feeling that, like Pavlov's dog, he would soon associate cellophane noodles with being stoned. He could feel Angie's eyes on him, a stare that weighed up his condition.

Zlata, not only a cold trail, had become an invisible wraith. Nothing from their database feeds or Tran Cam illuminated his path. Today the team focused on memflash results. Their tame IT guy projected some complex chart on the wall and chattered through the new leads. "Out of our twenty lambs right now, two of them have moved off-center. We have an appellate judge who ruled in two corporate regulatory cases for Industry, rather than with the NGOs who brought suit."

Legal coughed portentously. "I'm the profiler in this case. This judge is off his pattern. Most times, he favors the little guy and hammers businesses. I asked a friend in Eco-Law at Columbia, and he thought the opinions all pretty standard. But it doesn't smell right to me. There could be a wolf working here. We got six companies associated with the two cases." He had their attention—around the big conference table, all stared at him and some leaned forward, ready to pounce.

Angie asked, "Can you narrow it down?"

Legal's face wrinkled in delight. "No problem. Only one company is a plaintiff in both."

Thomas perked up and hauled himself out of the depth of the chair to the table edge. "What's your recommendation?"

"We ask Corporate Legal to take a gander at the company and see if it's involved with any other legal beagles this way and if all this just started. If we can get some confirming evidence the company is the bad-ass, you can take it to O'Brien to find out which corporate officer is the wolf."

Angie asked Thomas, "Would you object to having Garland look into the Judge? Perhaps recent movements that are out of the ordinary, a change in status of any family member, a break in the daily pattern?"

Thomas flashed on Mirko sprawled up dead against his desk. People died out there in the field. "That's a great idea. I don't want our team doing any footwork. Corporate Security can support us here."

Angie said, "Tell us about the other lamb."

IT stepped in again. "A senior editor at one of our metro dailies— very righteous except for whatever O'Brien has on him. His paper has been running this big exposé on waste dumping and a possible bribery scandal—public officials on the take. All of a sudden, reporters are assigned elsewhere, and the story goes cold."

Accounting held up her hand. "I profiled this one. This editor is a sensationalist, and he should be smelling blood in the water. It's a chance to damage a couple of councilmen, maybe get a City department head fired. Instead, the editor switched to feel-good news."

Thomas nodded. "Can't be the department head. Even in New York City, he wouldn't have enough money to buy the intel. Give me the two Council names, and I'll discuss them with O'Brien. He'll know who's most likely."

"Right," said Accounting, flashing out a grin of triumph. She passed a slip of paper down to him.

He scanned the names while he said, "Remember, Angie is the only one to see the entire list O'Brien gave us. I'd also like another twenty profiles started out of the remaining names. The more in play the bigger our chances of snaring a memdevice. How long would that take?" Knowing it was a lot of work, he gazed owl-like around the table.

Insurance, his bald head gleaming, said, "It takes a half-day to a day to learn the lamb and a couple of hours to set up sofbots—if we stick only with data feeds like newspapers and online news."

Angie asked, "Can we have another twenty within a couple of days then?" Nods around the table. "Let's jump on it. We're only as good as our last success, and we need to snare a memflash soon to stay in business."

Thomas's head hurt. His knuckles scrubbed deep into the hollow between his eyebrows. Soon he would get stoned.

Sibyl poured yogurt and nuts into the blender. "Why did you pick him?" She wagged the lid at the photo on the kitchen bar—a photo she had made in Phatal. A goofy grinning face beamed up at them—a bond specialist Robko had chosen from out of his customers.

"Dickie turned me on to him. He's a mouth. He can't stand silence and will say the first thing that pops into his head. Not the type to do transactions quiet-like."

"Now what happens?"

"Picking him out means I've found my teaser. Teasers lead you to a rack, and racks mean money. Still, we need the right tools." Hand on the door, he said, "Back in a heartflash. Behave yourself while I'm gone. And don't photo the neighbors. It makes them nervous."

He puttered deeper into East L.A. in the minivan. He parked in front of a pawnshop named Pachuco's, where he could keep an eye on the car through the shop's window. Sliding out and surveying the block, he tallied up the neighborhood's shifts in style. He spied fewer Latinos and more Anglos. New construction had leapt up like spring's flowers—some old residences in between the businesses had morphed into big four-squares. This part of East L.A. had begun the journey of gentrification, even on the doorstep of the gangs. He didn't like it.

Robko ducked inside, past a jangling bell, and found the Moth. The Moth stared at his approach through large eyes protected by thick glasses. His goatee, mustache, large sideburns, and receding hairline conspired to fuzz out around his head in a halo of fine hair. The Moth's color code ran to gray: gray skin, gray hair, gray teeth. He did indeed resemble a pine moth. The Moth blinked, his eyebrows waving as Robko approached the counter. "I think we've met, but maybe I'm wrong, and maybe things have changed. Like your name."

"Steve Gordon. I called earlier."

"Yes, Mr. Gordon. Glad you could still find the place."

"Who could forget? You've always had such interesting pawn."

"Hmm. Indeed." Eyebrows semaphored in the pawnshop stillness. Moth flying.

"Like I said on the phone, I wondered what you had in the way of radios."

"Interesting you should ask. For cars, you said?" He brought three paper bags out from under the counter. He opened one bag and placed a lozenge on the counter. "This radio"—he emphasized the word lovingly—"has a quarter mile range and very low power consumption—the mike sits on this end, and there's a magnet to hold it in place."

The Moth brought out a radio from the second bag, like a conjuring trick. "This one is very serious—for long-term monitoring. This behind-dash radio needs to be wired into a power source, and it has a clip lead that allows it to use the FM antenna in the car as a transmitter."

Audibly humming, he drew a third radio out of its crinkling paper bag. "I like this radio the best. I call it the 'Whisker' because of the six inch antenna." He teased the thin wire that sprang out of the casing. "You attach the mike anywhere you want—it's wireless and has its own power. The transmitter and antenna fit beautifully behind the bumper, but I have heard they can also slide inside the roof rack on SUVs." His

162

hands caressed the bug. "It's Israeli."

"What's the transmission distance?"

"Two miles."

"And the battery life?"

"About five days. They're lithium."

"How much for the Whisker?"

"For you, eight hundred but that includes batteries. I also have a digital receiver/recorder that matches the Whisker's frequency spectrum. It's three hundred."

"I'll take them both." He counted out twelve bills and left them on the counter. The Moth had an aversion to the touch of others.

"I only have a manual in Hebrew and French, but the drawings are good." The Moth dropped an old-fashioned sheaf of paper on the glass.

Robko glanced at the copied pages. "I can puzzle this out. I also thought I'd pick up a com-set."

"Ah, yes. Mmm. Mmm." The Moth poked around in a cabinet, his eyes darting back to Robko to ensure he didn't move.

"I only need two, not for a whole team."

The Moth returned to the counter with his hands full. He let out a full toothy smile, an awful sight. "Here we have our traditional model. The Russian Secret Service uses these. The radio clips onto your belt. Tape the mike on your neck or your wrist, and stick the wired earbud in. The transmitter encrypts based on a revolving code. It uses regular wireless network frequencies, but it's digital, and therefore hard to pick up on scan. A thousand dollars... for a pair of course."

"Anything less obvious?"

The Moth twisted his torso with delight. "I do have something new. It's made with smart phones like your iMob. The phone appears to have regular Bluetooth to plug in your ear, but with unique controls. You have a speed dial, a mute button, and a built in camera on the Tooth. The camera is video and can work in infrared. Comes two to a box, hooks up through regular mobile service but encrypts. Practically a consumer product and only three thousand for the set. Unique."

"I'll buy the smart phone coms." He counted out more cash. It disappeared below the counter. "Hmm, you wouldn't have some clean license plates would you? For a car and a motorcycle?"

"No for the motorcycle, yes for the car. It's off a wrecked vehicle and won't drop out into the system for ten, eleven months."

"How much?"

"One fifty, and a deal at that."

"Sure, the plate also." Robko dealt out more cash. With a whisk of a gray hand the money disappeared off the counter.

"Anything else this fine day? Weapons? Sleeping aids? Incendiary devices?" The Moth placed the two unsold bugs back into their bags and shoved them under the counter.

"Maybe later, as plans firm up."

Thomas didn't know why he hadn't done the phone thing before. He booked a room in a restaurant down in Little Italy where he would take his team to lunch. Ducking out early, he caught a cab down to Delancey and hopped off in the Bowery not far from Zlata's loft. He bought two pay-as-you-go mobiles in two different mini-shops and then walked down to the restaurant. He waited out front at the hostess podium.

When Angie and the crowd milled through the front door, he told them, "They're expecting us. Go on into the back room, and make your drink orders. I just have to rehash something with Ms. Tommo." He nodded to Angie. "Step up to the bar."

They leaned on the mahogany rail, and she tilted her face towards him, a glowing Mediterranean oval that charmed him. "What is it, Thomas?"

"Face the bottles, Angie. Legal and Insurance probably read lips." She did as he asked. "Slip this vidi in your purse. I've bought another for myself, and we'll use them for key calls. I turned off my regular vidi, so I can't be tracked. You might want to do the same."

She palmed the mobile. "I left my real phone in the office last night before I sneaked off to Staten Island. How we found Sibyl just popped into my head."

He texted her. "Here's my new number."

"You have a safe place to stay?"

"Yeah, I have a flop up in the Bronx."

"Flop? Your language becomes more colorful by the day."

He mugged and growled an old-time Bronx accent out of the corner of his mouth. "Yeah. Youse is gettin' da pik-cha."

She laughed, a bell trilling out.

He leaned closer. "Let's go entertain the troops. But before we do, I want to ask you to think about something. If you wanted to lock the Governor down, how would you do it? Just think about it again."

❦

They bugged the bond broker's German car easily enough—Robko used the operation as a training exercise for Sibyl. They disabled the alarm, defeated the locks, and placed the bug within ten minutes. Fun over, the real work began, following the jerk around. By the second day, Robko found Sibyl less than gracious.

"Boring, boooring. You could at least let me drive."

"You drive too fast. You'd be on his bumper all the time."

"Try me. I know the difference between shadowing and just belting down the Parkway."

He pulled over to the curb. "Okay, let's change over quick. He's at the light just ahead."

"Like I haven't memorized the ass end of his car." They swapped quick and smooth and caught back up. She had been right; she tailed better than he expected.

Robko picked up the receiver and screwed the earbud in. "He's on the vidi again—golf date—now he's got the tee time. Hanging up—calling for dinner reservations at Chez le Poconos or something."

"Robert, you don't have to keep up a running monologue. It's very irritating."

He hmmphed. "It's exactly what you did when you rode in this seat."

"Just tell me the good stuff. Appointments to meet celebrities. Phone sex. News about bonds."

"Sure."

She drove for fifteen minutes through stiff traffic. Silence filled the van except for road noise. "What's happening now?"

"Not phone sex."

"What then?"

"You didn't want to know." He wagged his finger at her, and she bit at the end of it.

She scowled. "Well, the occasional update would be good."

"You lucked out with the timing on the driver switch. He's

punched in a motivational sales course on his sat radio. Wait, incoming call—you'll like this. The office confirmed an armed delivery of bearer bonds."

"How much?"

He heard that quiet sound of greed in her voice, a smoothness like sexual arousal. "Two fifty. For a couple named Tony and Amanda Petersen. They've been notified and will drive in from Laurel Canyon this afternoon at three for pickup."

"I always wanted to ask, what do you do with bearer bonds?"

"Anything you do with cash. Illegal things. Also, bonds are far less bulky. Ordinary money in big bills is traceable, and of course, unhygienic."

"So where is Laurel Canyon?" She followed the broker's car through a left turn, timed it so they remained back a hundred yards and just clipped the yellow light.

He had his vidi out. "I'll look it up now. Here they are. They're in the book—I've got their address and phone now. Mulholland Drive. Let me see it on a map. 3D? Sure, why not. Beautiful house, Sibyl. It would be nice to visit."

"I don't think they'll invite you over."

"You guess? We'll slap on the landscaping sign and the new plate and drive by this afternoon, while the Petersens pick up their bonds. You can take surveillance photos with that beautiful camera."

"Why drive by at all?"

"I want to know who their security company is. That would eliminate a lot of alarm types. I need to focus us on the two or three alarms to prepare for. And there's some information we might want to buy from an old acquaintance, if we can tell him the company."

"When does it get dangerous? That's what I want to know."

Chapter Nineteen: The Known Devil

Thomas, Garland, LeFarge—all received the summons from the Personal Assistant to appear before O'Brien to report their successes and to be chastised for their slowness, none of them to be exempted. Garland and Thomas marched up to the PA's desk at the same time and shot each other an oblique glance. The PA scurried in front of them to the Governor's door and held it open. As they strode in, Don stopped with a jerk, one step in. Thomas caromed into him. Thomas peered over Don's shoulder to see three people immersed in O'Brien's magnificent couch: O'Brien himself, LeFarge, and sitting between them, a young woman. Don whispered, eyes wide, "Is that who I think it is?"

Thomas murmured in his ear, "Isobel Dupont, minus her goth-girl look. You said she had an accommodation with LeFarge."

"But I thought her as house slave, not out-and-about… much less anywhere in public with the Governor."

"Don, we look like fools, stuck here in the door." Garland took a couple of steps, swung back into stride. As they approached, O'Brien patted Isobel on her knee and whispered a word to her. She rose with a shrug and strolled towards the executive bathroom hidden behind the wall. As she ducked in, she glanced at Garland and Thomas over her shoulder, flat-faced, expressionless.

As the two newcomers joined them, O'Brien continued his conversation with LeFarge in a low voice. Garland wavered at O'Brien's elbow, standing at half attention, but Thomas dropped onto the couch beside LeFarge. "Morning, Egan."

"Just a minute, Tommy," said O'Brien. The Governor leaned into LeFarge's face. "So, you did get rid of those hotheads?"

LeFarge lolled in the couch, an arm thrown over the back. "No problem. The rest of the team is as volatile as a pack of bookkeepers.

We're ready to deploy as and where you say."

O'Brien pivoted, put his elbows on his knees, tipped that giant head up at Thomas and Garland. "Egan awaits information that can lead him to the memflashes and to Zlata. Information from you two. I know you'll have something to contribute this fine bright morning." He leaned back into the overstuffed couch and showed his teeth in a cheerless smile.

Thomas said, "Not anything conclusive for you today. The company we identified is definitely working a memflash to bend the judge. Now we need to figure out which officer has it."

"It'll be the CEO. I know him, the bastard," said O'Brien.

"Possible. But it could be the Chief Operating Officer. And there's a Board member who is the original founder's grandson and who likes to strut his stuff."

"So when will you know?" asked O'Brien.

"We're following the money. One of the three will have made a substantial withdrawal recently to buy the memdevice."

Nodding like a bobble-head doll, Garland said, "We're cooperating on this. All three men were in Belgium last week, and we confirmed an auction in Brussels occurred about the same time. Motive, opportunity, resources." He rocked from one foot to the other.

"So when will you know?" asked LeFarge.

Thomas replied, "Tomorrow probably, the day after for sure. Both Don and I would prefer the financial team under our General Counsel get the memdevice back, using the right pressure points."

LeFarge said, "That wouldn't be up to you now, would it?"

Garland reached out his hands towards O'Brien, diverting the Governor away from LeFarge. He looked like a supplicant standing there. "I propose we find the new owner first. There's lots of work left to do."

O'Brien said, "Next time find out about the auctions or sales before they happen, so I can send Thomas to work it. Moving on, what about Zlata?"

Thomas said, "The only new thing we have on Zlata is really about the priest." His eyes bored into LeFarge. "It turns out some family members with unsavory reputations have feelers out. They want his killer."

LeFarge ducked his head to hide a smirk.

Thomas plunged on. "Speaking of dangerous family members, isn't Ms. Dupont another risk for you? And us?"

LeFarge raised his eyes to Thomas and stared hard at him. "You take it head on, don't you, Steward."

Thomas felt lucky. "Simple question, LeFarge."

O'Brien grinned and scrutinized the two men. He watched to see which would break the hard stare first.

Garland shifted from foot to foot and made a shuffling sound in the deep carpet. "It is irregular. How much does she know?"

O'Brien waved him off. "Both Egan and I quite like the young woman. We have an understanding with her, and certain—constraints—have been placed upon her independence. Not that it's your business. Your business is finding Zlata and my property."

"Well," said Garland in a tight voice, "we better get to it then." He pivoted and headed for the door.

Thomas strolled out of the office. In retrospect it was all a case of "what have you done for me today?" He slipped a yellow pill in his mouth and swallowed it dry.

They crouched in the California thicket, halfway into a gully, and watched the house across the way. The chamisa breathed out an acrid, compelling perfume, dusting their clothes. The creosote bush Robko gripped smelled like tar. "You know, we don't need the money yet. One last time before we do this. We can delay. I'm willing to treat this as a future bank and make the withdrawal when we need it."

"We're not here because we need the money."

"Why are we here?"

"Because you remember stealing turns me on, and you want to make it with me."

"Well, that could be a motivator. I'll lead; you follow."

"How about I follow, you lead?"

Robko dropped further into the gully and scaled the other side. Under the house, he seized a steel column that supported the deck. Using his feet and hands, he shinnied up the post like a palm tree. He knew when Sibyl began her climb. The soles of her shoes made high-pitched squeaks, and he could hear her breath go ragged and heavy.

Now his head was just beneath the deck's underside. He reached his left hand up. He rolled up and under the railing, lay flat on the deck, and peered over the edge. He dropped his hand to her.

"About time," she said. She grabbed his wrist with first one hand then the other. Her weight loaded full on to his arm. She scrambled up his arm like a monkey and grabbed the bottom rail.

"You have your knee on my head."

"Lucky for you I'm so light."

They strode up to the doors. He bowed to her and extended his hand to the sheets of glass. "After you."

She fished in the pouch strapped to her waist. Within a minute, she had the face off an innocuous box and had clipped into the house's wires. Punching the buttons on the sequencer, she stared, hypnotized as it tried code after code. He watched the deck, the neighborhood, and the driveway at the end of the house. "Got it." The automatic controls opened the wall of glass and folded it back, forming concertinas at each end. The living room waited, a dark cave that lurked behind the deck.

They palmed flashlights and entered, searching for the floor safe they knew had been purchased four years before. The safe hid beneath a credenza—he toggled the switch on the back, and the left end wheeled humming into the room. "Go ahead. Just like the rehearsal."

She knelt in the space that had opened. A square cut out of the parquet revealed the face of the safe, quite large. She began to work.

He slipped off to cover the front. He hovered in the dark of the house, listening and intent. Through the open door, he could discern the faint hum of traffic, ever-present in Los Angeles. He could hear a passing flight out of LAX, and a clock in the hall ticking. He could catch the sound of a faint scratching and a high-speed whining. For five minutes he waited and watched the portico and parking pad outside. When the drill stopped, he slipped back to the living room.

"Ready," she said. He handed her the bulky gloves and the Dewar flask. She leaned well away and tipped the flask, slow, slow. Some of the nitrogen vaporized in midair. A drop of it bounced around on the safe front, boiling and jitterbugging about. A thin stream arced down into the hole in the safe front.

"Not too much. You don't want to break free into the interior. Not too little, or the works won't shatter and release the bars."

She shot him a sneer. "You've said that eighty-four times already,

170

you forty-watt ass. Is that enough?"

"Yes. If not, we'll soon know."

She corked the flask—she reached down and tried the lever, easing it sideways and then jerking it up. The bars shattered, and the safe opened.

She brought out a jewelry case first, then some watch cases, and with a flourish, the bearer bonds. Other documents lay secreted below, and those she shoved into the backpack with the bonds for future inspection. She cleaned up the scene while he stood in the door, listening to the front of the house. She wriggled into the backpack straps.

Robko said, "Congratulations. If you get away clean, you've done your first rack."

She grasped his face with both hands and gave him a kiss. Sudden, savage—a heavy crush on his mouth, and a deep pelvic rub. She released him with a shove, throwing him back. She pivoted towards the deck, to the swath of night sky and the lights of L.A.

At the top of the gully, he trundled the bike out from behind the manzanita. They mounted, and he fired up the Italian.

Wheeling down out of the mountains towards the coast, the pair swept through each set of bends, graceful and delicate. She leaned hard against his back, and her hands beat a tattoo on his thighs. She leaned over his shoulder to shout, "It's so good to be riding again. Let's drop the bag off at home, pack, and run down the coast to San Diego. Spend a couple of days."

"You're kidding. Five minutes after a job?"

"Where's your impulsiveness? You always get to be the irresponsible one. It's my turn."

They skated back into the brash city grid of Los Angeles, dazzling in its midnight lights after the dark hills. He eased to a stop at a light. "We've got a drop-off to make first. I've rented a lockup to keep the score."

"Rule twelve: don't sleep with the flash under your bed."

"Right, did that once too often. Then we'll ride down to Dago."

"Can we stay at the Coronado? It's been so long since we've been in a first class hotel."

Three times on the way to San Diego they passed traffic cameras serviced by Tran Cam, but the helmets and the temporary black paint sprayed onto the bike fooled the software. South of L.A., graff splayed across a concrete embankment above them as Robko arrowed down the freeway. Its message, waiting for him, said, "Love Speeds South to Crash in Passion." He was already thinking about her bottom, and that curve and tuck at the base of her spine.

Chapter Twenty: Come and Make Me Well

So they had money again, so what? Life didn't change, just the brand of champagne.

Wednesday, they cleaned the temporary paint out of every nook and cranny of the bike, and Robko turned the quarter-million in bonds into two hundred thousand in cash. Thursday through Saturday, the illegal bar set up and did business. Sunday, Robko worked a tough session moving the Phatal nightclub out of its warehouse, and Monday they sloughed along in a down day. The shop surrounded them, one third of their domain, the den where high-tech skankers puttered around and did much of nothing. They futzed among the clutter and the machine bits of their craft. The desktab was open showing Sibyl's recent photos scrolling by. She sang to herself, content. This irritated Robko, and he wished the crooning would stop—it interfered with the buzzing in his head. He said, "Are you sure those photos are safe?"

"In the cloud, encrypted, under another name. When I go legit, I don't want them tied back to whoring."

"Are you sure that wouldn't be a come-on?"

"One-shot celebrity. Not sustainable."

In front of him, he had a legal pad where he doodled. O'Brien lurked in the corner of the page—a bald head, angry eyes, and bear-like teeth. A rough sketch of the Artifact dominated the middle, and Steward's name appeared three times in block letters across the bottom. There was an outline of Georgia, with an arrow leading across to something that was supposed to be Manhattan. He made a little row of dots down one side. He put squares around the dots. As he churned it over and over, he also waited for a bit of intuition on what to do next. It clicked.

With the glimmer of an idea, he corkscrewed around and peered at her. The decision would depend as much on her as on him. She bent over the manual of an electronic safe, her homework for the week. Her shag hung round her head, off her neck; she twisted a strand of hair into a curl, released, and then teased again.

Let the idea come out naturally; let it walk first and then run as he told her about it. "So, want to jump on the bike, go down to the beach, watch the sunset?"

At his voice, she straightened up and pushed a mass of black hair back. "Like, a date? Sure."

"I thought you'd ask me for five hundred first."

A lazy smile, but he could see her canines. "I have my own money now."

They rolled out the motorcycle and brought a bottle of water, a blanket, and a bottle of wine and a glass for her. In the hot late-afternoon, light slanted sideways casting opaque shadows, blue-black. He motored them down to the beach without much rush, sliding along in the moment. Setting up not far off the parking lot, they leaned back on their elbows and stared off to the west. "So," she said, "what did you want to talk about?"

"I just needed to get out of the house."

"I don't think so, but I can wait." She did wait, and time stretched out for five minutes.

The surf had the same dull thump as his barb-slowed heartbeat. "It's O'Brien."

"Of course."

"He's stuck in my brain… in my throat."

"I've been thinking about it too, the history of it all. I mean, what else should your crew have expected? O'Brien just reacted to what you did." She leaned back into his shoulder, her hair tickling his nose.

He blew out a strand of her hair that had slipped into his mouth. "I broke in and stole the keys to the kingdom. It wasn't that big a thing."

"And the King sent his troops after you."

Leaning slightly away, he could see her face in profile, her eyes squinting out into the sunset. "Lot of damage since."

"You mean Carl and Isobel Dupont."

"I think they're both dead. I did nothing to prevent it. But they're not what bothers me the most. It's Mirko."

She slid down, her skull pushing under his collar bone. "Ah. Some things are hard to get through."

"Mirko was my friend. I lead them directly to him. Now he's

174

dead."

"And you're not."

He couldn't see her face now. She probably had adopted that guarded, reasonable countenance. "You think I have survivor guilt? Maybe I do, but it freezes my heart. I want this LeFarge, and I want O'Brien."

She said, "We have a good life now. You always say, 'Never make a stand if you can hide, and never hide if you can run.' What happened to my footloose skanker?"

"Don't you ever feel a sense of powerlessness?"

"Huh. I'm a woman in the hospitality trade."

"Point taken… but you changed that, got some control back."

She sniffed. "You said we were pretty much invulnerable since we ran away from everything in New York."

"True, but I need something more. I don't want to run anymore."

"Maybe people do change, a tiny bit. Maybe you're not such a lazy ass anymore. What do you want to do to O'Brien?"

"Hurt him, of course. Real bad. I want to bleed him out." He nodded, realizing now what he had been thinking for days. "Drink your wine."

The sun glimmered its way down nearly to the end by the time they spoke again. A dark line bisected the hot orange. The orb flattened out into an ellipse and lost its bottom half. The sky emitted a green flash. Robko took it as an omen. Money came green and flashy. The blue gray darkening that followed the setting sun—well, he lived in a dark world.

She said, "How do you hurt him? Especially while he's hunting us?"

"He wants the Artifact. Let's give it to him."

"A fake?"

He liked this part, could feel the grin breaking out across his face. "No, the real thing. There are two left. What we have to do is steal them and give one of them to him. That'll get him off our backs."

She held a finger up between them and the western view. "First, won't he know the Artifacts are gone?"

"Deception is everything. He'll know, but only when we show him the trick."

She snorted. She held up the second finger. "Second, won't he

175

figure out who stole the two remaining doo-dahs? Doesn't that put us back in the kill zone?"

"Well, we keep one for insurance."

"What do you mean?"

"Steward's files said there are two men O'Brien hates more than anyone else in the world, Carstairs and Thurgall. Probably because they're so much like him. Rich, powerful, manipulative people—only they've got a lot more gloss on them than O'Brien. I checked online. Carstairs is English and very upper class. Thurgall is California's next Howard Hughes or Joey Ellison."

"So O'Brien proves susceptible to jealousy. No surprise."

"You missed it. We use these two yo-yos for leverage. I tell O'Brien that if he crosses us, the third artifact goes to one of them."

"Oh." She thought about it. "So why give the second Artifact to him? Why not keep it if you have the insurance?"

"It's the deal we make. It's his consolation prize."

She wriggled—not sold yet. "Getting the second one back makes up for losing the first, and the third keeps him from coming after us? Do-si-do, around we go?"

"I hear your sarcasm. The second Artifact proves we have the third. The third is the important one, because we hang it over his head. Let's hope he's smart enough to follow the argument."

"He's smart enough to have an empire of stolen companies."

He pushed his chin down on top of her head. "We need a plan."

She crossed her ankles, lazy in the evening heat. "I thought you had a plan."

"Early days. I need to know where to find the Artifacts. I need to know how they're protected. I need to know how to rip them off without signaling that they're gone."

She snorted again. "That's a lot of needs."

"But we have some advantages."

"Name one."

"We have the basic security systems for several of his places. I'm betting on the lab in Georgia."

"That's one advantage…."

He shrugged, making her head bob. "We have time and money."

She rolled half over onto him, and nestled her face into his chest. "Let's spend yours first."

❀

Fall brought the rainy season to New York. Temperatures dropped, baseball began to wrap up as it headed into the Series; rain filled the gutters and floated the litter down into the storm drains. The quintessential center of the hip world may have been located in Manhattan, but even hip punkers and blinged-up drug lords carried umbrellas and scurried under the awnings.

Thomas could tell the team had turned hot, red hot. They ferreted out the links to two memory devices and then went on to crack another two. O'Brien obliged them for this success and gave them more names, more lambs. Their net grew. On the day they broke open a lead on their seventh memdevice, Thomas ferried the team down to the bar across the avenue to celebrate.

He wanted to talk to Angie off-line, out of the office. He had to maneuver around a bit as the team floated back and forth to the bar and through the tables, but at last he sauntered about the room beside her. "Haven't seen you much lately."

She wrapped her arm around him and squeezed. "I still haven't thanked you for the promotion and the raise."

"The title isn't great, but this pay grade takes home executive bonuses."

"The title is fine."

He linked his arm through hers and led her away from a noisy foursome. "Senior Operations Manager?" He snorted. "What you are is 'Spy Master of MI5.'"

"I like the title, and I love the money."

They strolled another dozen steps and wove round a waiter with a tray of champagne. Thomas cleared his throat. "So, you've been flying solo the last week or so."

She glanced over, offered a secret smile and patted his arm. "You don't need to see all the detail. Someone else should bring it together, while you think the deep thoughts."

"Such as?"

"Such as convincing LeFarge not to kill us."

He could read her face. How can he be so dense? "Yeah, that. We'll put a fail-safe in place. If one of us dies, there's evidence that

177

goes to the police. We tell him so."

"You know my objection," said Angie. "It takes down O'Brien—maybe—but LeFarge can always just disappear."

"Jean hasn't found the money trail yet, has she?"

"Good news there. She's close to wrapping it up. She wants to see us tomorrow."

He beamed. "Great. I worried that she was our mole."

"Not Jean. She's one of your fans."

He snorted. "Like I have a fan base."

"Sure. You've changed a bit, and they've changed with you. The ones that imitate you the most are your fans."

"Huh?"

"The black clothes, the spiky short hair? Strange hours, moody days. You don't look or act like a CEO anymore, unless it's a CEO in the movie business. And some of your team, they're changing to match."

"So I have a new tailor... or a new girlfriend... but you're saying the team is changing too?"

"Oh, yeah. Everyone thinks he's a predator now, and in chic New York black. Even our IT guy looks less NASA and more Manhattan. He wore an Italian blazer today."

"Cashmere. I noticed."

The crowd split them apart, but they circled back together and resumed.

He said, "Who do you think is our in-house traitor?"

"Let me fetch you a drink first."

"Tonic, then, and lime."

"You're not drinking much lately."

"Bad for my health."

"Bad for those pills," she said. When she returned, she nestled the tonic into his hand. "Don't be an idiot about this. You can't get away with it forever."

"I'm already a marked man. My fingerprints are all over a murder scene."

She made an exasperated sound, a "ghaak."

He knew enough to change the conversation. "You didn't answer. Who is our mole?"

"A better question is 'What is our mole?' If the spy in our midst is

178

merely ambitious, we have a leak that reports back to O'Brien. If the spy works for LeFarge, then Zlata dies; then possibly we die."

"It's O'Brien who calls within minutes after we discover something important."

She flashed out the crooked, ironic grin. "Yes. Reassuring, in a strange way."

"That's what I think too." He watched a knot of their people at the bar. They had clustered around the woman from Accounting, one of their first recruits. She broke out of the crowd and hustled over to him.

Her eyes shown bright in the bar's subdued lighting. "It may be nothing, but Tran Cam just fed us pictures of the right type of Italian bike in Los Angeles. There were two people riding it."

"Doesn't sound like 'nothing' to me. Sure about the motorcycle make?"

The woman nodded, her face radiant. Thomas clapped his hands for attention, "Everyone across the road and upstairs! Let's watch this play out together."

Robko and Sibyl lay tight together in their rehabilitated motel room, spooned up. He said, "I'm going to miss this place."

She did her best to distract him; she moved her buttocks very slightly, very slowly. "You would, gozo. Most people would be glad to move out. But what do you mean? Are we going right away?"

"Got to move back east if we're going after O'Brien. Tomorrow we'll go down and clean 'Steve Gordon' out and close his account. After that, I'll introduce you to the Moth. Great guy."

She glanced over her shoulder at him. "He didn't sound all that appealing when you described him."

"He'll be appealing enough when you buy legit I.D. from him."

"When do you want to leave?"

He slid his hand under the sheet and hitched it up around their shoulders. "Need to pack, rent a closed trailer for the bike, and throw a lot of our stuff in the dumpster. Lots of work. Day after tomorrow?"

"Okay by me. The sooner the better. Do we have to go through Utah? It's so boring and hot."

He dropped his head to nuzzle at the back of her neck. His voice was a little muffled. "Afraid so. We take the southern route this time. We're pointed at this place in Georgia. " He tolled through the towns, "Vegas, Salt Lake, Dallas, Atlanta. Depending on how it goes, Charlotte, Baltimore, New York."

"Vegas. I've always dreamed of Vegas. So trashy."

"You drive, I'll cruze, and I'll know what I want to do by the time we arrive."

"Planning on one of those mystic shaman dreams?"

Reaching up to stroke her temple, he said, "Chemically induced of course."

"Where will we stay in the City?"

"One of the luxury residence hotels, just for you. We'll have new names. We're flush; we're swimming in bond money. Upper Manhattan, near the Park?"

"Good clubbing up near Harlem. Hey, stop that. That's kind of private space you're probing there."

"Hmph. Early morning jimber. Purely accidental."

"Well, you could at least apologize."

"I've got a better idea."

The team clustered in their conference space, buzzing away. IT brought up the Tran Cam recordings on the giant screen. They all stared at the Italian bike, in its crimson red with custom white splash, tinged in blue, color that swept back over the fairings. "This is sighting number one, as they rode out of east L.A. A man and a woman for certain, but the first shots don't give us much more. I'll show you all the additional tracking, but it will help you to know they're headed to the beach." He showed them a variety of shots from different angles and places. They were able to get a good view of the bike, but the two riders wore helmets and nondescript clothes. "You probably picked up that we were wrong about Zlata—he is lazy. He still has a New York plate on the bike." Thomas heard a heavy sigh in the room as someone regretted all those hours sorting through DMV data feeds, searching new registrations. "Here's the beach. They parked about a hundred feet from the surveillance camera." He showed video and separated out three freeze frames. The camera revealed the couple as they parked, removed helmets, and rambled towards the sand. The man faced the wrong way the entire time.

Angie said, "Paste up the middle frame." It flicked back up to show the two seated on the bike as they peeled off helmets. The man's hands and headgear obscured his face. The woman already had her helmet off. "Zoom in on her. Now, can you paste up Sibyl Boxwood's photo file? Try the upper right one, the profile. Zoom that one for us."

They all stared at the two photos. Thomas said, "It could be her. The hair fools you—a blonde mop versus a longer black cut, kind of—"

Angie said, "It's called a punk mullet. That's her. I'm sure of it." The room buzzed; the staff agreed with Angie.

"Let's see the rest of it," said Thomas. The screen splashed up more video. Evening, and the bike crouched at the limit of visibility for the parking lot camera. The team could just see the couple mount and motor out the end of the lot.

"We catch them next as they ride back up into town. Software turfed up a distance shot from a cam on the other side of the Santa Monica Freeway. From there we got a photo on the Golden State Freeway, and another, and another. They exit the main road. This is Atwater Village—in northeast L.A., and here is my killer shot. They go past the Metrolink—see the station name? No other photos—they went to ground, home for the night. This is their neighborhood."

Thomas leaned forward on spread feet, calm under the reassurance of his yellow jackets. A quick, measuring scan around showed the staff jazzed to the limit. They appeared to vibrate in place, trembling in delight, buzzing like a hive. After months of mystery, Zlata had gone from the invisible man to a guy who lived within a mile or so of a specific train station. Calm, Thomas leaned over a staffer. "Please, could you get Don Garland on the phone? Tell him we've got a probable on Robko Zlata, and we'll need full ground support in California. Ask him to come in right away." He turned to Angie and raised an eyebrow. "Ms. Tommo, let's be quick to inform the Governor. If you would, call O'Brien out on Long Island, and let him know we have his quarry in sight." The team cheered, the end of a long manhunt.

"Mr. Garland wants to talk to you personally. No video—he's in purple silk pajamas," said the staffer. Giddy, she broke into a giggle.

"Don, Thomas here.—Yeah, we think we've got him. We found the motorbike.—Yes, a clever idea.—Northeast Los Angeles, Atwater

181

Village.—I agree, joint operation. What do you have on the ground?—That many? I forgot we had so many companies out there. Are you going out yourself?—No, I'll stay here, on top of the technology.—We'll pass all the current location data to your people now, and we'll let your people know anything we get as it comes in.—Sure, as soon as it happens. But, we'll be short-handed when we get live feed for people to watch. Can you bring a liaison in here with us? He can pick up from my people and let you know instantly.—No, I don't think I'll offer the same deal to LeFarge.—Yeah, best to wait until you're at least on board the plane before you tell him.—All right, we'll brief you fully when you get in here." He handed the phone back to the staffer.

Angie sidled up and murmured in his ear. "I convinced the Governor he needn't come in right away. He said he'd be here first thing in the morning, seven-ish, so we have ten hours to nail it. O'Brien also said he'd swing by and pick up LeFarge."

"Great. Okay, we'll live with it. Can you call our Tran Cam CEO on one of our burner phones? I want to make sure he gives us what we need."

She did so and handed the mobile over. "Find out the number of surveillance points he can give us in Atwater. I'll set up a shift schedule based on that."

Chapter Twenty-One: Guns on the Ground

O'Brien and LeFarge burst into the team's operation space escorted by Angie. O'Brien charged forward; his massive head swung from side to side, like a grizzly in a herd of deer. Thomas intercepted him and shook his hand.

"Tommy, your luck is back."

Thomas too, thought his luck was back. "Let me introduce you to the team. It'll be good for morale." They made the rounds while LeFarge ignored them and strode over to the digital map. LeFarge stared at Atwater Village as if one of the feeds would flash up Zlata's image.

Looping through the room shaking hands, finishing at the wall, Thomas stood the Governor up in front of the map. "We can tell you the story and show you the layout at the same time."

Like a dog barking at some threat, LeFarge jumped out. "Where's Garland?"

"He's in California. He took a corporate jet and a team out at midnight."

O'Brien caught LeFarge's eye. "Good man. Don's already on the ground, Egan."

Thomas signaled his techie over. "Can you take the Governor through the layout?"

"Glad to." IT had a laser-pointer that ran the board. "We first saw them as they left this area of Los Angeles… here," and he indicated a freeway camera location. "We tracked them to, and back from, the beach; they re-entered here, a different route. I confirmed the license plate—the bike carried Tim Boxwood's plate."

"Who?" O'Brien's voice sounded like a growl.

Thomas said, "One of Zlata's aliases. The point is we have a confirmed sighting."

IT picked up the tale again. "We now have live feed from four locations, here, here, here, and here." He flourished the pointer at red spots on the map. "Angie Tommo identified these six blocks as transient housing." More flourishes. "Census data also says eighty percent of the population in this neighborhood is non-white, so our chances go up; our couple should stick out like sore thumbs. Mr. Garland has deployed some unmarked vans on patrol and will start a ground search as soon as it's daylight out there. In the meantime, we watch the four cams and the train station from here."

Thomas leaned over to his guy. "They've covered the exits that we can't see?"

"Mr. Garland has guys on them. I'm afraid, Governor, that your buildings in California won't be well guarded today."

Angie added, "You should expect this to leak out. With all this manpower deployed...."

O'Brien grumphed and shook his head. "Screw 'em all, prying little pieces of dung."

Thomas grasped him by the elbow, fearing what the Governor would say next. "Perhaps, sir, we can continue the discussion in your office."

They rode upstairs and paced down the halls still silent in early morning. LeFarge strode behind them, unbidden. In his office, the Governor wheeled about, big as a house.

O'Brien slapped his hands together. "We've got the son of a bitch at last. Egan, scramble your troops. I'll call Garland and make sure he turns over operations to you."

Thomas objected, "Surely Garland has earned the right to take Zlata down?"

LeFarge whispered in O'Brien's ear. O'Brien grunted, nodded, and said to Thomas, "I told you at the beginning I wanted Don's hands clean."

"Don could use LeFarge as the backup threat," said Thomas.

The Governor said, "I don't need backup; I need a guarantee. I won't sideline LeFarge's team. Egan, get your Foreign Legion out to L.A. now."

Thomas tried one more shot. "We lost Zlata here in the City and in Ithaca because of the so-called Foreign Legion."

"I also remember you were in Ithaca, Tommy, and interfered with Egan's men."

"And we found Zlata for you again."

"You want thanks? Wait until he's under lock and key. My decision stands—Egan is going, and your team will support him. You can get back to your watching—we've got some work to do here."

O'Brien turned on the ball of his foot and stalked back to his desk. While O'Brien's back was turned, LeFarge pointed at Thomas's face and fired an imaginary pistol.

❦

In the elevator, Thomas shook two benzos into his hand and dumped them down on his anger to douse it. He charged off the elevator onto the computer floor, punched in the four-digit code to their office, and stuck his thumb on the pad. When the door slid open, he breathed deep and let it close back in front of him. Best to wait a minute.

By the time he flopped into a chair beside Angie in front of the digital map, his pulse had dropped back to normal, and he idled along on cruze. Angie perched in the chair, her desktab open. He leaned over to her, "LeFarge is on his way to the airport. You were right. O'Brien enjoys the mob-boss role. He'll do his Don Corleone bit through to the last act."

"Something I wouldn't have minded getting wrong."

"I've learned you're seldom wrong."

She shook her head, brushing off the compliment. "Got time to talk to Jean now?"

He jumped up, marched across the room, and leaned over Jean's shoulder. "Are you ready? I know we were supposed to meet this afternoon, but Ms. Tommo and I want to hear what you have to say as soon as possible."

Jean nodded yes and picked up her tablet. Thomas waved Angie over as they crossed the room; they converged on his desk space. Knee-to-knee in three chairs, they suffered the intimacy of an office cubicle. Jean balanced her tablet on her knees, so they could all see it.

Jean said, "You still want all of this to be confidential?" Thomas nodded, and she continued. "As you can imagine, a private militia is astonishingly expensive, so the costs can be disguised but not hidden.

Governor O'Brien has a shell company that handles the money—of course, an improper use of shareholder money." Thomas and Angie grinned at each other while Jean frowned. "The shell company expends fifteen thousand a month per mercenary for eight mercenaries. We have the mercenaries' bank numbers. They pay an additional thirty thousand a month for ex-Captain LeFarge. There have been performance bonuses that total another hundred thousand. I also detail equipment costs, a leased warehouse, and an old fire station rented for housing."

Thomas blinked. "How much does all that add up to?"

"It adds up to over two point six million a year without travel, vehicles, or expense accounts."

Angie said, "We guessed it wouldn't be cheap. So to summarize, you know the names and addresses of all the mercs, how much they're paid, where they keep their gear, and where they sleep when they're off duty."

Jean chuckled. "I even know LeFarge's favorite restaurant. And you'll find this amusing—the shell company deposits Captain LeFarge's salary in a joint account held with a Mrs. Jonathon LeFarge. LeFarge may be a dangerous man, but he lives with his mother."

"Funny," said Thomas. "I hadn't imagined LeFarge having a personal life, much less a mother."

Angie hmm'd. "We could pay for a hack at the right time to syphon all this money back."

Thomas nodded. "At the right time."

Jean didn't much want to hear that. She went on, "There's something else; I'm not sure if it's relevant. I found other irregular transactions in the shell company that will never stand up to audit. The largest abuse—Governor O'Brien pours fifty million dollars a year into a research facility in Georgia."

Angie said, "But all O'Brien's companies do some amount of research."

"Yes, and we have a lab in Georgia, a pharmacological facility. But—and I say but—the shell company funnels a great deal of money through the back door into this place."

Thomas said, "Whoa, don't know what that means. Might take some digesting." He frowned and picked at the starched crease in his jeans leg, distracted.

Angie began the wrap-up. She grinned, and touched the auditor on her shoulder. "Jean, this is all that we'd hoped for. It's a great piece of work."

"When this special task force is over, I'd like to file a report with the Head of Audit and our General Counsel," Jean said.

Thomas felt the shock run down his neck. "Not until it's all over, please."

Jean's smile dimpled out, a beam of cheerfulness. "Yes sir. Plus I don't want to look for a new job today. I'll transmit the summary set of files to your desktabs. I'd advise encrypting them."

Angie lagged behind. "Great stuff, but what do we do with it?"

Thomas shrugged. "Suck the money back into the shell company?"

"That shines the light on us, not them."

"Hire outsiders to do surveillance on the warehouse and fire station?"

She nodded. "Possible. But why, with LeFarge and his team in California?"

"And it doesn't catch them in the course of a crime. Expensive too. I bet it wouldn't pass Jean's audit."

Angie laughed. Then her grin faded.

Robko padded around the L.A. apartment, restless in the early morning hours. The road called him—he could see it all singing out to him, black pavement striped in white and yellow, green interstate signs flicking by. Outside, October's pre-dawn night lay warm and murmuring with traffic noise; they had all the windows open. Freeway sounds filled the rooms and made it impossible to lie back down. He decided to pack.

While Sibyl dreamed away the pre-dawn hours, or tried to, he emptied out their workshop into garbage bags and set them one by one near the front door. He separated into two piles, the keepers and the tossers. When he finished and the workshop lay empty and forlorn, he hassled the tosser bags into the minivan. The dawn's half-light obscured his activities from his neighbors. He drove to a nearby grade school and slung his trash into their dumpster.

At seven, he drove into East L.A. near the train tracks, where he knew a moving company that sold surplus trailers and trucks. He'd chosen this firm because the beat-up trailers all came in a tattered, anonymous white, painted over from the garish orange of the original company. He purchased the largest the minivan could drag, towed it back to the motel, and pulled it up parallel to their front door.

Unhooking the screen door, he wheeled the bike out and up the ramp into the trailer. He found it a piece of cake to strap the motorcycle down. He heaped bags all around the bike like a lake of black plastic. Lastly, he locked the roll-down door with a stout combination lock and went back in to wake Sibyl.

They left Atwater Village in the clear midmorning light. He slept in the front seat. Sibyl drove them past a white panel van, past someone selling carpet cleaner door-to-door, past the Metrolink. As she turned up the frontage road by the freeway, she saw graffiti painted below the bridge, scribing out, "Wandering Bird On The Wing." The trailer tire ran over a black spray can, squirting it out unobserved to clatter against the curb. Robko dozed through the omen.

Love and Pain

Chapter Twenty-Two: Locked Into the Depth of Night

Steward's team room bore a resemblance to a Las Vegas casino—no outside window distinguished day from night, no hint of outside reality intruded. Flashy equipment scrolled eye-catching displays; a bustle of people wore faces either hopeful or grim. A Vegas-like fragrance hung over all as a smell of institutional carpet, conflicting colognes, stale food, and that frisson of nervous perspiration. Thomas shuffled across the room and dropped into Angie's visitor chair. "This is really boring."

"You're not the one to complain, Thomas. You're not glued to camera feeds." She waved her hand towards the staff that stared into those screens.

"Don's had a day out there. Where's Zlata anyway?"

"I assume that's a rhetorical question."

He leaned over his knees, his hands clasped, and his forearms on his thighs. His heels drummed on the carpet. "I've made a decision."

"Sounds portentous."

"Since I don't have anything to do here, I'm going to have a peek at LeFarge's warehouse."

She stared at him. "You're joking."

"No—it's the perfect time. LeFarge and his boys are in California. Jean got us the address, but we haven't done anything with it yet."

Her frown chilled him to the marrow. No charming little girl here. "Ask Don's people to do it."

"And have them discover Carl Dupont's corpse stuffed into a refrigerator or buried in the basement? No, it needs to be someone who already knows about the murder."

"Thomas, you said we wouldn't send any of our team out into the field. Are you trying to prove something?"

"Maybe. But as counter evidence to your accusation, I've felt pretty shaky and apprehensive since they tried to kill me at the racquet club. This reconnoiter must be okay if a coward is up for it."

"Right. So you're ambling into their lair. Any reason I should approve of this expedition?" He gazed at that one eyebrow, arched clear up to the sky itself, and at the piercing, unamused eyes.

He ducked his head. "We might learn something. I'll call in while I'm out there. I'll back out if it looks like the bully boys are at home."

The warehouse and the fire station hid in general squalor on the edge of Bedford Stuyvesant, beyond the zone of gentrification in the old neighborhood, beyond the safe space and reliable cabs. He didn't slope off to spy in the corporate town car. He hopped out to Bed Stuy on the Fulton Street Subway and hiked the remaining blocks. He felt quite vigorous, swinging along on his mission, following the map on his burner phone.

The Foreign Legion rented an anonymous storehouse, a dinghy three-story on a gritty street of red brick warehouses. A padlocked garage door rusted beneath an old sign that said Cockaigne Industries. Cockaigne had painted the door black, but it had been tagged many times with graffiti. The top layer read, "Her Heart Is Pure Bitterness" in a bold red slash. He grinned and touched the text with his hand.

Thomas scouted for cameras as he wandered around the block twice—cams he would have ignored a year ago. The alley provided its buildings with truck docks, and he skirted through that also, a path that splashed through puddles floating with filth. He rattled the back door—locked. He looked around and found a fire escape with its ground floor ladder well up over his head. With some difficulty, he rolled a battered dumpster underneath it, closed the bent lid, and hauled himself on top with a grunt. Gazing down, he spotted a streak of yellow slime on his black jeans. He teetered on the shaky support—the whole thing rolled a couple of inches, and he waved his arms for balance. His fingers could just graze the bottom rung.

He gave a spring and caught the bar with both hands. He chinned himself but hung there stymied—he didn't have the strength to clamber on up. Staring at his own knuckles, he gasped for air, feet dangling. With a squeal, the ladder broke free of its years-old rust. His feet hit; he let go. The ladder rattled all the way down and smashed his left foot.

He found the windows locked on both the second and third floor. He couldn't find a way in from the roof. He grimaced. He searched his pockets and found nothing useful. He kicked the roof parapet and swore at his humiliating defeat.

On the way down, he spotted the putty on a third story windowpane, rimming the glass in white, different than the black ancient surrounds of the other panes. An elastic ear stuck out, and he tugged at it. Someone had been through here before. He unzipped the putty, caught the glass before it fell. He reached in, unlocked the window. With difficulty, he forced the window up on its decrepit dirt-crusted tracks. Triumphant, he wiggled across the sill, picking up more filth on his jeans.

He crouched beneath the third floor ceiling, dirty beams but inches above his head. He canvassed the space but left the small rooms un-inspected—their padlocks, encased in dirt, hung limp in stout old hasps. He descended to the second floor, relieved to find fourteen-foot ceilings. There a vast room had been abandoned by humanity. Only a couple of dismal toilets crouched naked in one corner. He knelt at the top of the stairs, listened, and crept down. His heart sounded as loud as a punk band—anyone nearby would hear it. Lucky for him and his heart, the floor below held no mercenary.

LeFarge's army did indeed operate out of here. Two large black SUVs with tinted windows hunkered near the front warehouse door. To the side squatted a mechanic's bench, littered with tools, clamps, and ammunition in various sizes. They had stacked large plastic storage tubs—he lifted the lid of one and discovered several bulletproof vests. Another tub yielded up digital radios with earbuds hanging off coiled wires. He wrinkled his forehead, thought about it, and decided. He hung one on his belt and stored the mike and earphone in an inside pocket—there might come a time when he needed access to the Foreign Legion's chitchat. He wished he knew something about channels.

He found three desktabs on their chargers. When he turned them on, he found their thumbprint locks awaiting someone else's whorls. He was stymied.

He shrugged, then stared around the large space. He wondered what to look for. A waste of time, a wasted trip. He wandered over to a shipping container. He swung half the end open to let light into the black space within. The smell assaulted his nose. He stepped up into the container, and his shoes made scratching sounds on the dirty floor.

He found a cot, a blanket on the floor, and a five-gallon bucket full of dried excrement. Someone had been kept here, locked away. The captors had left a chain padlocked to a tie-down on the wall, left in laziness or readiness, he could not tell. Its other end lay slack on the floor with another padlock hooked through a loop, waiting.

The air hung very silent in that container, very heavy. The metal walls pushed inward; the ceiling hovered dark above his head. He spun on his feet and ran through the door. He closed the container up. Surprised, he heard his own breath ripping ragged, in and out, gasping.

He had nothing but the stolen radio—no ideas, no evidence, no plan. He trudged back over to the gunsmith bench and rummaged. Like snakes, they lurked there, wrapped in rags in the clutter—he picked up two pistols. The slides said they were 380s. After some study, he ejected the clips, saw bullets at the top of each, and reinserted them in the butt of each gun, slapping the bottom. He heard a click—he guessed that was good. Thomas settled one in each of the front pockets of his jacket. Now he had some manhood. He returned to the stairs to leave by his window.

The warehouse door rattled and he sprinted up the stairs, hesitating at the top. He lay down on the landing to peer into the space below. From his aerie, he gaped at the limo as it slid in, stared at the driver as he climbed out, and closed the door. Recognition struck when he saw the man stride to the back of the car—LeFarge! The bastard was supposed to be on his way to California.

LeFarge hauled Isobel Dupont out. He marched her across the floor with hands in a rigid grip around her arm. He stood her up in front of the shipping container. "Open it." She struggled with the handles and swung the door back.

Thomas eyed them as they were limned against the faded light from the front windows. LeFarge leaned into the woman, their two heads inches apart. Broken words drifted up the stairs to Thomas, fragments tight and angry. Isobel shook her head. LeFarge dragged her into the door of the container. She broke. Her shoulders fell; her head drooped. LeFarge talked to her for a minute more. As he did so, he reached up and pushed her hair back with one hand, back behind her ear. LeFarge caressed her; he consoled her. Dropping the gesture, he

194

frog-marched her back to the car.

O'Brien waited by the back door. The three were shoulder to shoulder. Thomas stared as O'Brien's hands rose up behind the woman's head and jerked her into his kiss. The Governor kept her smashed to him, spoke, and grinned an ursine grimace. She nodded. The two men shoved her into the car.

In the long, low light of a fall dawn, Sibyl and Robko left their mid-price, Vegas motel room, and drew the door shut behind them. They slid into the van, she on the left and he on the right. She simpered and reached over to pat his hand. "Did we go to the bathroom before we got in the car?"

This was good; he liked this acting. He whined, "Are we there yet? Can we stop to eat soon?"

"Be a good boy, and we'll pick a place for tonight that has a swimming pool."

"Better a pool hall."

They followed the railroad tracks southeast, made a right, and picked up the entrance ramp to the freeway. They passed under one of Nevada's electronic speed signs, one that monitored traffic, one that announced time delays and informed drivers of upcoming problems. Its camera looked down upon them. Somewhere in Connecticut, code running in a giant rack-mounted computer recognized an aged minivan and a junky trailer. It saw two people in hats and sunglasses. The software failed to make the leap of identification. But this software could learn.

Chapter Twenty-Three: Fall from Grace

W hat do you mean, he's gone!" Dennis Malley O'Brien balanced
at his desk, both hands on each side of the phone, and shouted
down into it. Thomas roosted in one of the dwarf chairs across from the
Governor. He watched the great head hang down towards the speaker
and camera. "You crap-covered scrotum!" The desktop flecked with
spittle.

Thomas couldn't see the phone screen, but he could hear clearly.
Garland's voice quavered on the other end. "We've been on location
four days and haven't found him. It's a sure bet Zlata has slipped past
us again." Don cleared his throat. "We did find two apartments that had
just been vacated without notice. Each had a couple living there, but we
don't know which couple was our target. We've found the transient
population here is remarkably suspicious."

"What the hell does that mean?"

LeFarge, another disembodied voice from California, said, "It
means they wouldn't tell you shit if the stink was in the air."

"Captain LeFarge is correct. Our efforts to I.D. one of these two
couples as Zlata and Boxwood have not worked out. We had an
incident between a LeFarge employee and one of the Latino men here,
and word has spread through the community. Anyone who is a stranger
here—anyone—gets blank stares and no answers."

Thomas asked with his blandest voice, "What kind of incident?"

LeFarge's voice rattled up through the speaker. "No big thing. One
of my men could distinguish a lie when he heard it and brought some
pressure to bear. He didn't appreciate being jerked around."

Appalled, Thomas flashed a glance at the Governor but held his
silence. The Governor didn't even react. O'Brien didn't care about the
battered man or the community's hostility. "Forget the apartments.

196

They're not in the goddamn apartments, so who cares," said the Governor.

"Yessir." Garland had nothing left to say.

O'Brien asked, "Are you tracking Zlata again? Do you have him on the radar?"

Thomas replied, "My department, that. Tran Cam didn't spot them as they left Atwater Village and has not reported any hits."

"Brilliant. Frickin' brilliant."

Thomas plowed on. "If they're not on the bike, we may not get a clear sighting of them for some time. We have to write off the bike as a tool to find them, and we have to go on facial recognition software alone. It'll be tough."

O'Brien's face clouded up like a storm front. "Specifics, Thomas. What are you telling me?"

"We think we would catch them on camera in places like ATM machines, hotels, and restaurants, that type of place. Tran Cam coverage in those sectors is limited. It just doesn't have a lot of restaurant customers."

O'Brien got quiet as Garland described further local efforts. Garland didn't have much to say, but he took a long time to say it. The Governor interrupted, "Stop."

Garland did stop. LeFarge interpreted it as a chance to get a word in. "He may still be here in California. We'll continue working L.A. until Steward finds Zlata again. Either way, we're on it. The Polack can't stay ahead of us forever."

"I—said—stop. Your operation out there is dead. Bring the troops home. We'll discuss if there should be some personnel changes when you get back. And I mean leadership changes." O'Brien tapped the vidi's screen, and the call ended. He swiveled his big head up towards Thomas and asked, "Well?"

"LeFarge is killing my good luck."

"Maybe."

"Do you want a postmortem or a guess on what happens next?"

"I don't give Mary's Sacred Veil for your stupid look-back. How do we get back on Zlata's tail?"

"Hard work, same as before."

"And what is your opinion on the performance of your two peers?"

Thomas coughed. "Garland does well for a man who suddenly

197

finds himself in charge of a spy agency. You know my opinion of LeFarge."

"You want me to fire him."

"You can't. Everything he's done he did in your name. You can't fire a murderer who could bring you down."

"The thought had crossed my mind. I got a goddamn tiger by the tail."

"You could have him killed, but then you might have a saber-tooth tiger by the tail. It escalates."

"And I thought you were my moralist."

"Not me, sir. I'm your pragmatist."

"And what about you, Thomas? Should I replace you?"

"I've run a clean operation, sir, and I've found Zlata for you twice. If you want to send me back to Acquisitions, I'll go right away."

"I'm not bitching about your smarts or your hard work, Thomas. You used to be lucky. Now it's Zlata who's lucky. You may be the wrong horse to back."

They made Dallas by the third day as they idled across America. Modifying their old pattern, they stayed out of both cheap and high priced hotels. As a change-up, he chose a resort associated with an exclusive golf course outside the metroplex. They checked into a bungalow.

Dumping the suitcases on the bed, he said, "Any objection if we stay a couple of days?"

"I like the sound of that." She ambled through their living room and out the back where the deck cantilevered out over a fairway.

He followed. "It's time to change our look again. They may know the old Robko and Sibyl, so we'd better switch out. We need to go shopping."

"Ooh, I know. You could be tall this time."

"Ouch. I could be blond. You'll have to do the eyebrow too. And I could grow a goatee… or a beard."

"That won't grow in blond."

"True."

"Can I be a redhead?"

198

"I always liked banging redheads."

"Instead, you got a hothead. Well, I told you all men have their kinky fantasies. Maybe I should go as a man, just for you."

"We're going to Georgia, you know, before we get to NYC. Times haven't changed that much. Out-of-state gays traveling the back roads of the South—we might solve O'Brien's problem for him."

"I could still go as the man, and you could go as the woman."

He shot her a look and then decided to drop it. He strode back into the bungalow. "We can talk it out tonight. Let's shower and call room service."

"What would you like?"

"It's Texas. Organically raised steak for you of course, but order vegetables and a starter for me. Fish if they have it. Clean living for me." He sauntered on in to the palatial bathroom, stripped, and cranked on the shower. He stood beneath the multiple jets. In a minute or two, she strolled in behind and pressed up against his back. He said, "Hothead, huh?"

"We don't have much time. Room Service is on the way." He turned around to face her, the water spraying them from all sides. He began to shampoo her hair. She soaped his chest. Even in this moment, she said, "Loan me five hundred dollars. I'm good for it. You can trust me."

Room Service arrived just as they finished toweling off. The waiter, noncommittal about a couple of guests wrapped in bathrobes, set up a table on the deck, placed out dishes under cover, and served out a glass of Bordeaux on Sibyl's side. He seated Sibyl, accepted a tip from Robko, and slid gracefully away.

Robko gazed at her across the table—a small woman barricaded behind a large steak. She fought it tenaciously. He shredded his way through his green stuff.

She had also ordered cheesecake for two with exotic chocolate. He dissected his cheesecake with a fork and spread it around the plate while hers disappeared. She nibbled at her chocolate. "Straight up, they say, with a red wine chaser back. Chocolate and wine, a match made in heaven."

He sniffed.

She sloshed the wine around in her glass before belting it back. "Have you been thinking about the score?"

199

He pushed his plate back. "No, I've been thinking about your other career, all these pictures you keep snapping. And you never keep the pretty ones."

She sneered, "I did photography in art school. The really beautiful photos are immediate, visceral. Often ugly. Pretty is what your mamma took at your tenth birthday party."

"Huh?"

"You ever see photos by Weegee or Diane Arbus?"

"I have no idea who you're talking about."

"Of course not. Weegee photographed dead bodies on the pavement. Arbus photographed midgets."

"What happens to all your photos, especially the ones of dead midgets?"

She glanced at him, then at the empty wineglass. "When the wrinkles set in, when my career is over? Then I'm going to get gallery shows set up as a Richard Avedon or Tommy Chan. Be a name." She sloshed more red into her glass.

"I thought you wanted to be a thief?"

"I want it all. I want to live to be a hundred and be rich and powerful. I want fame and lovers forty years younger."

He looked out off the balcony into the orange light of sunset. He just wanted O'Brien. "How about you? Have you been thinking about the job?"

"No. I've been thinking about you. How come you're not a petty criminal with two tours in the pen? You should be broke half the time and screwing around with small stuff."

"I am all that... exactly what you said."

"For an impoverished loser, you treat a girl pretty nice."

He shrugged. "I got some breaks; that's all."

"Tell me about it."

"I don't do the bio, even within a crew. But you're different; you still have my five hundred dollars and half the bond money. I'll sell you the story."

"Will you take it in trade?"

He shot her an amused glance. "I'll pay for sex or drugs, but I like it better when you give them to me for free."

"So tell me about the lucky breaks." She eyed his dessert plate.

He handed it to her. "First break? Figuring out who I was early on.

Everybody else around me loved a punch-up. The dickheads thought knives were cool and bought cheap-ass guns that blew up in their hands. Those turf wars in high school showed me I had no guts for blood and violence. Lucky I've got that streak of cowardice, I guess."

"But you can hang by your fingertips from a balcony six floors up?"

"As long as no one steps on them."

"So you found out you don't like guns and knives. What happened next?"

"Well, Mirko and I…." He stopped and stared off at the golf fairway.

She caressed his hand. "Still hurts, doesn't it?"

He slid his hand back and blew past her question. "Mirko and I got high most days with a friend who had an older brother. Big brother stole cars and delivered them to a chop shop—and made a good living. We got involved in ripping cars too and did it for a while. I dropped out of high school about then. Between Mirko and me, we made and spent more money than our school superintendent ever took home."

The corner of her mouth twitched up. "The American Dream."

"Mirko arranged it so we could move up, and we joined a high-end car gang. They smuggled cars into Central America and sold them to 'legitimate' businessmen who didn't want to pay the import fees. We found the downside—we were both over eighteen. Mirko got copped one night. They caught him hot-wiring a limo. This was in a parking garage in downtown Chi. He couldn't get the beast out before they sealed him in. He did beat the hell out of the limo trying, though. That was the first time he went up."

"The first time?"

She had pitched her voice noncommittal, neutral. He admired her control, after most of a bottle of wine.

"Mirko had an aptitude for jail. He prospered in there, but jail scared the hell out of me. I couldn't imagine going in."

"Of course. Then what?"

"I had time to kill while he did his time. I moved to New York—Chicago was too hot—and met a fence, so I switched to B and E."

"B and E?"

"Breaking and entering. Again, luck was with me. My fence paid much better for high-end stuff, so I raised my sights from TVs and microwaves to jewels, antiques, collector shotguns, that type of thing. That's when I taught myself to read."

"You—taught—yourself—to—read."

"Yeah, I dropped out of school as a junior, and I had been able to fake my way through to that point. But to be a good thief, I had to read and understand all those manuals on alarm systems, locks, vaults—all the stuff they use to keep you out. Of course, that means I can spell magnetic induction, but I can't spell philosophical."

"Still, to teach yourself to read—"

"I had some motivation the second time around. I enjoyed the challenge of finessing all those lockouts, and I liked working alone. After a while, I found out climbing came natural to me, so I took some of the money and went off to mountaineering school to get real about it. Some of that turned out useful."

"I don't see you on a mountain." She polished off the last inch of wine.

"Well, no. You know, they expect you to get up at six in the morning? I preferred six in the evening. All those slick young mountain dicks drank like fish; at that time, I toked more than a four-man rock band. I had just started down the no-win slope into pills."

"The slope that led to your present sorry state?" She forked some of his cheesecake into her mouth. "Unique skill set."

"My biggest skill is the ability to wiggle through a mouse hole and not get the screaming meemies. Comes easy for me, but I worked once with a blaster—a guy who blows safes—who went utter gaga in some ducting. I left him in there, the sparky, begging for the authorities to jerk him out and arrest him."

"So how did you learn about moving money around, and about new identities and bearer bonds?"

"My fence. He agreed to educate me on the roll, as long as a steady stream of merchandise showed up. After a while, they copped him for receiving stolen goods. I visited him up at Riker's Island, and he connected me in with the next level, the serious crews. I liked the work—I didn't have to do the planning, just show up and do as I was told. Well, it was nice until the O'Brien job."

"Hmm. We don't travel tomorrow, so I'm up for more wine." She ambled off to the bar refrigerator and sauntered back with two small bottles. "One for me, and one for me."

202

"You could have brought me something."

"Okay. Red, blue, yellow, shitty brown?"

"The klonos, I think."

She sashayed into the bathroom, trailing the ties of her robe on the floor, and wandered back with two pills and some water. "What about my five hundred?"

Chapter Twenty-Four: You Are My Constant Pride

The rough, raised weave smelled like soap and wool—dry and dusty. Robko eased open an eye and stared across the carpet towards, what? The rug hung over him like his ceiling; the drapery in front of him hung upside down. He twitched and blinked that one exposed eye; the world flipped over. He found himself huddled on the carpet in a bedroom in a bungalow on a golf course in Dallas. Of course. The buzz had receded. Time to amp it up. He rose onto his hands and knees to discover the bed ruffle. His hand levered him up—Sibyl lay in front of him on her side, naked, asleep. She snored through her mouth, gentle rasping in and out. He lurched to his feet and ambled into the bathroom. Party drugs lay loose across the counter. Spotting her wine glass, he filled it with water. He picked up a designer barb and perched it waiting on his tongue. A pause. He added a vallie. Vicodin, why not?

Her voice bullied him from a vast, empty space, far away. He couldn't quite focus his eyes. "Robert, what did you take? Pay attention." She slapped his face, and he felt the shaking she gave him, but at arm's length. She could have been shaking anybody. "What did you take?"

He fought for a breath. Things colored up blue-black around the edges. "One of each. A Chinese buffet." His tongue moved in his mouth like paste; the words oozed out like glue.

"Oh shit, oh shit. You gozo. Here," she tugged him, jerking him across a slick white surface.

He squinted up his eyes. She heard his tongue flog around in his mouth, but nothing made sense.

"I can't understand you—you're so screwed up you can't even talk. Here's the toilet. Puke."

"Wha?"

"Here. I can help." She thrust her finger down his throat and, sure enough, his body quaked, and his throat gagged. A life-restoring vomit. When he had finished, she mopped his face and mouth and threw the towel into the corner. "C'mon, stand up." She struggled to get him to his feet. They staggered forward into the bedroom.

He spotted the bed and fell forward onto it. She tugged at his shoulders, thrust her hands under his arms, and jerked. She couldn't heave him up; he had gone limp, his eyes closed. She threw on her bathrobe and ran to the bungalow door.

A gardener strolled by, a coil of hose over his shoulder, a bucket in his hand. She demanded, "Hey, you! Come here." He approached her, sidling a bit, an expression on his face like he would rather run. "I need your help."

"Sí, como no." He glanced back over his shoulder, searching for a way out.

"What's your name?"

"Constantine."

"Okay, Connie, I need your help to walk a man around the room. Come on in. Two hundred dollars."

He understood the money. Constantine shuffled into the bungalow and allowed her to close the door.

"Back here in the bedroom. Get him up; get his arm over your shoulder. Now walk him... back and forth."

"Sí, pero, he barely breathe."

"I'll help with that. Robert, hang on." She ran into the bathroom, found his kit, dumped out the naloxone and a syringe. She ran back into the bedroom. Constantine toiled across the room as he carried a limp, half-naked man. She stabbed the needle into his upper buttock and pressed the plunger. "Walk him, walk him. Robert, snap out of it. You have to help." His feet dragged along with floppy uncontrolled twitches. "Come on, Connie, we have to sweat it out of his system."

"Qué ha tenido?"

"Shut up. None of your business."

"Qué lo malo." For a half hour, the brown man carried a sagging pallid Anglo back and forth, urged on by a strident, diminutive woman.

Robko's head swung up, his mouth sucked for air, and he wheezed. "Water."

"Keep him moving. I'll bring water." She brought a glass from the bathroom. They paused, poured it into his mouth, and watched his convulsive swallow. Robko threw it back up along with some yellow slime onto Constantine's pants.

"Ah, señor," Connie said.

She said, "Three hundred dollars. It's okay."

"He wakes up. Mire, he breathes better." Robko wrenched his arm back from around the gardener's neck and tried a couple of stumbling steps.

"I got it, Sibyl. I can walk." Robko lurched around the room, bumped into the dresser, and turned. "G-g-gangway," he stuttered. He waved his hands and faltered across the room. Constantine backed out of the way.

Sibyl said to the gardener, "We're done here. I'll get your money." She fished in the dresser and brought out a roll of bills.

Constantine said to her back, "Four hundred. Tambien, I keep quiet."

She marched over to him, handed him money with her left hand, and seized his index finger with her right. Constantine's knees bent, and he let out a sharp hiss. She told him, "It's three hundred."

He dropped the money and swung at her, punched her hard in the eye.

She bent the finger back within an inch of his wrist. He dropped to his knees with a cry. "Hit me again, why don't you? You don't punch worth a damn. Three hundred, and you'll keep your mouth shut, bien. If you don't, I'll burn your house, kill your children, and then I'll shoot you. Muerto, sí?"

"Sí."

"Pick up the money." He fished for the money with his free hand. She glared down into his face. "Just so you remember what I promised." With a pop, she dislocated his finger.

The gray-haired old butler brought Thomas down to the den and said, "Wait here. Governor O'Brien will be with you shortly." The door closed with a whisper.

He could smell the sticky, sweet fragrance of lilies that erupted up out of a massive vase on a side table. A wall of French doors stretched behind the flowers. They opened onto a swath of Long Island grass. He moved past the flowers to the glass. Out there on the green, a group of Adirondack chairs scattered, chalk white against the manicured browning grass. A big man in black loomed halfway between the chairs and the house, hands clasped behind him. Above the back of a chair, Thomas made out a head, recognized dark hair, and contemplated a woman who gazed out over the water. A fog lay thick offshore. He opened the door and strode across the grass, past the bruiser in the suit.

Intuition paid off—Isobel Dupont curled up in her chair, shoulders hunched, knees up, feet on the seat. He dropped into the chair beside her. She glanced over, sharp, irritated. "Do I know you?"

"You've seen me before. In O'Brien's office."

"Hmm?"

"You're Carl Dupont's daughter, aren't you?"

"What's it to you?"

"Changed sides, did you?"

She didn't answer. Time stretched out.

"Right. None of my business." He turned away towards the Sound, stuck out his legs, and scooted down into the seat in a slump. They both pretended to watch the fog.

Her voice was low, muffled. "I made some compromises."

"Compromises?"

"Yes." She snapped her head around and snarled at him. "Like screwing LeFarge so he wouldn't kill me."

"Tough trade-off."

"Happens to women all over the world. I'm not the first, and I won't be the last."

"This is Long Island, not the Sudan."

"Might as well be Africa."

"They kill women in the Sudan, after they finish with the rape."

Her chin swung up, and she gazed calmly into the fog. "He's not done yet."

He let silence fill a count or two. "How's O'Brien fit in?"

She threw a sardonic glance at him. "I got promoted. Wife Number Three flew off to Paris a couple of months ago and doesn't look to be coming back. Egan handed me over, and O'Brien installed me here."

The fog sidled in over the next few minutes. He cleared his throat.

207

"Anything I can do?"

"You work for O'Brien, right?" Her voice sounded brittle and ugly. She could crack.

"Yes." That hurt to admit.

With a glare like death, she said, "So what's the offer? You getting in line with the other two?"

"No. Just wanted to help."

"Right. Piss off." She unfolded her knees, straightened out of her chair, and stalked across the lawn to the house. The guard followed her in.

"It's been two days, gozo."

"Yeah, feels more like a year." Robko lay in the giant bed, sunk into the mattress, splayed in a cross shape. He had pillows stuffed against the left and right sides of his head. "Did you know there's a faint portrait of the devil in the ceiling, like someone had painted him in black and then buried him in white?"

Sibyl flicked a quick glance up. "You're hallucinating."

"I wish. He's wearing a top hat and a long coat, and his tail snakes out clear to the bathroom. It's an omen."

Sibyl wrinkled her nose at the Mephitic atmosphere. "Jeez, two days without a shower and a dozen vomitations. I'm not moving back in here until you do something about it."

"Yeah." His hand dug at his hair. "My scalp feels kind of crusty."

"And don't think a shower gets you off the hook. You stink in so many ways. I'm definitely not over being mad at you."

"I'm entitled to the little slip now and then. We're all human. The Church says 'Fallibility is the state of man.'"

"Screw the Church, you asshole. You goddamn OD'd! Suicide is a sin, you know."

"If I go stand in the shower, will you stop shouting?"

She snorted. "I'm going shopping. Want anything?"

"Khaki. My disguise requires khaki."

"Okay, you got it. But first, prove to me you're not going back to sleep."

He lurched up and shuffled five feet towards her headed for the bathroom door. "Are the yellows in there? I could do with a smoother about now."

She delivered the punch from her waist clear up into his jaw. It knocked him over the corner of the dresser and onto the floor. Pale as parchment, she stood over him, shaking. The cords in her neck stood out like wire. "You're unbelievable. Absolutely unbelievable." She spun on her heel and marched out.

When she returned, loaded up with bags and boxes, she found him back in bed. She leaned against the doorjamb and stared at him, suspicious. "Sober?"

"God yes. Feels unnatural. And my jaw hurts."

"Good. Don't forget I'm the one with the black eye, not you. Should have been your black eye." She cocked her head towards the living room. "Let's move to the couch. It's time you shifted your lazy ass back to work."

She led the way and sprawled out with her foot on the coffee table. "You asked me three days ago if I had been thinking about the job."

"I don't recall it, but if you say I did, I did. Let's talk about it."

"You're a skank as well as a skanker."

He waited.

"These Artifacts, they require something to run them—they have to plug into something."

"Yes, and those weird-ass connections mean it's specialized. Plus you have to load them up somehow. Together that means sensor gear on the human being and a huge computer."

She tilted her head. "Not something you'd tote around in a messenger bag or a briefcase."

"You're thinking what I'm thinking."

She nodded. "To load an Artifact or to use an Artifact requires a lab."

"Right. The lab in Georgia, which is what I'm saying."

"What if you're wrong?"

He smirked. "What if I'm right? So much easier that way."

"But once Artifacts are loaded, they could be stored anywhere?"

"Yes, even a penthouse office in lower Manhattan."

She twitched like she had been shocked. "Sarcasm won't win me back to your side."

"Sorry."

"Wouldn't it make sense then if your office had been robbed—I mean, keep your empty spares where you load them? Where you have a high level of security?"

"I think so."

"Now I believe in Georgia. What's this place like?" She curled her feet up under her and leaned towards him.

He grinned—she was hooked. "Well, first, it's out in the fields. A paved county road runs down one side, and there's a long fenced driveway that leads to the front guard shack." He picked up their stolen desktab. "Here, let me show you. See, they have the usual two ring fences with the dog run in between. There could be some advantage to break in from the woods but a lot of work to slip past the fences and the dogs. These doo-dads symbolize robotic cameras in the corners and halfway down the fence line. Could be they work on motion detectors."

"I'm not keen on barbed wire."

He flapped a hand. "If we broke in that way, we'd go through or under, not over."

"So the fence sucks. You'll find another way in."

He stretched out his arms, his fingers laced and his knuckles cracking. "I need to go see. Can't do much here."

She nodded her head. "Let's swing down to Georgia and pick us up an Artifact or two."

"Just like take-out, phone the order in?"

"I wish. You ready to travel?"

"I'd like a couple of days of gym time first, to build some edge back."

"Don't take too long. They could eventually figure it out and be waiting for us."

Chapter Twenty-Five: Lab Rats

When Thomas got back from Long Island, Angie was sitting at his desk in his little cubicle off the electronic boards. She had his middle drawer open and her feet propped up on it, a cup of coffee cradled in her hands. She said, "Any luck with O'Brien?"

He shrugged his shoulders. "More of the same. But I did get to talk to Isobel Dupont. Young woman needs some help."

Angie raised an eyebrow. "Collecting strays?"

He said, "That was remarkably cold." He waved his hand at the desk drawers. "Did you find anything of interest in there?

"What are the white ones?"

"They're sodies, or Sodium amylobarbitone. Hypno-sedative. Try one."

She rolled her eyes. "No thank you, sir. I've got something serious to talk to you about."

"Shoot."

"You may not like that verb when I'm done." She waved him to a chair, then rolled forward a foot until they were knee to knee.

"This sounds ominous."

She fished out a piece of paper from off the desk. "Do you know Allen?"

"Who?"

"O'Brien's PA."

He ripped out his crooked grin. "Oh. I thought his name was O'Brien's PA."

"You're not going to be laughing when you see what he gave me. You see, Allen's gay, and he knows my little secret. We've got a bond."

"Like a fraternity?"

She glared at him like he was a recalcitrant child. "Just stop it, and listen. He gave me an image off his copy machine, out of the memory bank. It's not good news. Here, I printed it out."

She handed it to him. He scanned it. A list of names, eight in all. The first two had a line drawn through them—a note for each, "Auto," and "Fall from deck." His name was last on the list. He stared at her. "What is this?"

"I went to our employee data bank. Seven of these people work for us in Georgia, with titles like Laboratory Technician. Two have just died, and employee death-benefits are kicking in for the families. I think these seven are the auxiliaries that helped build the Artifact. I bet LeFarge is killing them, one by one. I would guess O'Brien ordered up at least the first seven."

"But maybe not the eighth."

"Does it matter?"

Under the truck, Sibyl couldn't see Robko—she could barely see her own knees or her hands in black gloves. The tires hissed away, a sibilant rumble close to her head. The blacktop slipped past them smelling like creosote. They lay in cradles hung from the truck frame.

Through the Bluetooth headset he whispered to her, "Front door coming up."

They swayed as the truck turned into the compound.

"Those cameras set in the ground. We made a mistake—they're bound to spot us under the truck," she whispered.

"Naah. Black cloth cradles, low light, black clothes. Relax."

The truck stopped at the gatehouse. They couldn't hear any conversation over the idling engine, but she imagined the driver conferring with the guard. A huge flash of light—the driveway all around lit up from dark to blinding in the blink of an eye.

"Just be still," he whispered. "Some guard with a jimber for the job turned on the lights above the apron. This helps hide us."

The truck rolled forward, past the lights and into the compound. She whispered back, "I nearly peed my pants."

"Side effect of the job."

"We did it!"

"Only the front gate. There's more to come."

Robko and Sibyl lay quiet as ghosts in the slings while the driver shut the truck down and the guard searched the cab and the back. The stink of diesel dissipated as the breeze pushed the fumes away.

He whispered, "Wait for it. They'll pull around to the big lab building." The driver swung up into the cab, fired up the engine, and drove them about a half mile around the complex. "The second he stops… before he starts backing," he whispered.

The truck shuddered to a halt. They rolled out of the cradles and landed on their hands and knees. The truck began to back.

"Jesus! He's turning! He'll crush us!" she hissed. They rolled out the right side between the wheels of the trailer and tractor. They scuttled, low to the ground, until a transformer against the building concealed them.

"You okay?"

Her breath shuddered out hard. "I didn't think it would be that scary."

"Piece of cake. The guards are always bored, so if they see, they see by accident."

"I meant the truck tires."

"I know what you meant. Ace, seriously ace! Pumps up the old adrenaline."

He led the way over to a small wing that jutted out from the main building block. "Wait here." He wedged his back and shoulders into the corner, splayed his hands, knees, and feet out onto the walls and sidled upwards. Three floors later, he disappeared over the roof's edge. In a moment, he dropped a line. She clipped into the loop and closed her eyes. Faced into the corner, she cat-walked up the wall while the rope tugged her up. She bounced and swayed, struck her shoulders first on one side of the V and then the other. She didn't open her eyes until the rope changed angle. She clambered over the edge, thirty feet up.

"You're a pro," he said as he coiled up the line.

Irritation flashed through her like fire—he wasn't even breathing hard. "It was worse than the truck wheels."

"The next part is the loud part." He scrambled over on his haunches to the air conditioning, a mass of blowers and a snarl of two-foot tubes. "It ain't Hollywood. In the real world, security always ignores the AC."

"God! The blowers are huge."

"That's good for us. Nice fat ducting." They knelt and applied themselves to screws and a panel. A black square, two by two, yawned open in front of them. "Okay...." He led the way, lighting up the duct with a lamp strapped to his forehead. The fans howled and the frigid air pushed hard behind them. The wind made her eyes water.

She shouted into her Bluetooth, "This is awful. I have to sneeze." She did, for the next hundred feet. She damped it with her sleeve.

"Shush," his disembodied voice said in her ear.

"Right, asshole! Let's get out of this ducting. I can hear my teeth chatter."

He fished out a pair of shears and cut a three-foot long hole out of the duct's side. "No way to be quiet with this one." With some banging and reverberation, he folded a rectangle of metal out. "Now we're out in the ceiling, but we'll be coming back through here."

"Crawling back into that wind... great."

Robko could see her, all angular in the grid work of the ceiling, cradling her little flashlight. He crawled along to her in the dark, his head-mounted lamp flashing back and forth. "Fixed it. Security cameras are telling lies to the guards. How are you doing?"

"I hate this. I'm going to fall one way or the other." She breathed short sharp huffs.

"Brace with your other hand on the steel deck above, like I showed you."

"That's how I cut my hand on a screw."

"It will be easier going back."

"Yeah, right."

"Let's see what else they have in store for us." He wedged up the edge of a ceiling tile, inserted his camera, and inspected his iMob. "Uh-huh. Uh-huh." He twisted it around.

"What?"

"As bad as I thought. One more defense—lasers." He fished up the tile and set it aside. He jammed his toes against the wall below and lowered himself. "Come on down. I'll turn on the lights."

He steadied her as she hung and dropped from the ceiling, her toes sliding down the wall. She found herself inside the lab, in front of a steel door, in a square marked out on the floor by the door. "Don't step out of the box," he said.

"Duuh."

He pointed at the security cameras up in the four corners. "Don't worry. They're watching reruns." He handed her vinyl gloves.

The lab sprawled out in front of them, big and cluttered. One wall held cages full of white mice; some of them rustled, quiet but awake in their pine shavings. The left wall housed four large cages of chimpanzees. All slept but one—he contemplated Sibyl and Robko while he made small crooning sounds and picked at his ear. Towards the end of the room a dentist's chair trailed wiring harnesses into a junction box.

"There it is... the Frankenstein machine," she said. "I expected a giant computer, not that screen thingy beside it."

"It's probably hooked to something big somewhere."

"So where are the Artifacts?"

"Personally I would keep them in that vault over there, on the back wall." He pointed at a twenty-by-twenty steel cage with a solid door.

"So where are these lasers?"

"There's a regular grid—see the emitters along the top of the wall? You can't see the beams with the regular lights on."

He watched her blink rapidly, her shoulders hunched, her fists in tight balls. Bottled-up stress. No wonder she was so caustic.

"Now what?" She shook her hands like she was shaking blood down to the fingertips.

"We turn the lasers off. I see the push button for 'em on the wall over by the vault. First person in the lab each morning would walk through the beams and switch off the system. The alarm will be on a delay."

She clapped her hands and gave out a shaky laugh. "So go turn them off."

"Bit more tricky than that. Security would know, even if the alarm doesn't sound. Red lights on the board." He knelt and fished more gear out of his backpack.

"So you have to wiggle through the beams, like in the movies?"

"Not me. You." He handed her a night vision mask like ski goggles and tugged on his own.

"Why me?"

"Because you whined about the air conditioning."

215

"Right. Thanks." She turned on the goggles, flipped off the regular lights in the lab, and saw—a tracery of light beams across the room.

He nudged her. "See the hole in their defense? They didn't train beams across the lab bench. You can wriggle down the counter."

"Me? I thought you were joking."

"Why not you? You're smaller than me. Besides, if you trip the alarm, we were fated to fail. If you don't, then we were fated to win, and you get to keep the five hundred dollars."

"I'm about to have a heart attack."

"Calm down. Think it through. Act it out in your mind."

"I have to pee."

"No, you don't. It's the excitement."

She crouched on the floor and stared into the geometry of the beams. "Don't rush me." Several deep breaths. She sidled forward to the first lab bench, stepped over one ray, and ducked beneath another. She hopped up onto the bench and slithered onto her stomach. She had a clear path most of the way down into the lab. Only at one point did she have to inch under an angled beam.

Her ghost voice breathed in his ear, "God, I hate you, you gozo."

At the far end, she hopped down from the bench, lay down on the floor, and rolled under the last net of light. Rising up by the steel cage, she slapped the red alarm button. The grid disappeared. "Turn on the lights."

"Your wish is my command. Now we better hot-wire the button so they think the lasers are still on." He started down the room towards her.

"There's another button here on the wall. It says, 'Pressure Alarm.' What the hell is that?"

He froze. "That means there are floor sensors. No mention of them on the plans."

"Pressure plates that I could have triggered—while I was rolling around?"

"Uh-huh. But our luck held. Fortune was with us."

"Jesus! Sometimes you're such a jerk." She slapped that button too.

216

Chapter Twenty-Six: A Ship without a Sailor

The coffee bar stank of grounds and burnt milk. It had seized a normally pleasurable smell and amped it up until the nose couldn't tolerate it and shut down. At a booth in the back, Angie and Thomas waited for exotic NYC drinks. They needed a half-hour of small talk, a half-hour away from the office pressure cooker. As casually as he could, he asked, "You seeing anyone?"

"The theft caught me between relationships. Good thing too, since I've had no time for a personal life. And you?"

He gave a shrug. "Nothing except casual. Tighty-whitey prep girls. A singer in a band."

"That your type?"

He shook his head. "I thought you were my type. What about you?"

She indicated the black barista clacking up in heels with their confectionary coffees. "She's my type." She paused, waited for the ritual of the saucers, cups, and spoons. They watched the broad shoulders and the cornrowed hair sway away.

He admitted, "Statuesque."

She laughed out loud, astonished he got it. "Ace. Ace-and-a-half." For a couple of beats, she mixed foam into the coffee with a tiny spoon. "Thomas, you asked me how you would set a brake on the Governor?"

"Yes, nudge him our way. Pressure him to fire LeFarge. That type of thing."

"As long as LeFarge remains on the scene, it's going to be tough. And he's not giving up his meal ticket."

He gave half a shrug. "I've beat my head on that wall too."

"You should install a different kind of failsafe, something for if it all goes wrong."

"Hmm, the get-out-of-jail-free card?"

She tapped the table and lectured him in her voice of reason. "A persuader that would make O'Brien protect you rather than throw you to the wolves. You should record him when you two talk about anything dubious or illegal."

He banged his fist on the table. His eyes glazed as he thought about her suggestion, her brilliant suggestion. "That could work. Something to bargain with when we're talking to the Federal prosecutors. Something we can threaten him with after the arrest. Damn, how could we have missed it? Record him, huh?"

"Only for the dirty stuff."

"Hmm. That's all we talk about. You don't see us using it for day-to-day?"

She shot him the knowing grin. "Not with O'Brien. If he knew what you were doing, he'd scrub you out right away. Even in company takeovers, his motto has been…." She held her hand out to him, inviting the answer.

"Remove the man; remove the problem."

"Yes."

Robko and Sibyl knelt in front of the vault and stared at the electronic lock, a fingerprint reader with an evil red light. She rocked back on her heels. "I thought you expected a combination lock?"

"I did. I brought the drill and a listening probe."

"Are we stymied?"

"No. Remember what we did to Steward's desktab in Ithaca? I need something like talcum powder." They both ranged up and down the room, searching in cupboards below the lab benches.

She said, "A whopping big box of artificial sweetener? Looks like rat poison, but it should work."

"Sure." They circled through the room, dusting for prints. "This lock reads thumbs. Thumbprints show up on things you pick up. Beakers, coffee cups, baseball bats, marital aids, that type of thing." They found ten smudges for every clear print, and of course, thumbprints were in the minority.

She discovered a full, perfect print on a bottle of water. "All right!" he said. "Now, let's lift it with this packing tape." He handed her the roll.

She stared at him but took it. She eased a piece of tape onto the print and carried the tape to the lock.

"Go ahead. You've seen it done. Just don't get it upside down."

The light turned green. "I did it!" She laughed. "That ought to be worth something to you."

He could see her infectious grin and her eyes, open round, delighted with success. "Why do I think it's five hundred dollars?"

They opened the door to the cage. Besides memflashes, files, loaded test tube racks and drugs, the vault held a bonanza of Artifacts.

She prodded at a rack of small lucite boxes with her forefinger. "Look at these itty-bitty ones. Weird."

"Those are the mouse-size versions, don't you think? I wonder if they fill up the Artifacts with tiny mouse lives or try to load up one mouse with another's brain?"

Her finger traced back and forth across the small plastic boxes. "How can we find out? That would explain a lot about O'Brien and why he wants to keep this for himself. I mean, storing yourself is one thing. Stealing a body is another."

"Nasty thought. O'Brien's brain riding around in some kid's head-case."

She glanced down at the floor. Her eyes came up to meet his. "Would you do it? I think I would. Plenty of brain-dead pretty girls out there."

"Really? Murder?"

She shrugged. "I'd think about it. Especially when I hit sixty."

"Anyway, we don't know if they can do it."

She held her hands up at shoulder level, palms up. "No, seriously. How can we find out? If they're close to a solution, the value of the Artifacts skyrockets. And the danger."

He tugged at his eyebrow. "We read their lab records, the memdevices lying here."

"Yes! I found a box of new flashchips back over there. Something to copy to. I'll grab a desktab and start with the latest."

"Good idea. You'll make us rich yet.

"While I slave away, what will you do?"

"Break into this cabinet here. They'd keep their really good paraphernalia in that. It's just a single-keyed lock." He slipped out a book of picks and chose his standard probe. "Too fat." Sliding out a probe with a long triangular point, he tried again. "There's one pin—can't reach the second." He chose another thin-tipped pick with a shorter triangle. "Uh, yeah honey, that's it. Too easy."

She let out a tchaa sound. "Would you please hush? Don't you know it's rude to talk to yourself when you have to share space with your co-workers?"

"Don't go all giddy. Any luck with the memdevices?"

"They're downloading fine."

He opened the door with a simple handle. "Man-sized Artifacts! I've seen these babies before."

She gazed into the box where two large Artifacts nestled in foam. "Okay, now what?"

"You pack them away. I want to fake up decoys, something that will satisfy a quick scan."

"Secretive gozo, aren't you? There's a box of Artifact parts in the first bench. Second or third drawer."

Robko found parts and assembled two boxes. "You haven't seen any crystal packing, have you?"

"Not me. You could empty out Mouse Artifacts."

"No, they'd catch that. I'll use your artificial sweetener." He packed the fakes, snuggled them into the rectangular foam pads and locked the cabinet. "Ready?"

"Ready." She swung the vault closed. "Now what?"

"Clean up where we dusted for prints."

"What if we let the chimp out instead? Like his door wasn't locked? Anything messed up gets blamed on him."

"A stroke of genius! After that, you can guess the drill. Crawl back up in the ceiling and wriggle our little asses back down the shaft into the air conditioner blast. And last but not least, explain the alarms being off by tripping the circuit breakers for the building."

"And get out."

"And get out. We saw them park the trailer at the dock and leave it. It should still be there. We'll slide up in the cloth cradles and wait for the truck to come back."

"What if it sits there for days?"

"Okay already. I'll check manifests."

She bobbed her head. "Let's hope it doesn't turn too cold tonight.

Sleeping in those cradles could get nippy."

"Want to share a cradle? Purely to avoid hypothermia."

"Purely?" she said, eyebrow cocked up.

※

"We're on the wrong tack," Thomas said. Florescent lights rained down a warm yellow that denied the midnight hour. They slouched around the cluttered conference table. Over at the electronic wall, another three teammates monitored Tran Cam data.

Angie picked up the bottle of scotch she had brought and poured another shot into her coffee cup. "That's what I want to hear... that we're doing it all wrong."

Thomas loved it. She could have been so right for him. "No, I'm serious here. We can make a new start. What if we chased this guy based on his profile? If you tell me what we know about him, you're telling me what he will do. Then we watch where he goes to do it, not the whole damn world."

"Want a drink?"

"Sorry, I can't. I'm on a good flight right now. Don't want to crash land."

She rolled her eyes. "You mean you don't want to poison yourself and die in your own vomit. Okay, here goes... creeping up on thirty-four-years-old but acts twenty-one. Party animal, professional thief, appears to do a couple of jobs a year, then fritters away all his money in between. Loves motorcycles and speed, which should demonstrate aggressive tendencies, but otherwise appears passive—the second or third stringer on a job, not the lead. He can live in a loft with expensive possessions or a flea trap in Chinatown."

Thomas grinned, egged her on. "Keep going."

Angie coughed and snuck a peek at him. "A loser addicted to barbiturates."

"Bite me, Ms. Tommo."

"I'm here at midnight just to be insulted?"

"Keep going."

"He could wiggle under a crack in the door and hang by his fingers from thumb tacks in the bulletin board. Short, small, and muscular."

"Uh, huh. Keep going."

221

"Runs around with a prostitute and married her. Has no hang-ups about her career. She worked all the time he lived with her—so he must not care."

"Interesting. Amoral, but probably not a pimp."

"If she's his type, then he likes the kind that dresses in black, lives to shock you, and looks like your fifteen-year-old kid sister... or brother."

"I don't get anything there."

"No, because you're pure hetero. Zlata is also ethnic. He's real Polish, from one of the old neighborhoods. Had a best friend from his school days, but hadn't seen him since said friend went into The Church. Hasn't been near home and friends since the friend died and he ran."

"Didn't die—was murdered. Anything else?"

"Won't give up the Artifact. Insanely lucky—he's beaten a very expensive team over and over."

Thomas winced. She was right, as usual.

"Okay, your turn," she said, and sipped at her scotch.

"He's on the run, but he's smart enough to know he can't run forever. He hasn't tried to negotiate, so he must have something else in mind."

She twirled a pencil in a circle on the tabletop. "Makes sense."

Thomas paused, continued. "He may have stashed money here and there—the accounts we seized showed about fifty grand each. We keep cutting the money off behind him, so he must be low on funds."

"Maybe. It's a plausible progression."

"If he runs out of money, he goes back to work. If that's the case, Zlata not only evades us—he practices his profession at the same time. Very cool head."

She snorted. "It's the barbiturates. They're calming."

He stared across the table at her, watching the way her hair made shadows around her face, revealing it as she flipped her hair back. "They work for me. So we've never seen him act aggressively, but we've never seen him cornered. Would he pick up a gun? Under what circumstances?"

"Problematic. Approach with care." She stretched and glanced over at the three staffers who manned surveillance consoles, then turned back. "That all you got?"

222

"Hmm, critical. Some might say harsh. Here's my last point. Why has he never practiced his profession on us? He's got to want to hurt us bad by now."

"He already has the Artifact, even if he doesn't know what it is."

"I made it pretty clear to Father Mirko; the Artifact was Zlata's ticket out, and Zlata didn't buy it."

"So?"

"Why didn't he give it up?" Thomas leaned forward, locked his fingers together, and sighed. His eyes flew open—he jerked bolt upright, pointed a finger at her. "Because he doesn't have it!"

Angie jumped on it. "You're right. He sold it. We've been chasing the wrong man. We should be after the guy who bought the Artifact from Zlata."

"Why didn't he steal it back? Is he more afraid of the new owner than of O'Brien?"

"Speculative."

"Indeed. Then back to our best guess. Zlata doesn't have the Artifact anymore, but he knows it's his way out."

"So what?"

"He needs an Artifact. Not THE Artifact."

She shook her head. Then cocking her face over, she smoothed the lipstick in the corner of her mouth. "You've got something there. But do you want Zlata or the Mister X who has the original Holy Grail, O'Brien's loaded Artifact?"

"Zlata knows X. We don't."

"Okay, we need him no matter what, and he needs an Artifact."

"Zlata will be coming to steal an Artifact from O'Brien. He'll use it to change the game."

She drummed her fingers on the arm of the chair. "Yes. Maybe. We should search our own house."

"Damn! This last month we've combed the metropolitan US with Tran Cam—in the hope the woman or Zlata would stroll into an airport or a bank. But he's coming to us."

"Even if you're right, we can't ask thousands of employees to watch out for Zlata. We could never explain it."

"No, but Tran Cam software could scan our own cameras."

She jerked her head. "Oh." They both thought about it. "It's Georgia. Remember Jean and the fifty million dollars? That's where

O'Brien had his Artifacts built."

"Has to be. We'll hook the Georgia cameras into here, have the software watch."

"So what does this mean?" She shot him the knowing glance. "Not operationally. I mean, politically."

"We have to tell Garland."

Angie nodded. "But not about the Artifact. And we don't tell LeFarge anything."

"Right. One other thing."

"What's that?"

"I used to think LeFarge was our biggest vulnerability. Now I think it's O'Brien. You agree?"

She laughed. "For sure. He'll be the death of us."

Thomas felt his mouth fake a smile, but it was a skeleton's grin.

Chapter Twenty-Seven: Club Gonos

Down in an industrial yard in New Jersey at midnight, close to the corridor that sucked the commuters along into NYC, Robko and Sibyl stashed the trailer and the motorcycle. They had gone to a self-storage business where Robko had once concealed the rewards of a specialty rack. An eccentric owner of fifty chicken stands had misplaced his Wild West gun collection. Robko searched for the right fence, so he had to keep the lock-up for some time. In his weekly checks, he found that the yard was run by a Pole out of Chi, a careful, quiet man who became his friend.

It wasn't going well. She had raised the door and stood by, trying to guide him and the trailer in a simple backing maneuver. He had lined up to the right of the aisle, prepared to turn the ninety degrees left and slide into the storage unit. Theoretically the trailer would fit, but he had yet to prove it.

She shook her head. He had backed and filled so many times that the trailer door was centered on a concrete post of the next storage unit over, and the van was practically touching the doors on the other side. She'd shouted till her throat hurt, but the slump-shouldered figure in the driver's seat over-corrected every time. "Tchaa. I can't stand it." She strode up to the driver's window and repeated, "I can't stand it."

"You can't stand it? You're not doing the work. Maybe if we unhitched the trailer and rolled it in."

"Only if you want to unload it first. It's too heavy. All those cars you stole, you never had to back up?"

"No, you just drive them out straight ahead. I never even had to parallel park."

"Get out of the car."

"What?"

"I said—get out of the car."

He opened the door and clambered out. He came across as whipped, hanging his head. She jumped in and slammed the door. She turned hard left, and with a jerk headed off down the aisle. Now that she was in charge, she felt a grin pop onto her face. She hummed as she drove clear around the block of units and came back to their lock-up, centered in the middle of the aisle. She cranked first one way to start the turn, then the other to straighten out. The trailer centered up on the door. She pulled forward to straighten up the van, then as she peered left and right at the side mirrors, she backed the trailer smoothly into the unit.

"How the hell did you do that?"

"I grew up with horses. I've been backing trailers since I was fourteen."

In the end, the Bronx flop turned out to be just another place: the difference was that Thomas was locked up with himself. He didn't mind the faded furnishings, the old-fashioned bathroom, or the kitchen with a buildup of grease and grime in every crack. He didn't mind the sour smell of take-out in every other apartment or the stale fragrance of urine in the stairwells. Here he would be himself for as long as he could stand it.

Like the other inhabitants, he found life in his rooms less troubled than life outside them. Rather than cultivate other people, he talked to himself. He hid from LeFarge. There was safety in solitude.

Nine at night. In the elevator lobby, he kicked something into the corner. He wandered over to find a jink pipe, tarred with its last burn. "Drain Cleaner," he said aloud. "Thunderbolt." Coming down the graffitied corridor from the elevator, he saw the bare light bulb that blazed in its socket outside his door. "Edison's security," he said. He peered up at the door jamb and saw the edge of black paper protruding out against the brown enameled door. "No one in or out." He read new graff scratched deep into his door, "My Kingdom Is Gone."

"Really charming. Obscure too. Should look that up."

Inside, he threw a frozen pizza into the microwave and spilled a couple of pills onto the countertop. He flipped on the TV. He scanned around channels while the microwave groaned. "Nothing."

In an hour, he felt as dark and small as the room. He picked up his throwaway and, blanking the video, dialed Angie. No need for her to see what a dump this was. "Angie, still at work?"

"Just walking through the shift change for the surveillance team."

"We had a good day, didn't we?"

"Yes. Memdevice number nine arrived back and is under lock and key. The humdrum searches didn't produce anything new, but your ideas on chasing Zlata inside O'Brien's empire have perked up the whole place."

"Our ideas."

"You make the intellectual leap; I execute. I don't have to do strategy."

He could imagine her, pacing back and forth in front of the electronic wall, waving good night to her departing troops. "You're very humble tonight."

"Oh, and did I mention, I keep you from falling apart?"

"Speaking of falling apart, I need to break free. I can feel the walls closing in."

"You're not talking about clubbing again, are you?"

"It's all about looking for Zlata, in case he's back in town. I've done ten clubs in twenty days. It's time to get lucky."

"You know the private detectives are also looking."

"Waste of money. They don't have the feel. I picked up the name of a new club up near Central Park yesterday—it's wild enough to draw him. Want to grab a cab and meet me there? Not like it's a date."

He could hear her chuckle on the other end. "You got that right."

About nine, Robko and Sibyl rambled over to the new club from their high-rise residence hotel. Robko had found the club venue that morning when he asked the doorman, "What bar would terrify you to learn your daughter hung out there?"

The answer bounced back quick and sure. "Club Gonorrhea. Other side of the Park."

As they stepped up to the brute at the door, Sibyl said, "I wish my mother could see this, an exclusive, bouncer-protected, sexually transmitted disease. Oh, the irony of it all."

227

"All the signs are good. A bruiser on the door, a lot of people dressed in black, and the pavement outside jumping up and down from the bass."

"I wouldn't want to live in the apartments upstairs."

He dropped a fin on the guy at the door, and they slipped into the front of the queue. "This is just to show our appreciation."

"Of course, sir. You won't remember me, but I'm Freddy. You dropped into the Dumpster a couple of times when I worked the door there."

Sibyl glanced at Robko. "And I don't think he means your place in Chinatown either."

He snuggled her arm and leaned his head over to touch hers. "I'm betting you think you're funny and all."

Inside, the Club owners had decorated the place in sheet aluminum spattered in red paint. He inhaled a muddy river of perfume and cologne, sharpened up by the tang of spilled wine. When they gazed up, they viewed the usual ducts and lights painted black. They also stared at upside-down furniture attached to the ceiling.

She said, "Makes me dizzy."

"Try it while you're flying on something pharmaceutical—it's a mind-neuker. I feel like I'm walking on my Ma's ceiling." He could feel an associated memory teasing at the back of his brain, but the klono he had swallowed kept it at bay, mysterious and delicious.

She started snapping pictures—two hipsters visibly preened for her camera.

The band portrayed itself as a New-York-tripper on a hillbilly turnaround. Two men swapped through a succession of instruments and traded vocals back and forth while a drummer attacked the world's smallest trap set. The nasal tenors droned on about the hills of North Carolina, the virtues of home, and the methamphetamine cure for love sickness. Three horn players gave the whole mix a Motown vibe. She leaned in to Robko's ear. "It's possibly the worst band I've ever paid a cover for. It's Elmo Goes to Hollywood and Plays with La Cantina Brass."

"This isn't the real band. The real band is in the back."

"Huh?"

"See on the back wall... set far apart?"

She peered through the gloom. Three doors painted with spatter-

and-drip. Each door had its own label, Doors Number One, Two, and Three."

"Door One," he shouted in her ear, "is a martini, cigar, and hookah bar designed to give you black lung and cirrhosis in under two hours. Door Two leads out a back patio bar, which will still be packed even after first snow. And Door Number Three...."

"— is where the real band plays. How did you know?"

"I videoed this afternoon. Talked to a woman who claimed to be Joan Jett."

"Impossible. She'd have to be seventy-five by now."

"Mick is still alive. Shall we see what's behind Door Number Three?" They wended their way back—the thick gluey crowd, more interested in the lobby band, slowed them in a quicksand of revelry.

Door Three banged open abruptly and a mob of twentysomethings boiled out. Door Three drowned out North Carolina with a tidal wave made of power thrash hyped on steel drums. They let the mob by before wiggling down the corridor.

Thomas and Angie had met at the front bar and percolated into the back. She had given the band an hour of her time based on the lead singer. Angie told him that the singer looked a lot like a young Blondie and appeared alluringly surly. After the hour though, Angie pointed down into her drink.

He bent toward her. "What?"

The ice had melted. He stared. A standing wave of bulls-eyes made a resonant connection—a psychic link between her scotch-and-soda and the bass player.

"I'd like a civilized drink," she shouted, "in a civilized place, where the staff doesn't smell of hair gel and sweat."

"Are you sure? It gets better the later you stay." The band perched on scaffolding above their head, not six feet away. He could smell perspiration dripping off the band. The music rolled out so loud, his senses felt confused, like the sweat had mixed with the percussion.

"You mean as I get drunker and the music gets louder?" The crowd seethed around them, jostled them as they scrunched together around their tiny table.

229

Making a trumpet of his hands, he shouted into her ear. "I hear the third set has been used for the soundtrack of an indie sci-fi movie—*The Destruction of Tokyo*."

"Then I'm definitely sure. You'll buy me a bottle of champagne, and we'll get two rooms in one of those exclusive Central Park hotels. We can be in to work early tomorrow."

He shrugged, jumped up, and turned to lead the way. As they wove down the hall through a crowd to the lobby bar, he shouted to her over his shoulder, "I bet the Fire Marshal didn't sign off on this hallway." With a jarring thump, he ran full into someone. It was Zlata! Zlata had sandy hair and two eyebrows instead of one, but it was him all the same. Thomas held his palm up. Zlata paused and rocked on his heels. From his greater height, Thomas leaned down and shouted, "We haven't met, but we know each other. I'm Thomas Steward, and you're Robert Thomas Dragomir Zlata.

A honey-haired woman stepped past Zlata and seized Thomas's hand. He found himself on his knees on the floor, with a high likelihood of his thumb and index finger snapping. With her other hand, she grabbed him by the scruff of hair on top of his head and jerked his chin up and his head back.

"Sibyl," shouted Angie, grabbing her shoulder. "Don't do it. He's trying to save you, like he tried to save Mirko."

The crowd backed up behind them in the hall. Robko heard, "Make a hole… out of the way, assholes." Volume and temperature were rising. He didn't give a shit. Robko watched the two women glare each other down. He wondered—would it escalate to a fight? He spotted the moment the tension broke—there, Sibyl cocked her head, the other woman nodded. With a guttural snarl, Sibyl released the tall man kneeling before her. She wiped the hair gel off her hand onto his shoulder.

Robko swayed on his feet, both from the scene and from the trank. "Thomas Steward, huh? Get up, you're blocking the road." He jammed a hand under Thomas's armpit and threw him back on his feet. "We'll want to talk." He shouldered the man to the right, towards the restrooms.

Sibyl crowded up behind him. "Jesus, if there was ever a time to run, Robert, this is it!"

"No. Let's see what happens. Where did you learn to do that thing with his thumb, anyway?"

"It's part of my profession, handling the clientele."

"That's how you treat the clients?"

The woman behind Sibyl said, "I bet some of them like it."

They huddled together, a foursome crowded into a small restroom hallway of a basement club in NYC. "Now this is funny," said Robko. "How did you find us?"

Thomas held out his hands palm up. "I've been stalking the clubs. We listen to the same music. It's a small borough."

Sibyl said, "Yeah, only about five million people."

Robko pointed at Angie. "What did she mean?"

Thomas shook his head. "Mean what?"

"That's what I'm asking."

"I didn't hear—I was distracted." He nodded towards Sibyl. "She was ripping my hand off."

Angie leaned towards Robko. "I said… Thomas plans on saving you."

Thomas's mouth fell open.

She shot him a pitying glance. "Oh please. It's the only way to explain how you behaved in Ithaca."

Robko stared hard at the two before him, first right, then left, and considered what each one might be thinking. "We need somewhere to sit down, some place where the drunks don't bump us on the way to the crapper."

They settled on a hotel bar nearby. They agreed they needed time to talk with their partners first. "See you there," Thomas said.

Robko nodded. "If she doesn't talk me out of it. Otherwise, good-bye—it's been a shocker."

Thomas and Angie led off. They stepped down the pavement in the chilled October air. There was an organic smell mixed in with the usual bus fumes and urine tinge of city atmosphere. Thomas thought it might be rotting chestnut leaves.

She linked her arm through his so she could peep over his shoulder and watch the couple behind.

He said, "What are they doing?"

"Fighting. Well, she's hissing at him."

"Hope they get it sorted out before they join us."

Angie said, "What do you hope to get out of this?"

"Frequent flier miles?"

"Seriously."

With a huge grin, he laid out his brilliant idea. "The name of the man who has the Artifact now."

"That would be something."

Her tone flattened him out. She acted less than impressed by his brilliance. "Of course, Robko has to gain something in return for telling us. A hundred thousand and immunity might be okay with him."

"But—can you make that promise?"

"The question is whether I can keep it. I need LeFarge on a chain, and I need a guarantee from O'Brien."

"But LeFarge has his talons into O'Brien." She clawed the air with her free hand and seized her own throat.

"Yeah, just like that... and don't think Dennis Malley O'Brien appreciates it either. He's wondered how to get rid of LeFarge when all this ends. I could just let nature take its course, and even hurry it up a bit."

"But Thomas—" she said.

He sighed. "You're full of objections tonight."

"You're the Governor's go-to guy. He'll ask you to arrange the killing."

"I wonder if I've sunk that low." He dropped his head, shook it, and laughed.

"You could think of it as self-defense."

"Yes, but would I be rationalizing? Better to face it—I would love LeFarge to be killed. I want him dead more than I want to run my own company." They nodded at the doorman, turned into the hotel, and strolled across the marble and steel space to the lobby bar.

She peeked over her shoulder again. "They're coming in now."

"I know. I can see them in the reflection."

"Getting crafty, are we?"

"I saw it on TV. I've been practicing to see if LeFarge or his goons

232

are following me." They asked for a four-top table away from the windows and ordered champagne and a tonic-and-lime. Angie made sure it was a good champagne.

Thomas said, "It'll be a minute. Since we chose the hotel, he'll scout the lobby and check for exits. I've certainly got time...." He fished a bluebird out of his pocket and threw it to the back of his tongue. He swallowed it dry and grimaced as it stuck in his throat.

"I wish you wouldn't do that, not right now. It really pisses me off."

※

Robko made reasonably certain they could escape if needed—he spotted three bolt-holes. He and Sibyl hesitated in the door and then threaded their way through the bar to the table in the back. Sibyl eased into the chair opposite the Italian-looking woman. Robko pulled the last chair out across from Thomas. He kept his legs out from under the table, kept back where he had room. It reminded Robko of two chess games at the same table. A waiter bustled over, delivered a bucket of champagne, a flute, and a lowball with ice and lime floating in it. He hovered, waiting to hear from Robko and Sibyl.

Thomas leaned forward on his forearms and clasped his hands together. "It's occurred to me not everyone has been introduced. I'm Thomas Steward, and this is Angelina Tommo. Angie, let me introduce you to Robko Zlata and Sibyl Boxwood."

Robko nodded solemnly, feeling like an owl. He already knew Thomas, had in fact ransacked his possessions. This Angie was new to him.

Angie waved her hand at the bucket and said to the other woman, "Do you want to share my champ?"

Sibyl ripped out an evil little grin. "You read my mind."

They all turned to Robko. "Thanks, I'll just have a club soda." The waiter disappeared. "So, you work for O'Brien."

"You already knew that," said Thomas. "What's more important—I represent the good-cop side of the conversation. There's a bad cop who also works for O'Brien."

In spite of himself, Robko said, "Captain Egan LeFarge."

"You are well informed."

"Sometimes." Did Thomas know his desktab had been downloaded in Ithaca? The blond man hadn't said anything revealing yet.

"I believe you used to have something O'Brien prizes highly. It's a small Lucite box with some white contents. It's called the Artifact. I've already asked you for it once before, through the priest."

"You make two assumptions. One, that I once had this Artifact, and two, that I've passed it on."

Thomas said, "You're fishing to see what Father Mirko told me. That's an easy one—your friend was loyal. Logic says the Artifact has moved on."

Robko bent his swizzle straw in half, tied it into one knot, a second, and a third. "Well, I admit I don't have it."

The tall man watched him, solemn, remote. "Progress. Now I'll give you something in return. Nobody in O'Brien's organization knows you're in New York except Angie and me. I can make that part of the deal."

"Deal?" asked Sibyl.

"I'm ready to offer you a lot of money for the current location of the Artifact."

Robko sputtered into his club soda. "Maybe you won't after I tell you."

Angie explained, "We surmise you sold the Artifact to someone very powerful. We believe you're more—cautious—about offending your customer than offending O'Brien."

Robko watched Sibyl scratch at the white tablecloth with one carmine-colored nail. They both knew how wrong Angie was. "You make a lot of assumptions, don't you?"

The tall, blond man said, "Deductions, more-like. They led us to Chinatown, to Ithaca, and to Atwater Village."

Robko and Sibyl shot each other a hooded glance. They hadn't known about Thomas and California—a dangerous man if he had tracked them that far.

"So what I can do," continued Thomas, "is offer you one hundred thousand dollars for the name of the man who bought the Artifact from you."

Robko answered, "A hundred flip is pretty lightweight, don't you think? We do know what the Artifact does. It's an electronic soul, and we know O'Brien has downloaded himself into it."

Sibyl added, "And even if it was more than a hundred, how could we ever spend it? The bad cop wants us dead, not bought off."

Thomas barely moved his head in acknowledgement. "Ah. Two objections. I'll deal with the last one first. LeFarge is blind without Angie and me; he depends on us for intel. Unless you do something stupid, LeFarge won't be able to find you on his own."

"Lovely. We get to stay on the run," said Sibyl.

Robko sat still as a stone. He thought, *Make the tall man work harder.*

"The Governor could be flexible on price as long as he gets value for dollar."

Robko felt his pulse kick up. The tall blond man had missed it. Steward thought it was about the money. Robko said, "Are you O'Brien's exclusive negotiator?"

"Yes."

Robko caught Angie's twitch. "Well, that was a no. Maybe you can arrange to be the sole negotiator when you talk to your boss."

"But what would I tell him?"

"You've already agreed not to mention we're here in the City— your opening move. Tell him two more things. We have to have his protection, unconditionally."

"That can be arranged if the return on investment is high enough."

"The second thing, the deal structures different than you laid out." Robko watched the blond man incline his head over the table cloth, like a crane.

Thomas said, "How so?"

"The first Artifact didn't get sold—it got destroyed." Sibyl's shoe cracked into his shin. "Down the sink, into the river."

Angie shook her head. "So you have nothing to bargain with."

Buried in an awful silence, the four of them watched each other. The ice in the bucket settled around the champagne, louder than breaking glass.

The blond man made a laconic flicking motion with his hand. "That changes my plan, but not my objective. I still want to get you and this woman out from under, somehow."

That stopped the conversation. Robko hid his surprise by sipping at his club soda. He tried on an attitude of nonchalance. "Why?"

"No reason you would believe."

"You gotta give us a reason to trust you."

"Trust me… or face LeFarge. But you have to give me something to work with."

"Okay."

"Okay, what? Something to work with, or back on the run?"

"Okay, we can lay out something. While the first Artifact is gone, we have the second and third. We will return one of them to you… for fifteen million dollars. Bearer bonds. I like bearer bonds. No wire transfers you can follow."

Thomas rocked back in his chair; his forehead wrinkled up like tree bark. "Second and third?"

Angie, no negotiator, chuckled. "How did you get them?"

Sibyl coughed to block her own laugh. "Inside info. Picked them up in Georgia. They're still there as far as the locals know."

Thomas said, "You demanded millions. And you said you'd return one of them. Why not ask double the money and turn over both?"

Robko tented his fingers. "The third is our insurance policy. If anything happens to us…."

"So melodramatic," said Sibyl, "but so true." She drained her flute.

Robko said, "If we don't make the usual vidi call on a regular basis, the third Artifact goes direct to O'Brien's rivals."

"And who would you think that is?" asked Angie.

"Carstairs in London. Or Thurgall in San Diego. They'd have the resources to develop it."

Robko could see a grin teasing the corner of Thomas's mouth. The tall man said, "Wow. I think you have an opening gambit. Let's see what our side offers in response. I'll call the Governor." He picked a table near the door and faced away from them. Robko focused on his back, trying to read something from the set of the shoulders, the tilt of the head.

Angie fished the champagne out of the bucket, let the water drip off, and offered Sibyl a refill. "And I thought tonight might be boring. What shall we chat about? Where did you two lovebirds meet?"

Thomas videoed O'Brien's priority number. "Sir, Thomas here. I've got some interesting news." Thomas could see O'Brien on the iMob,

236

dressed in a full tuxedo, leaning over the camera. A gilded ceiling framed O'Brien's ursine head. *Dinner at the mansion?*

"Wait, I'm in a party; let me leave the table." Thomas heard the rustle of cloth as O'Brien clasped the vidi to his body, then dead air. Finally, "Go ahead." It appeared O'Brien had locked himself in the toilet—blue, hand-painted tiles flocked with fleur-de-lis framed his squat face.

"I'm going to voice-only and off speaker. I'm not alone here." He switched the speaker and screen off and held the device to his ear.

"What do you have? A new lead on a memdevice?"

"No, sir, much better. I'm in contact with Robko Zlata."

"What! Where is he? Can you lay your hands on him?"

"No sir. I don't know where he is—he called me. He blocked Caller I.D."

"Damn. Why did he call? Does he want to sell the Artifact?"

"I only have bad news, I'm afraid, but I do have a way forward. The Artifact was destroyed."

"What! He killed my Soul?" O'Brien was barking into the phone.

"In a manner of speaking. He destroyed a recording of you. There's more. He has stolen two other Artifacts from your lab in Georgia." Thomas shoved the iMob tight against his ear. He counted. One. Two. Three.

O'Brien's voice sounded level, dry. "You called it bad news. You don't exaggerate."

"We can have one of the Artifacts back...," he took a breath. "for fifteen million dollars."

"And the other? I have to have them all."

The crisis point. "He keeps the third as a hostage. If we renege, he turns it over to Thurgall. Or Carstairs."

"Goddamn! I'll have that little son-of-a-bitch's balls!"

"Maybe. Most probably not. He has a pretty strong hand, don't you think?"

"I need to consider this. I'll call you back in five minutes."

This was bad. O'Brien never considered anything; he made snap judgments. This was a stall.

Thomas hurried on before O'Brien cut him off. "I know it's distasteful, but think about it. For a flat fee, you get the Artifact back, and it's no longer roaming around out there. You get it exclusively; we don't have to hunt Zlata anymore, and the problem goes away."

"He wins and I lose. I told you, I'll call you back. Stay ready." O'Brien cut the connection. Thomas glanced at the time on the face of his mobile and trudged back to the table. "He said maybe. He'll call back. So what have you kids been talking about?"

"Italian shoes," said Sibyl.

Robko gave a twisted grin. "We've been dancing around whether or not to trust you."

"Hmm. I have the same question about you, you know." Thomas stared at him.

Robko said, "I'm an open book. I steal things and sell them; then I live off the money. I'm a trustworthy thief with a heart of gold."

This guy was more and more interesting. "And how do you see us?"

"You steal things too, only legally. Steal big enough, and it's called a takeover."

Thomas laughed. "You have a pretty good idea about it—we do steal companies." He tapped the tablecloth. "We'll all have to give it some thought, about this trust thing."

"Right. You could be my inside man, or you could be leading me into a trap."

"And you could ditch me halfway through the deal, and O'Brien would probably have me killed."

"It has occurred to me we could take our business elsewhere." Robko gazed across the room, his face as smooth as glass, his eyes opaque.

"But that leaves your issues with O'Brien unresolved." Thomas's phone rang. "Excuse me. I should take this call, don't you think?" He tapped on the screen, held the phone up to his ear. "Yes?" He strolled away from the table, towards the bar.

"O'Brien here. Are you sure he'll make the deal?"

"No guarantees. Definite risk. LeFarge killed his best friend, and we've hounded him across America. We've pretty much ruined his life. The reason he'd take the deal is first, he gets rich and second, you're off his back."

"Hmm. You're trying to convince me to buy my own Artifact back."

"You've already spent a lot trying to seize it. Buying it is a lot less

238

work and more certain." All true, but would O'Brien get past his power trip and see the obvious?

"And he keeps the third." O'Brien's voice sounded like it was full of grit.

"Build another one."

"That's not it, and you know it. He holds the third one over my head."

"Then, take all the action away. After we retrieve what we can, take the Artifacts public. Sell them like TVs, like iMobs."

"Bull. That's only money. Can you imagine how much power I would have as the only immortal on a planet of the dying?"

"Ah. That's what I figured." *Just go on-and-on while the rest of us feed the worm.*

"Immortals need servants and agents too, Thomas. You're taken care of, as long as you protect the secret."

Thomas grimaced. He wanted to run a company, not play butler for O'Brien. "What do you need in order to proceed with this negotiation?"

"I need to know the two Artifacts have in truth been taken."

Thomas's words came so quick they stumbled. "I don't think you should alert the staff at your lab. It could leak out into office gossip."

"Give me some credit here. I sent the lab director to check, just a minute ago. Only he will know."

"What else? What are my instructions as your negotiator?"

"First, offer him ten mill, and settle at twelve and a half."

"Understood."

"And tell him it takes time to get that much cash together."

"So it does."

"No, not really."

"Interesting." Vanity makes people tell you the damnedest things. O'Brien had millions in hand—under the mattress?

"Using the cash as an alibi buys me a couple of days. Tell him he has to bring the Artifact to me personally, at my mansion out on Long Island."

"He won't go for it. He'll want an exchange on neutral ground."

"Tell him he can have his money at my house, and I'll throw his mother in for free."

"You kidnapped his mother?" Thomas's mind stumbled; he felt dizzy. O'Brien must have been working on this before the phone call, flushing Zlata out in his own wicked way.

"We began moving on it yesterday. LeFarge flew out to transport her back, and his man on the ground in Chicago may already have her, locked in the trunk of a car."

"Dennis, this is a very big mistake. Just give him the money out in the open. Don't snatch his mom."

"No. He might have gone to the Feds—"

"Doubtful. He's selling you something he stole. He wants money, not to bring you down."

"He's jerking me around and getting exactly what he wants." O'Brien sounded sure, not angry. "At least that's what he thinks."

"There's something you're not telling me."

"We'll make my deal, not his. I will give him a couple of mill for the second artifact—no skin off my nose. Then I start another negotiation on the spot. His dear old mom for the third artifact. Call me back when the little shit agrees to my price and my meeting place."

Silence shouted down the line. Thomas found himself at the window of the bar, staring out at the sidewalk and into the avenue beyond. For fully a minute, he held the dead phone to his ear. He turned and rejoined the table.

Robko watched the tall blond man in black, at ease, ambling back to the table.

"I've found a way around your trust issues," Thomas said.

Sibyl slapped her hands on the table. "What did he say?"

"Enough. Enough to get you to trust me."

She tossed her hair. "I can't think of a thing you could say that would earn our trust."

Thomas turned to Robko. "I can—full disclosure on my side and betrayal of my boss. O'Brien agrees to pay. Not the full fifteen—rather two. The horrible wrinkle is that he has Mrs. Zlata and will squeeze the third Artifact out of you in return for her life. He says he will pay you for the second Artifact, but somehow I doubt it. If it hasn't occurred to him yet, it will. He can take both Artifacts and pay nothing. He'll instruct LeFarge to kill your mother, and you, and Ms. Boxwood here."

Robko sat still, as motionless as death.

240

"As for me trusting you not to run, all that changed when your mother came into play."

Robko felt his head pound, his pulse like a hammer. He could hear his own voice, a long way away. "Do you know for sure he has my Ma?"

"No, not positively. LeFarge is on his way to Chicago to transport her back. O'Brien believed she had already been taken, but he wasn't certain."

Robko snatched out a vidi and called. After some time, he said, "No answer."

He dialed another number. The screen flicked on, and the interior of his mother's bar opened out. A young woman with french-fried blonde hair crowded the screen, her nose growing ludicrously huge. "Mira's Bar and Grill."

"Yeah, can I speak to Mrs. Zlata? This is her son, Robko."

"You're the son? Funny, I thought you would look like a real devil. She's not working tonight."

"Okay, gotta go." He punched in a third set of numbers. A heavy woman wrapped in an apron answered, her hair coiled and pinned up on her head. He jammed the phone in his ear. "Ciotka Mircea, it's your nephew Robko.—Yes, it's been a while. Listen, my Ma may be in trouble. I've tried calling the apartment, but there's no answer. Could you run across the street and up the stairs to check?—I'll call her phone in a couple of minutes.—Okay, thank you." He hung up. They all waited, quiet. In two minutes, he dialed again. "It's Robko.—It was? Unlocked or kicked open?—That's bad. It's best if you call 911. Right away. And Ciotka, don't say anything about me, okay?—Yes, I'll call later, I promise." He stared at Thomas. "He's snatched her. Now what?"

Fortune Turned

Chapter Twenty-Eight: Ephemeral Nature of Light

Thomas sank into the overstuffed chair and disappeared into its depths. He picked at the piping that ran around the cushion, fingers busy, nervous. He had made the decision. Then others took over. Things began to accelerate towards a point of incandescence, or blackness.

Suffolk County would have been a great summer holiday, but in November a cold wind blew off the water, and the locals had set, grim expressions. Through an open door into the next room, Thomas spied on Robko as he prepared gear and nestled it into a backpack. Angie perched at the desk in their room and called Garland on her iMob. Thomas watched the curve of her back, the bob of her head. He could pick out Garland's voice only as a murmur.

"Don, Angie Tommo here. I need a favor.—You know how you alerted me when LeFarge scrambled out to Ithaca?—We need the same again, a low risk thing. Could your people track his mobile for me today?—That's right. We just want to avoid any more, hmm, criminal responses to our information gathering.—Well, I can tell you that every time LeFarge swings into action, Thomas, you, and I get more jail time piled up.—This is really important, Don. We've done some favors for you in the past.—You'll do it?—Good. Your mobile has this number now. You can reach me day or night on it."

Satisfied she had persuaded Garland to do what she wanted, Thomas tuned out. Sibyl appeared in the open door carrying a first aid kit. "Only the standard stuff, Mr. Steward. Do you think we'll need anything else?"

"Call me Thomas. Anything worse, we'll need an ambulance, not Band-Aids. Mrs. Zlata—the thing that occurs to me—she'll need a change of clothes. If you could, ask Zlata what size his mother is and buy something for her to wear once we have her back here."

"Robert won't know, but I've met her and can guess. Sweatsuit and underwear, I think. I'll ask my phone to map me to the nearest department store."

He glanced at his iMob to check the time. "Be back by three—Robko and I leave for the marina then."

"Like we all don't know the timetable. You're both turds for leaving me behind."

He coughed into his hand to avoid the laugh. "I can live with that. Make sure you gas up the van while you're out. If we leave in a hurry, we may not want to stop for a long time."

"Yes sir, Mr. Boss Man, sir."

"And Sibyl...."

"Yeah?"

"Thanks."

Thomas knew he had to make the call, but he delayed, ran the possibilities through his mind. He knew it was a stall, just over-rehearsing. He gave a sigh and laughed at himself. He tapped his iMob and called O'Brien's private vidi. The Governor was backlit by some huge windows—Thomas couldn't really make out his face. "Hi, Thomas here. I just spoke to him. He's unaware you have his mother, as far as I can tell. He agrees to the deal, and he agrees to the meeting place."

"Why? You didn't think he'd go for it."

"I don't know why. Perhaps the size of the payout has made him foolish."

"Any chance we can just grab him now?"

Thomas shot a glance at Robko in the next room. "No, we don't know where he is. We know he's not too far though if he can be at your door on time. In-state, on his way into town?"

The Governor's head cocked over. It looked like a bowling ball in the half-light. "He goddamn better bring the Artifacts."

"I assume he won't bring the third Artifact. We'll have to send someone to retrieve it. It could be me, if you want."

"Naah. I'll send Egan direct from here."

"Should I come out to the house?"

"What, you and your scruples? Leave it to me and Egan."

Thomas tried on a smile, hoping it didn't look too fake. "Has LeFarge arrived yet?"

O'Brien leaned forward into the screen. "Why do you want to know? You his keeper?"

"No, I don't need to know where he is, just confirming loose ends. About ten in the morning you can expect Zlata at your front gate. Call if you need anything."

O'Brien disconnected.

Angie caught Thomas before he could move. "Corporate reports LeFarge is back in New York, in Manhattan. Not Long Island."

"Where do you think they have Zlata's mother?"

"If Security had said Bed Stuy rather than Manhattan, I would think their warehouse or fire station. But Manhattan? That says to me LeFarge sent his guys on with Zlata's mother and stopped off in town to do some business."

"Business? A few quick errands after a kidnap?" He couldn't fault her logic, but logic could fail.

"Think about it—they'll want the old woman there at the meeting to apply visible pressure."

"All right, once we leave here, call me if LeFarge heads towards the estate."

"Set your phone to vibrate."

"Already is."

"Something else." She jerked her head towards the other bedroom and dropped her voice. "Most of my cash and a card have disappeared. And I saw our Mr. Zlata hide a roll of bills in Sibyl's handbag."

Thomas delivered a crooked grin. "Isn't that sweet—he wants to make sure she's provided for."

"Does this mean you can't trust him?"

"You think I trust him? Mention it to Sibyl; ask for your money back. Her reaction should be interesting."

Zlata popped through the door with a metal hoop in his hand, about the size of a medium pizza. "Okay, Thomas. Down on the carpet and rehearse. This is the pipe size you'll crawl through. Next, we'll review the house plans again."

Dreamlike, the Adirondack chair floated white, luminescing on the brown grass by the water, catching light from the setting sun. They could see it for the last ten minutes as Thomas rowed across the cove. As he snatched glimpses over his shoulder, it gave him some flickering memory from childhood, some recollection of a similar luminescence on an Illinois lake long ago. A good feeling washed up into him as he tugged at the oars. He gave himself over to the repetitive motion. Robko perched in the back. He was hunched over with his butt planted on a cold, hard thwart in a stolen boat, one with the improbable name "Bright Lily" painted on its stern. Thomas remembered lilies on his mother's piano, remembered playing with toy soldiers under the black, comforting beast. Good omen.

Thomas coasted the last ten feet, so the prow kissed the breakwater that marked the edge of the estate and held the sea at bay. He backpedaled on one oar, so the boat came 'round. Robko sprang up, carrying the painter, and lay behind the slight berm to hide. Thomas followed, and they tied the boat up to a stake they had also stolen.

Robko said to Thomas, "Last chance. No need for you to risk it in there. You can wait for my return at the hotel... or your office."

Thomas thought, *And you could take the money, and Sibyl, and your mother, and run again.* He shook his head. "I'm going."

Robko splayed his hands out. "Seriously? You're not ready for this."

"Look, you don't know anything about boats. You needed me to get here. I need you to get me in."

Robko shrugged. "Easy for me... harder for you. You're sure there are no dogs?"

"No, the dogs would be a threat to the grandchildren."

He caught Robko's grin in the dusk. The flash of his mink-like teeth shown out. "If you're wrong—"

"Trust me. It's just the rent-a-cops and the security systems in the plans."

"And a six-pack of mercenaries and maybe LeFarge. Piece of cake. Time to move."

Robko led the way to the spear-topped wrought-iron fence and along its length. "Here, the drainage culvert. I'll wriggle through first. I'll drag the backpack behind me on a line. You slide in behind me on your back once I'm out the other side. Roll your shoulders back and forth like I taught you, and don't get your hips stuck. You'll bang your knees, but keep pushing with those big feet."

248

Thomas stared at the culvert end. "That's got to be smaller than fifteen inches." A lot smaller than he had expected.

Robko fished cutters out of the bag and held them up. "For the screen on the other end. What you really mean, Thomas, is a fifteen-inch pipe in the dusk shows up as smaller than the hoop you messed with in a brightly lit room. Don't worry; they'll jerk you out if you get stuck—and kill you." He lay on his stomach, extended the bolt cutters in front of him, and wiggled into the pipe like an eel.

With a heavy sigh, Thomas lay on his back and gatored into the pipe. A fetid smell surrounded him. He did bang his knees. A lot. In the middle, his shoulders and neck getting gritty with mud, he lost it. He slammed his head into the top of the pipe trying to sit up. He thrashed with his hands. His breath was a hoarse voice of panic. But then, he thought of the little man gone on ahead, getting his mother, running again while Thomas died in the pipe. The bastard.

At the other end, Robko hauled him out and pushed him into a bank of tall-growing currants. "See, wasn't so bad. Shuck out of those coveralls. They're covered in muck."

"Not so bad for you. You're a small guy. I have your promise we don't escape out the same way?"

"No promises. Now stuff both sets of coveralls back in the pipe." Robko pulled on night vision goggles and held out a pair for Thomas. "Still a lot of ambient light, but it will turn dark quick. I want to approach the house while daylight cameras are blind, before Security switches to infrared." In the dusk, the goggles made a glimmering curve across the top of his face. "Now, stick this bluetooth in your ear. I'll call your vidi."

They left the currant bushes and scrambled along the grass on their hands and knees to the terrace. Thomas heard the whisper in his ear. "The plans say they have proximity detectors every ten feet. We can make a path through them. Help me spot the first one."

"There. Two feet in front of you. It's a small black plastic cap at tile level."

"Gotcha," Robko whispered. "We'll avoid the house corners—floodlights on motion detectors. Place your feet where I do, and walk soft." They moved in a zigzag back and forth across the terrace. As they gained the house, Robko moved along the wall. "Not the doors or the regular windows. I want the sauna window. Saunas are hostile

249

environments for alarms—all the heat and moisture. They always turn off spa sensors, inside and out."

"Sure, like you said. But why do you have to tell me all this again?"

"I want you focused on me and the job, not your fear. Here we are." He chinned himself up to the high small window. "Yeah, as I expected. I need up on your shoulders, so squat down and take me onboard."

Thomas grunted with the weight. "What would you have done if I hadn't been here?"

"Climbed up to the brick cornicing and hung upside down." Robko had small tools in his hand. "Okay, they may be turned off, but let's shunt them out anyway. First the latch." He inserted a putty knife and with a twist, opened the lock. "Taping the contacts now. Good thing I'm a pro."

"You're a heavy pro."

"You're out of shape." Robko lurched up off of Thomas's shoulders and slithered into the small window. His voice, quiet and amused, echoed back through the dark rectangle. "Your turn."

Thomas strained himself up to the sill. He grunted and scrabbled with his toe tips and found himself on a face-first slide into the sauna. He puddled up on a bench as he landed. "How long do we have to wait here?"

"A long time. Until the house quiets down. Dusk helped sneak us in, but it's still early evening. We can wash the mud from the pipe off first and then settle down for a nap."

Thomas could feel muscles in his shoulders and even in his back twitch. Keyed up, hell, on fire. He couldn't make it through hours like this—he popped a yellow sleeper into his mouth.

Robko said in a whisper, "Don't you just love this stuff? I love a rack."

"Really? I'm so jittery I could puke." All of this just to keep an eye on the thief, to make sure it didn't all go wrong.

"Pity. Don't hurl on me."

Seven hours. Robko nudged him. "Safe enough to move."

Thomas went off to pee in the toilet adjacent to the sauna. "What's first, money or Mother?"

"If you're right, then she's locked up in the garage apartment, far away from the vault. We don't want to drag her around the house."

"If we're right about her location...."

Robko's voice was a murmur in the dark. "If not, we have to search everywhere. She'll have a guard—that'll give it away."

"Still sounds like a crap idea."

"Make the plan, repeat the plan, work the plan. Money, Ma, car."

Robko thought, *Same glitzy office he has in Manhattan. O'Brien must have a jimber for this type of thing.*

The walk-in vault hid behind a wall in his office, a wall covered by an ornate bookcase. Robko removed a handful of books at eye-level on one end and motioned to Thomas to do the same on the other end. "Search for a release. One end will be hinged, one will have a catch. If you find it, don't do anything; just tell me."

"I've spotted the catch," said Thomas. "It's a lever in the back of the case."

Robko joined him. "No alarm. How phunk! Amateurs."

The vault lay behind, protected by a single combination dial. Robko said, "Just like in the plans. Forty years old. I know it well." He positioned a punch by the dial and hammered in a dimple. He began to drill. In two minutes, he ran through the steel into the door. After that, short work. He inserted a tube and an earpiece and clicked his way through the combination. "Bearer bonds and cash only." He jerked four collapsible bags from the backpack, unzipped them, and shook them open.

The hidden vault revealed itself as big, as large as a Tribeca efficiency. "Holy Christ!" said Thomas. He had paced in ahead of Zlata to find art racked against the wall, a gun safe, jewelry boxes, and shelves covered in money and bonds. "There's a lot of paper in here."

"The bearer bonds are $5000 face value, but the money is in $100's. Bulky." Robko shuffled through two of the bundles. "Old money, not sequential. He must have hoarded it up for years. Look for another bag—there's too much for these."

"He's got aluminum suitcases."

"Better than nothing."

251

Thomas felt like a moose stumbling along behind the Polish thief. Zlata made no sound; Thomas made plenty. They toted the money through the quiet house, detoured away from O'Brien's private wing, and skirted the servants' quarters. They kept their eyes open for Ma Zlata's guard as they advanced.

The attached garage linked to the house through the kitchen, and they followed stairs up to the quarters above. At the top landing, Robko snuck his head forward by millimeters to peer around the corner. He moved back, pointed to his eyes, and pointed at Thomas. Thomas peered around the corner. A guard parked in a chair, leaned back against the wall, sleeping.

Robko slipped back down the stairs into the kitchen, Thomas on his heels. "We have to take this guy. Kram!"

"Is there a problem?"

"I just—hate the rough stuff. When we grab him, keep him down in the chair. Pin him to the wall."

Robko fished into his breast pocket and produced a syringe. He yanked the cap off and held his finger to his lips. The two men slunk back up the stairs, sidled into flanking positions on each side of the guard. With a mutual nod, they attacked him. Thomas seized him by the throat and wrist and tried to pin him into the chair and against the wall. Robko grabbed the other wrist and jammed the needle into his forearm.

The mercenary awoke with a bound, shook both men off like water off a dog. Thomas found himself on the floor while the guard kicked him in the gut, hard—and kept on kicking. The man towered over Thomas and dug under his arm. He pried a gun out. Robko jumped on the merc's back. Before the guard could shoot Thomas, the drug took over. The guard sank to his knees, carried Robko down with him, and collapsed onto Thomas.

"Christ!" said Robko. "I hate shit like this. You okay?"

"He's crushing me. You're no help. Roll him off me."

Inside the garage apartment, they found Robko's Ma, bolt upright in a chair, handcuffed to an old-fashioned radiator.

Thomas tried on a reassuring smile and said to Ma Zlata, "Hello again. We met in Chicago months ago."

She ignored him. Ma Zlata was not the nurturing big-lapped,

grandmother type. Life had shaped her small and hard, all elbows and knees. Sour wrinkles of dissatisfaction surrounded her mouth, and her upper lip had been corrugated by time. Henna hair surrounded her face.

Her head craned up at Robko. "Robko! I heard noise out in the hall. I hoped it would be you."

"I came to get you as soon as I could, Ma."

"It's your fault I'm here, isn't it, Robko? Your father may have been a crook, but at least he worked soft crime. You deal with all these thugs."

Zlata dropped to his knees and ferreted out the bolt cutters. He snipped the chain on the cuffs and released his mother from the radiator. He said, "They didn't clamp down too tight on these—I can wiggle the cutters under." With a grunting effort, he sheared the hardened steel. The bracelets fell away.

She said, "I'm going to the can right now. See if you can find me a cigarette. I haven't had one in hours."

In her absence, they dragged the guard into the bedroom, used zip ties to bind him, strapped tape over his mouth, and removed his handgun. Groaning with effort, they rolled him back behind a bed and straightened up, their faces beaded in sweat. "Do me a favor," said Zlata. "Help me find her that cigarette. It will improve her mood."

The guard, the room, the pockets of her coat held no cigarette. Thomas thought, *How bad can she be?*

The old woman stomped out of the bathroom. "All right, Robko. No cigi? Mary's bleeding heart! I'm dying here for a cigarette. What happens now?"

"We sneak down to the garage below and steal the biggest vehicle. We drive it out and crash the gates. We have friends who will meet us about ten blocks away."

"And I can go home?"

Thomas said, "Yes, this will finish it, one way or another." He tried to pat her on the shoulder; she wriggled out from under his hand like he had a plague.

"I'm talking to my son. Is that right, Robko, what he says?"

All right, Thomas thought, *She can be pretty hard-assed.*

Robko said, "I don't know. But I know we have to get you out of here."

Thomas said, "Maybe you should take her on down to the garage

253

and pick a car or truck. I'll ferry the rest of the bags." Zlata nodded, hoisted an aluminum suitcase, and grasped his mother by the arm.

She jerked away. "I ain't some old lady. I can walk by myself."

Robko ushered her down the stairs to the kitchen and to the garage hallway, shushing her all the way. He eased open the door to the garage stairs. Too late. A large man carrying an automatic weapon trudged up the stairs. He saw them and broke into a lumber. Robko locked the door and retreated up the short hallway to the kitchen, only to find another big man with a large gun. With a secretive glance up the stairs to the apartment, Robko glimpsed Thomas frozen on the landing. With a sigh, Robko dropped the case and raised his hands. All eyes were on him.

They pushed his Ma into a chair and jammed him up against the kitchen island, dug through every pocket, banged his balls searching his pants for a gun. As Robko lay bent over on his face with a gun pushed into his ear, one of the mercenaries videoed LeFarge. "Boss, it's Johnnie at the house."

"Yeah, I'll be there in a couple of hours."

"No, that's not why I called. We caught us a sneak thief. Same guy we expected tomorrow." Johnnie turned the screen around to show Robko pinned to the counter. "He was headed for the garage."

"Good. Great. Glad you got him—that saves us a lot of work tomorrow."

"He has the old woman and a suitcase full of bonds."

LeFarge's laugh rang out tinny in the kitchen. "My, my, Mr. Zlata. We can't trust you at all, can we? It's a shame we're on opposite sides."

"What'll we do now, boss?"

"I'll jump in the SUV and be right out. It'll take an hour. You wake up the Governor and lock everybody down in his study. No servants. Call me en-route when you've got everything in place."

"Roger that." Johnnie strode over to a landline on the kitchen wall.

The mercs dragged Robko and his mother to O'Brien's office and pushed them through the door. O'Brien leaned on the desk arrayed in paisley pajamas, swaddled in a silk bathrobe. Isobel Dupont huddled on the couch, dressed in a large man's shirt, her pale legs tucked up under her.

The Governor resembled a bear in a blanket. He recognized Robko and turned a pomegranate color. "What the hell is going on? What's that?" He indicated the aluminum case, and the merc brought it to him.

O'Brien threw it up on the desk. He popped the snaps and ripped up the lid. He gawked. Spinning on his heel, he swung the bookcase back and stared at the hole drilled in the vault door, the handle in the open position. They all watched his broad back. They waited to see what he would do.

O'Brien didn't even check inside. He turned, marched across the room, and thrust his face down into Robko's. "Where's the rest of my money?" He pitched his voice low, almost conversational, but there was a fleck of spittle that leapt out.

Robko prayed Thomas was already on the move. "It's in the bedroom where you kept my Ma."

O'Brien swung his big head towards the woman on the couch. "Isobel, did you know about this?" Still purple in the face, O'Brien spoke in a quiet voice, but with a growl.

She threw her dark hair back from her face. "How could I? You've had me under lock and key."

O'Brien swung his bulk back to Robko. "That right?"

"I broke in to bust out my Ma. Not her." Even staring straight at O'Brien, Robko tried to keep the whole room in focus. He spied one merc whispering to the other.

The mercenary approached the Governor. "We're supposed to call LeFarge. He's in the car on his way."

O'Brien, never prying his eyes away from Zlata, said, "Sure, go ahead."

The guard brought out his vidi and called. He toggled LeFarge onto speaker, "This is the situation, Boss. We've hogtied this Zlata guy and his mother, like I said. We've also scooped up a shiny suitcase, and Zlata says there's more in the apartment over the garage."

LeFarge's voice, tinny and artificial said, "How much more?"

O'Brien said, "Is that you, Egan? Not much, another suitcase maybe."

Robko stirred the pot. "Five bags. Maybe twenty million all

255

together, a lot of it in bonds. I had to make multiple trips to carry it all, and that's when your guys grabbed me."

A two-beat pause. LeFarge said, "Ah, Mr. Polack. Twenty mill? Does Zlata have the two devices on him?"

O'Brien grabbed the phone. "How did you know about the Artifact?"

LeFarge sounded cheerful. "Basic surveillance, Governor. But how many does Zlata have with him?"

"Just one." The merc handed up a Lucite box to O'Brien.

Robko's jaw hurt, he was biting down so hard. A shame he hadn't made a counterfeit.

"One is as good as two in these circumstances," said the hollow voice.

O'Brien replied, "I have to disagree with you on that, Egan. I need both of them."

"You do, but I don't. Men, this is what I want you to do. Shoot O'Brien in the gut, so he bleeds out nice and slow."

O'Brien's voice was sharp. "Egan, that's not funny."

LeFarge said, "I didn't mean it to be funny. I'm taking the money and the Artifact. Flashing millions around in front of me! Paying me chicken shit. My crew deserves better, and we're going to take it."

O'Brien's face fell open like the red maw of a grizzly. He displayed a string of spit from a canine to a lower tooth.

LeFarge repeated, "Shoot him." The merc closest to O'Brien fired twice. In the closed room, the gunshots deafened them all. O'Brien fell screaming to the floor, but it sounded thin, distant.

Isobel uttered a small shriek. Robko's mother gawped at O'Brien and staggered back a step from the man and his growing pool of blood.

LeFarge's voice rose out of the vidi. "Kill Zlata right now. I'm sick and tired of him. Then his mother." The mercenary leveled the gun at Robko and smiled. Nothing left to do but watch the end of the gun.

Stuck on the stairs, I watch Robko raise his hands, watch the whole thing go to hell. I can't believe we struggled this far only to have everything fall apart in a kitchen, like some soap opera. I see the tough old woman scrunched down in a chair and Robko laid out over the counter like meat being prepped for the grill. And me… hiding like a coward. Back, back, back up as quiet as I can, set the money down, and crouch at the top. Listen. Why don't these idiots realize one of them is missing, is up here tied up? When they do, they'll be up the stairs. They're calling someone. Bad news, it's LeFarge. Some IQ comes in play now. Dragging Mom and Robko away into the house. What should I do?

It pops into my head—prepare the getaway and then get them away. First, take the money, the bags and the suitcases. Run them down to the garage. Door. Steps. Stumbling. There's the one I want, an SUV the size of a delivery truck. Black and maybe armored. A huge massive chrome front. And it's parked near the door. I need a key, a key, not in the ignition. Ah, there, the chauffeur has a board with all the keys. This one, this one, no this one. That's it. Now open the back. Back and forth, throw in four bags and a suitcase. Now to go save Robko. Bad odds. Bad odds. Creep through this house like I know what I'm doing. Voices ahead. Follow the voices. They're in the office. O'Brien has discovered we snatched the twenty million. And that prick LeFarge giving orders over the phone. Running things over the damn phone from his damn car. There's Zlata and his mom stood up against the window. O'Brien near to her by the desk. The ass waves his hands. I bet he doesn't feel very much in charge now. The mercenaries' broad backs are like the shoulders of bulls. Facing into the room away from me… Oh Christ! LeFarge will cowboy the whole thing; he'll kill everybody and take the money. Why the hell doesn't O'Brien realize he's about to be dead? They shot him! Dig the gun out—the guard's gun. Pull it out—jerk it out! Pull the slide part back; jam a bullet into the chamber. LeFarge orders Zlata's death, and then it's her turn. Now or never. My heart is about to explode. Run into the room. Jam the gun into the back of the head of the first bull. Fire. Kill him! The gun kicks in my hand like it will fly away. Now I will get shot instead of Robko. I jerk the gun towards the second bull. Throw a shot his way. Miss! He doesn't turn at all. He holds that pistol out at Robko. His gun booms. Thank God he missed! No, a horrible red flower blooms—opening up Robko's face. He flies back. The son of a bitch! I'll kill him! Two feet away. Shoot once… shoot twice. His head flies apart.

I can hear her voice—Robko, Robko. Ma Zlata kneels beside him where he is crumpled up on the floor near the windows. She is keening, wailing like a cold winter wind. She gathers him up, holds him to her. I step forward over the dead mercenary and come to her side. She has buried her face in his collarbone; she cries, she cries. His head lolls back, the hair hanging loose and bloody in back. Curdles of gray streak through the blood, the back of his head shattered. I look down into his face. The bullet hole is the thickness of my thumb, ringed in black. His eyes open, his mouth loose—he looks surprised.

Thomas called Angie from inside the garage. "Angie, it's all gone bad. I've got Ma Zlata and Isobel Dupont. I'll come out the way we planned. O'Brien's regular security will be on my ass quick.—No, listen. Stay where you are. Call 911 from that pay phone across from you, and tell the Bluemen two of O'Brien's employees have shot him and a visitor. Tell them they need an ambulance. Tell them O'Brien is bleeding to death.—Robko? He's not coming back."

Thomas had the old woman seat-belted in beside him. He cranked the ignition. Isobel, huddled in the back seat, chanted over and over, "Get us out, get us out, get us out."

He drove straight through the garage doors and over the pieces and burst out into the open. From the right, someone ran towards him, pistol out. He turned left off the garage apron and howled down the drive, took out the wrought iron gates with the SUV, and cracked the windshield into crazed stars.

Chapter Twenty-Nine: I Shall Reign

Two broken women in a hotel room: Zlata's mother and Sibyl. The old woman was silent, hunched over on the side of a bed, staring at the dresser. Sibyl, curled in a ball behind the old woman, wept tears and snot, eyes pinched into crinkles, face bright red. A forgotten tissue was balled up in her hand.

A string of deaths, all in his hands. A long thread of abysmal luck. No way he could stay—best to run. Thomas could hear his own dead-flat voice. "Angie, drive me into Brooklyn, to the bus station." The entire way he huddled against the minivan door, stared out first at the expressway and then at the streets as they rolled by. In the last two or three blocks, he said to Angie, "Here's where we stand. Sibyl gave me the two Artifacts for the twenty million dollars."

He mustered up the energy to keep talking. "I suppose ten of it already belonged to her and five to you. Help her through the next days. Help her run. Make sure we can reach her. Buy her a burner phone, and memorize her number."

"But what about you? What about me?"

"I'm finished in O'Brien's empire. If he dies, it's bad, and if he lives it's worse. From here, I sell the Artifacts. Half the money is yours. If I make it, I'll see you get your share."

"That's it? You just slink away?"

"I've killed four men altogether, two in Sibyl's apartment, and two last night. Most criminals don't launch their careers so dramatically."

She had another objection, her face pinched and hard. "You can't leave Isobel and Zlata's mother behind with LeFarge after them. They want to go home. LeFarge will tie up his loose ends. He'll find them and kill them."

"I know. I have to handle him too."

She jerked to a stop at the bus station, sandwiched behind a cab and the trashcans.

He clambered out. He leaned back into the van and said to Angie, "We had a great partnership. I'll miss working with you."

"Stay then, Thomas. Ride it out. Deny everything."

"They're going to put the three crime scenes together. I left my prints all over Father Mirko's office and Sibyl Boxwood's condo. I'll be on the hook for the homicides at the mansion—I'm the number one suspect, aren't I?"

Tears broke into her eyes. She bit her lip. "You always did choose poorly for yourself. You're doing it again."

"No doubt. But at least I leave you in the clear. They'll focus on the missing player." He patted her on the shoulder.

She stared to the left, gripping the wheel hard, then glared at him. "How can such a smart guy end up so stupid?"

"Just lucky I guess."

She grabbed him by the cuff. "Get back in the damn car. No more of this noble bullshit!"

He thought at that second he might cry, for himself, for Robko. It had all slipped out of his hands. But in the back of his mind, there arose a tease, a wiggle of a notion. "I've finally acquired my own multi-million dollar company. Only problem is that I'm my sole employee." He straightened up and picked up his bag off the curb.

Angie leaned across the minivan so she could gaze up into his face. "Okay, okay. Have it your way. At least let me know how it goes for you out there. If you're any good at this new life, maybe I'll quit my job and work for you. Somebody needs to pick up after you."

"If I'm any good, you're rich. But if you can, clean up after me this one last time. Take care of our friends and our team." He nodded, ducked his head, and shuffled towards the bus station. Glancing back, he caught sight of the minivan trundling away. One survivor.

Forty-four hours and a half-dozen transfers later, he climbed down off the bus in a Minnesota town in the Iron Range. Once long ago, his mother had brought him here to a lake for the summer. It was as good a way to choose a destination as any.

He had expected a bus station, but it turned out to be a diner named

"River and Range." Whether that could be translated to a good omen or bad, he couldn't tell. The café showed him people with sheepskin-lined boots, ratty flannel shirts, stained jackets, and smiles on their faces. They held tight to each other, joked, and laughed in the warmth of a diner while blue snow plummeted down outside. It took a while to work up to anger, but that anger carried him through a tuna melt and chips and then coffee—who the hell did they think they were? What right did they have to happiness in the midst of poverty?

He checked into the motel next door, one of those that advertised its sun dome. The motel had been built around a large covered swimming pool with its own waterside village. A black man ran the front desk, a guy somehow familiar. Behind the counter, he wore a long coat and gloves—the moist air in the lobby was a degree or two warmer than outside. He handed Thomas a key. "Cheer up, sir. Spring will follow the hardest winter."

Thomas climbed the stairs to his room and fell into bed. The TV flickered in the corner. He watched the concrete ceiling for ten hours, while he napped off and on.

Dragging on his clothes, he carried his burner phone down to the poolside. Perched on a bench in the big atrium, he deliberated over the next irreversible step. He felt like the bird on a wire, watching the world from a great height. *In the end,* he thought, *it all comes down to whether you feel lucky or not, if you sense things will turn your way.*

He blanked the video. He dialed. O'Brien's rival picked up. "Carstairs here. I can't see your caller I.D."

"Some phones shouldn't have fingerprints. My name is Jimmy Cabot."

"Your name isn't familiar. How did you get this number?"

"From Dennis Malley O'Brien's security people."

The man on the other end cleared his throat. "I'm listening."

"I have something to sell, from one of O'Brien's labs. It's not patented, and it will end up big. The biggest consumer item of the next hundred years." The concrete bench sucked the warmth out of his buttocks; the air cloaked him moist and dank. A bizarre, uncomfortable place. He grinned, enjoying himself.

"What exactly are you selling?"

Thomas felt his jaw clench—this was the moment. Time to deliver. "Not the idea. The actual prototype and laboratory records for the last six months on its manufacture, development and tested uses."

"The prototype. Of what?"

"A device that can download and store an entire human mind." Thomas let it sink in.

"Really?" Carstairs sounded tight, unconvinced. "Are you a crackpot?"

Thomas snorted. Carstairs turned out to be predictable. "Wrong question. Any answer I give has to be 'No, I'm not a crackpot.' You can ask a better question—was O'Brien crazy? You heard about the shootout on Long Island three days ago? It was all about this device. O'Brien traveled the full mile for this. He risked it all, and now he'll pay the dime."

"How do I know any of this is real?"

"We could meet. You could bring one scientist or engineer with you and inspect the device and selected records."

"Assuming all this turns out legit, why wouldn't I just take the idea away and develop it myself?"

Thomas choked down on his laugh and inhaled. "Because it will be the biggest race for the most enormous market since vidi phones hit the shelves. You don't have the years it would take to develop from scratch." He could feel the adrenaline; it rocketed around in his blood. It made him feel tough, smart.

"I don't follow."

"Everything changes once this device hits the market. People will see it as a way to store their loved ones and archive their youth. Their whole lives, with instant recall. Their real family tree."

"Why should I care about genealogy?"

"You're not listening. Engineers will see it as a way to create androids for hostile environments. Companies will want it as a way to hold on to their intellectual property. Some people will use it as immortality. It will open up brand new professions in legal, advertising, peripheral manufacture, robotics. The market will move at the speed of light."

"Maybe," said Carstairs.

"You can't keep this a secret now; O'Brien has lost control. Every lab rat that worked on the device will parley it into a career with another company. You're already out of time."

Carstairs hemmed. "Who are you? One of the lab rats? One of

O'Brien's inner circle?"

"I was O'Brien's fixer."

"Huh. What's your price?"

Thomas felt his mouth quirk up in a lopsided grin. Halfway there. "Ten million wired offshore at the meeting, upon agreement. An additional fifty million on delivery. I have easy terms—anonymity for me. Also, we do the deal face to face."

"This sounds a lot like industrial espionage."

"Yes."

"I'll grant you your meeting, but I won't be present," said Carstairs.

Show him it's serious, thought Thomas. "Sorry, no intermediaries."

Carstairs grunted. There was a long pause. "Then you have to give me a strong reason to risk entrapment. Up front."

"What if I provide correspondence from the VP of Research to O'Brien?"

Thomas could sense the distrust, the frown, the shake of the head. "Could be faked."

"Could be real."

"Not enough."

What a cowardly little man. "I have clandestine video of O'Brien talking to me about it."

"Ah. Dennis with his pants down. Send it to me." His voice had evened out, even loosened up.

"Coming to your phone now." Carstairs was hooked.

"I'll dig into this and consider it. Talk to a couple of my people. Then we'll talk. Talk about meeting, about my engineers. A guarantee that this device works... talk about the money."

So it wouldn't be a meeting in a coffee shop, a quick look-see, and we're off. Probably a shakeout in a lab. Would Carstairs have his own army? "Sure. If I were you, I'd want to do a detailed check of the thing too. But that will cost you more, not less. And I'll need guarantees also."

"How can I reach you?"

"I'll call again in six hours."

"One last thing," Carstairs said, "just to speed up checking you out."

"If you can."

"Were you there when O'Brien was shot?"

"You mean, did I kill him for the device? No, you can't leverage me that way." Thomas tapped the screen to end the call.

Next, he called Thurgall. The conversation played through much the same way. How alike the two men ended up being. And he had priced the deal right—any less, and they wouldn't have believed it.

Thomas perched on the bench in the sun dome for a long time. Eight thirty in the morning, Central time. He picked up his pre-paid vidi again and placed the call. Again he blanked the video. The line clicked, and he heard Chicago. "Yo. Hold a second." Thomas could hear the man shout, "No, you idjit. That pallet is vodka—it goes next aisle over." The voice boomed onto the line. "Kazimierz Liquors. What can you do for me?" Testosterone. Old school.

"Hello. I'm trying to reach Dag Kazimierz."

"You got him."

"I called because you're Mirko Kazimierz's brother."

The man on the other end said nothing.

"I knew Mirko."

"I'm listening."

"I was there when he died." Thomas stared out over the pool and watched small wisps of steam rise up into the chilled air. An image of a church office in Ithaca—the priest slumped on the floor—threaded up into his mind, followed the steam upward.

"Not on this line."

"Sorry?"

Dag said, "We don't talk on this line. Unblock your caller I.D., so I can see you. Don't say your number; show me."

Frowning, Thomas did so. "Now I have to trash this phone."

"Tough shit. Hang onto it for a few minutes. I'll call you when I'm someplace secure. Gimme five."

Thomas waited by the pool. For five minutes, then another five. His throwaway rang.

"Who are you?"

"My name is Jimmy Cabot."

"That don't mean nothin' to me."

"What does matter is my connection to your brother's murder."

"Did you do it?" The voice cut like a carbon steel knife.

"Kind of. Indirectly." Thomas rested his forehead on his knuckles, elbow on his knee.

"You got balls calling me to say something like that, Jimmy."

Thomas imagined a hard, hard man, bent over a burner phone in a safe room somewhere, on the lookout for someone to murder. "I didn't intend it to happen. I followed Robko Zlata's trail, and it led to your brother. I fed the Zlata info back to my organization, and your brother's killer followed me to Father Mirko."

"Zlata? Mirko said he was on the run. Why you telling me this?"

"I want you to know the shooter's name. He's Egan LeFarge."

"Can you spell that?"

"I'll type it in for you." Busy with the thumbs.

"Bullcrap name. Frickin' Frenchman." There was a sneer in the voice, under the anger.

"He's ex-military, a mercenary living in New York City; works special security."

"That's not a problem. We got reach there." Dag sounded confident.

"He has a crew."

"That's no problem either."

Thomas thought, *Don't go in cold—pay attention to me.* "Listen, this is a bad-assed crew. They killed Robko Zlata also."

"Mercs, like this LeFarge?"

"Yes."

The man on the other end laughed, an ugly sound. "Mercs is wussies. They get used to automatic weapons, and all they know is spray and pray. They don't know how to work in close."

"Right."

Dag said, "How do I know you're feeding me the straight stuff?"

"He's after me, too."

"Got you scared?"

"Definitely. I can give you the background file on this if you want, and there's details you can check out. It would also include surveillance material that I have—make him more accessible."

"Send them now."

Thomas said, "Give me a second." He tapped the screen and made the drop. "Do you see it?"

"Wait. Checking now. So here's a file on this guy. Big deal, Jimmy."

265

"Now that you have the file, you have time to read it; check it out." Thomas thought, *Harder to sell than Carstairs.*

"I don't know you. I don't trust this info."

"This is the best chance you have. You don't seem to care much."

Dag's voice barked back down the line. "I want the man who killed my brother—killed a priest for Christ's sake!"

"Your brother forgave LeFarge."

"My brother took the Holy Orders. I didn't."

Good… that was what he wanted to hear. "We understand each other." He pictured Dag scowling, gripping the mobile like it could give him back a lost brother.

Dag's voice dropped a pitch, got soft… more threatening. "From here on out, don't try to help me. If your dope checks out, you done all you need to do. If it don't, you got a serious problem."

"One other thing. An old lady lives in LeFarge's house. She didn't have anything to do with it, so don't harm her."

"What? You think we're the frickin' Chechnyans? Thanks for the call. I'll keep your name and number in case you're screwing me. If you're straight, I'll lose it. Don't call again, Jimmy."

Jimmy pitched the phone into the pool.

About the Author

Scott Archer Jones is currently living and working on his sixth novel in northern New Mexico, after stints in the Netherlands, Scotland, and Norway plus less exotic locations. He's worked for a power company, grocers, a lumberyard, an energy company (for a very long time), and a winery. Now he's on the masthead of the Prague Revue, and launched a novel last year with Southern Yellow Pine, *Jupiter and Gilgamesh, a Novel of Sumeria and Texas*. The book was a finalist in four categories in the New Mexico – Arizona Book Awards

Scott cuts all his own firewood, lives a mile from his nearest neighbor and writes grant applications for the community. He is the Treasurer of Shuter Library of Angel Fire, a private 501.C3, and he desperately needs your money to keep the doors open.

https://www.facebook.com/ScottArcherJones

CPSIA information can be obtained
at www.ICGtesting.com
Printed in the USA
FFOW05n1109250215

9 781940 869339